PR

"A stirring tribute to the American codebreakers who helped identify spies during the Cold War, Healey's novel offers up a joyful ensemble of women at the top of their game while also providing a nuanced look at the motives behind those who chose to betray their country. This is a terrific read: ripe with romance, filled with nail-biting suspense, and a celebration of the power of female friendship."
—Fiona Davis, *New York Times* bestselling author of *The Stolen Queen*

"Jane Healey knocks it out of the park with her new heavy hitter *The Women of Arlington Hall*. This page-turner has all the goodies historical fiction lovers will devour: Cold War espionage; a brilliant, fiery female codebreaker; spies in love (yes, please); girl code; passion; and suspense. Catherine (Cat) Killeen, just out of Radcliffe, is accepted into the special Russian Section intelligence unit to help foil the Russians' plot to steal atomic secrets from the United States in the 1940s. A woman of her time and *ahead* of her time, Cat stops at nothing to reconstruct the elusive KGB codebook and track down those Russian spies living in America, who infiltrated the highest levels of government—even if the price tag is her own life. Healey doesn't miss a beat merging real-life events with fictional flair and rich plot twists. Lots of recognizable Cold War players make cameos: Herbert Hoover, Klaus Fuchs, Julius and Ethel Rosenberg. Unputdownable. Healey at her very best."
—Lisa Barr, *New York Times* bestselling author of *The Goddess of Warsaw*

"With *The Women of Arlington Hall*, author Jane Healey brings historical fiction readers everything we look for in an enthralling read. Healey weaves deep and meticulous research on the Cold War–era codebreakers into a page-turning plot replete with spies, romance, intellectual puzzles, little-understood historical events, betrayals, and suspense. Alongside a heroine who, appealingly, is both brainy and still finding her way in life, we learn about the complex world of post–World War II political intrigue, even as she navigates the twists and turns of her personal life. A fascinating, fun, and compelling read."

—Joy Jordan-Lake, bestselling author of *Echoes of Us*

THE WOMEN OF ARLINGTON HALL

OTHER BOOKS BY JANE HEALEY

The Saturday Evening Girls Club
The Beantown Girls
The Secret Stealers
Goodnight from Paris

THE WOMEN OF ARLINGTON HALL

a novel

JANE HEALEY

This is a work of fiction. Names, characters, organizations, places, events, and incidents are either products of the author's imagination or are used fictitiously.

Text copyright © 2025 by Jane Healey Ungashick
All rights reserved.

No part of this book may be reproduced, or stored in a retrieval system, or transmitted in any form or by any means, electronic, mechanical, photocopying, recording, or otherwise, without express written permission of the publisher.

Published by Lake Union Publishing, Seattle

www.apub.com

Amazon, the Amazon logo, and Lake Union Publishing are trademarks of Amazon.com, Inc., or its affiliates.

EU product safety contact:
Amazon Media EU S. à r.l.
38, avenue John F. Kennedy, L-1855 Luxembourg
amazonpublishing-gpsr@amazon.com

ISBN-13: 9781662526503 (paperback)
ISBN-13: 9781662526510 (digital)

Cover design by Faceout Studio, Amanda Hudson
Cover image: © Lucky-photographer, © VValD, © Leigh Prather / Shutterstock; © Science History Images / Alamy; © Eyesblink

Printed in the United States of America

For my daughters, Ellie and Madeleine, who inspire me every day.

It may be roundly asserted that human ingenuity cannot concoct a cipher which human ingenuity cannot resolve.

—*Edgar Allan Poe*

There are at the present time two great nations in the world . . . the Russians and the Americans . . . Their starting point is different, and their courses are not the same, yet each of them seems marked out by the will of Heaven to sway the destinies of half the globe.

—*François-René de Chateaubriand, 1802*

Part One

Chapter One

Monday, September 15, 1947
Arlington, Virginia

As the taxicab drove away, I stood with my purse hanging over my elbow like a weighted pendulum, my big brown leather suitcase next to me as I gaped at what appeared to be a small city surrounded by a fortress. Armed guards stationed along the perimeter of the fence stood watch as hundreds of military officers, as well as civilian men and women, arrived to start their workday, showing their security badges to the guard stationed at the main entrance.

I shook my head, taking it all in, not quite believing I was here. After everything that had happened over the past few months, I had finally arrived at Arlington Hall.

"Excuse me, miss. Can you please show me your credentials?" A stocky young guard approached me, and I realized I must look ridiculous standing there with my suitcase, just staring at everything.

"Oh, sorry, I . . . I don't have them yet. But I am supposed to be here. Today is my first day," I said, trying not to sound too eager.

"What's your name?"

"Catherine Killeen."

"Follow me, Catherine Killeen."

He took my suitcase, led me to the guard booth next to the main entrance, stepped inside, and made a phone call. I knew for certain this was my start date, yet still I watched him and resisted the urge to nervously pick at my nail polish, considering my options if the person on the other end of the line said they'd never heard of me.

"You're to go up to the main building. Someone will greet you upon entering," the guard said upon hanging up. "Are you okay with that suitcase? Do you need someone to help you?"

"I'm fine, thank you," I said with a quiet sigh of relief as he let me pass through the gate.

A minute later I regretted not taking the guard up on his offer. The winding path to the main building was longer than it looked, especially for someone dragging a clunky suitcase. When I finally reached the entrance, I had to hoist it, step by step, up the stairs to the front doors, all while awkwardly holding my purse under my elbow. Despite the early hour, the humidity was oppressive, and now I was red-faced and sweaty for my first day of work.

Formerly an all-girls school, the stately main building of the Arlington Hall government complex had a beige brick facade and a three-story portico adorned with massive white columns. Catching my breath, I walked through the front doors into a grand foyer with an impressive central staircase, detailed moldings, and French doors. The air smelled of musty books and polished wood, and there were industrial fans strategically placed in a vain attempt to cool down the building's interior.

"Catherine Killeen?" A woman with reddish-brown hair, an angular face, and thick, black-framed glasses greeted me as soon as I entered.

"Yes, hello," I said, taking off my straw hat and reaching out to shake her hand. "Please call me Cat . . ."

"I am Margaret Sherwood, in charge of orientation," she said in a clipped tone, after the briefest handshake. "Follow me to the drawing room, please. Your Arlington Hall employee orientation will begin in about fifteen minutes."

"Sounds good, thank you," I said.

"Why do you have your suitcase with you?" she asked, glancing at it over her glasses as I tried to keep up with her brisk pace. "Don't you have a place to stay?"

"No, I stayed in a hotel near Union Station because I arrived late last night," I said. "But I . . . my professor led me to believe that housing arrangements would be made for me?"

"No, no," Margaret said with a tsk. "Your professor was wrong. I swear some of these academics who recruit for this program do not pay attention to the logistical details at *all*."

I stopped walking, jolted by her words. I couldn't afford another night at the Phoenix Park Hotel. Where on earth would I go?

"So, you're telling me that there's no housing for me here?" I said, a little lightheaded from panic.

Steps ahead, Margaret whirled around and looked at me.

"No, I'm afraid nothing was arranged ahead of time for you," she said, her tone less shrill, more sympathetic.

"Sorry, I obviously should have confirmed housing beforehand," I said, trying not to sound as alarmed as I felt. "Professor Burke can be oblivious."

"Well," she said with another tsk, "I suppose I can give you some suggestions at the end of the day, Ms. Killeen."

"Thank you, I really appreciate that," I said, giving her a tight smile as we started walking again.

She led me down one of the corridors into a drawing room where a dozen women were sitting at circular tables. I sat down at an empty one in the far corner of the room and shoved my suitcase underneath it, relieved to have a moment to collect myself. I tucked a stray curl back into my bun and took a compact out of my purse, reapplying some light-red lipstick and blotting the perspiration off my cheeks with a tissue. My normally pale face was still flushed a deep pink from the walk, making the small constellation of freckles across my nose less prominent.

Ten minutes later, Margaret Sherwood returned with a half dozen more women, and I cringed when I realized not one of them was carrying a suitcase. I was the only one who had moved hundreds of miles from home without confirmed lodging. A petite woman hurried over and took a seat next to me, as Margaret handed out papers to each of us, along with black ballpoint pens.

"Effie LeBlanc," the woman said with a Southern accent I couldn't quite place. She had wide-set, pale-blue eyes, and her ash-blond hair was pulled back with a red silk headband. I shook her hand, and she nodded at Margaret. "Honestly, she could pass for one of the high schoolers I taught back in New Orleans, but she's a little scary, isn't she?"

"More than a little," I said with a smile. "Cat Killeen, so nice to meet you."

"Good morning, ladies, and welcome to Arlington Hall, official headquarters of the Army Security Agency, ASA for short," Margaret said. "We will go through some paperwork, then I'll take you to get your identification badges."

She held up two badges for show-and-tell and continued speaking.

"These badges are your security credentials, and you must show them every morning upon entering the main gates, as well as any other buildings. The color at the bottom of your badge shows your level of access. First rule to remember: You are never allowed to have your picture taken with the badges on, or to wear them outside these facilities.

"After you're issued your credentials, you'll attend several lectures from top military officers on topics of critical importance for all new employees. Then myself or another supervisor will interview you. Finally, you'll receive details on what department and building to report to for training tomorrow. Any questions before we begin?"

After our murmurs of no and some head shaking, she continued.

"The first document in front of you is the United States Loyalty Oath," Margaret said. "Please read it over and sign it."

The loyalty oath asked that we swear to "defend the Constitution of the United States against all enemies, foreign and domestic" and that we take this obligation "freely, without any mental reservation or purpose of evasion."

I signed it, with my own theories as to what enemies we were defending against now that the war was over.

"The second document in front of you is the United States Secrecy Oath." She held one up to show us, walking among the tables, looking each of us in the eye as she passed.

"You must sign this oath, swearing that you will never discuss your activities here outside of your official duties—not now, not ever, even after you are no longer working here. This includes with your family members. If anyone asks you what you do here, you tell them you are a secretary and you do the basic tasks that secretaries do—sharpen pencils, file papers, type—you get the idea. When you pray at night, you give God thanks that you're a secretary, because He doesn't even need to know what you do."

Effie stifled the smallest laugh at this, but she stopped when Margaret glared at her.

My family knew I hadn't moved all the way here to become a secretary. I'd have to come up with a better cover story for them than sharpening government pencils.

"To be clear," Margaret continued, "discussing your activities here with anyone on the outside opens you up to prosecution under the Espionage Act. And—I'm required to say this to all new hires—understand that you will not be spared the full consequences of treason against the United States simply because you are a woman. And yes, the punishment for treason is execution. If you are uncomfortable with these terms, you are free to leave the premises now, and we will rescind your offer of employment."

She paused for a moment, letting the gravity of her words sink in.

"Now," she said, "would anyone like to leave?"

We all shook our heads no. *The punishment for treason is execution.* The words unnerved me, and I could tell, looking around the room, that I wasn't the only one. The consequences were dire for revealing our "activities" to anyone, but we still didn't even know what these activities *were*.

"Okay, then please sign your papers, and I will come around to pick them up," she said, getting back to business.

"So do you have any idea what your job is here?" Effie asked under her breath as we signed.

"I've got a vague idea," I whispered back. "The professor who recruited me said that it was top secret and that I was a good fit, and I'd learn the details when I arrived. But apparently, we're not learning anything from Margaret."

"We're in the same boat, then," Effie said, nodding. "And I guess we're really in it now, whatever in the world *it* is."

"No doubt," I said as I looked over the papers to make sure I hadn't missed anything.

I couldn't stop bouncing my knee because my nerves were getting the best of me. I had no place to stay and no idea what my job was, and I was pretty sure I had just signed my life away to the US government. I grasped the Saint Rita medallion around my neck and said a silent prayer to her. Seeing as she was the patron saint of lost causes, it wouldn't hurt to have her on my side today.

I was just about to ask Effie about her living arrangements, but she spoke first.

"So where are you from, Cat?" she asked as she handed her paperwork to Margaret.

"Cambridge, Massachusetts. Am I supposed to even tell you that? I feel like I'm already in trouble, and I haven't even started yet," I said with sarcasm.

"No kidding. I think we're fine, if we don't get on no-nonsense Margaret's bad side," Effie replied. As if hearing this, Margaret looked right at us and asked the group to gather our things and follow her.

Chapter Two

I held up a sign with my name in large block letters above my newly assigned employee number, 4819, and the photographer took two pictures—one of me facing him and one of me in profile.

After we had received our credentials, all the new recruits attended lectures given by various army officers on the importance of secrecy and security, basic work protocols, and emergency measures, among a few other dry topics.

Then Margaret led us on a tour of several workspaces within the main building: massive, musty-smelling rooms lined with dark wooden file cabinets and jammed with people, mostly women, sitting at long tables, some with graph paper, index cards, and sheets of paper, others surrounded by huge binders or standing in front of corkboards.

Beyond the main building and despite the military guards and barbed wire fencing, Arlington Hall had a campus-like feel, with a recreation center, a bowling alley, a barbershop, a dispensary, and a theater as well. There were also some more modern, hastily constructed office buildings that had been built during the war.

It had been a long, tedious day, and by that afternoon I was back in the drawing room with several of the other new employees, sipping a cup of coffee and awaiting my interview with Margaret.

"I think the military uses that last officer's lecture as a form of torture," Effie said as she sat down next to me. "It was all I could do to keep my eyes open."

"Completely agree." I grinned back at her and, taking another sip of coffee, added, "So Effie, how'd you end up here?"

"I taught one year of high school mathematics at a huge public school in the city, and on the last day of school I came home and called my mama, told her I would rather shovel horse manure for a living than teach," she said. It was clear she'd told this story before. "I couldn't bear the thought of going back. A friend from home has a job here. He was the one who told me I should take the civil service exam and see if I'd be a fit. And . . . here I am. What about you?"

I explained to her how Professor Burke, my professor at Radcliffe, had approached me about taking a civil service exam for top secret "specialized government work having to do with national security."

I had sat for the exam with seven other Radcliffe women and a dozen Harvard men.

"He told us he selected us to take the exam because we were in the top ten percent of our class, and we represented the kind of traits the government was looking for," I said. "And if we did well on the exam, we could take a special seminar with him during the spring semester that might lead to positions here in DC. I didn't even know if I wanted to get a job in DC, but I'm competitive when it comes to tests. I really just wanted to get the best score on that exam."

"And did you?" Effie asked.

"Almost," I said. "I scored the second highest. One of the Harvard men beat me. He wouldn't let me live it down the rest of the year. Just obnoxious."

"I know the type. Tulane, where I went, was full of them," Effie said. "I've been meaning to ask, where exactly are you staying?"

I explained my housing predicament.

"Oh no, sugar, I'm sorry to hear that," Effie said, sympathy in her eyes. "I moved into Idaho Hall a few days ago. They might have a couple rooms in my building available. But you'll need to pay cash up front."

"I've got some cash. Is it an apartment building?"

"No, it's one of the women's dormitories at Arlington Farms. There's a bunch of them, built during the war. And I've got to warn you, since you went to Radcliffe, it is *not* fancy. You'll have your own room, but the bathrooms are shared. They even keep us on a schedule for showers."

"I grew up on the top floor of a triple-decker with my father and three older brothers," I said. "I am not accustomed to luxury accommodations, trust me."

"Well, in that case, meet me here when we're both finished for the day. You can come check it out for yourself," Effie said, and I was so relieved I wanted to hug her.

"Catherine Killeen?" Margaret called my name from the front of the drawing room, and I raised my hand.

"Please come with me. You can take your coffee," Margaret said.

"Your turn in the hot seat," Effie said with a wink. "Good luck."

I thanked her and followed Margaret to an office at the opposite end of the corridor. We sat across from each other at her desk, and she took out a thick folder with my name on it.

"You took the course on cryptology, organized by the army, with a Professor Burke?"

My mind briefly flashed back to my first day in eccentric Professor Burke's seminar.

"*Welcome to Harvard's highly selective and top secret cryptology seminar, formed in partnership with the US military. Please refer to the definitions on the board.*"

Cryptology—the broad science of codes and ciphers

Code—a fixed relationship between one set of symbols for another

Cipher—a rule for altering letters in a message

Cryptography—the art of creating codes to encrypt messages

Cryptanalysis—the science of breaking codes, deciphering those encrypted messages to recover their meaning

"I did," I said, recalling the exhilaration of being selected for something so covert, among just a few Radcliffe women and a dozen Harvard men. "There were several of us from Harvard and Radcliffe who took it in the spring."

"And you're the only one here from that group?"

"Yes," I said.

"And remind me, what was your major?"

"Math, with minors in French and Russian."

She nodded and opened the folder.

"As you may have been told, when you accepted the offer to work here, a team from the Federal Bureau of Investigation conducted a routine background check on you. School and work references, police and birth records. They are remarkably thorough. I don't have the entire report here, mind you—that's above my pay grade, so to speak."

"Um, okay," I said. I imagined FBI men sifting through every part of my personal life, trying to find . . . what? I tried to guess what they had discovered about me that could have prevented me from working here.

I'd lived in my family's home my entire life and had just graduated from one of the best colleges for women in the country. Until now, my life had been scandal-free, except for my breakup with Andrew, which only interested the neighborhood gossips.

"You're not married. Are you . . . are you currently engaged?" she asked, looking over a page in the folder.

"No," I said, feeling my face start to burn. "I was supposed to get married in June, but I called it off the morning of . . ."

"You called off your wedding to an Andrew Foley. Yes, that's in here, just checking to make sure you hadn't changed your mind."

"Oh," I said, stunned that she knew. "And no, I . . . I definitely haven't changed my mind."

My brand-new ivory satin wedding dress was still hanging in my closet at home with the tags on it. I heard one of the nosiest women on our block had dubbed me "the runaway bride of Line Street." I should never have let it get that far. The devastated look on my ex-fiancé Andrew's face when I told him flashed through my mind, and it still pained me. And I had vowed to my father I would pay him back for the money he lost.

"The higher-ups here prefer women who are unattached," Margaret said, bringing me back to the present. "Less problematic, you know."

"That makes sense," I said, nodding, though my mind was still on my guilt, on Andrew, and on the mess I had made of my life that day. All of it done so I could come here. Time would tell if it had all been worth it.

"Well, good," Margaret said, making a note. "Moving on, do you enjoy crossword puzzles and word games?"

"I do, very much," I said, glad to change the subject.

"I have a crossword here. Would you mind doing it for me, right now, while I time you?"

"Oh . . . I'd be happy to," I said.

She handed me a pencil and a sheet with a crossword puzzle that was on par with the most difficult ones I'd tackled in *The New York Times Magazine*. I leaned over the desk. Margaret clicked her stopwatch and told me to begin.

As soon as I was immersed in the puzzle, everything but the paper in front of me fell away. For a few peaceful minutes, my mind wasn't racing with thoughts about the background check that included such personal, and somewhat painful, details. For the first time since I left home, I wasn't fretting about where I was going to live or about leaving my family.

Puzzles had always focused and calmed my mind, and, from a young age, I had a knack for them. By the time I was eight years old, I was faster than my older brothers in timed crossword puzzle contests. By age ten, I was beating my father too.

I tracked the clues with my left hand and scanned the boxes with my right, trying to identify patterns and filling in words. A few inspired guesses led me to the correct words before even looking at the clues. I murmured to myself as I erased and backtracked, penciled letters into boxes again, until I was down to one last clue: "bee's landing place," five letters. I filled in the letters *P-E-T-A-L*.

"Done," I said, putting my pencil down with satisfaction.

"What? You've finished it? Already?" Margaret looked up from what she was reading and hit the stopwatch. Her eyes wide, she looked from me to the crossword.

"I am—look, here," I said, sliding the crossword over to her, my small, neat handwriting filling in each box. "There are tricks you learn in terms of speed."

"But . . . but you finished that puzzle in five minutes and twenty-nine seconds," Margaret said, frowning at the stopwatch as if it could be wrong. "That's unbelievable."

"It's not my best time ever," I said. "It was a fairly complex crossword, though."

"It's the best time I've ever seen in the two years I've done these intake interviews," Margaret said. "I'd have to check to be exact, but you've broken the record by at least two minutes."

"Oh," I said, feeling my face grow warm. "I've been doing them a long time."

"Tell me, can you describe what it feels like when you're working on a puzzle?" Margaret asked, sitting back and looking at me as if for the first time.

"What it feels like?" I repeated the question and looked up at a tiny crack in the ceiling above us, trying to find the words. "It's like everything goes quiet, and I'm . . . I know this sounds a little crazy, but it's like I'm *inside* the puzzle. Everything falls away. My family used to joke about it. They said when I'm working on a crossword, they could blare a fire engine siren in my ear, and I wouldn't even notice."

"Interesting," Margaret said with a genuine smile as she took some notes. "One more question. Do you have any creative pursuits? Are you musical at all?"

"I took piano lessons from the time I was five until I went to college. And I sing. With my brother's band, traditional Irish folk music. I'm curious, why do you ask?"

"For years we've been trying to determine the characteristics that make someone good at cryptanalysis, at codebreaking," Margaret said, jotting down a few more notes. "There's no proving ground for this kind of work. And it's fascinating because some PhDs come here and just can't get the hang of it, and then we've had high school dropouts who have a natural ability. Musical talent and a knack for word games are attributes that many of the stronger codebreakers possess. Although we had a concert pianist a year ago who was completely inept at it. He didn't last a month."

"Interesting," I said, hoping I wouldn't suffer the fate of the pianist.

"I think so," she said. "Now, to go over the rest of your background check."

She noted that Professor Burke had said I had an unusual intelligence and referred to me as one of his "star pupils with a near photographic memory," which made me blush again. Several other teachers wrote glowing recommendations, describing me as "hardworking, conscientious, and persistent." There was even one from Sister Agnes, who had been my supervisor when I taught Sunday school at St. Mary's Church.

Hearing these kind words from people in my life was exactly what I needed at that moment. For the first time all day, I felt like I was meant to be here, and it calmed me.

"Overall, your background check was stellar, but the FBI flagged a couple of details in your family history, so it took a little longer for you to get clearance."

"What details?" I frowned, my brief surge in confidence evaporating.

"Mind you, as I said, I don't have your entire background check here . . ." she said. "But for one, your father is not native-born."

"No," I said. "He was born in Ireland, but he's an American citizen now."

"Yes, and he's a pillar of his community and demonstrably loyal and patriotic to his adopted country. Your brothers Michael, Seamus, and Richard are all decorated war veterans. Your family has an outstanding reputation in the city of Cambridge. They cleared that one up quickly. And I'm sorry for the loss of your oldest brother, Richard."

I looked down at my lap and paused before speaking. So was I. Four years, and this unexpected mention of Richie's death still took my breath away, his absence in my life an ache that time had not healed.

"Thank . . . thank you," I said. Eager to change the subject, I asked, "What's the other issue?"

"It's your mother's family."

"What?" I sat back in my chair, not able to hide my shock. "My . . . my mother died in childbirth when she had me. She was born here. Her family disowned her when she married my father because he was Irish Catholic, and poor. I . . . They've never been a part of my life."

"Your mother's brother Peter Walker lives in New York City," Margaret said. "He is a respected academic, a scientist and physics professor at Columbia."

"But?" I said, because she paused for a moment, looking down at the file.

"*But* he's also a member of CPUSA, the Communist Party of the United States. This is not something they want to discover in a candidate's background."

"He's what?" I said, a bitter taste in my mouth. This person who had never wanted to be part of my life was now somehow impacting it. "But this is ridiculous. I've never met him. How can he be an issue when I have had nothing to do with him, or any of my mother's family? Is this going to be a problem?"

Peter Walker. It was jarring to hear this woman say my uncle's name when I hadn't spoken about him to anyone, even my father, in years. How much did Margaret know? Did she know where my mother's family had immigrated from? Of course she did.

"No, it's not a problem, you still have the job. I'm sorry, I didn't mean to alarm you. You wouldn't be here if you didn't finally receive clearance. The FBI was able to establish that you and your family have never had any contact with Mr. Walker," Margaret said.

"Well . . . good," I said, sitting up, finally taking a breath. "So, I can start training tomorrow still?"

"Of course," Margaret said. "But understand, in your time working here? If you are ever eligible for a promotion or new projects, your uncle may come up again. Since Truman announced this whole loyalty program for federal employees last spring, things have gotten a little stringent, to say the least."

"Thank you, I understand," I said. At this point, I just wanted to get through this first week. I was tapping my foot so fast that Margaret glanced down at it, and I stopped.

"Sorry, it's just nerves. Could you please tell me about the project that I'm going to be working on? I only know it's some sort of codebreaking, but for what?"

Margaret riffled through a different folder on her desk.

"Here it is," she said. "Yes, you're where I guessed they'd place you. You have been assigned to work with the unit in Building B. That is where you will report in the morning. A woman named Gene Grady will meet you, and you'll begin your training with her."

"Building B, thank you . . ." She had told me exactly nothing. "But what does the unit *do*?"

"I'm sorry, but I . . . I don't have the clearance to know many details regarding that group. Very few people here do," Margaret said. She seemed embarrassed to admit it. "What I do know is that, what they're working on? It will make that crossword puzzle you just finished seem as simple as duck soup."

Chapter Three

When I was about five years old, my father told me the story of my mother, and to this day I cherished it as much as my favorite childhood fairy tales.

Before she became Annie Killeen, my mother was Anna Walker, born in America, from a wealthy Jewish family in New York City. Her father, Daniel, was a successful furrier, her mother a seamstress. Her older brother, Peter, attended Columbia University and graduated summa cum laude with a degree in physics. At the top of her high school class, Anna had her parents' support to go to college, rare in those days, and she enrolled in nursing school.

She met my father, Joseph Killeen, after he had returned from the Great War a decorated Navy veteran and was starting his career as a Cambridge firefighter. Anna had recently finished nursing school at the New England Hospital for Women and Children and was living near his fire station in East Cambridge with two fellow nursing students.

One hot and humid August evening, she walked by the fire station, and he was sitting outside with a couple other firemen, drinking sodas and smoking cigarettes. It was, according to everyone who knew them, love at first sight. She married my father within a year, despite her family disowning her because he was Irish Catholic and "didn't have two dimes to rub together." And so Anna Walker became Joseph Killeen's beloved wife, Annie.

I replayed their love story in my mind as I looked at the small black-and-white framed photo of my mother that I had brought with me to Virginia. I traced her face, as I had hundreds of times before. Looking at the picture, I felt a quiet hurt in my heart, a longing that only motherless daughters know.

Annie Killeen is frozen in time in the black-and-white photo, twenty-two years old, sitting on Castle Island Beach in South Boston, laughing at something someone is saying behind the camera. She is the same age I am now, and our similarities are undeniable: thick, ebony curls and pale skin, the same prominent cheekbones, blue eyes, and bow lips. One of the only real differences between us is the smattering of freckles across my nose. My father always said that was the only thing about my face he could take credit for.

What would she think of the choices I had made that had brought me here? And the evergreen question: What would she think of *me*?

A staccato knock on the door made me jump.

"Catherine, are you up?" Effie called.

"I am," I said.

She handed me a white paper bag as I opened the door. "In case you're hungry. It's a stale powdered donut." She smiled and shrugged. "But that was the best of the options this morning, and there weren't many left."

"Thank you so much," I said, though I was too nervous to eat.

"Just wanted to make sure you didn't oversleep. The bus to Arlington Hall will be here in twenty minutes. You've been assigned to Building B too, right?"

"I have," I nodded.

"Great, maybe we can have lunch together. Meet you downstairs?"

"Sounds good, see you there," I said, shutting the door.

I put the photo back on my tiny nightstand, next to the one of me, my father, Mickey, Seamus, and Richie at my uncle's bar. Waking up, I had needed a moment to remember where I was, and then the homesickness had washed over me. I ached for my well-worn cream-colored cotton blankets at home, my simple pale-blue room, the smell of bacon grease coming from the kitchen where my brother was making breakfast. And I still longed for what home was like when our house was full, before Richie died in the war.

My room was on the second floor of Idaho Hall, in the group of government dorms known as Arlington Farms. It was decorated with garish pink-and-green floral print curtains and a matching bedspread. It was clean and larger than my closet-sized room at home, furnished with a tall bamboo dresser with a mirror and an upholstered light-pink chaise lounge. The last girl who had stayed in the room had been a heavy smoker, and I had kept my window wide open all night to try to air it out.

As I arrived with Effie the night before, the receptionist had told me that she had a room for me and the rent was $24.50 a month, up front, in cash, if I wanted it. Given it was my only option, I handed her the money and headed to bed.

Built five years prior to accommodate all the "government girls" moving to DC for jobs, the gray, two-story residential dormitories at Arlington Farms were spread out across several acres, and each one was named for a state. Idaho Hall was, as Effie had promised, the opposite of fancy, but overall, it exceeded my expectations. It had a cafeteria and multiple snack bars, there was a kitchenette and laundry area on each floor, and the common area included a game room, a store selling food staples and cosmetics, and lounges with partitioned dating cubicles like they have at some drugstores.

I finished getting ready and found Effie waiting in the common area with some other women, and I was overjoyed to see an urn of fresh coffee on the table nearby.

"How'd you sleep?" she asked after I had helped myself to a cup.

"Not great. But the room's fine. Thank you again. It's just there's too much to think about." I paused before adding, "And if we're going to be friends, I have to confess something."

"What?" Effie said, amused.

"That was the second night I've ever slept away from home." I cringed.

"Ever?" Effie asked, her eyes wide.

"*Ever*," I said, wincing at her shock. "I know, it's pathetic, honestly."

"But you didn't live at Radcliffe?"

"No," I said. "I could literally *walk* to Radcliffe. It didn't make sense for me to live there. I could barely afford tuition as it was."

"No wonder you couldn't sleep," Effie said.

"Being next to the bathroom also doesn't help," I said, making a face. "The walls are thin."

"Maybe you can move rooms at some point," Effie said. She looked me up and down and shook her head before adding, "Second night away from home. Cat from Cambridge, I think you've got some living to do."

I was about to tell her I agreed when a striking young woman with auburn hair in a low chignon came up to us just as we were heading out the door to catch the bus.

"Good morning, Effie," the woman said with a smile.

"Hey, Dale," Effie said. "Cat, this is Dale. She lives across the hall from me. She's from Alabama. Cat's from Massachusetts."

We shook hands and shared our stories. Dale Motlow had graduated from the State Teachers College in Troy, Alabama, and she had been working at Arlington Hall for a year. She was also a former beauty pageant queen, second runner-up for Miss Alabama, which was not a surprise given her gorgeous figure and porcelain skin. When I told her where I had graduated from, her eyes lit up.

"You know, last weekend, I was out with some of the girls in our hall, and we met a couple fellas who just graduated from Harvard," Dale said. "One of them was so handsome—total movie star looks. His name was John. Do you know a John from Harvard who looks exactly like Gregory Peck?"

"There were a lot of Johns at Harvard," I said, recalling a half dozen off the top of my head, all of them from varying degrees of wealth and privilege, including my irritating rival from Professor Burke's cryptology seminar. I wasn't enough of a fan of Gregory Peck to know if there was a look-alike in the bunch. "Did you get his last name?"

"I wish I did," Dale said. "I did make a point of telling him that a group of us usually head to the Liberty Pub after work on Fridays, so I'm hoping he shows up. You both should join us too, meet some of the other gals who work at A-Hall."

"Oh, we are definitely coming," Effie said as the bus was pulling up. "Cat could really use some nights out on the town, right, Cat?"

"Whatever you say, Effie," I said with a laugh as we climbed onto the bus, though the comment made me bristle. I'd been singing at bars and Irish pubs with my brother's band from the time I was sixteen. I wasn't as sheltered as Effie appeared to think.

As the bus pulled out of the driveway of Idaho Hall and Dale and Effie continued chatting, I was distracted by the sense of unease that had plagued me since the day before. Looking out at my unfamiliar surroundings, I ruminated about how little I knew about my mother's family and, for the first time, was troubled by what other people might know.

If the FBI knew that my mother's brother was a member of the American Communist Party, then they certainly knew that my mother's parents, Daniel and Irina, had immigrated to the US as young newlyweds in the late 1800s from Anapa, a town on the northwestern coast of the Black Sea. In Russia. And, fearing discrimination when they arrived in New York City, they had Americanized their last name from the original *Volker* to *Walker*.

They had to have discovered all this, but what else had they found out? I'm sure there were things they had discovered about my mother's family that I had no idea about. I had stopped asking my father about the Walkers years ago, and now the FBI had more information about them than I did. When you grow up knowing so little about one side of your family tree, you're always trying to fill in the branches in your mind, to make sense of a huge, unknown aspect of your identity. If I asked Margaret, or someone higher up, to see my whole file, would they show it to me? My guess was no.

And though I was ultimately cleared to work at Arlington Hall, it was still unsettling, having a piece of my personal history matter so much.

"You ready for your first real day?" Effie asked as we got off the bus and lined up to go through the security checkpoint along with Dale.

"I think so. Maybe? I'm just anxious to get started. I hate being the new person in anything," I said.

Even on my first day of Radcliffe, I hadn't been this jittery, and it wasn't just because of my family history. In college, I had never doubted my academic abilities. It was the social aspect that was difficult to navigate. Being a commuter student from a working-class family, I was an outsider among girls who came from families with old money and all the connections that entailed. I was the only firefighter's daughter among them.

Today, for the first time ever, it was the actual *work* that was worrying me. Had anything in my background truly prepared me for this? If a concert pianist could fail at it, certainly I could too.

"Once you get used to all the security, Arlington Hall is a great place to work," Dale said after we had passed through the gates. She told us more about the campus, pointing out the recreation center, the beauty parlor, and car repair shop.

"The mess hall's down there. I'm in the main building. Where'd they assign you two?"

"We're both in Building B," I said.

"Good luck. We'll all make plans for Friday night," Dale said.

We said goodbye to Dale and headed to our assigned location. Buildings A and B were built on a slope behind Arlington Hall and stood in sharp contrast to the classic architecture of the main school building. They were identical, massive, bland, two-story buildings made up of long corridors with perpendicular wings, constructed quickly during the war to accommodate the thousands of workers being hired by the Army Security Agency from all over the country.

"Who are you supposed to report to?" I asked.

"Sam something. I can't believe I can't remember his last name," Effie said. Her face had gone pale.

We walked into the lobby, once again showing our credentials to a guard upon entering. I was going to ask him where we should go, when an impeccably dressed woman with shiny chestnut-brown hair came through a door and gave us a warm smile. She looked like she had just stepped out of a bandbox.

"Which one of you is Catherine?" the woman said, and I put up my hand.

"I'm Gene Grady. Welcome to the team," she said, holding out her hand. "So glad to have you on board."

"Nice to meet you," I said. "I'm looking forward to getting started."

"You must be Effie, then," Gene said, and Effie nodded as they shook hands. "You're in Sam's group, the IBM group, on the second floor. He said he'll be out to greet you in just a minute."

Effie gave me a thumbs-up as Gene led me down the hall.

"Let me show you around our unit, and then we'll find somewhere quiet to talk, and I'll tell you what I have in mind to get you oriented with everything we're doing here," she said.

I thanked her as she took me into a room as big as a bowling alley with high ceilings and with massive windows lining each side, the smell of ink and Lysol mingling in the air. The room was partitioned into different work sections, and there was a quiet buzz of several dozen people working individually and in small groups. Lining all four walls of the room, and even acting as partitions themselves, were file cabinets, many of them close to bursting.

"Over there in the corner are the two reading sections," Gene said, pointing to the opposite side of the room, where behind a partition several people were seated at tables, concentrating deeply on the documents in front of them. "In the middle here is the traffic section. That helps keep us all organized. And I work in the back room, where we do the high-level troubleshooting stuff. Hey Bill, is the smaller conference room empty?" Gene asked a stocky, middle-aged man walking toward us.

"Yes, empty for now," Bill said in a European accent I couldn't place. He had black, wiry eyebrows, and the top of his bald head was slick with sweat. "New recruit? Bill Weissman, pleasure to meet you."

"Nice to meet you too," I said. He stepped in a little too close when he shook my hand, and I could smell his sour breath.

As he walked away, I glanced over at the traffic section to see a woman around my age with long black hair and olive skin scowling at him. She caught my eye and quickly turned back to her work.

Gene and I made our way to a cramped conference room lined with even more cabinets and sat down across from each other at a long oak table as a fan in the corner blew stale, warm air around us. She reached into a drawer and pulled out notebooks and pens for each of us.

"I know you took the course in cryptology at Harvard, which is excellent. You're ahead of the game in terms of training," Gene said. "What has anyone told you about the work we do in this unit?"

"Nothing," I said. "I know it's some kind of codebreaking, but I have no idea beyond that."

"Oh gosh, you must be dying to know at this point," Gene said.

"That would be an understatement," I said with a quiet laugh.

"Welcome to the Russian section," Gene said. "Although outside these walls it's referred to only as the 'Special Problems section.' It began here in '43. I was one of the first employees assigned to the group. All these file cabinets are filled with thousands upon thousands of encoded telegrams between Moscow and Soviet diplomats stationed all over the world. The US intercepted them between 1941 and 1946. Because they were sent by regular commercial telegraph, wartime censorship allowed the US to receive copies of all cables. And everyone out there in this unit has one mission: to break the Soviet code system so we can read these messages."

And there it was, like the last word in a puzzle that is just beyond my understanding and then in a flash becomes as clear as a billboard: Russia.

It was the largest Soviet country, and I was now a part of the Russian section at Arlington Hall. I had considered this possibility as soon as Margaret had uttered my uncle's name.

I blinked, absorbing this information, my arms covered in goose pimples. *This.* This was why I had taken the risk, why I had upended my entire life and moved down here. For a once-in-a-lifetime opportunity exactly like this.

I hoped she didn't notice my nervous foot-tapping under the table, because, as I considered all the possibilities of the role, I couldn't deny the quiet hum of anxiety beneath my excitement.

"Fascinating," I said.

"It can be, but I must warn you, it can also be maddening and tedious," Gene said with a rueful smile. "The Russians' code has long been considered unbreakable, much more innovative and sophisticated than the German or Japanese systems. One analogy we've used to describe their cryptography: It's as if they locked the door once, locked it again, and then, just to be sure nobody could get in, they threw away the key."

"But if you have such a large team here," I said, "you must be making some progress?"

"It's been hard fought, but we have," Gene nodded. "Bill Friedman, the army's legendary chief of cryptology, has hired some of the best cryptologists in the world, including the renowned cryptanalyst Meredith Gardner, our resident genius. We've also recruited smart graduates like yourself. We've discovered a chink in the code's armor. And it's led to some breakthroughs. Let's just say you've arrived at an exciting time, for lots of reasons."

"I'm thrilled to hear it," I said. "And . . . what are we hoping to find in breaking this code? What kind of information?"

"That's the first question everyone asks, naturally," Gene said. "In the past couple of years, it's become apparent, through more than one intelligence source, that the Soviets had a vast network of spies here in the US during the war, some even within the upper echelons of government."

"So, you . . . you want to discover who they are from these messages. You want their names," I said, guessing that this was partly why President Truman was so paranoid, ordering extensive "loyalty checks" for all government employees.

"Bottom line, yes, we're trying to find out who they were, exactly what kind of intelligence they gathered. There's a lot more to it, but that's it in a nutshell. On that note, we should get started. I want to walk you through some of the basics of how the Soviet code system works and our various methods." She stood up from the table and went to the chalkboard behind her. "And then we'll talk about your schedule for the week. I'm going to have you spend time in all the groups, to gain a clear understanding of what each of them does."

"Sounds perfect," I said.

I watched her as she began to write rows of numbers in delicate, elegant handwriting. When Professor Burke had recommended me for this role, it had broken something open in me. I hadn't even realized opportunities like this existed for women. And once I knew there was a job out there, waiting just for me, I couldn't let it go. The thought of getting married and teaching had felt more and more suffocating by the day.

I could draw a direct line between the news of Richie's death and my engagement to my high school sweetheart. My wedding was meant to be something to make my father happy, to fill the void in our lives after Richie's death had hit us all like a tornado, ripping out the foundation of our family.

But, as the wedding date got closer, I started to grow more and more panicked, picturing myself twenty years in the future, living on the same block in the same city, never reaching for anything more, never taking a risk for something beyond my small life. I had chosen to get married to try to make my father happy, but in the process I had lost myself.

In the end there was only one obvious choice to make: Say yes to this job and finally, for probably the first time in my life, say no to what was expected of me. I realized that the most important before-and-after moments in life don't happen to you; they're the ones you make happen. I just wished it hadn't taken me until my wedding day to know for certain what I wanted.

And now that I was here, I desperately wanted to become an invaluable member of this team. Even at Radcliffe, I hadn't met many women who shared this yearning I had, to be part of something bigger than myself. Watching Gene Grady at the board, I knew that was about to change.

Gene turned back to me, blocks of numbers in groups of five, four rows across, three rows down on the board behind her. And as I began studying them, I decided the issue could wait. There was a puzzle in front of me, and it was too tantalizing, like the biggest present waiting to be unwrapped.

"So, what do you think, Catherine, are you ready to start working on the biggest top secret intelligence project in America?" Gene smiled at me, brown eyes sparkling.

"More than you can imagine," I said, smiling back.

"Then let's begin."

Chapter Four

Friday, September 19, 1947

The Friday night crowd at the Liberty Pub was an eclectic mix of DC-area college students and young professionals like us. The floors were strewn with sawdust, and the exposed brick walls were covered with black-and-white photos, event posters, and weight belts from the storied boxing career of the owner before he had hung up his gloves for the last time. The timing of the Liberty's opening had coincided nicely with the end of Prohibition—a "We Want Beer" protest sign on the mirror behind the bar a reminder of those dry days.

On a narrow stage, a group of five musicians was warming up, all older men around my father's age, with some combination of graying or receding hair, two of them so similar in their fire-hydrant-like build and round Irish faces that they had to be brothers. There was a fiddler, a banjo player, and a guitarist, along with a flautist. The bodhran player, with the single-headed frame drum on his knee, left no doubt that this was a traditional Irish folk band, just like my brother Mickey's.

I closed my eyes as I listened to the notes of the craggy-faced fiddler warming up. The combination of music along with the smells of spilt beer, cigarette smoke, and kitchen grease put me right back at my uncle's pub, and a wave of homesickness washed over me.

I had survived my first week at Arlington Hall, and all I had wanted to do after work Friday was head to Idaho Hall to get in line for the shower and go to bed. But Effie and Dale had reminded me of my promise earlier in the week.

"You aren't falling asleep on me, are you, Cat?" Effie said, back from the bar with rum and Cokes for the three of us.

"Not yet," I said. "Sorry to be a stick in the mud, it's just been a heck of a week. Too much to think about; it's hard to turn off my brain."

"That's why we're here, to put it all aside for a while, have some fun." Dale flashed a dazzling smile and held up her glass. "Cheers, ladies, you made it through week one."

The three of us clinked glasses as Dale strained her neck and scanned the crowd for the John from Harvard she had told us about. A few men openly stared back, desperate for a smile or a wink from her.

"One thing you'll learn about DC: There is so much fantastic music in this town," Dale said, pointing to the guys on the stage. "You're Irish. I think you'll like these guys—they're so talented."

"I'm sure I will," I said. "I actually sing in a band pretty similar to this one back home. My brother and his friends started it in high school."

"Get out of town!" Effie said, swatting my arm. "You? Sing in a *band*? I tell you, my friend, you are just full of surprises, I thought I had you pegged."

"I know you did, but going to an all-women's college isn't the same as growing up in a convent," I said.

"Well, *that's* certainly true, given your runaway bride story," Effie said.

"Oh, I want to hear the runaway bride story—do tell. Hold on, though, there's some of the girls from work," Dale said. She whistled and waved at a group of women that had just walked in the front door. I recognized a few faces from Building B.

"I'm going to go find a ladies' room to freshen up before meeting everyone," I said, putting my drink down.

I followed the sign to the ladies' room, heading down the narrow, dimly lit hallway at the back of the bar. It was across from the swinging

The Women of Arlington Hall

door to the kitchen, and there were muffled sounds of clanging pans and the smell of frying burgers wafting through the air.

I thought of my dad and my brothers back in Boston; Mickey and the band were probably warming up onstage at my uncle's pub right now. Longing for that warm, familiar feeling of home, I again questioned whether the decision to come down here had been the right one for my life or an impulsive choice to escape the fallout of my canceled nuptials.

I was still preoccupied with my thoughts, my head down looking in my purse, as I walked out of the ladies' room and slammed right into someone, stumbling backward. The man I'd run into grabbed me by my elbow.

"You all right? I'm so sorry," he said, and I whipped my head up because I recognized the distinct, low-pitched voice. And then I recognized him—thick, wavy black hair, big, dark eyes, a strong jawline, and his imposing build, over six feet tall and the kind of handsome that made the two women walking into the ladies' room do a double take.

"Catherine *Killeen*? Killeen! I can't believe it's you. What on earth are you doing in DC?" Jonathan Dardis said. I opened my mouth to say something but closed it, speechless in disbelief.

Jonathan Dardis, the only Harvard classmate who had outperformed me in Professor Burke's cryptology seminar, was standing in front of me at a pub in DC.

"Wait, aren't you supposed to be married?" He took his hand off my elbow and looked down at my ring finger.

"What are you doing here?" I said, not able to hide my irritation. "Aren't *you* supposed to be in New York City?"

"I got a much better offer, and ended up moving here instead," Jonathan said, shrugging with his usual casual arrogance. "What happened to the wedding?"

"I . . ." I said, unsure what to say and what to leave unsaid. We were former classmates, not friends. "I guess you could say I got a better offer too. Let's just leave it at that."

"Wow," he said, shaking his head. "What kind of . . . Wait, are you working in DC too?"

"I am, in Virginia, actually. At Arlington Hall," I said.

"Oh right, of course that makes sense," Jonathan said, nodding. "I turned down that job."

"What? No, I don't think so," I said, but as soon as the words came out of my mouth, it dawned on me. "Oh. *Of course* they offered it to you first."

We were the two best students in the class. But he was a man, which gave him a career advantage that I would never have. He was always going to be offered any job first.

"Yup," Jonathan said, and then he broke out into a huge grin. "Wait, you're not still mad that I got a higher score than you on the final, are you?"

"No," I lied. "That's ridiculous. It was months ago now, and it doesn't matter."

"You are, I can tell—it still burns you. You were always so competitive with me," he said, laughing.

"What?" I looked at him and frowned. "More like the other way around."

"Sure, whatever you say, Killeen," he said, still grinning. I was about to protest again when he put his hand on my elbow again. "Listen, can I buy you a drink for almost knocking you over? Hold on . . . do you live at Idaho Hall? Are you here with Dale Motlow?"

"Yes, yes, I am," I said, closing my eyes for a second. "Oh God. You're her Jon from Harvard. You're Dale's Jon. Well, I mean, not that you *belong* to Dale, but . . . you met her recently?"

"Yes, she said she would be here tonight," Jonathan said. "Has she talked about me?"

"A little," I said. I didn't mention that she had compared him to Gregory Peck. Did he look like a young Gregory Peck? Maybe in a certain light. But no need to inflate his ego even more by telling him that.

"So, she's here already?" Jonathan said. "Are you two good friends?"

"Well, I only just met her, but she seems nice."

"She's gorgeous, isn't she? Do you . . . do you think she's smart?"

"She is very pretty. Do I think she's smart?" I raised my eyebrows at the question. "She's not dumb. I mean, she works at Arlington Hall. They don't hire just anyone off the street. And let's be honest, that's never mattered to you before. Why start now?"

I wouldn't have thought that was important to Jonathan Dardis. He had a well-earned reputation for dating around. From what I knew of him, curves were a common characteristic among the women he dated. Intelligence? Not so much.

"Ouch! That's harsh, Killeen," he said, though he was clearly amused. "Do you two work together there?"

"We're in different buildings," I said, and with a sigh I pointed to the opposite end of the bar where Effie and Dale were sitting. "Come on, I'll take you back to our table."

"Let me get the guys I'm with, and we'll come over," Jonathan said, and then he gave me his crooked smile and shook his head. "Cat Killeen in DC."

"Indeed, I am," I said. "But you still haven't told me how you ended up here?"

"I changed my mind about the New York job, and ended up heading to Quantico, Virginia, for training right after graduation," Jonathan said, obvious pride in his voice. "I'm a newly minted G-man, an agent at the FBI."

"Congratulations. Wow, FBI . . ." I looked up at him, frowning. "I'm sorry, I just can't believe you're standing here right now. That we're both in the same city."

"Ha, you thought you were rid of me." He winked.

"What kind of work are you doing at the FBI?" I ignored the wink.

"That's classified, ma'am," he said, lowering his voice. "But I bet I can guess what you're working on."

"Even if you could, I couldn't tell you if your guess was correct."

"Are you working with Meredith Gardner?"

"Why? Do you know him?" I squinted at him.

"No. But he's legendary. The FBI cryptanalysis section practically has a shrine devoted to him."

"He's in my section, and you know that's all I can say," I said. "They literally remind us daily of the United States Secrecy Oath we signed."

"Oh, come on, Killeen, I almost *had* your job there," he said.

"Yes, you mentioned," I said, irked that he said it again. "You were offered it first, I was second choice."

"Oh, calm down," he said, rolling his eyes. "All I'm saying is, given I almost got the job, I've got a sense of what you're probably working on."

"I am calm. And maybe you do, but then you definitely know I can't talk about it."

"All right, all right. You can't talk about it. For now. Who knows, maybe at some point you will be able to." Jonathan gave me a smirk that I knew all too well, like he knew something I didn't. Which was unlikely, but still aggravated me.

"What? What does . . ." I started to respond when his smirk turned into a broad grin. He was doing it to tease me, to get my back up, as he had in class so many times before. I groaned, refusing to take the bait. "Never mind, let's go see your Southern belle."

∽

An hour later, Dale, Effie, and I were sitting around two tables pushed together with Jonathan and three of his friends from the FBI, as well as a handful of girls from Arlington Hall. The band was playing "Drowsy Maggie," a favorite of my brother Mickey's band, and the tune was a visceral reminder of home, equal parts comfort and ache. The area in front of the stage was now cleared of tables, and a few couples were dancing.

When we sat down, Effie had introduced me to Gia Manzo and Rosemary Biddle, two women I had seen around the Russian section in Building B, who happened to live on the same floor as her at Idaho.

Gia was the olive-skinned, raven-haired girl I remembered from my first day when Gene had given me the tour. Up close she had startling hazel eyes and spoke with an unmistakable New York accent. Rosemary was built like a dancer, tall and willowy, with pale skin and bobbed platinum hair that fell in a perfect curtain, accenting her prominent cheekbones.

"So, Cat from Boston, you went to Harvard with him?" Gia asked, nodding across the table at Jonathan.

"Radcliffe actually, that's the women's college," I said, then felt silly for correcting her because it was essentially the same to anyone on the outside.

"Sure, sure," Gia said, not impressed. "I didn't go to college."

"What did you do before this?" I asked.

"Worked at my sister's beauty shop in Queens," Gia said. "One of the last girls that worked in Building B was a total snob, appalled I got hired without a college degree. She lasted three months."

"She *was* a snob, but that wasn't why she didn't last," Rosemary said. Her voice had a distinct, raspy quality like the Hollywood actress Lauren Bacall. "She was just dreadful at the job."

"I've seen a lot of new ones come and go in weeks or months. Doesn't matter whether they went to college or not," Gia said. "This work can't be taught. No telling who's good at it until you get here."

"So we've been told," I said, and Effie and I glanced at each other nervously. I thought of Margaret's speech on our first day.

"You'll both know soon enough if it's for you," Rosemary said, her tone less cynical than Gia's. "And if it's not, don't be too hard on yourself."

The band finished playing just as Dale let out a roar of laughter at something Jonathan said to her, causing us all to look up.

"Not going to lie, he's as handsome as Dale said," Gia said in a low voice, as she glanced in their direction. "I'd burn toast for him in the morning."

"Gia, don't be ridiculous," Rosemary said, taking a drag of her cigarette.

"You don't agree?" Gia said, eyebrows raised.

"Well, *I* agree," Effie said. "Not my type, but no denying he's great-looking."

"I suppose he is," Rosemary said, tilting her head, openly evaluating him. "But he also seems quite aware of it."

"Exactly. So arrogant," I said, thinking how much he would love overhearing this conversation.

"He may have met his match in that department with Dale," Gia said. "Miss pageant queen."

Dale had her hand on Jonathan's elbow, leaning in, her chest against his arm and again laughing at something he said. At that moment, Jonathan caught my eye and winked at me again—so typical. He seemed genuinely happy that we had run into each other, but my feelings were mixed at best. And I couldn't let go of the fact that he had been offered my job at Arlington Hall.

"Explain this to me again: You two were in the same classes at Harvard?" Dale said, catching the wink and still leaning into him as if her life depended on it.

"Just one class. Most of the classes at Harvard and Radcliffe were separate," Jonathan said.

"Thank God, one class with you and the rest of those Harvard men was enough," I said. I was teasing, but it was not a lie.

"Wow, again? You wound me with your words," Jonathan said. Holding a hand up to his heart, he nodded at Dale. "Killeen's still mad because I was the only one who scored higher than her on the final exam."

"By just three points." I instantly regretting saying it, because it only proved he was right.

"Ha, see? You know exactly how many points. I knew you were still mad." Jonathan beamed.

"Jon, did you ever hear Cat sing with her brother's band?" Effie asked.

"I . . . I can't say I ever did," he said, hesitating. "Though I heard about it. It was part of her whole mystique at Harvard."

"Mystique?" I gasped and laughed out loud. "What on earth are you talking about? I—"

"Jon, you promised me a dance." Dale interrupted me, stood up, and offered her hand as the band started playing "Maid behind the Bar."

"We'll finish this conversation later, Killeen," he said as they headed to the small dance floor.

"Not if Dale can help it," Gia said with a sly smile.

"Were you two good friends back at school?" Rosemary asked.

"Friends? No, not at all," I scoffed. "Just very competitive classmates, never friends."

"Well, maybe that will change now that you're both here," Effie said.

"Doubtful," I said, as I watched Jonathan put his arm around Dale's waist, feeling a pang of something like jealousy in spite of myself.

Chapter Five

Friday, October 3, 1947

"We are going out tonight, my friend, even if you're planning on working *again* this weekend," Effie said, adjusting her wide, pale-pink floral headscarf over her hair as we hurried through security and down the path to Building B on a muggy early October morning. She had yet to wear the same hair accessory more than once since I'd met her. "Was that night at the Liberty the last time you went anywhere?"

"As a matter of fact, it was," I said, feeling almost guilty. "But I had to work last weekend. There's so much I need to learn. I'm the total rookie on this team, and I hate that."

It was true, but I was using it as an excuse, too. I had also thrown myself into work as a distraction from my homesickness, which had only gotten worse. I had spent long days shadowing the different groups in the Russian section, learning all that I could, and choosing to spend the last two weekends in Building B, declining social invitations from Effie and some of the other women at Idaho Hall. Every night before bed, I spent hours reviewing the "homework" that Gene had assigned me, wanting to prove my worth and impress her with my innate abilities. But now I was feeling lonelier than ever, longing for home, living for letters from my father or brothers and still questioning if I had made a massive mistake taking this job, despite the rare opportunity that it was.

The Women of Arlington Hall

"Honey, we *all* have a lot to learn. Every day I leave here exhausted. All the new information they're throwing at me, it's been brutal," Effie said. "Trust me, getting out will do you some good. Dale's organized a group to go to the rooftop of the Cairo Hotel. We're meeting your friend Jonathan and—"

"He's not my friend," I interrupted her a little too sharply.

"Uh, *right*." Effie smiled. "Anyway, we're meeting up with *not your friend* Jonathan and some of his FBI coworkers. You're coming with us tonight. I won't take no for an answer."

"Fine, I'll go," I said with a dramatic sigh. "As long as you help me figure out what dress to wear. I'm kind of hopeless when it comes to fashion."

"Deal," Effie said as we entered Building B. We said our goodbyes, and I headed to the building's café to get a cup of coffee before my morning meeting with Gene.

My expectations had been far too high when I heard about the café in the basement. It was a dingy, narrow room off the main corridor, next to the doorway that led to a fireproof vault that took up the rest of the floor. The café consisted of four scratched-up, orange Formica tables with flimsy metal chairs, a coffee and tea station, a Coca-Cola machine, and a vertical glass bakery cabinet of muffins and donuts that was stocked with fresh goods twice a week at most.

When I walked in, Gia was sitting at the last table in the back. She had her head tilted up to the ceiling, and she was holding an ice pack that concealed her entire face, but I recognized her long, dark hair in a high ponytail hanging over the back of the chair.

I was pouring coffee out of the industrial-sized stainless steel urn when a voice in my ear made me jump and spill coffee all over my mug and down my hand.

"Ow!" I said, shaking the hot coffee off my hand as I turned and looked up to see an unusually tall young man standing behind me. He was well over six feet tall but had a dimpled, youthful face and thick, sandy-brown hair with an untamed cowlick in the front. But the oddest thing was, he was wearing only a white T-shirt, orange boxer shorts, and a pair of brown loafers with no socks.

"Oh, I am so sorry, so, so sorry. I didn't mean to startle you," he said, holding his hands up. "Are you okay?"

"I'll be fine. But are *you* okay? Why on earth aren't you wearing any clothes?" I said, raising my eyebrows.

"Oh yeah, don't mind this getup," he said with a grin. "I biked to work today, and my clothes are so sweaty. I'm not used to this Virginia humidity, even in October. It's so stupid, I should have brought a change, but I didn't. Anyway, I'm drying out my clothes. It happens."

He shrugged like this was the most normal thing to do in a workplace, and I wanted to ask if this was something he did often, but he kept talking.

"I just came in to tell you the Coke machine is rigged, so Cokes are free. I rigged it, or you might say I broke the Coca-Cola code." He said this with an exaggerated wink.

"Um . . . thanks, I'll remember that," I said, struggling to have a normal conversation with this giant man-child in his underwear.

"I'm Cecil," he said, holding out his hand. "Cecil Peterson."

"Cat Killeen," I said, shaking his hand even though mine was still damp with coffee. "Nice to meet you."

"Have you ever seen a UFO, Cat?" he asked.

"I'm sorry, a what?" I said.

"UFOs, unidentified flying objects? Supersonic flying saucers?" he said. "Like the ones a pilot in Washington state reported in June? The pilot's name was . . ."

"Kenneth Arnold, from Boise, Idaho?" I replied, and his dimpled face lit up with delight. "I happened to read an article about it. I remember it clearly because it was so strange. In the *Chicago Sun*, in June, right?"

"Yes, that's the one!" Cecil said. "I . . . I can't believe you know."

"Arnold reported seeing—wait, I'll tell you what I remember . . ." I said. "Nine bright, saucerlike objects flying at ten thousand feet between Mount Rainier and Mount Adams, in Washington state, their speed estimated at an incredible twelve hundred miles an hour."

"Yes, exactly." He laughed. "So, are you a UFO aficionado too? Have you ever seen one yourself?"

"I'm not. And I have definitely never seen one." I said with a smile, amused at his obvious enthusiasm. "Why, have you?"

"Yup." He gave a solemn nod. "Last summer, on my parents' farm in Iowa. Three of them on the horizon right after dusk, just sitting there in a row. People all over Iowa reported seeing them."

"And what happened next?"

"They were there, and then they just . . ." He raised his hands in a floating motion, his eyes looking off into a distant galaxy that only he could see.

"Wow," I said, because I had no idea what else to say.

"You're new, right?" he said, snapping out of his UFO trance. I just nodded in response as he kept talking. "I've been here four years, dropped out of college. I took an IQ test with the army and ended up in this place, if you can believe it. A few years ago, I solved some stuff for Meredith that no one else could solve. So, I'm a permanent part of the team now. Have you met Meredith yet?"

"I have not," I said. "Not yet."

I had seen the "resident genius," as Gene referred to him, locked away in his corner office most days when I walked by it, oddly fragrant pipe smoke wafting from his doorway. He was the de facto leader of the Russian section and the primary reason the group had finally made some huge progress.

"Well, I'm sure you've heard all about what an absolute legend he is. He's my idol. You think you have a good memory? Meredith's brain is . . ." He put his hands on both sides of his head and made an exploding motion, complete with sound effects. "He speaks twelve languages, including Old Church Slavonic and Sanskrit of all things. And when the Japanese team needed more help during the war, he taught himself Japanese."

"That's incredible," I said. I had learned that Meredith Gardner's linguistic abilities were something that the team in Building B loved to boast about, and the number of languages he spoke was a moving target of anywhere from eight to sixteen, depending on who you asked.

"What's incredible is that he learned it—like was fluent in Japanese—in only *three months*. Can you believe it?"

"I truly cannot," I said. This was a new kernel of information that made me even more intimidated about meeting Cecil's idol.

"I only speak Russian, though I'd like to pick up another . . ." Cecil stopped at the sound of a metal chair screeching and looked over at Gia.

"Ah, there she is," he said, dropping his voice to a whisper. "Giada Manzo. The girl I'm going to marry. Ain't she a beauty?"

"Oh, congratulations. You're . . . you're engaged?" I said. Gia hadn't mentioned having a fiancé.

"Not yet, but someday." He nodded, looking over at her. "Meredith met his wife, Blanche, here; there's been some other love connections in this place. It's going to happen."

At that moment, Gia took the ice pack off her face and glared at Cecil.

"Cecil Peterson, if you just told Cat that you're going to marry me, I swear I will string you up on one of those dogwoods outside," Gia said. "Don't think I won't. It doesn't matter that you're the size of the Jolly Green Giant. And for the love of God put some clothes on!"

"And that's *my* cue to go," Cecil said, grinning at me before calling out, "Nice to meet you, Cat. Love you, Gia. See you soon!"

"Not if I see you first," Gia yelled back as she blotted her face with a napkin.

"Nice to meet you," I called out after him.

"Was it really? *Nice* to meet him, I mean?" she said, eyebrows raised. "The guy was in his underwear. And I bet he was talking about UFOs, right?"

"You are correct," I said, smiling. "I didn't mind, though. I think he was impressed that I knew about the incident in Washington state. He's very excited about that one."

"Oh, I've heard all about it, trust me. Cecil's brilliant, but he's an odd duck," Gia said. "And the thing you need to understand is, he's not even the oddest duck in this joint. This place is run by the army, but sometimes it feels more like a nuthouse."

"Good to know," I said, still amused as I walked over to her table and sat down. I nodded to the ice pack. "And . . . can I get you anything?"

More people were now coming into the café to get their morning coffee or tea.

"I'm good, thanks. Headache's almost gone," Gia said. She was wearing a bright purple dress paired with several gold bangle bracelets and a chunky jade beaded necklace, the type of statement jewelry I could never pull off.

"Cigarette?" she said, taking a cigarette case out of her purse.

"No thanks, I don't smoke," I said.

"You might after working here a little longer," she said with sarcasm.

"Hey, ladies! G, I'll take one of those cigarettes." Rosemary came up to Gia's table and joined us, helping herself to a cigarette.

Gia proceeded to tell Rosemary about my introduction to Cecil.

"Despite the fact that he wasn't fully clothed, Cecil's harmless," Rosemary said, laughing. "And actually sweet, and I definitely can't say that for everyone here."

"That's for sure," Gia said.

"I'd better run." I glanced at the clock and stood up. "I've got my last one-on-one session with Gene. She called it my 'final exam.'"

"Oh boy, good luck with that," Gia said, tapping her cigarette in the ashtray. "Not sure if anyone told you, but that's like the first big gauntlet they judge you on here. You don't pass the test with Gene, you could be on the next train home to Cambridge."

"Gia, don't scare her, good Lord," Rosemary said, giving her a little shove.

"Is it true, though? Have people been sent home for not passing?" I asked. Gia's words had hit a nerve. I felt like I had prepared, but I hadn't considered it in the context of a make-or-break career moment.

"No . . ." Rosemary hesitated. "Well, only a couple of people . . . maybe more than a couple."

"At least six that we know of, Rosie—be honest." Gia gave her a look.

"Okay, that's true," Rosemary said, and when she saw the worried look on my face, she added, "But don't worry, Cat, I'm sure you'll do just fine."

Chapter Six

Gene was one of the original members of the Russian section, and in the first months, the team had sorted the thousands of encrypted Soviet telegrams in America's possession by both diplomatic mission and cryptographic system. They discovered there were five unique systems. Two of these were for mundane diplomatic and trade communications. However, it quickly became clear that the other three systems were being utilized for nefarious purposes by Soviet military intelligence and the KGB, the Soviets' espionage agency. And since that time, the team had focused on deciphering the telegrams from those systems, focusing particular attention on the KGB telegrams between KGB headquarters, referred to as Moscow Center, and the KGB's foreign stations, otherwise known as *rezidenturas*.

These Russian rezidenturas were located all over the world. In the United States, they operated primarily in secret, under the legitimate cover of the Soviet consulates in New York City and San Francisco, as well as the Soviet embassy in DC. The KGB spies working in the US often posed as diplomats, journalists for the Soviet press agency, or trade representatives of Soviet companies operating here.

In the early days, the Russian section likened the encrypted telegrams between Moscow Center and the rezidenturas to a jigsaw puzzle with a million black pieces, because the Soviets were using an incredibly sophisticated double-encrypted method called the "one-time pad" code system. In this system, a message for Moscow Center would be written out in Russian and delivered to a code clerk at one of the rezidenturas—such as the Soviet consulate in New York. The code clerk would first turn to the KGB codebook. The codebook had hundreds of words, as well as letters of the alphabet. Each one of the words and letters corresponded to a five-digit number group. The first step in the cipher process would be to convert the words in the message into five-digit number groups from the codebook.

Once that was done, the clerk would turn to his one-time cipher pad—this was a sheet with more random five-digit number groups—to *double*-encrypt the message. There were supposed to be only two copies of this one-time cipher pad in the world—one for the clerk sending the telegram and one for the receiver in Moscow. A sheet in the one-time pad was supposed to be used only once and then destroyed by both the sender and the receiver.

However, sometime during the war, the Soviets made a mistake. They ran short of cipher material and distributed triplicate copies of the one-time pads. And, thanks to painstaking, methodical work scouring the coded telegrams for repetitive number sequences, the Russian section discovered this, resulting in their first big breakthrough. When the genius cryptanalyst Meredith Gardner joined the Russian section after the war, the team started to "match" the telegrams that had been enciphered using these triplicate pads.

It was during this time that Meredith made the most game-changing discovery to date. Every codebook has a finite vocabulary. So, when a sender must include a proper name, he must spell out the word, letter by letter, prefixing the word with *Spell* and ending the word with *End spell*. With the help of duplicate one-time pads, as well as the use of a partially burnt Russian codebook that had been found on a battlefield in Finland, Gardner figured out the codes for the words *Spell* and *End spell*. This was the "chink in the armor," the critical discovery that Gene had described on my first day.

"The *Spell* and *End spell* indicators were the Russians' 'code within a code,'" I said in conclusion, and I hoped it was Gene's last question because I was starting to get hoarse from explaining everything she had taught me. "The Soviet cipher clerks had a *separate* dictionary that assigned five-digit code groups to *English* letters that had to be transmitted. This was a key weakness, the pathway into breaking the Soviet codes. And Meredith and the team, with the help of the IBM group upstairs, have been reconstructing the Soviets' KGB codebook ever since."

I wiped my brow and tried to ignore the trickle of sweat dripping down my back, more nervous than I had anticipated, especially because my discussion with Gia and Rosemary right before had made me feel like this "final exam" was more critical to keeping my job than I realized. The fan in the corner of the conference room was anemic, blowing air around but somehow making it feel even stuffier.

"Excellent explanation," Gene said, clapping her hands together. "I'll be honest, you understand it far better than most new employees do at this stage. You already grasp some of the nuances of the work, so well done to you."

"Thank you," I said, exhaling.

"Now, can I give you a short message to encrypt using their system?"

"Of course," I said, grateful that this part of the review would be written, as I was sick of the sound of my own voice.

Gene got up and wrote a message on the chalkboard:

ATTACK AT DAWN.

I grabbed the codebook used for training and wrote out the four-digit number groups that corresponded with each word, as well as the period at the end of the message:

0441 (ATTACK) 0412 (AT) 2123 (DAWN) 9000 (.)

Then I turned the first code "lock" by transforming the four-digit words into five-digit codes by tacking the initial digit of the second four-digit group onto the end of the first group:

The Women of Arlington Hall

04410 41221 23900 00000

Next, I consulted the Russian section's own one-time pad for four random five-digit codes:

23402 89524 94742 00425

And, as I started to direct all my attention to the message, my nerves faded. I became calm, completely focused my energy, and absorbed myself in the assignment, and everything else fell away except the task in front of me.

To encipher the message even further, I added the original five-digit codes and the random one-time pad additives together using the Fibonacci method, a fancy term for a rather simple system of noncarrying math where no numbers carry over from one column to the next:

04410 41221 23900 00000

23402 89524 94742 00425

27812 20745 17642 00425

Finally, in front of the code, I added the five-digit code on the upper left-hand corner of the one-time pad page that I was using (67182), so the recipient would know which page to look at in their own copy of the one-time pad.

Gene was right. It was so complex, yet ultimately simple if you paid careful attention to how it was done. This encryption process felt intuitive, almost effortless, and there was a joy in the process that was hard to articulate. I had discovered over the years that this happened when I was truly passionate about the work in front of me, like I was now. In college, it happened when I was solving sophisticated problem sets in my multivariable calculus class or translating short stories by Dostoevsky from their original Russian. Solving complex crossword puzzles and singing with my brother's band gave me a different but similar sense of exhilaration, because those pursuits came more naturally to me, whereas calculus, Russian translations, and codebreaking required deeper intellectual focus by design.

I wrote out the final code on the board, the chalk growing hot in my palm:

(67182) 27812 20745 17642 00425

I put my chalk down and exhaled. It had taken no time at all.

"Well, you flew through that one. And this is perfect," Gene said with a smile as she reviewed my work on the board, comparing it to the ciphers in front of her. "It's all correct. I should have given you a harder one."

I just nodded. I knew it was correct, but it was a relief to hear it from her.

"Cat, how are you feeling about everything?" she asked, motioning for me to sit across from her. "I know it's a little like being back at school, with all the studying you've had to do since you arrived."

"I'm feeling well overall," I said. "Still a little bit like a fish out of water, but ready to get into the real work. If you think I'm ready."

"I do," she said. "Let's review a little more after lunch? I'm going to have you work with the troubleshooting team to start."

"Sounds great, thank you," I said, feeling relieved.

"Besides the work, are you settling in? Have you met everyone in the section yet?"

I started to answer when we were interrupted by a knock on the conference room door. Meredith Gardner, the legend himself, burst into the room without waiting. He had a long face, full lips, and ears that stuck out a bit underneath his dark brown curly hair, which was cut short but sticking up a little in the front, as if he had been pulling at it. His outfit, consisting of a light-blue button-down shirt, cream-colored vest, and bowtie, made him stand out as more fashionable than other men in the building. He was holding a pipe in one hand and a manila folder overflowing with papers in the other.

"Gene, I need you to call a meeting this afternoon," Meredith said in a tight voice, not bothering with a greeting. "It's urgent—one o'clock, right after lunch."

"Uh . . . okay, of course," Gene said, and then, looking at me, she added, "Have you met Catherine Killeen yet? She's the newest member of the team."

"Your reputation precedes you, Mr. Gardner, it's very nice to meet you," I said, standing up to shake his hand, thrilled to finally be formally introduced.

"What?" Meredith frowned and backed away from me like I was spreading a disease, not offering a hand in return. He looked at me and then back at Gene, perplexed. "I'm sorry, I don't have time right now . . . one o'clock, Gene? Okay? The whole team. We've got some new developments we need to discuss."

I felt my face burn. The genius team leader had no interest in even meeting me—not exactly a positive sign.

"See you then." Gene sighed and gave me an apologetic look. "Please don't take that personally. He is the most brilliant person you will ever meet, but it's better you understand this now—sometimes he's . . . he's a little lacking in social skills, especially when he's stressed about something, which he clearly is today."

"Okay, I'll try not to," I said, looking at the doorway where he had just stood, my face still warm from embarrassment.

"You'll be coming to that meeting with me as well," Gene said. "It's rare that Meredith gets this excited about anything, so whatever it is, I'm guessing it's going to matter to all of us."

Chapter Seven

"I'm sure you're not the only one he's done that to," Effie said. "I have heard he's a quirky character. My boss described him as 'a salty genius with more than a little spice.'"

"Or maybe he's just a genius who's rude," I said, taking a bite of my bologna sandwich, still brooding, reliving my introduction to Meredith in my mind. We were sitting outside Building B, at one of the few wooden picnic tables under the large oak trees, coveted at lunch for the shade they offered.

Just then, Rosemary and Gia walked out the front of Building B carrying to-go lunch boxes from the cafeteria, looking for an open table. Effie waved them over.

"How'd the grilling with Gene go?" Rosemary asked as they sat down to join us.

"Fine until the end," I said, explaining my encounter with Meredith again.

"Oh, sweetheart, we should have warned you," Gia said, laughing and shaking her head, unwrapping a cheese and tomato sandwich on white bread. "He is one prickly individual. You get used to his demeanor, but it can come as a shock at first."

"It took him four months to remember my name," Rosemary said.

"Really?"

"Really," Rosemary said. "And he still calls me Roseanne once in a while."

"Honestly, we should make bets to see how long it takes him to learn yours," Gia said. "I think it was at least six months for me."

"Well, thank you both for telling me. I feel a little better now," I said. It was nice to know his behavior was more universal and not directed solely at me.

"So, did you two talk to Dale? We're going out tonight, and I cannot wait," Effie said. "The rooftop of the Cairo Hotel? There'll be a big band and dancing, and it has a gorgeous view of the city."

"Absolutely," Gia said. "And Rosemary is in too, even though she's about to tell you she's not."

"What? That's not . . ." Rosemary aimed a fake scowl at Gia. "I mean, yeah, I was going to maybe just go to a movie with Margaret. You've met Margaret—she was in charge of your orientation. We started working at Arlington Hall the same week."

"Please come out with us. Margaret too if she wants," Effie said. "Cat has been holed up here, working way too hard, in my opinion. She needs a night out with girlfriends."

"Well, in that case, I'm in," Rosemary said, smiling at me.

"Thank you, ladies," I said, taking a sip of Coke, looking forward now to the distraction from my nagging homesickness.

We chatted more about the dress code for the evening and other weekend plans outside of work, and then Gia looked at her watch.

"We better finish up," Gia said. "If you thought Meredith was rude when you met him, you should see him if you're ever late for a meeting."

∽

I sat with Gene in the back of the large conference room on the second floor of Building B. The windows were all open, and there were three fans blowing, and, as an eclectic stream of people filed in, Gene whispered me their names and a little bit about their background.

Most of them were women around my age, a couple of math majors out of Smith and Vassar, a few former teachers. One very young woman named Opal had won a national puzzle competition and was recruited right out of high school. There were some middle-aged men scattered around the group as well, including three career army officers, a former partner at an NYC law firm, and an electrical engineer from MIT. Cecil Peterson came in and gave me an enthusiastic wave. He was fully clothed, but now his feet were bare. Effie was there with Sam Ringwald, a distinguished, white-haired, older gentleman who was the head of the IBM group.

William Weissman, whom I had met on my first day, gave us a nod as he walked by.

"What's his story?" I whispered to Gene.

"Oh, Bill? He's been here since the end of the war, served in the army as a translator and cryptologist in Italy and Africa, now he's a linguistic advisor for us."

"I couldn't place his accent when we met. Where's he from?"

"Unclear. He refers to his background as 'exotic,'" Gene said, rolling her eyes. "He's fluent in Russian and reads Arabic. To be honest, I forget where he's originally from. And I should also warn you he's very flirtatious, *thinks* he's quite the charmer. Don't be afraid to put him in his place if he comes on too strong."

"Got it," I said.

I was about to ask her if she had been given an inkling as to what the meeting was about when Meredith walked in with Frank Richards, the chief of the intelligence division of ASA, as the murmuring in the room increased in volume by a fraction. One of the top executives in the organization, Frank was a burly war veteran, built like an aging linebacker, his salt-and-pepper hair cut in a short military style.

"Frank rarely attends meetings," Gene said, with raised eyebrows.

Meredith Gardner stood with Frank at the front of the room looking through the pages in his hands, a little hunched over, as if trying to make himself smaller. Frank, on the other hand, was greeting and talking to some of the people sitting nearby including Cecil. Judging from Frank's expression and the beet-red color of Cecil's face, he had admonished him about his lack of footwear.

"Good afternoon, everyone. Let's get started," Frank said, clearing his throat at one o'clock on the dot. His stance was similar to that of a coach giving his team a game day pep talk, and something about his furrowed brow and pushed-in nose was reminiscent of a bulldog. "First, I don't need to remind you that you are involved in one of the most secret and sensitive intelligence projects in the world. You all know the oath you've taken, and you know that violating that oath is punishable by death."

Frank paused and rubbed his hands together as a few people around the room nodded at this statement with somber expressions. Meredith had yet to look up from reading his pages.

"On that happy note, let's get to the main reason we called you in today," Frank continued. "Since Meredith's breakthrough discovery of the *spell, end spell* indicators in the telegrams, many of you have been working tirelessly over the past several months, using all the techniques available to us, to unearth some of the English words and proper names in these messages. In the last couple of days, Meredith uncovered some intelligence that will illuminate just how critical the work we are doing in this building is to America's national security. We both agreed he should share it with the team this afternoon.

"Now, I know he's not a fan of speaking in front of groups, but as I told Meredith, this is his main event, and as we all know, he understands this work more than literally anyone on the planet. And with that I'll hand it over to you, Meredith."

Meredith nodded, cleared his throat in an almost exaggerated way, turned his back to everyone, and started writing furiously on the chalkboard in long, jagged letters.

CARTHAGE = WASHINGTON, DC

TYRE = NEW YORK CITY

SIDON = LONDON

BABYLON = SAN FRANCISCO

"So as some of you know, we've discovered the code names the Russians used for several of the major cities in the US and abroad. These four we've known for some time," Meredith said in a soft voice.

As he wrote these on the board, a few people in the group gave each other questioning looks. Clearly this discovery was not new to many of them, including Gene. They wanted Meredith to get to the point.

"Now I know you're all wondering why I called you here today. It's not like we need to have an all-hands meeting every time we make a little progress," Meredith said, and a few people chuckled. He paused. The tips of his ears were bright pink, his hand slightly shaking as he held up a piece of paper to read. "So, here we go, the following is part of a message, that I just deciphered from a telegram from the Soviet consulate in New York City to Moscow Center. Keep in mind that this is dated December 1944:

"'Enumerates the following scientists that are working on the problem: Hans Bethe, Niels Bohr, Edward Teller, Arthur Compton.'"

Meredith cleared his throat and held up his hand to indicate he wasn't finished, as the pink on his ears spread to his cheeks.

"'Enrico Fermi, Ernest Lawrence, Harold Urey . . .'" Meredith continued, reading off a total of seventeen names. A couple of people in the room gasped in recognition.

"But I know those names," Cecil blurted out from the front row as soon as Meredith was finished.

"Yes, Cecil." Meredith gave Cecil a nod. "I think most of us have heard of at least one or two of them. But why don't you tell everyone who they are?"

"Niels Bohr, Urey . . . they're some of the most brilliant physicists in the world . . ." Cecil's voice wavered. "They were handpicked by

The Women of Arlington Hall

Oppenheimer for the Manhattan Project, part of the group that built the atom bomb."

"That is correct," Meredith said just above a whisper, his expression grave. I glanced over at Gene, and she had her hand over her mouth.

"They were working on America's most closely guarded secret during the war," Frank said, stepping forward. "These scientists conducted critical research in the top secret laboratories in Los Alamos, New Mexico, and at the Oak Ridge, Tennessee, scientific compound, and some of them were also involved in research at Chicago, Columbia, and Berkeley universities. We have long suspected, but now it is clear, that the Soviets had spies in the US who knew about the Manhattan Project . . . as early as '44. And during that time, they were sending coded messages back to Russia about *our* atomic secrets.

"This begs the question . . ." Meredith paused, his voice louder now but shaky, his anger palpable in every word. "If they knew all these scientists' names, what else do they know? How much more of our scientific intelligence did they steal? Was it enough . . . did they steal enough from us to build their own bomb?"

The question hung in the stale air of the conference room, which was silent except for the whirring of the fans and the buzz of a few black flies hovering around the ceiling lights. My arms had broken out in goose pimples. I looked around at the shocked expressions in the room. Effie's boss, Sam, had been standing the whole time, and now his face had turned as white as his hair.

"Obviously, that is the question that has been weighing on our minds. If the Russians have the bomb, that changes everything. The global balance of power is turned on its head. America's atomic monopoly is over," Frank said, taking over for Meredith, who had his hands crossed over his chest, his mouth a tight, angry line. "It's not hyperbole to say the world will never be the same.

"And that's why we cannot keep this information to ourselves any longer. Over the next three weeks, we are going to compile a special report memorandum for a few high-level Army Security Agency officials about all that we've discovered so far. But we need to make it as comprehensive as possible, so I want all of you to throw everything at this—mine old messages, exploit the weaknesses we've already discovered, utilize the IBM group's capabilities as part of these efforts, of course.

"This probably goes without saying, but I'm going to say it anyway: This will be the most important work we've ever done as a team. Nothing comes close. Meredith is putting together a project plan. We'll review this on Monday. Plan on some late nights. Any questions?"

As Frank scanned the room, we all stayed silent.

"All right, people. More on Monday. Class dismissed," Frank said.

Everyone started getting up to leave, quietly absorbing this stunning intelligence, and people's expressions ranged from angry to contemplative to deeply worried. The Soviets had been stealing atomic secrets from us, possibly enough to develop their own bomb, and the profound implications of that possibility were almost too much to comprehend.

I felt proud to be a part of it, but also like an impostor. The idea of this work was still daunting. Many of these experts had been working on breaking the Soviet codes for several years. Would I ever feel like an integral part of this? Would Meredith Gardner ever care to know my name?

Effie's stunned expression mirrored my own, and when we caught each other's eye across the room, we exchanged a look, as if to say, *How in the world did we end up here?*

Chapter Eight

That night, Effie and I went to meet our friends at the Cairo Hotel in Dupont Circle, in downtown Washington, DC, a little after eight o'clock. The streets were packed with people, and music floated out of a couple of the nightclubs on the street, a muted cacophony of jazz and blues, Dixieland and bluegrass. Music always improved my mood, and there was a festive feeling in the air as throngs of people of all ages made their way down the street, laughing and chatting, groups calling out to one another. I was happy I had agreed to a night out. It was an antidote to both my homesickness and the heavy revelations from Meredith and Frank at Arlington Hall earlier that day.

Effie looked adorable in a red-and-white sleeveless polka-dot dress with a full skirt, her hair swept into a low chignon with a red bow. I had chosen a black cotton dress with a boat neck and cap sleeves and had pulled my hair up in my usual bun. Compared to Effie's, my outfit now seemed downright drab, and though she had kindly assured me it was perfect, I made a note to myself that it was time to shop for some new clothes.

In the middle of the Cairo's rooftop garden, there was a fifteen-piece band situated on risers, in front of a large parquet dance floor with gold lanterns strung on wires above it. Circular tables with black tablecloths were scattered along the rooftop's edges, tucked among green velvet boxwood topiaries wrapped in tiny white twinkly lights.

Dale, Gia, and Rosemary waved us over to their table up in the corner. The Cairo was the tallest building in town and offered a stunning view of the lights of the DC skyline.

"Well, this is exactly what I needed, a drink with a view," Effie said after the waiter brought over our drinks.

"Amen," said Dale as we all gazed out at the spotlights illuminating the Washington Monument in the distance, its backdrop a breathtaking orange-and-pink autumn evening sky streaked with wispy ribbons of clouds.

"So before you got here we were talking. You two have only been here a few weeks. Has anyone told you about the vodka Collins rule?" Gia raised her eyebrows, looking back and forth between me and Effie. She was wearing a striking raspberry-colored A-line dress and a chunky, double-stranded, beaded pearl necklace, dark hair in a low bun.

"The what?" Effie asked.

"No, what is it?" I said, frowning at her.

"Some of the girls at Arlington Hall came up with it for when we're out together at night," Gia explained. "The rule is for any time a stranger starts talking to you and seems *too* interested in where you work or what you do. If a man starts asking you probing questions or you just get a bad feeling, you tell the rest of the girls you're with that you're ordering a vodka Collins."

"And then what, we hightail it out of there?" Effie said.

"*Discreetly* hightail it out," Rosemary said with a small laugh. "It's not like we all run for the door. We meet in the bathroom and come up with a plan to discreetly leave."

"Have you ever had to use this rule?" I asked.

"Fortunately no," Gia said, and Rosemary shook her head.

"I haven't either," Dale said. "But I know that some of the other girls have. Not everyone in this town is on America's side."

Dale bent down to get her cigarettes out of her purse, and Effie gave me a look like, *No kidding*. Dale didn't even work in Building B. She had no idea what we'd just learned that afternoon.

"He's here." Dale's face brightened. She stood up and waved, as I turned to see Jonathan with two other young men standing near the rooftop's entrance, searching the crowd.

Jonathan's face lit up when he saw Dale coming over to get them, kissing her on the cheek in greeting as she took his hand to lead him back to the table. Her auburn hair fell over one shoulder in perfect pin curl waves like Lana Turner, and the two of them looked like a couple out of a Hollywood movie, a fact I found mildly irritating.

"Killeen, nice to see you out on the town again," Jonathan said, nodding at me. "Ladies, let me introduce you to two of my friends from the Bureau."

Louis was a tall redhead with a face full of freckles, apparently a brand-new recruit from Wisconsin who could have passed for a high schooler, and Archie was a British FBI liaison, a floppy-haired brunette with large blue eyes behind nickel-framed glasses.

An hour later, we added chairs as a couple more of Jonathan's coworkers joined us, and our table was crammed with highball and martini glasses, ashtrays and dishes of nuts and olives, as we chatted in small groups and listened to the sounds of the in-house band play favorites from Benny Goodman and the Glenn Miller Orchestra.

"Now aren't you glad you came out?" Effie smiled at me.

"Yes, especially after that meeting today," I said, as we watched a frustrated Gia try to show Louis the steps to the Lindy Hop.

"Dale," Gia pleaded when the song was finished, holding Louis by the elbow. "You're the trained dancer. Please, teach him the Lindy Hop while I go to the ladies' room. For the love of God, save this boy from *himself*."

"All right, if you put it that way, come on, Louis, let's give you some tips," Dale said, laughing and grabbing Louis by the hand. She put her mai tai down on the table and headed out to the dance floor. Pointing at Jonathan, she blew him a kiss and added, "I'll be back to get you for the next one."

"Come on, Killeen," Jonathan said, standing up and holding out his hand. "One dance with your old classmate?"

"Oh no, that's okay," I said, feeling my face grow hot.

"For the love of God, go dance," Effie said, giving me a shove. "I'm dragging Archie out there as soon as he comes back from getting drinks."

"Well, all right, sure, one dance," I said as Jonathan grabbed hold of my hand and led me out on the dance floor, just as the band's female vocalist started to sing the ballad "To Each His Own."

"Oh, this isn't a Lindy Hop kind of song," I said, frantically looking around for Dale. "Do you want to switch with Dale? I could dance with Louis. Because this is more of a slow song and—"

"Shh . . ." he said, holding a finger to his lips. "Dale's fine. Trust me on that."

And I caught my breath when he put his hand on my waist, the scent of his familiar cologne, a not unpleasant combination of sandalwood and leather, lingering in the air between us. I remembered it from the times we had sat near each other in class. A couple of my Radcliffe classmates had gushed about it all semester.

"Just relax, Killeen." He grinned at me, and all I could think was how many hearts he had broken with that smile. "The war is over, we're in this amazing city, time to quiet that nonstop mind of yours and have fun. When was the last time you just had a good time for the sake of it?"

"Honestly? It's . . . it's been a while," I said after a moment because it was true. Aside from the one night at the Liberty Pub, I had not just gone out and had fun since long before I called off my wedding. Fun had not been a priority in my life for a long time.

"I think that should change. You've got a new lease on life, and no more fiancé . . . which I'm guessing was your idea?" He looked at me at this last part, and I nodded.

"It was definitely my idea," I said.

"Poor guy . . . what—"

"I see things are going well with Dale." I nodded in her direction.

He shook his head and paused before he spoke.

"Dale is a nice gal—beautiful, obviously. Very . . . *Southern*." He gave me an exasperated smile and shrugged. "So, back to you, why did you call off the wedding? I'm just curious. It was such a surprise to see you here. He was your high school sweetheart, Boston College grad on his way to BC Law. And you had a teaching job already, didn't you?"

"I did," I said, surprised that he remembered those details of my life. "The closer I got to the wedding day . . . I kept imagining myself waking up at fifty years old, having lived on the same block my entire life. Unfulfilled, unhappy . . .

"So, when Professor Burke recommended me for the job opportunity here, that was my ticket out. I never, ever should have waited until the morning of the wedding to call it off, though. That I will always regret. Poor Andrew . . ."

"Yeah, you just explained why you broke it off, before ever mentioning poor Andrew's name," Jonathan said, cringing.

"I guess that should tell you everything, then." I sighed. I thought back on that terrible morning, my wedding dress, with the tags from Filene's Basement still on it, hanging on my bedroom door. My bouquet of baby-blue hydrangeas wilting in the fridge as I sat at my kitchen table, telling Andrew I couldn't go through with it. The yelling and tears before he stormed out of the house, my father and brothers' stunned expressions, looking at me as if I had lost my mind.

"I had to stay with him when he went off to war, and getting engaged when he got back was just the next step, and for a while I convinced myself it was the right one. And my dad, I wanted to give him some happiness, after . . . after my brother."

"I knew about that too," Jonathan said, his voice soft, sympathy in his eyes. "I'm so incredibly sorry you lost Richard."

"Thanks," I said, looking away. "It's been four years, and I feel like I can finally mention him without . . . but . . . yeah . . ."

I stopped talking and swallowed, my throat thick.

"I understand. I lost a couple friends when I was over there, right in front of me," he said, squeezing the hand he was holding. "But . . . I . . . I know that's not the same as a brother . . . again, I'm sorry."

"Thank you," I said and, ready to change the subject, added, "So, back to you, is it serious with Dale?"

"Oh, I guess this is tit for tat, then?" he said.

"Sure, why not?" I teased.

"It is not serious with Dale. But it's fun," Jonathan said. "I just moved here, I'm focused on the new job, not looking for anything serious."

"Jonathan Dardis, have you ever in your entire life looked for anything serious with any woman?" I laughed.

"Not really." He shook his head, smiling.

"I thought so—*such* a Lothario." I nodded, amused. He had broken the hearts of at least two girls in my class at Radcliffe. Probably more.

"Listen, Killeen, all kidding aside. I know we were never really friends. But it's so nice seeing a familiar face from home—well, kind of from home—here, you know what I mean? Anyway, maybe . . . maybe we could be friends now?"

He said this just as the song ended, and I found myself wishing our dance wasn't quite over yet. I couldn't deny that it *was* nice knowing someone here who had known me before this, even if it was just as classmates. Friends would be fine. It was dating Jonathan that was pure trouble. I'd leave that to Dale.

"Maybe we could be, Dardis," I said, nodding, and when I looked up at him, he gazed into my eyes with such kindness and intensity that I lost my train of thought for a second. "That . . . that would be . . ."

"Come on, handsome, it's my turn." Dale came up behind us and gave me an insincere pageant queen smile, grabbing Jonathan by the elbow and pulling him to the other side of the dance floor. His damn cologne lingered in the air, and now I had a better understanding of why those girls in our class had swooned.

Chapter Nine

Friday, October 17, 1947

Dear Cat,

I'm sorry I've only written a couple letters. You know I'm not much of a writer. But as Dad reminded me, I only have one sister. You know he's pretty good when it comes to laying on the guilt.

How are things in Washington, DC? Have you run into Truman yet? Will you ever be able to tell us what the heck it is that you do in this fancy government job? Even if you can't, Dad will keep bragging about you to the guys down at the firehouse. It's starting to get a little embarrassing, to be honest.

Mickey and the band miss you. I hope you can at least come home occasionally to sing with them. Mickey thinks he's a good enough lead singer, but as usual he's the only one who thinks that.

To answer the question in your last letter, yes, I am still having the nightmares. Last night's was different, though not in a good way. Richie was there in Salerno with me. I was in a field, three of my guys were down, and I was trying to save them. At first, I didn't recognize Rich because he was so far away, but when I did, I started screaming at him to stay down. He put his hand up to his ear like he couldn't hear me. I was trying to save my guys but got up to go after him, because he was in the middle of the field like a sitting duck, and he yelled, "Seamus! Save who you can save!"

And then I woke up. Save who you can save. I couldn't save half the men I wanted to—that's something I'll never, ever get over. I'd just like the nightmares to end.

Mrs. Sheehan says that our lost loved ones visit us in our dreams when they want to communicate with us again. But Mrs. Sheehan also thought that the pigeon that flew into her kitchen during Lent last year was the sign of the Holy Spirit, so I'm taking her words with a grain of salt. I admit I'd like to think he was trying to visit me. It's been four years, but sometimes I still miss him so much I can hardly breathe.

I can't even ask Dad or Mick about this stuff because it's too damn hard. But at least I can talk about it with you. I know you miss him as much as I do. There'll never be another like Richie Killeen. I miss his imitations—do you remember his impression of Father Curran? We would all be rolling on the floor laughing. He had the best laugh, didn't he? What I would give to hear his laugh one more time.

Anyway, enough about poor Rich. I'm trying to think of the latest neighborhood news. Oh, your friend Annie Driscoll is having another baby—that makes three for her, right? And Christine O'Shea from your class at St. Mary's just got engaged to Tommy Costa. Her parents are not happy that she's marrying a Portuguese fella.

One other piece of gossip I wasn't going to share, but I think you should know . . . I ran into Andrew last week in the North End. He was with a girl, and it was definitely someone that was not just a friend, let's put it that way. He introduced me, her name was Garland, and I only remembered it because . . . What kind of name is Garland? She's a nurse in Boston, that's all I got about her.

I don't know, Cat. I mean, we all grew up with Andrew, but let's just say I kind of understood when you didn't marry him. And now? Well, if you've had doubts about your decision, get over that, because he's clearly moving on already.

We all miss you, Kitty Cat. I'm sure Dad will write soon. Mickey, well, he's even worse than me when it comes to letters.

Love,
Seamus

One of my tears fell on the letter, smudging the word *pigeon*. I was exhausted from working long days, and that was making me overly emotional. The familiar ache of homesickness that I'd managed to keep in check had come rushing back into my chest as soon as I had picked up the letter in my box at Idaho Hall. I missed my late brother Richie in waves. Some days I wouldn't think about him at all, and other days he would be on my mind from the moment I woke up in the morning. I had never dreamed about him, though.

"Hey, Cat." I looked up at the sound of Rosemary's voice. She was holding a bagged lunch, looking pristine in navy slacks and a silk blouse, not a hair in her platinum bob out of place. Her smile faded when she saw my face. "Oh no, are you okay?"

"I'm fine." I wiped the dampness from my face, motioning for her to sit down across from me at our favorite picnic table in the shade. "I finally got a letter from my older brother, Seamus. It was . . . well, here, I'll let you read it."

"Are you sure?" She frowned as I held out the letter to her.

"Positive. It's too much to explain, you'll see," I said.

I watched as Rosemary read the letter, at one point looking up at me, sympathy in her eyes.

"Wow, that's . . ." she said when she finished. "Cat, I had no idea you had lost a brother in the war."

"Yeah, my oldest brother. Richie," I said, taking a deep breath to try to keep from tearing up again. "He was stationed in the Pacific, Solomon Islands."

"I'm so sorry. I can't begin to imagine your loss." She reached over to squeeze my hand.

"Thank you," I said, smiling with teary eyes. "I . . . I don't know. It's still hard sometimes. And that's the most Seamus has talked about it to me in a long time. And then of course there's the part at the end about my ex, Andrew. That was *interesting*."

"To say the least," Rosemary said, smirking as she unpacked her lunch. "Does it bother you? That he's dating already?"

"Honestly, no," I said. "It's a relief in a way, to know that he's moving on. I just still feel guilt for letting it get that far, to the day of our wedding, I mean . . ."

"At least you didn't marry him, though, right? I know too many friends who've done that," Rosemary said, lighting up a cigarette, her lunch untouched. "After I graduated Bryn Mawr, my parents basically tried to force me into an arranged marriage. This poor fella Gerald. He was . . . he was fine, I guess, came from one of the right families in Philadelphia, but I had zero interest in marrying him. My dad offered to buy me a house if I would at least go on a few dates. A *house*, do you believe that?"

"Honestly, I cannot," I gasped, laughing. It was clear Rosemary came from money, as evidenced by her understated, gorgeously tailored wardrobe of Claire McCardell clothing and her Patek Philippe gold watch, among other clues. But the detail about the house confirmed she was even wealthier than any of us suspected.

"It's why I moved down here," she said. "I needed a change. I needed an adventure."

"I'm up for an adventure," Effie said, walking up to the table and plopping herself down next to me, taking a bite of a Granny Smith apple. "And Cat, I can't believe I didn't tell you this on the bus this morning, but I have some great news."

"I could use some. What is it?" I asked.

"There's a girl moving out on our floor. I already asked, and you can have her room!" Effie said, and she was right: After many nights lying awake because of the toilets flushing on the other side of my wall, this was excellent news.

"That's amazing. Thank you for asking for me," I said, cheered by the idea of living with friends.

"Excellent, we'll all be on the same floor," Rosemary said. "Although I'll be honest, ladies, I'm not sure how many more months I can stand living in Idaho. The thin walls, the crowded bathroom mirrors? Work's been too all-consuming to think about it, but at some point, I'm going to have to look for an apartment."

"Oh, come on, Rosie, Cat hasn't even moved to our floor yet, and you're talking about leaving," Effie said, giving her an exaggerated pout.

"Well, it's not happening anytime soon," Rosemary said, getting up from the table. "And our meeting is about to start now. We better go. We can talk after."

"Right," I said. Tensions in Building B had been high since the last meeting with Meredith and Frank.

Rumor had it that Meredith had been sleeping in his office, and he wasn't the only one, as everyone assigned to the "Russian Problem" had been working long hours to gather as much intelligence as we could for Meredith and Frank's report. We had now compiled undeniable evidence that the Russians had infiltrated the Manhattan Project and had likely been stealing critical atomic secrets from us during the war. Remembering

Frank's words, I found it chilling to contemplate what that meant. It felt like we were trying to put together a million-piece mosaic—attempting to create a full picture of not only what specific scientific intelligence the Soviets had stolen, but also how they had done it.

"I'm exhausted," Effie said. "I hope Frank's happy with what we've got so far."

"Don't we all?" Rosemary said. "And you're not alone. I saw Cecil face down asleep at his desk late yesterday afternoon."

"Also, I don't know about you all, but I feel like I've lived in this stuffy building for a couple weeks," Effie said. "Oh, and I was working late last night and went to get a Coke in the café, and I saw two rats scurry down the hall heading toward the vault. I ran screaming up the stairs."

"I saw one behind one of the file cabinets on the second floor the other night," I cringed. "So disgusting."

"*Disgusting.*" Rosemary made a face. "They keep saying they'll take care of the problem, bring in an exterminator, and they never do."

"Yup, after the rats and all this overtime, I think we are well due for a night out this Saturday," Effie said as we entered Building B. "No excuses from either of you."

"Oh, trust me, I don't have any, even though I'm as spent as you are," Rosemary said.

"Great, Gia and Dale are in, and Dale's Jon, and some of his friends," Effie said.

"Huh, so Dale and Jon are still an item," Rosemary said. "Dale's known to be kind of fickle when it comes to men. I'm a little surprised. Cat, what was he like at Harvard?"

"Honestly? Arrogant, and a flirtatious charmer. Jonathan Dardis was the guy every girl wanted to date, but he never dated any of them for long."

"Maybe he really has met his match in Dale," Effie said as she reapplied her lipstick. "I'm not sure I've met a more confident gal in my life."

"Agree. They're perfect for each other," I said as we entered the conference room.

Chapter Ten

Even if I could write Seamus back and tell him the truth about my work here, about the global significance of it, he'd never believe me. The first weeks at Arlington Hall had humbled me. I had spent most of my life, which up to now had been in school settings, confident that I was one of the smartest people in the room. That's why I remembered that Jonathan had beat me by three points on our last cryptology exam. In my entire life, I had rarely taken second place when it came to academic or intellectual pursuits.

But being a new team member of the Russian section, being in this collective group of brilliant minds like Meredith, Gene, and even the quirky Cecil, among world-renowned linguists, mathematicians, and engineers—this place was an entirely different ball game.

After the first month, I still felt like somewhat of an impostor, and my recent series of bad dreams involved Gene or Frank sitting me down in that stuffy little cabinet-filled conference room and firing me because I wasn't cutting it.

So far, I had been assigned to the Russian section's troubleshooting team. The hours were long, and I stayed longer, attempting to master the combination of techniques the team used most often. These included crib-dragging or looking through thousands of telegrams for already-known keywords within a message's ciphered text, with the assistance of the IBM group.

The IBM crew also helped us by conducting frequency analyses of unknown codes, to try to find clues about their meaning based on where they were placed in a message. And the final key aspect of the process was exploiting the weaknesses in the Soviet codes that Meredith had already unearthed.

The work required patience, persistence, and more mental energy than anything I'd ever worked on before. It was at times maddening and other times fascinating. Someone described it as digging for a needle in an entire field of haystacks, and it was a painfully appropriate analogy.

Sitting in the back of the conference room, waiting for the meeting to begin, I was going over what the team had compiled, at least what I knew of it, wondering if it was enough in Frank and Meredith's eyes. It seemed there was still an incredible amount of information in these Soviet messages that we didn't know, and it was unclear how long it would take the team to get there. Months? Years?

"Hey, Cat, impressive work this week, by the way. You're an unbelievably fast learner, even for this place." Cecil interrupted my thoughts as he came bounding up to me. He was wearing normal clothes and loafers today, along with an enormous white sun visor.

"Aw, thanks, Cecil, you just made my day." I smiled, straining to look up at him—at six foot seven, he was over a foot taller than me. "What's with the visor, by the way? Were you just out in the sun?"

"No, of course not." He looked at me as if it was an absurd question. "So, you know how there's a bowling alley here? They're starting a league, and I'm forming a team. You are my second recruit. Gia was my first."

"For the love of God, Cecil, I am not joining your bowling team," Gia said, sitting down next to me with a sigh. "And take the visor off. No one wears those indoors. You look ridiculous."

She was wearing a striking tangerine dress today that flattered her olive skin, reminding me that my own bland wardrobe still desperately needed an upgrade.

"Aw, come on, Gia, it might be fun." I nudged her, and she shot me a look. Cecil was like that kid in the playground that nobody would play with, and his earnestness tugged at my heart. He didn't seem to have many friends at Arlington Hall.

"I knew you'd say yes, Cat, you're the best." Cecil beamed and clapped his hands together. "Gia, you'll come around to it, I just know you will. Next Saturday we start. Rosemary, are you in?"

"In what?" Rosemary raised an eyebrow at me and Gia as she pulled over a chair to sit with us.

"She's in," I said, giving Rosemary a wink. "You can include Effie too, though she's over with her team, so we'll tell her later."

"Yes! We're going to have a great ol' time," Cecil said, and his obvious delight made even Gia crack a slight smile. "I'm even going to get us custom designed team bowling *shirts*."

"He is by far the oddest person I've ever met," Gia said as we watched him walk to his favorite seat at the front. "And I'm from New York City, so that's saying something."

"All right, everyone. I think we're all here, so let's get started," Frank said, again standing at the front of the room with Meredith. They were a study in contrasts: burly Frank, the sleeves of his button-down shirt rolled up like he was about to get into a bar fight, and nattily dressed Meredith, in a beige vest and plaid bow tie, a pipe sticking out of the side of his mouth, looking like he'd rather be anywhere than standing in front of us.

"I'm required to remind you at the start of these meetings that revealing this highly classified intelligence to anyone is punishable by death," Frank said, rubbing his hands together. "So, with that said, happy Friday. I'm going to have Meredith kick things off."

"I want to thank you all for burning the midnight oil," Meredith said. "You've all done extraordinary work. I have always approached the kind of work we do here with a certain joy, and maybe that's why I've gotten pretty good at it."

There were smiles in the audience at the obvious understatement.

"Since discovering the scientists' names, however, our work here has taken us in a chilling direction. And I'm . . . I'm still coming to grips with that. We're not in Kansas anymore. And as Frank always reminds us, we've got to be more careful than ever about never revealing what we know to anyone outside these walls." Meredith gave a sad smile. "That said, let's review what we're planning to include in Special Report Number One of the newly dubbed Venona Project. If any of you want to add context or have questions, please chime in. Yes, Rosemary?"

"What's the Venona Project?" Rosemary asked.

"It's what we're calling the 'Russian Problem' from now on. For security's sake, we needed a name for it that wasn't descriptive," Frank answered.

"But what's *Venona* stand for?" Cecil called out.

"Nothing. I made it up." Meredith smiled and shrugged, and a few people laughed. He then started writing on the board as he continued talking. "Since making more progress after breaking the *spell* and *end spell* code, we've discovered more of the code names the Soviets use in their communications—for locations, for US politicians, and for the sender and recipients of the coded messages, including:

KAPITAN—President Roosevelt

ARSENAL—US War Department

THE BANK—US State Department

"The code names represent a new, mysterious vocabulary for us to solve.

"There are hundreds of them, and yes, some of these code names are for Soviet intelligence officers, agents, and sources who were operating here in American during the war," Frank said, getting up and once again talking to us like we were in a locker room before the biggest game of our lives. "We need to keep working harder than ever. Always with these two questions at top of mind: How did they acquire those seventeen scientists' names from the Manhattan Project? And most importantly, what other secrets related to the atomic bomb were they able to steal?

"Cecil, I know you've been able to decode some Soviet KGB tradecraft terms and meanings—why don't we review those, because they'll help in our search moving forward. Will you come up to the board and help me out?"

"Yes, chief, definitely." Cecil jumped up, knocking over his chair as he ran to the chalkboard before Frank even finished the sentence. When he reached the front of the room he looked back at me. "Hey, Cat, want to help me with this? Your handwriting is better, and you should get just as much credit for the work."

"Cat, get up there," Rosemary whispered, nudging me with her elbow.

I stood and walked to the front of the room, all eyes on me, feeling a little weak in the knees, my face flushed. I had met most everyone at that point, but I still caught a few curious stares from those that I hadn't.

"You write, I'll explain." Cecil handed me a piece of chalk and smiled at me encouragingly. "These terms should help us categorize the code names and maybe give us clues to their real identities."

I had been hesitant when Cecil had asked me if I wanted to work with him, but it turned out to be my first real foray into codebreaking, no longer just shadowing and observing other people. Many of my late nights over the past couple of weeks had been spent working with him, drinking far too many cups of bitter coffee and snacking on his seemingly unlimited supply of Dots gumdrops and Necco Wafers candies. Cecil's command of the Russian language was excellent, and he had been in the section from the start, so he not only understood the various codebreaking methods used but had also helped develop some of them. He was a character, but no one would question his brilliance. He was born for this kind of work. He was right. I had picked up a great deal from him in a short time. The least I could do was join his bowling team.

Probationers—KGB agents

Fellow countrymen—Members of the American Communist Party

Workers—KGB officers

Put on ice—Deactivate an agent

Legend—Cover story

Shoemaker—Forger of false passports

My hand was trembling a little as I continued to write out the many words we had discovered. As I wrote, Cecil explained our methodology for finding the terms and their definitions.

"Thank you, Cecil, and . . . uh . . . Catrina," Meredith said when we were finished, and Effie coughed into her hand, stifling a laugh, as I walked back to my seat. I sat down, still shaking from nerves.

"Nice job, *Catrina*," Gia whispered with a wink, and Rosemary just rolled her eyes and smiled.

"Meredith, Gene will work with you to write up what I'm calling 'Venona Special Report Number One' with all that we have so far—the scientists' names, the terms Cecil and *Catherine* just listed, and every code name we've discovered so far. All of it. I want it ready to send no later than early next week, Wednesday at the latest," Frank said.

Meredith's arms were crossed, visibly frustrated by this announcement, but he said nothing.

"Excuse me, Frank?" Bill Weissman cleared his throat. "I just want some clarity—are we to understand that some of these spies are still here, in the US? Do you believe they're still at it?"

"Yes, I'm sure some of them are, and new ones have replaced some of the agents who were here during the war years," Frank said, acting like it was absurd to consider otherwise. "That's what Meredith meant when he said we were entering uncharted territory. These messages might be a few years old, but it's likely some of the Soviet agents mentioned by code name are still working here. That's why it's time to, discreetly, inform the higher-ups at the ASA and FBI."

Meredith shifted uncomfortably, shoving his pipe in his mouth as if to stop himself from speaking. His whole demeanor made it clear he did not agree, but Frank continued talking.

"The thing we all need to remember is, the Russians are playing chess while we are playing tic-tac-toe." He looked around the room, his expression grave. "They are very old hands at the espionage game. It is in their history and their blood. Compared to us and the British? They are *masters* at this."

A chill went through me. Nobody spoke. We all just glanced around at each other, absorbing this information. Frank paused and looked up at the clock above the chalkboard.

"I've got to head up to the Capitol," he said, concluding the meeting. "That's enough for now. Needless to say, we've *still* got our work cut out for us, and we're just getting started. Class dismissed."

Chapter Eleven

That evening I walked upstairs from the café, with a free, ice-cold Coke from the rigged Coke machine in hand. It was after six, and the normally chaotic open office area of the Russian section was empty. It never felt as peaceful during the workday, and I had found I enjoyed staying late just to sit at my tiny desk in the corner and work in the calm quiet. It was Friday, and I knew I should go back to Idaho Hall and relax with some of the girls, maybe start packing my things to move to my new room. But I had been going over a new, partially decoded and translated message that I couldn't stop thinking about. It was the mention of one woman's name that I kept turning over in my mind.

"I know what you're saying, Frank, but I just want a little more time. We're close to making some more breakthroughs, and I want to be as thorough as possible."

The door to Meredith's office was open, and I heard his voice loud and clear.

"And as I've said before, Gardner, the clock started ticking as soon as you read me those scientists' names," Frank said. "We don't *have* more time. We need to run this up the food chain to the colonel. He can decide if we share it with J. Edgar Hoover."

"Meredith, we'll include a number of caveats about what we've discovered, what we have here, and what we don't yet know," Gene said. "Frank's right, we can't keep a lid on this anymore, for all the reasons we've discussed."

"All right," Meredith said, exhaling. "If we have to do this, you still don't think we should include the White House?"

"No, I'm worried about leaks. I don't trust some of the people who work there, based on some intelligence from the FBI," Frank said. "I want to keep this as contained as possible."

This discussion was not for my ears, so I tiptoed over to my desk, to gather my things before they knew there was anyone else still on the floor, only to trip and bang my knee against Rosemary's desk, letting out a loud, reflexive curse from the pain.

"Who's there?" Frank barked.

"Cat, what on earth are you still doing here on a Friday?" Gene said, leaning out of the office, her chestnut hair perfectly coiffed, burgundy shirtwaist dress pristine even at this late hour.

"I was just going over some things," I said, cringing and rubbing my knee, which was radiating pain. "I'm sorry, I'm heading out now. Just getting my purse."

"No please, come in here for a second," she said, waving me over with a smile.

"I don't want to interrupt . . ." I said, but Gene gave me a look that said she wasn't taking no for an answer.

"Grab a seat." Gene motioned to a folding chair in the corner of Meredith's office, and I dragged it over and sat down.

"Um . . . okay, and good evening," I said, looking at Frank and Meredith, as my foot started tapping of its own volition.

"Good evening, young lady," Frank said, frowning at me.

"I'm sorry, but what is she doing here?" Meredith frowned at Gene, as if I couldn't hear him.

"Meredith, as you know, Catherine is new and so far has proven to be one of the hardest working employees that we have," Gene said.

"Oh, thank you," I said.

"You're welcome," Gene said. "And I'll only keep you a minute. We were just going over details of Special Report Number One that's going up the chain of command to Colonel Carpenter, head of ASA, and the Army's G-2 special intelligence group."

"Um . . . okay," I said, and Meredith let out a big sigh.

"The reason I asked you to come in"—Gene shot Meredith a warning look—"is because I have a new assignment for you, and you're going to be working with Meredith more closely as a result."

"What? What assignment?" Meredith said, sitting back in his chair and throwing up his hands. "What are you talking about, Gene? We haven't even discussed—"

"Let me finish," Gene said, holding up her hand to him, and Meredith closed his mouth. "I'm putting Cat in charge of the new master book of code names we discussed the other day. You said you needed someone dedicated to it, Meredith."

Meredith and Gene locked eyes for a moment, and I thought he was about to continue to argue, but instead he let out a big sigh and nodded at her to continue.

"Cat, you'll track every code name the team discovers in the deciphered messages from KGB officials in New York City, DC, and San Francisco to Moscow Center, otherwise known as KGB headquarters," Gene said. "You will note every appearance of them by message number and date and, when discovered, the code name's actual identity. This will be our bible as we continue to mine these messages for clues about the Soviet agents, officers, and sources in the US. What do you think?"

"I'd . . . I'd love to take that on, thank you," I nodded, happy for the assignment, despite Meredith's sour expression.

"Great," Gene said. "It's settled, then."

"Don't screw it up, sweetheart," Frank said, looking at me with a skepticism that knocked the pride right out of me. "It's too important."

"Exactly," Meredith said. "You've only been here what? Two weeks?"

"Actually, almost five." I stood up and looked both of them in the eye. They barely knew my name, and they clearly doubted my abilities, and that aggravated me. "I promise you both, I won't screw it up."

"I *know* you'll do a terrific job with it," Gene said. "We can talk more about it on Monday."

"And I'm sorry to interrupt your meeting," I said. "Have a good weekend."

We said our goodbyes, and I walked out of Meredith's office but stopped short, startled by the sight of Bill Weissman at the other end of the room, hat and brown leather briefcase in hand, standing over Cecil's desk.

"Bill, hello," I said in a raised voice. Bill looked up at me, a possible flash of anger in his eyes, but his face transformed into its usual charming grin so fast I couldn't be sure.

"Catherine, burning the midnight oil again too, I see?" he said.

"Not quite," I said, walking toward him. "I'm heading out soon. I thought I was the only one here besides those three. Did you need something from Cecil's desk?"

"No, no, it can wait till Monday," he said, putting on his gray felt fedora. "Are you walking out now? Would you like me to wait for you? Walk you to the bus station?"

"That's kind of you, but you go ahead," I said. "I've got to pack up my things."

We said goodnight, and he left without even stopping by Meredith's office to say goodbye, which struck me as strange. After I was sure he'd left the building, I walked over to Cecil's desk, to see what Bill might have been looking at, but it was organized chaos, a mess of his favorite yellow legal pads, towering piles of gray file folders and scattered *While You Were Out* slips, so I couldn't begin to guess what Bill had been eyeing.

I returned to my own desk to pack up, grabbing my purse and picking up the file with that new name I had discovered and the possibilities it held. And I made a snap decision.

"Hi, again," I said, knocking on Meredith's doorframe, and judging from their looks of exasperation, I was testing not only Meredith's patience but Frank's too. "I'm heading out, but the reason I'm here so late is a piece of a message that I have been working on. I came across something tonight I think is important."

"Something that can't wait until Monday?" Frank asked, hand on his bald head. "We're just leaving ourselves."

"I . . . I think no, it can't," I said, trying not to second-guess myself.

"What, pray tell, is this 'revelation'?" Meredith said in a bored tone with a dramatic wave of his hand.

"The code name Liberal has been mentioned six times from October to December of 1944. And, so far, he's believed to be one of the key Soviet agents connected with the plot to steal atomic secrets," I said.

"Yes, sweetheart, we all know about Liberal," Frank said, interrupting me. "So why don't we—"

"I know you know, but that's not the interesting part," I said, holding up the file in my hand. "I was going to say I found a mention of Liberal in a new message from late November. And when I deciphered and translated it, I realized one of the words is a first name, a woman's name, within the *Spell* and *End spell* indicators. I think . . . I think it's a really interesting clue: *Liberal speaks of his wife Ethel, aged twenty-nine, married five years.* Liberal's wife's *real* name is Ethel," I said.

Gene was nodding and smiling at me in approval.

"Ethel," Frank said, nodding. "You're right, that's a new lead for us."

"Thanks," I said, blushing with pride despite myself.

"You mean it's a lead the FBI could work with," Gene said. Giving Meredith a pointed look, she added, "*If* the colonel makes that decision. But he can't make that decision unless we send him the special report."

Meredith said nothing to me. He just stood up, grabbed a piece of chalk, and started writing, from memory, the other decoded messages that mentioned the agent Liberal, including their dates and message numbers.

"I'm going to need you to stay a little later, Cathy," he said over his shoulder. "I want to go back and review everything we've got on Liberal so far."

"It's . . . that's fine, I'll grab my notebook." I didn't correct him, and Gene didn't either. She just gave me an amused look and shook her head. The fact that he wanted to work with me was a start. He'd remember my name soon enough. I'd make sure of it.

Chapter Twelve

Saturday, October 18, 1947

"Sugar, we need to take you shopping. You've worked a bunch of overtime since you got here. I think you can afford at least one new dress, maybe two?" Effie said as she stood in front of the closet of my new room on the second floor of Idaho, rifling through my clothes, trying to determine what I should wear out that night. She was wearing a violet peplum-style dress, with a matching headband, naturally.

"I know," I said. "I've never had a clue when it comes to fashion."

"Or . . . color, apparently," Effie said, taking out a navy-blue dress and holding it up. "How many black, navy-blue, and beige clothes does one girl need? That's it, next weekend we're taking you shopping at that department store, Woodies."

"Who's going to Woodies? I'll go." Gia poked her head into my room, wearing a marigold floral dress, her long, dark hair pulled up in the front, cascading down her shoulders in the back.

"Lovely dress, Gia. Yes, you should come. We need to help Cat pick out some clothes that don't make her look like she's a novice at the convent," Effie said.

"Ouch, that's a little harsh, don't you think, Effie?" I said, giving her a playful shove, as I took out the same black dress I had worn to the Cairo. "I'll just wear this again. We're only going to the pub—it's not exactly fancy."

"It is a little harsh but . . . not untrue," Gia said, eyeing my black dress with pity. She took it out of my hands and put it back in the closet. "Wait a sec, I'll be right back."

Gia returned carrying a hot-pink dress with a black patent leather belt.

"I think we're about the same size," she said, as she held it up against me. "Try it on."

"I love it. Definitely try it on, Cat," Effie said. "And Gia, how do you have more dresses than Queen Elizabeth? Is your family as rich as Rosemary's?"

"Ha! Definitely not," Gia said as she helped pull the dress over my head. "But my sister Carmen is a great seamstress, so she's made a lot of my dresses for cheap. Ah, there we go, that looks gorgeous on you. You should wear pink more often."

I turned to look at myself in the full-length mirror on the back of the door. It was a dress I'd never have picked out on my own, but I had to admit it was flattering. The belted waist and the flared skirt made me look shapelier than I really was.

"Thank you, you really don't mind me borrowing it?" I said, looking at the back of it in the mirror.

"Not at all," Gia said with a wave of her hand. "I even have lipstick to match that you can borrow. And you should wear your hair down for a change, show off those curls."

"Do you think so? I feel like they're kind of unruly," I said, running my hands through them.

"I agree with G. Just pull your hair up in front like Gia's, leave it down in the back," Effie said, grabbing my hairbrush and twisting my hair up in front with two barrettes. "There. Lovely."

"Ladies, are you ready?" Dale said, peeking in. "Taxi's going to be here any minute. Oh! Great dress, Cat."

Minutes later, the four of us were squished into the back of a taxi heading to the Liberty, the young taxi driver obviously delighted to have a car full of women on a Saturday night.

"Wait, I thought Rosemary was going too. Where is she?" I asked.

"I think she's meeting us there with Margaret Sherwood, that gal who led orientation," Effie said. "I find Margaret to be a bit much. But she and Rosemary are close friends. Archie and Jonathan are meeting us there too, right, Dale?" Effie said, straining to check her red lipstick in the rearview mirror.

"Yes," Dale said with a huge smile. Per usual, she was radiant, this time in a deep-blue dress with pale-blue piping.

"I saw you walking him out last night." Gia looked across at Dale. "Is it getting serious?"

"I wouldn't say that," Dale said with a coy expression. "He's a Yankee *and* a Catholic. My daddy would hate him, but that's why I moved away from home. So my family can't monitor every aspect of my social life. And I must say, girls, he is one hell of a kisser."

"Who? Your daddy or Jonathan?" Gia teased, and we all started laughing, even the taxi driver.

"Gia!" Dale said, giving her a playful punch on the shoulder.

"He speaks *very* highly of you, Cat," Dale said, nodding at me.

"Who does?" I raised an eyebrow, trying to banish the vaguely unpleasant thought of her and Jonathan locked in a passionate embrace.

"Jon, silly," Dale said.

"I find that a little hard to believe," I replied.

"No, really," Dale said. "He said you were kind of intense and competitive..."

"Well, I'll give him that," I said. "But he was even more competitive than me."

"He also told me the guys in the class were intimidated by you, because you were—I believe the words were 'scary smart and so pretty.'"

"Now that's ridiculous." I rolled my eyes. My face was turning hot, and it had nothing to do with the stuffy taxi.

"Cat, take the compliment," Dale said, holding her compact and reapplying her lipstick as we turned onto Q Street. "I wouldn't lie about it. And it's a good thing I'm not the jealous type."

"Scary smart and so pretty—no surprise to me they thought that," Effie said as we pulled up to the Liberty.

"Me neither." Gia grabbed my hand to help me climb out of the cab.

"Aw, thanks, friends." I smiled, and it dawned on me that my homesickness was finally fading into the background of my daily life. I had fascinating work and a group of girlfriends, something I had never found in high school or college, for the simple reason that I'd never quite fit in, in either place. In high school, most of the girls in my class were talking marriage and babies by senior year, and only three of us went on to college.

At Radcliffe, many of my classmates abided by rules that I didn't know existed—rules from an upper-class society playbook ingrained in them thanks to being educated at schools like Miss Porter's and Dana Hall, and from attending debutante balls in Newport or spending summers in places like the Hamptons or Nantucket.

As the four of us walked into the pub together talking and laughing, I felt a sense of ease and comfort with these girls from Idaho Hall. They were a piece in the puzzle that was my life, that I hadn't even realized was missing.

∼

An hour later, we were sitting around the same table we had sat at the last time we were at the Liberty. White cotton cobwebs and black felt spiders adorned the walls along with all the boxing paraphernalia, and plastic orange pumpkin garland was draped across the top of the mirror that ran the length of the Liberty's long, polished oak bar. The smells of frying oil and stale beer, and the sight of the band joking with one another as they tuned their instruments, made me wistful for my uncle's bar and my brother's band. Singing with Mickey and the guys, learning the classic Irish folk songs, the harmonies and arrangements, had been an outlet, an escape I didn't realize I would miss so much.

"So how are you, Cat?" Rosemary said, interrupting my thoughts. She had arrived with Margaret Sherwood shortly after we had. "You seemed a little distracted today when we were moving all your stuff upstairs. Is it that news from home, about your fiancé?"

"Ex-fiancé," I said. "Important distinction. And I . . ."

"What news?" Gia interrupted me. "Fill me in first, please."

I explained what Seamus had reported in his letter, and her eyes grew wide.

"Wow. No flies on your ex," Gia said, her mouth in a twist.

"No flies at all," I said as I looked up to see Jonathan and Dale chatting with one of his colleagues from the Bureau, her arm around his elbow. He had arrived shortly after we had, thick, dark hair freshly cut. Effie had shown me a picture of Gregory Peck in *Photoplay* magazine, and I had to admit there was a strong resemblance. As if he sensed being watched, he glanced over and caught my eye, and I turned to Gia and pretended not to notice.

"But I'm surprised at how little I've thought about the Andrew news. I've been thinking about work, honestly. Something came up last night. I know we can't talk about it here."

"Absolutely not," Rosemary said. "Tonight we are discussing fun and trivial things only. Speaking of, Archie the Brit seems smitten with Effie. Can you ask Jonathan more about him? Make sure he's a decent guy?"

Archie and Effie were standing at the bar chatting with Margaret. Archie was looking down at Effie, adjusting his glasses as he laughed at something she said.

"All I know from Eff is he went to Cambridge, has three sisters, and is not here permanently. I can ask Jonathan, although I think Eff can handle herself," I said.

"Speaking of Jonathan," Gia said, lowering her voice and leaning in. "This is bordering on gossip. Okay, it's *totally* gossip. So, Dale is dating Jonathan, and obviously likes kissing him, as I myself have witnessed more times than I care to count, but . . ."

"Spill it, Gia," Rosemary said.

"The other night after work, I met a friend from home for drinks. He works as an aide to Senator Wagner from New York," Gia said.

"And?" I said.

"And *he* is friends with the congressional aide from . . . Alabama, like Dale," Gia said. "And that aide from Alabama—Roy something—claims he's romancing a bombshell pageant queen who works here in town."

"I mean, the South does love their pageants, though, right?" I said, caring way more about this piece of gossip than I should, while trying to poke holes in her theory. "It's possible there's another pageant queen in the city."

"Come on, Cat, you really think that?" Rosemary said with a laugh.

"I don't know . . . I just don't think we should jump to conclusions," I said. "Dale and Jonathan have been spending a lot of time together."

"We'll discuss this later," Gia said under her breath. "She's coming back over with Margaret."

"Ladies, there are some very handsome FBI men here tonight. You need to meet some of them," Dale said, her cheeks flushed as she sat down next to Rosemary and took a big sip of her mai tai, such an odd choice of drink at a pub. Just then, the crowd started cheering as the band launched into "Whiskey in the Jar," and I got up to get another round of drinks.

As I was ordering, Jonathan spotted me at the bar and waved me over to where he was standing, making space next to him.

"Hey, Cat, good to see you," Jonathan said with a warm smile. He looked me up and down. "Now that is a *great* dress."

"Oh, thanks, it's Gia's," I said, my stomach doing a tiny flip thinking of Dale's words in the cab.

"Tell me your order," he said.

"Oh, but it's my turn to buy for the girls." I held up my purse.

"I'll get this round, I insist," he said. "I'm glad I caught you alone. Could we . . . could we grab our own drinks and talk—for just a quick minute? Confidentially?"

"Sure, I guess," I said, both curious and a little uneasy.

"Louis!" Jonathan called out to the tall redhead we had met at the Cairo, and Louis, who was standing with a group nearby, made his way over.

"Nice to see you again, Catherine. What's up, Dardis?" Louis said.

"Bring these drinks to those gorgeous ladies at the table over there, okay?"

"Absolutely." Louis smiled and winked, deftly picking up the two rum and Cokes along with his pint.

Jonathan led me over to the corner of the bar near the back hallway, pulling out the last available barstool for me. I thought of what Gia had just said about Dale's possible dalliance. Her aide friend's information was probably totally off base, just idle gossip. She shouldn't have even told us.

"I tell you, sometimes I can't believe I'm here, can you?" Jonathan said, the delight in his eyes making him look much younger than twenty-five. "Living and working in one of the greatest cities in the world."

"Sometimes I really can't," I said, and maybe it was the drinks, or the warmth of the bar and the Irish tunes that always made things better, but I knew how he was feeling. It was exhilarating to be here—and it was the first time in my life I had ever felt this kind of independence, this freedom.

"I tell you, after I got back from the war, I said, whatever I end up doing, it's going to be a part of something bigger. My dad was crushed when I told him I wasn't going to go to law school or join the family firm. But for a stubborn old Irish fella, he got over it. He was just glad to have me back in one piece."

"Don't I understand that," I said in a quiet voice. "You took the road less traveled."

"And that has made all the difference." He smiled. "I love that Frost poem."

"Me too."

I knew he had served in the army, in Europe. A shrapnel injury to the leg had brought him back home for good. Harvard had saved his space until he returned, as they had for many veterans of the war.

"As I mentioned, canceling my wedding, ending up here?" I said. "It can all be traced back to the war, to Richie . . . to Richie's death."

"How is your other brother, the one . . . the one who came back?" he asked.

"Oh, Seamus?" I thought of his recent letter. I couldn't wait to hug him again. "He's . . . okay. He has these terrible nightmares, and I can tell he still feels this awful guilt over surviving when so many didn't."

"I know all about that." Jonathan nodded. "The nightmares *and* the guilt."

"I'm sorry," I said softly.

We were quiet for a moment, lost in our thoughts, listening to the music, as the band launched into "Seven Drunken Nights," another pub favorite.

"Do you know this one?" Jonathan asked.

"I know all of them, Dardis." I laughed. "The lyrics, arrangements, harmonies. I didn't just sing in the band, I basically grew up in my uncle's pub, so . . ."

"You need to ask these guys if you can sing with them some night," he said. "Don't you miss it?"

"I do, more than I thought I would. But I could never do that, I'm sure they'd think I was crazy," I said, glancing back at the table where my friends were sitting. "What exactly did you need to talk to me about? Because Dale's glancing over here looking a little peeved. We should go sit—"

"Okay, real quick, can I tell you a story?" He took a sip of his drink, smiling and holding up a finger, signaling to Dale we'd be there in a minute. Her expression was less than thrilled.

"Um . . . okay," I frowned at him. "Quick story."

"In 1945, an American woman named Elizabeth Bentley walked into the New Haven, Connecticut office of the FBI. She was a New

Englander and a Vassar grad, and she told the FBI she was willing to provide information in exchange for immunity from prosecution."

"What kind of information?"

"First let me *tell* the story. God, you were like this when we were in class too," he said, teasing.

"All right, I'll shut up. Sorry," I said. "But get to the point."

"The woman claimed she had extensive information about Soviet spies operating in the United States. She was willing to give the FBI all this information *if* they granted her immunity. She stated she knew this information because she was a Soviet spy herself."

I could feel the goose pimples on my arms, the hairs on the back of my neck standing up. I looked him in the eyes and shook my head.

"Jonathan . . . no. *No.* Why are you . . ." I said. I started to walk away, but he grabbed my elbow, and I stopped.

"Cat, just . . . please hear me out," he said, still holding onto my arm, our faces a couple of inches from each other, close enough that I could smell the rum on his breath, that damn cologne too.

"I don't want to know any more. You shouldn't be telling me this!" I hissed, looking around. He had been talking in a low voice, directly into my ear. But I was still paranoid that somebody could have overheard him. "You shouldn't be telling *anyone* this . . . You could get fired. Or worse . . . they could . . ."

"But I trust you implicitly," he said.

"Why? How?" I said, feeling the warmth of his hand gripping my arm, his dark eyes looking into mine with an intensity and trust that unnerved me. *Scary smart and so pretty.* The words echoed in my brain. "We barely know each other. We were in one class together."

"Yes, we were at the top of our class in a very specific seminar on cryptology. And I know whatever I tell you will stay between us. You're such a straight arrow, and I need you to hear this. You and I . . . I can't tell you how I know, but I *know* we're working two sides of the same problem. The Russian Problem. And I think we could help each—"

I tried to signal with my eyes that Dale was coming up behind him, but it didn't register.

"What in the world are you two discussing?" Dale interrupted Jonathan, and he dropped my elbow like it was on fire, while I weighed the gravity of his words.

"Just catching up on some news from home," I said, and it sounded like such a generic lie I cringed. And now I couldn't help wanting to know the entire Elizabeth Bentley story.

The team had made so much progress, but there was an undercurrent of tension in the Russian section, a feeling of constantly chasing ghosts that we would never be able to catch.

I thought of the most recent clue, *Liberal speaks of his wife Ethel, aged twenty-nine, married five years.* Maybe the FBI could help lead us to some of the real spies behind the code names.

"We were just coming back, sweetheart," Jonathan said, putting his arm around Dale and giving her a kiss on the cheek, which seemed to placate her. "Cat was just asking me more about my coworker Louis over there, and whether he had a girlfriend back in Wisconsin. She loves ginger-haired guys, don't you, Cat?"

"Wait, what? I . . ." I started to say that this was not true at all, but Dale interrupted me.

"Cat, why didn't you tell me?" Dale said. "We've got to get you two talking. Come on."

"Oh yeah, I mean . . . okay, sure," I said, figuring it was better to just play along for now. Dale took Jonathan's hand, and we headed back to the table.

When Dale wasn't looking, I narrowed my eyes and gave Jonathan a dirty look and mouthed, *Thanks.* He just winked back at me.

Chapter Thirteen

Wednesday, November 5, 1947

Per Frank's orders, "Venona Project Special Analysis Report Number One" was given to the heads of the ASA and G-2 the weekend following our meeting. And for the next couple of weeks, all of us in the Russian section worked as hard as ever, while also waiting for some sign from Frank or Meredith that the report had been read, that those in authority understood the gravity of our discoveries so far.

Since our talk at the Liberty, I'd only seen Jonathan Dardis in passing a few times, when he was leaving Idaho Hall with Dale, and we hadn't had any chances to talk again. But I kept thinking of his words that night and the woman named Elizabeth Bentley who had confessed to being a Soviet spy. The more I considered it, the more I desperately wanted to know everything about her, to learn what he knew, to see if it would help our cause in Building B.

It was the first Wednesday in November, and Gia, Rosemary, and I were sitting at our usual picnic table under the trees. The autumn air was crisp, but the sun was shining, and that was enough for us to take a break from the confines of Building B.

"I thought something would have happened by now, didn't you?" I said, keeping my voice low. "We just sent a report regarding the Russians stealing atomic secrets during the war. What could be more critical to America's national security than that?"

"But maybe things are happening, and we haven't been informed yet," Rosemary said, examining her chicken salad sandwich. "None of us are exactly in the 'need to know' category."

"It's the federal government." Gia shrugged. "They don't do anything fast."

"Speaking of fast, why is Cecil running over here like he's being chased?" Rosemary said. Gia and I turned to see Cecil galloping down the path from Arlington Hall like a giraffe, barely holding on to the large cardboard box in his hands.

"Ladies, I'm so glad I caught you at lunch," Cecil said, taking a deep breath and dropping the box on the picnic table. "They have arrived, just in time for Saturday. Wait till you see."

"What the heck are you talking about?" Gia said.

"Gia, remember, the bowling tournament is Saturday," I said giving her a look, hoping she would be kind.

"Yes," Cecil said. "Our bowling shirts arrived. I even had them monogrammed. Here, look."

He rummaged through the box and held up a bright purple shirt with gold trim on the sleeves and collar. The name *GIA* was emblazoned on the front breast pocket. He turned the shirt around, and on the back there was a large cartoon picture of a UFO, the words *The Flying Saucers* underneath. The shirts were so loud, so over-the-top in color and design, I gasped and bit my tongue to keep from laughing.

"Oh, wow!" Gia said, pulling herself back from the table, looking at the shirt as if it might bite *her*.

"Do you like them, Cat?" Cecil looked at me, earnest and hopeful. "I designed them myself."

"How could I . . . How could I *not?*" I said. "No team will have shirts anything like this. Not even close."

"They're fabulous," Rosemary said, reassuring him. She took one out of the box and held it up to her slim frame. "They're so . . . so bright, they can probably be *seen* from outer space. Did you get one for Effie?"

"I just gave it to her," Cecil said, beaming as he passed them out to us. "Effie was supposed to join the Pin Pals, the IBM group team, because they needed one more player, but she got out of it. We're bowling against them, the Lane Rangers from Building A, and the Alley Gators—they're the accountants in Arlington Hall. See you Saturday at five at the bowling alley. This is going to be so much fun!"

"There is no way on God's green earth I am wearing that thing," Gia said after we watched him hurry into Building B.

"Why not?" I said, teasing. "You love bright colors."

"Oh, Gia *come on*, look how thrilled he was," Rosemary said, taking a cigarette from her. "I'm going to wear it, even though it might be the first purple thing I've worn since grammar school."

"Also, I don't think Cecil gets out much. Please do it," I said.

"I like bright colors, but these are . . . Also, the Flying Saucers? Seriously?" She raised her eyebrows as she turned the shirt over to look at the back.

"Come on, it's funny," I said. "And it's definitely better than the Pin Pals."

"Have you gals ever bowled before? I used to go with some friends on Sundays at Bryn Mawr," Rosemary said.

"Only a few times in my life," I said. "Cecil might cut me from the team after Saturday. What about you, Gia?"

"I've bowled a bit," Gia said with a sigh, getting up and throwing out her lunch. "And because you're making me feel bad for the guy, I'll stay on the team. But both of you owe me a drink after."

"Deal," Rosemary and I said at the same time, laughing as we headed inside.

∼

That afternoon, Rosemary and I were in Meredith's office, attempting to assist him with what he called his "hunt for the great white whale." Little by little, he was reconstructing the KGB's codebook, which was essentially the dictionary they used for sending words and phrases in English. In the world of cryptanalysis, this was known as "book breaking." It was the oldest and most challenging form of codebreaking. If he succeeded, we'd have a dictionary that would allow us to read the text of all or at least most of the telegrams that were sent or received from Moscow Center to its KGB agents and informants stationed overseas during the war years.

A few of us would go into his office at least a couple days a week, sitting amid mountains of file folders and his preferred gray notebooks as we tried to help him exploit the weaknesses he had already discovered. Book breaking had its own proven strategies, and Meredith was a master of all of them.

It was all reminiscent of the most challenging of crossword puzzles—a discovery of a vowel could unlock more than one word. The placement of a word could end up revealing a familiar phrase. At times the process could be thrilling but, more often, it was painstakingly tedious.

Meredith stood at his bulletin board, deep in thought, as we all reviewed the data written out on index cards pinned in neat columns. The first column contained the original KGB messages with their impenetrable, five-digit blocks of numbers. The second held what the experts called the "message prints"—these were the messages reduced to their basic code groups, without the concealing encipher from the original messages. The third contained the IBM group's invaluable index of each five-digit code, including their various locations and which codes appeared more than once in the cable message traffic. Finally, there was the frequency analysis list—where we ranked the blocks of code by how often they appeared in messages, listing the most frequently used ones up top.

"A linguistics professor at the University of Texas once said, 'If you change the way you look at something, the thing you look at changes.' I always think about that when I'm stuck. Consider the pieces of the whole in a different way, rearrange them, shake out another clue. Find any weaknesses and exploit them." He paused, still facing the board, sleeves rolled up, pipe hanging out of his mouth, the not unpleasant aroma of Middleton's Cherry Blend tobacco in the air.

"You understand, we're not stopping until we can read entire messages," he mumbled, still moving things around. "The words from the Russians' English dictionary we have so far? These are just the beginning."

He often said things like this, more to himself than to anyone else. Rosemary started to ask a question but stopped at the sound of voices coming from outside Meredith's office. Frank had entered the Russian section with Colonel Carpenter, the head of the ASA. He was a tall, silver-haired older gentleman with an intimidating presence, particularly when he was wearing his uniform, as he was today. Two other men followed behind the colonel. One was also quite tall and looked to be in his thirties, wearing a charcoal gray suit and wire-rimmed glasses. I gaped at the other man, recognizing him from the cover of a recent issue of *Newsweek* magazine. He was stocky, with slicked-back black hair and dark, bulging eyes, wearing a perfectly tailored, expensive-looking beige suit.

"Uh . . . Meredith?" I said.

"One minute, I need to get this all down," he said in an irritated tone as he wrote something on the chalkboard.

"Is that . . . ?" Rosemary looked at me.

"Oh yes. Yes, it is," I said, gritting my teeth and nodding.

"No, Meredith, you really need to see who's here," Rosemary said, straining her neck to get a better look.

"Who? We're in the middle of something here. What could be more important . . ." He turned and threw his chalk down. But when he spotted the group walking toward the conference room, his face went white. Frank knocked and opened the office door.

"Meredith, can you please join me in the large conference room?" Frank said. It was an order, not a request. "It looks like your special report is finally getting some attention. And where the heck is Gene?"

"Gene had to leave this morning for an emergency dentist appointment," I said. "Root canal."

"She's never out. Of all days," Frank said, closing his eyes, his fingers squeezing the bridge of his nose. "Rosemary, grab your notebook and pen. I need you to be Gene in this meeting and take the best notes you can."

"All right, I'll meet you in there," Rosemary said, but as she stood up, he looked her up and down.

"Oh no. No." He exhaled, looking at Rosemary's outfit in horror. "Hoover hates seeing women in pants. Cat, you're wearing a dress. Get your things—you're going to have to be Gene instead."

"Frank, that's ridiculous," Rosemary said, eyes wide in disbelief.

"Seriously? Why would that matter?" I said, looking at Rosemary in her beautifully tailored navy slacks and gray silk blouse. "Rosemary's outfit is gorgeous."

"Sorry, Rosemary, it's just one of his quirks that I do not want to deal with today, of all days," Frank said. "See you in there, Cat."

"J. Edgar *Hoover* can go pound sand." Rosemary bit her lip, furious.

"Honestly," I said. "You should just come in with me. What's he going to say?"

"Oh no. I don't even think Frank wants me to walk by the conference room," Rosemary said with a cynical laugh as she got up. "Good luck, my friend. Let me know how it goes."

Meredith hadn't said a word this whole time. He was staring at the board or something beyond it, lost in thought and even paler than before.

"Meredith?" I said. "Are you okay? Do you need some water?"

"What?" Meredith said, coming out of his daze.

"I think we'd better head to the conference room," I said, feeling like I might throw up.

"Yes," he said, grabbing some files and a notebook to bring with him, still looking frazzled.

J. Edgar Hoover, the director of the FBI, was one of the most famous and powerful men in the United States government. He had distractingly thick black eyebrows, and when I walked into the conference room and introduced myself, he stood up and shook my hand, and his stern expression relaxed into a tight smile for a brief second. I knew from newspaper articles that he was short, but he was even shorter in person than I expected. I was five foot five, and he was a couple inches taller at most.

The man with Hoover was Bob Lamphere, one of the senior members of the FBI's Soviet espionage section. He was broad-shouldered, a few inches taller than Hoover, with a square jaw and brown eyes, handsome in a rugged, Midwestern sort of way, with an open smile and a much friendlier demeanor than Hoover. Meredith appeared visibly unimpressed with either man, and I could tell this made both Frank and the colonel uneasy.

As soon as everyone was settled around the table, Hoover began to speak.

"The colonel brought your report, your Venona Project Special Report, to my attention, and it is alarming to say the least," Hoover said. "It has also reinforced my suspicions about just how much and for how long the Soviets have been infiltrating our country, spying on us. Over the past few years, we have had clues and uncorroborated testimony, but what you have here? This is finally proof that the Soviets penetrated the Manhattan Project. And I fear it's just the tip of the iceberg."

"The first thing Hoover and I discussed is who should be given this information," the colonel said, leaning forward in his chair, his fingers a pyramid. "The larger the distribution list, the more likely the Soviets will find out what you've uncovered, so we're going to keep it contained to just a small group: the FBI Soviet espionage unit and a couple top officials at G-2 military intelligence for now. And I believe we have no choice but to inform a couple of our high-level contacts in British intelligence as well."

"You aren't going to inform the president?" Frank asked.

"No, absolutely not," Hoover said, shaking his head. "We have reasons to believe there might be a Soviet agent working in the White House."

Meredith cleared his throat rather loudly, and we all turned to look at him.

"As I said in the report," Meredith said, speaking for the first time, "the code names, what we've been able to discover so far—we've only scratched the surface, creating more questions than answers. We have much more work—"

"That's why I've assigned Lamphere to work closely with you and your team on this," Hoover said, interrupting him. "Sharing information from the FBI, discovering the real names behind the code names, and ultimately launching investigations into suspected individuals."

"With all due respect, director," Meredith said, blinking at him, frustration in his voice. "I think the Russian section has more to do on our *own*, before we're ready to work with the FBI. We need more time. Many of the messages are still full of gaps."

"Mr. Gardner, that is not your decision to make," Hoover said, making it clear this was not up for debate. "The FBI is involved going forward."

"Meredith, I understand your perspective, but this has already been decided," Colonel Carpenter said.

"We've got a growing team in the Soviet espionage section." Bob Lamphere spoke up for the first time, smiling at Meredith, trying to assuage him. "Lindsay Philmore, one of the rising stars in British intelligence, will be coming over, working out of the British consulate; Jonathan Dardis, a brilliant young veteran and Harvard graduate, is my right-hand man; Archie Spencer . . ."

The mention of Jonathan's name caught me off guard for a brief second, even though I knew I shouldn't be surprised given what he had said at the Liberty.

"I know we're working two sides of the same problem."

It made sense, of course we were given that he had been offered my role on Meredith's team before joining the FBI. And now I had the exact context for why he had been so eager to talk to me about Elizabeth Bentley.

"Cat? Are you getting all of this?" Frank was looking at me, eyebrows raised.

"Yes, of course," I said, focusing back on the present.

"Good, so Bob, you'll be returning in the next few days to meet with Meredith," Hoover said.

"Absolutely," Bob said, nodding at Meredith, who was staring at the ceiling.

More was discussed about the details of the memo, and what progress we had made in the weeks since we had sent it. When things appeared to be winding down, Frank held up his hand.

"I have said this to both Hoover and the colonel prior to this meeting, but before we convene, I need to emphasize it again," Frank said. "It is critically important that what Meredith and the team are working on, in breaking the Soviet code system, remains top secret. In other words, *if* the FBI launches investigations based on these deciphered messages, you can *never* disclose these messages as a source. And they must never be used in court either."

"Yes, exactly," Meredith said, throwing his hands up, relieved that Frank was making this point clear. "From an intelligence standpoint, the value of these decryptions lies in their secrecy—the Soviets can never know what we can read and see. It's our one true advantage over them."

"And I promise you, the FBI intends to protect that advantage," Hoover said, standing up from the table and looking at his watch. "If investigations are launched, if, God willing, we end up in court, we will only state this information has 'come from a highly sensitive source of known reliability,' or words of that nature. We're extremely good at this, Gardner. Your secret project here will be safe with us."

The rest of the men left, but Meredith remained at the conference room table, hands behind his head, staring up at the ceiling again, as if waiting for divine intervention. I held the Saint Rita medallion around my neck between my thumb and forefinger and debated whether I should try to talk to him. But watching him, it was clear that he wasn't anywhere that I could reach at the moment.

I quietly gathered my things and stepped out of the conference room, when he called out my name.

"Catherine?"

"Yes?" I said, leaning in the doorway as he turned to look at me, an enigmatic expression on his face.

"Everything's going to change now," he said, his voice resigned. "For the Russian section."

"I know," I said, in a gentle voice because he seemed tormented by the thoughts running through his head, at what the future was about to bring via Hoover and the FBI. "But we've been waiting for someone to pay attention and do something, and now they are. This is all good . . . Right?"

"That's the thing," he said, his expression grim. "I'm not convinced that it is."

Chapter Fourteen

Saturday, November 8, 1947

Much to Cecil's delight, the Flying Saucers placed second in our first-ever Army Security Agency bowling tournament on Saturday. Our victory was thanks in large part to Gia, who had failed to mention that her father had been the longtime president of the Italian American Bowling League of New York City and she had been bowling since the age of five. She even brought her own pale-pink bowling ball in a monogrammed two-tone pink leather bag.

After it was over, Effie and I went back to Idaho Hall to change out of our garish bowling shirts before heading out for the evening. Gia and Rosemary had been smart enough to bring a change of clothes to the tournament and had gone straight to dinner at a local Italian place with Margaret, Cecil, and some other bowlers.

Effie had a date with Archie Spencer. And though I had planned to meet up with the group that had gone to dinner, after a hot shower, I decided to call it a night, write a couple letters to my dad and brothers, and go to bed early. I had just put my favorite flannel pajamas on when there was a knock on my door.

"Hey, sugar," Effie said, handing me an envelope. She had changed into a royal-blue A-line dress that brought out her eyes and had pulled her hair into a bun accented by a matching ribbon.

"You look so pretty," I said.

"Thank you." She smiled, posing for me. "Archie brought this to give to you. From Jonathan."

"What?" I said, looking down at the jagged handwriting. I recognized it from class.

"I was ordered to deliver it right away." She shrugged. "Why are you in your pajamas?"

"I've decided I'm staying in," I said. "I'm beat after this week."

"You sure about that? Maybe this note will change your mind." Effie gave a nod to the envelope, and I opened it.

> Killeen—
> Heard you had a couple of unexpected visitors at Building B yesterday. I think it's time we finished that conversation from our last time at the Liberty. Meet me there tonight. I'll be there by eight.
> Jonathan

"Is this an invite or a demand?" I frowned at the letter. "It's just like him, *Meet me*. Not *Would you like to meet me?* Or *Please meet me if you are available*..."

"Well? Are you going to meet him?" Effie asked, reading over my shoulder. "You know what? You absolutely should. I know that meeting yesterday rattled you. I mean of course it did, how could it not? It was J. Edgar Hoover, for the love of God. He's like Washington's biggest power broker. I dropped some files off to Meredith afterward, and he was still shell-shocked."

"We both were," I said.

"So . . . are you going to meet him?" she asked.

"I don't know," I groaned. "I'm tired, but I'm also too curious. I know we can't discuss everything, obviously, but still . . ."

"Then throw one of your new dresses on and go," Effie said. "It's Saturday night, it'll do you good."

She went over to my closet and pulled out another dress she had helped me pick out, in a color and style I never would have chosen on my own. It was candy-apple red with a full skirt, pleated above and below the bust with a waist panel to create a "nipped in" look, according to the saleswoman.

"Here, this one, it's fabulous on you," Effie said.

"Do you think Dale will get the wrong idea if she hears about it?" I said. "I mean, it's just a drink, and I knew him from before."

Dale had gone home to Alabama for the weekend for a wedding of one of her sorority sisters.

"Dale's supremely confident in herself and her effect on men. She won't give it a second thought," Effie said, pausing for a moment. "And listen, we've all heard the rumors about her and the congressional aide. Who also happens to be away this weekend."

"Really?" I raised my eyebrows at this.

"*Really.*" Effie grimaced.

"But Jonathan's in the FBI. Does she honestly think he won't find out?"

"I have no idea," Effie said and then, looking at the clock on my nightstand, added, "but now I've got to go, because Archie's waiting for me, and he's going to wonder what's taking so long. Go. And, you know, maybe have a good time? Don't treat it as just work. You're better at having fun than you think, my friend."

An hour later, I stepped inside the Liberty. The sounds of the fiddler warming up made me wistful for home. I couldn't wait to see my father and brothers at Christmas.

Scanning the crowd, I ordered a drink and was asking the bartender if he'd seen someone of Jonathan's description when I felt a tap on my shoulder.

"You're here," Jonathan said, beaming at me. I had to admit, he looked ridiculously handsome, wearing a pristine white shirt under a navy-blue suit jacket. "I gave it fifty-fifty that you would show up. Come on, I got us a table away from the stage. It's not so loud."

He paid for my drink and led me by the elbow to a booth on the second-floor landing, where we had a bird's-eye view of the entire bar.

"Is that a new dress?" he asked as soon as we sat down.

"As a matter of fact, it is," I said.

"I don't think I've ever seen you in red."

"This is actually the first red dress I've ever owned. And thanks," I said, feeling my face flush, flattered that he had noticed.

"So, Dale's home this weekend?" I asked.

"Yeah, she's in a wedding—sorority friend," he said, taking a sip of his beer. He looked back at me. "Dale's . . . she's fun . . . but we didn't come here to talk about Dale."

"No," I said. "And you're right, after the meeting yesterday, I needed this drink. Thanks for the invitation. So . . . do you know everything that was discussed?"

"Oh yes," he said. Lowering his voice, he added, "Of course it's not like Hoover didn't know what you all were working on, but that special report even shocked him."

"What did you hear about how the meeting went—overall, I mean?"

"I heard Bob Lamphere's version. Why don't you tell me how you think it went?"

I gave him the play-by-play, also keeping my voice low because Arlington Hall had made me always have my guard up in public places. He listened intently as I struggled to explain Meredith.

"He's as brilliant as you've heard, but can be temperamental," I said. "He works harder than anyone I've ever met. And he's territorial about this work. I think he's worried about where things are going to go from here, his lack of control, now that the . . . now that you-all are involved."

I looked around the bar, paranoid to say FBI.

"That's basically what I heard," Jonathan said. "But Bob is a terrific guy, whip-smart and hardworking too, and he's a charmer. That's part of what makes him so good at his job. I'm sure he'll be good friends with Meredith by the end of the week."

"And *I* think you're way too optimistic about that, but we'll see," I said with a laugh. "Look, I want to hear your story from last time we were here, about that . . . about Elizabeth Bentley. I need to know what you know."

"Yes," he said, elbows on the table. With his finger he traced a jagged, ridged line someone had carved.

"I feel okay talking about it, now that our groups are officially working together," I said.

"I figured," he said, and teasing he added, "I didn't mean to get you upset that night. It's just that, even if we *were* sharing information unofficially, I know you'd never tell."

"Yeah, yeah," I said, with a wave of my hand. "But now I need to know. Tell me everything."

"She joined the Communist Party while in graduate school at Columbia . . ." he said. "What? You just got the strangest look on your face."

"I'm . . ." I said. "I'm fine, it's just, I have an estranged uncle who works at Columbia and is also a member of the CPUSA."

I told him the story about Peter Walker and my background check.

"I knew about your mom," he said in a soft voice. "But wow, did you know about your uncle before you came here?"

"I've always known *of* him, but we've never met," I said.

"That must have been odd to have him come up in your background check," he said.

"It was very odd, but in the end I was cleared," I said. "Anyway, when you mention Columbia and the Communist Party in the same sentence, of course it makes me wonder if they knew each other."

"I read her statement. It's over a hundred pages long, and she never mentions anyone from her Columbia days."

"So their paths probably never crossed," I said. "Anyway, sorry to get distracted. Now tell me the rest."

Jonathan explained that shortly after that, Bentley met Jacob Golos, a Soviet KGB operative based in New York. The two began an intense affair, even though Golos had a wife in Moscow and a mistress in

Brooklyn. Bentley became Golos's courier for a vast network of contacts, gathering information from spies placed in government scientific labs, the Treasury Department, and, again allegedly, even the White House.

When Golos died unexpectedly in '43, Elizabeth took over managing the network. But the pressure of the role led Elizabeth to alcoholism and extreme paranoia. And as an American, rather than a Russian-born spy, she feared that Moscow Center might not want her around for long.

"What . . . She thought they would kill her?" I asked, shuddering at the thought.

"Yes," Jonathan said. "When she came to the FBI, she named over seventy Soviet agents and sources and also listed a dozen US government agencies whose secrets were being shared with the KGB on a regular basis."

Jonathan took another sip of his beer, and we just looked at each other for a moment before he continued. "You can imagine what Hoover thinks of Bentley's allegations. They are incredible and incendiary, but there was only one problem with Bentley's confession. What do you think it was?"

"Hmm . . . Based on some things Hoover said, I'm guessing she had nothing to back up all these allegations," I said. "You've got no corroborating evidence."

"Bingo, we have nothing," Jonathan said. "And that has frustrated Hoover to no end. But your team might be able to help us finally determine whether Bentley's telling the truth."

"Because if we can corroborate what Elizabeth Bentley has told the FBI with any information our team has uncovered, we might finally be able to track down some of these Soviet agents, *if* they're still in the US."

"Now you're talking, Killeen," Jonathan said with a smile, pointing at me with his glass.

This partnership with the FBI was far from one-sided. We weren't just giving them leads to chase down. They had pieces of information that could help us make more progress with deciphering the KGB messages, and with Meredith's "white whale," re-creating their codebook.

"So, word is you've become Meredith's right-hand woman."

"I'm not sure about that," I said, although I had developed an understanding of Meredith, of how his mind worked as well as his quirks. And I'd proven myself to some degree, unearthing some critical intelligence in my first few months in Building B, "Liberal's wife Ethel" being one of several key clues I'd discovered.

"Trust me, if that's what I hear, it's true. So, what do you say? Think you and I can work together and help our teams, and our bosses, work together?"

"Maybe . . ." I said, and his face fell. "What I mean is, I'm willing to try. To start, you need to really give your boss some background about Meredith. He's going to be a tough nut to crack."

"Good, glad you're willing to try. And yes, I'll talk to him," Jonathan said.

"Okay," I said, and with a single, lingering look, we understood each other. But the flutters in my chest compelled me to look away, focusing on the Irish band performing onstage.

"This band is growing on me," he said.

"They're really talented," I said.

"I mean, they're not as good as your brother's band, especially when you sing with them, but . . ."

"Wait . . ." I looked over at him again, smiling, one eyebrow raised. "What are you talking about, Dardis? You said you'd never heard me sing,"

"I . . . okay, you busted me," he rubbed his hand over his face, embarrassed. "It was long before we crossed paths. During my first year of college, prior to my trip to Europe. A bunch of us were coming from a Red Sox game. We ducked into Killeen's for a beer because it was raining buckets. We sat in a booth in the back, you were singing with the band that night, and well . . ."

"Well, what? Come on, out with it," I said, still smiling, but now I was tapping my foot, nervously anticipating what he was about to say.

"You were brilliant, naturally." He leaned closer. "That year was hard, worrying about going to war, devastated about friends getting killed. It was such . . . it was a terrible time . . . I went to hear you and the band a few times over the next few months. It was my favorite escape, if that makes sense."

"I'm sorry, I . . . I honestly don't remember ever seeing you there." I blushed at his compliment, frowning, searching my memory for his face in the audience years ago. "I've got a pretty good memory, and I feel like I should . . ."

"Oh, my buddies and I, we kept to ourselves, sat in the back usually," he said.

"I still can't believe it," I said and then gave him a shove. "You *lied* to me."

"Yes, well, now you know my secret. I was a fan of your music, your singing, before we knew each other." He took a sip of his drink. "I thought you were a professional singer. So when you turned up on campus, it was a total surprise."

"You remembered who I was?" I asked, skeptical. "Just from seeing me sing at Killeen's a couple times?"

"Catherine Killeen, anyone who has seen you up onstage could never forget your voice, never forget *you*. I told you before, it was part of your mystique with the guys at Harvard," he said in a quiet voice, nodding at me.

"Oh please, and I told *you* that's ridiculous," I said, looking away, hoping he couldn't tell how much I was blushing in the dim lights of the pub.

"Okay, all right, don't believe me. Anyway, we should toast," he said, holding up his glass. "I think this is the beginning of a beautiful friendship."

I started laughing again as we clinked glasses.

"What? What's funny?" he said, a huge grin on his face.

"No." I pointed a finger at him. "Did you . . . did you *really* just quote *Casablanca* to me?"

"So, what if I did?" he said, laughing now too.

"Is that one of the lines you use with all the ladies?"

"Actually, no," he said, giving me that crooked smile that had broken so many hearts at Harvard. "That line's just for you."

Chapter Fifteen

Monday, November 10, 1947

Before we left the Liberty, I had given Jonathan some more tips on working with Meredith that I insisted he pass on to Bob.

"Look, you and I are smart people, right?" I said. "But Meredith Gardner is operating on a different plane from just about everyone in the world. I have never in my life met anyone who is a genius like him. But also, he's a loner, is incredibly introverted, and can be prickly—mostly because he hates to be distracted from his work."

"Sounds like fun," Jonathan said. "Also sounds like you're making excuses for him."

"Maybe I am, but it's because I understand him now," I said. "He likes ideas and words and puzzles. And his singular obsession is solving *unsolvable* problems. He takes . . . he takes knowing, as Frank has said. This is not a man that you can take out for a beer and bond with over college football. He's . . . he's going to be difficult."

So, when Lamphere walked into the Russian section on the following Monday morning, I hoped Jonathan had given him enough background to prep him for his first meeting with Meredith. He looked handsome in a navy double-breasted suit, crisp, pale-blue shirt, and striped tie, and he greeted various people in the office with a warm smile and tip of the hat. A couple of the young secretaries openly stared at him after he walked by them, giggling and talking behind their hands.

"Good morning," he said to me, Gia, Rosemary, and Effie. We were sitting around Gia's desk, going through the latest reports Effie had brought over from the IBM group. "I didn't realize there was a secret female army over here at Arlington Hall. Catherine, I know we met last week, but I haven't met any of you. Hi, I'm Bob Lamphere from the FBI."

Everyone introduced themselves and shook Bob's hand.

"Effie LeBlanc, right? You're Archie's girl," Bob said. "It's nice to finally meet you. He's told me so much about you."

"Um . . . I . . . I guess I am, and likewise," Effie said, startled by his words. "Lovely to meet you, sir."

"Please, all of you, call me Bob. *Sir* makes me feel old." He grinned. "I'm looking forward to working with you. I've got a meeting with Meredith at ten to kick things off. That's his office in the corner, yes?"

"I'll bring you over," I said, getting up. "His light's off, but I know he's in there."

I knocked on Meredith's door. He didn't answer, though I could see him through the glass, hunched over his desk. Bob looked at me, knocked a little louder, but still Meredith didn't respond.

"I think I'm just going to pop my head in," he whispered, taking his hat off, revealing jet-black hair receding slightly at the temples.

"Good luck." I nodded to him and went back to Gia's desk.

"Guess we'll see how this goes." I winced, holding up my hands with fingers crossed.

"Oh, it's going to be an utter disaster," Gia said with her usual cynicism. "He's been complaining about the FBI all week. Hey, can we move our work to your desk so we can eavesdrop, Rosemary? It's the closest to his door."

"We will do no such thing," Rosemary said in a firm voice before adding, "though honestly I'd love to."

"Meredith was in a particularly foul mood when I dropped off some files to him earlier this morning," Effie said. "Does Bob know what Meredith can be like?"

"Jonathan was supposed to warn him," I said.

"Did you tell him about the dead-fish voice?" Gia asked.

"What?" I said, frowning at her.

"Oh, even my group knows about that," Effie said. "When he talks in the dead-fish voice, it means he has zero interest in what you have to say."

"Huh." I remembered several occasions when Meredith had sounded like that. "I've heard it, I just didn't know it had a name."

Not even ten minutes later, Bob stepped out of Meredith's office, and Meredith slammed the door behind him.

Bob had an amused smile on his face and, to his credit, did not appear the slightest bit ruffled as he put his hat back on, stopping by to see us on his way out.

"Leaving so soon?" Gia said, followed by "Ow!" because I kicked her under the table for the rude comment.

"I guess we'll give it another try in a few days," Bob said, his tone unfazed. "He wasn't in the mood for much talk today."

"Please don't take it personally," Effie said, and Rosemary and I, and even Gia, chimed in with similar sentiments.

After he left the Russian section, I decided to follow him.

"Bob?" I said, catching him in front of Building B.

"Yes?" he said with a smile.

"I don't know if Jonathan told you anything . . ."

"He did, thank you," Bob said. "So did Gene and Frank. I know it might take a little time with Meredith. But I'm confident I'll get there."

∼

For the next few weeks, Bob Lamphere came by every couple of days to meet with Meredith. And each meeting, if you could call them that, lasted about ten minutes. Bob, to his credit, did not give up, even though Meredith grew more reticent each time Bob came by. Everyone else in the office really enjoyed getting to know the gregarious FBI agent. He was funny and kind, and his wife had just had a new baby, so he proudly showed us new pictures of his infant son.

The Monday after Thanksgiving, Bob arrived just as Meredith was storming out of the office, blurting out something to Bob about a prior meeting as he rushed by him. This time even Gia took pity, because Bob couldn't hide his frustration.

"He likes sherry," Gia said. "Maybe bring him a bottle?"

"Oh, and he loves Middleton Cherry Blend tobacco," Effie said, biting her nail before adding, "I'm sorry, I'm not sure how buying him tobacco or sherry would really help your cause, though."

"Thank you, ladies," Bob said. "I have no choice but to keep trying. My job is on the line here."

I had run into Jonathan at Idaho Hall the night before while he was waiting for Dale. And he had informed me that Bob was receiving tremendous pressure from Hoover for not making more progress with the ASA, specifically not making more progress with Meredith.

"Maybe tell Meredith that Hoover himself is going to march back into your building again and read him the riot act," Jonathan said. "Trust me, he doesn't want to be on Hoover's bad side."

"I don't doubt that," I'd said. At that point Dale had come downstairs and whisked Jonathan away mid-conversation, which annoyed me more than it should have.

That afternoon, long after Bob left, Meredith came back, ignoring everyone as he headed straight into his office and slammed the door.

"That's it," I said, getting up from my desk.

"What are you going to do?" Rosemary said.

"I have no idea, but this is getting ridiculous. He knows what's at stake, and everyone is just . . . just putting up with his stubborn behavior because he is who he is. I'm going to talk to him."

"Good luck with that," Rosemary said. "I could run down to the rec center, get you a helmet before you head in there?"

"That's something Gia would say," I said, looking at his closed office door.

"In all seriousness." Rosemary stood up. "I'll go with you. It shouldn't be any of our jobs to do this."

"Thanks, maybe two against one will be better," I said.

"All right, let's go," she said, as if we were heading into battle.

I rapped on Meredith's door. When he didn't answer, I walked in anyway.

"What the . . . Catherine, Rosemary," he said, frowning. "Please go away. I'm busy. And if this is about the FBI and Lamphere, don't bother. Gene just talked to me about it over lunch, and I'm not in the mood for any more lecturing."

"Meredith," I said. "I know your reservations about working with the FBI, but you cannot stonewall Bob Lamphere forever. Sooner or later, you're going to have to work with him. And it's killing all of us to see him keep trying and have you behave this way."

Meredith put his hands over his face.

"You know more than anyone, our progress has slowed down . . ." Rosemary said, taking the words out of my mouth. I thought of the spy code-named Liberal and his wife named Ethel. We'd uncovered many more code names of Russian spies since then, but not nearly as many clues as to their real identities.

"Some days it feels like we're wasting precious time," I said.

"We are not wasting time!" Meredith bellowed, slamming his hand on his desk. It was the first time I'd heard him yell, and Rosemary and I both jumped, startled by it.

"I am still doing the work," he continued, his voice still loud but no longer yelling. "We are making progress. This work, as you know, takes patience and persistence."

"Yes," I said, keeping my tone even and calm. "But we could also be working *smarter* if we worked with the FBI."

"But I don't . . . I don't trust Hoover," he said, pushing back from his desk. "I don't like him either. He's an anti-communist zealot. He's way too political, interested in his own power above everything else."

"That all may be true, but um, he's the *director of the FBI*," Rosemary said, grimacing. "And by the way, Bob Lamphere is not Hoover."

"Rosemary's right," I said. "We've all gotten to know him. Bob's a good person and has the country's interests at heart. I think you can sense that about him. The FBI Soviet espionage group has been working the same problem from a different angle. They want the same things we want. To identify these atomic spies, among many other Soviet agents."

"You always talk about codebreaking requiring 'collective brain power,'" Rosemary added. I thought we had made our points, but I wasn't sure it would matter.

He glared at us, and I braced myself for him to start ranting again.

"And I also don't like giving up control," he said, his voice soft now. "I've been here four years. This started out as the most challenging intellectual exercise of my career. Like solving the biggest and most complex language puzzle the world ever created. The Russian code system has been described as almost mathematical in its abstract beauty, and I have come to believe that to be true.

"But as I've said before, when I discovered that list of Manhattan Project scientists, I knew that we'd entered a darker territory. The real-world implications of our discoveries now? They've . . . they have been hard to accept. It's absolutely horrifying. It's . . . it's not what I signed up for."

"I know," I said, and Rosemary just nodded.

"Anyway, I apologize for yelling," Meredith said. "I know your intentions are good. And I also know if I don't start cooperating with Bob soon, I could end up fired."

"Please. They'd *never* fire you," I said with a smile.

"Oh, you never know." He grinned, knowing I was right. "Anyway, your points are taken. I'll . . . I'll work on my . . . approach with Bob."

"Good," Rosemary said. "That's a start."

Rosemary walked out, and I was just about to follow, but instead I asked the question I'd been curious about since the day Hoover had shown up at Building B.

"Meredith, if you could get anything from the FBI, any sort of intelligence that would help our cause, what would you want from them?"

"Oh, that's a very easy answer," Meredith said. He told me in detail what he was looking for, and I took mental notes in my head.

"If they could get me that? That could change the whole game for us," he continued. "But I wouldn't even bother asking."

"But why not? Isn't it worth at least asking?" I said.

"Catherine, it's impossible they have that kind of intelligence," he said, his tone kind but somewhat condescending. "They could only get that information by breaking into the Russian consulate. Which is completely illegal."

Chapter Sixteen

Saturday, December 6, 1947

On Friday night, Effie arranged for a large group of us to go dancing at the Cairo Hotel again, this time in their grand ballroom.

"Is Archie going home with you for Christmas?" I asked as we climbed into a taxi.

"No, he's not," Effie said. "I think the culture shock would be too much for him. Also, introducing him to my parents? Well, that means it's serious. And look, he's charming and kind, and who doesn't love that accent, but when Bob referred to me as 'Archie's girl'? I'm just . . . I didn't come here looking for a husband, I came here looking for a life."

"Oh, do I understand that." I laughed.

"I know you do, runaway bride," Effie teased.

"I'm dreading going home for the holidays." Gia sighed.

"Why?" I asked.

"I'm getting pressured," she said. "My parents want me back in New York. Permanently. To help manage the beauty shop, inventory and accounting, all of it."

"But what about your sisters?" I asked.

"My sisters are too busy having babies to help," Gia said. "Also, I know this sounds harsh, but none of them are that smart. They're all great with hair but a disaster with numbers."

"You can't leave us," Effie said, wrapping her arm around Gia's elbow. "It's bad enough that Rosemary is moving out."

Rosemary had just informed us that she had finally made the decision to leave dorm life, moving into an apartment in Georgetown with Margaret in January.

"You absolutely can't," I said. "And what about poor Cecil? He'll be devastated."

"Oh please," Gia said, rolling her eyes as we got out of the cab. "Trust me, I don't want to leave. Believe it or not, I'd miss Idaho Hall, and you two."

"Aw, so sentimental, G, thanks," Effie said as the hotel doorman tipped his hat and opened the front door for us.

"And Jonathan is definitely coming tonight?" I asked as we walked up through the hotel's art deco–inspired lobby, which was accented by white marble Egyptian columns, dark polished wood furniture, and burgundy velvet floor-to-ceiling curtains. It smelled of floor polish and some vaguely exotic perfume, a combination of cinnamon and musk.

"He is," Effie said. "Archie said he's coming, along with a few others from the FBI, and maybe a couple of friends from the British consulate. Rosemary and Margaret are meeting us here, probably some of the IBM girls too."

"Why are you asking about Jonathan?" Gia said, teasing.

"What? It's nothing like that, he's with Dale," I said, getting more defensive than I should. "I just want to talk about the whole Bob and Meredith situation."

"Is he, though? *With* Dale, I mean?" Gia said, tilting her head, frowning.

"Gia, enough with the gossip," Effie said, giving her a pointed look.

"It's not gossip if it's just between the three of us," Gia said.

"It's totally still gossip," Effie said. "But go ahead, tell her."

"Is this about the congressional aide rumor?" I said. "If it is . . ."

"Not a rumor, I'm afraid," Effie said.

"It's only a matter of time before she breaks up with him," Gia said. "I still don't know how he can't know."

"The aide, whose name is Roy, apparently has enormous political ambitions," Effie said. "And their daddies are friendly. Their parents go to the same country club, the same Baptist church. It's a match made in Southern-fried Alabama heaven."

"You didn't even tell her the best part," Gia said, with a mischievous smile.

"Oh no. How can there be a best part?" I said. "Poor Jonathan. If this is all true, she needs to break it off with him. It's not right to string him along."

"Roy's last name is Gale," Gia said, with a mischievous smile. "If they get married, her name is going to be *Dale Gale*. Isn't that amazing?"

"Okay, that's enough, they might already be here," Effie said as we entered the crowded ballroom. It was a grand room with high ceilings and crystal chandeliers that gave off a warm, ambient light that reflected off massive windows flanked with the same velvet curtains as the lobby. A large, raised stage with a twenty-five-piece orchestra overlooked the dance floor. Each table had a Christmas-themed arrangement, and two twenty-foot-tall Christmas trees flanked the stage, decorated with gold tinsel and hundreds of red-and-green bubble lights. Even the chandeliers were adorned with faux partridges and pears.

"There you are, ladies. Come with me." Archie greeted us all with kisses, putting an arm around Effie as he led us to a large table on the opposite side of the room. Rosemary and Margaret were there, as well as Louis and a couple of new fellas who I assumed were also from the FBI.

"Welcome, ladies. Great choice, Eff," Rosemary said.

"Agree, this is such a terrific spot," Margaret said. She was wearing pearl-framed glasses tonight and a black dress with detailed embroidery that flattered her petite figure, and I was struck by how much more relaxed she was outside of Arlington Hall.

"Where's Jonathan?" Effie asked, clearly asking on my behalf as we sat down.

"He's out somewhere with Dale, but they might be by later," Archie said as the waitress came over and took our drink orders, and I tried not to feel disappointed by the word *might*.

As the evening progressed, the energy in the ballroom felt charged. Everyone seemed to be having a fabulous time. Maybe it was due to the festiveness of the décor for the holiday season or the gorgeous full-piece orchestra and free-flowing drinks, but something about the night felt magical. I even danced with Louis a couple times, relieved to discover his dancing had improved.

A couple of hours after we arrived, a surprise guest appeared at the ballroom's entrance, looking a little lost, his eyes searching the dance floor and tables for familiar faces. His sandy-brown hair was slicked back, and he wore an impeccable charcoal-gray suit with broad lapels and a tie covered in bright yellow sunflowers. I gasped and hurried over to him.

"Cecil?" I beamed at him. "Is that really you?"

"Cat! You're here!" He leaned down to give me a kiss on the cheek.

"You look so dashing, my friend," I said.

"Thank you," he said, nervously smoothing out his jacket. "Do you like the tie?"

"I *love* the tie."

"I think sunflowers are unapologetically optimistic."

"I guess that's true." I laughed. "Are you looking for . . . ?"

"Gia. She invited me," he interrupted, nodding, and I tried not to show my surprise.

"Oh . . . oh, that's great. I am so glad you came," I said, pointing back at our table. I caught Gia's eye, and she just gave me a wink.

"Gosh, she's gorgeous," Cecil said, gazing at Gia as he talked. "She invited me on the condition that I only bring up UFOs once tonight. So, I brought a list of other things to talk about with people."

He took a piece of notebook paper out of his pocket to show me.

"Put that away. I promise you won't need it," I said. "It's a nice group of people over there. Go. I'll be back soon."

"Thank you," he said, grinning ear to ear like a little kid. "You know, I've . . . I've never really had a group of friends before, like you and the other gals."

"Can I be honest, Cecil?" I said, patting him on the arm, touched by his earnestness. "I never have either."

"Really?" he said.

"*Really,*" I said.

I watched him walk over. Effie jumped up and gave him a big kiss on the cheek as Rosemary signaled the waitress to order him a drink and Gia pulled out a seat for him right next to her. What I had said was true. I finally understood how it felt to be part of a group of friends, to have people at your table.

"Hey, Killeen."

I whirled around, smiling at the sound of Jonathan's voice my ear. "Jonathan, Dale. You both made it."

"I dragged him to a cocktail party in Georgetown for an hour. A friend from home was hosting. It was a pretty dull affair," Dale said, looking around. "This place looks way more fun."

As a couple, they looked like they were straight out of a *Vogue* magazine: He was in an impeccable black suit, hair slicked back, and she was in a blue satin dress that accented her every curve, her hair in tumbling waves.

"Hey, is that another new dress?" He stepped back and whistled as Dale wrapped her arm around his, leaning into him in the territorial way I'd seen before, making me question, once again, if the congressional aide rumors were actually true.

"Yes, Gia helped me pick this one out," I said. It was plum-colored velvet with an off-the-shoulder neckline. "And Effie talked me into buying it. It was on sale."

"It's stunning," he said, one eyebrow raised. "Your friends have good taste."

"Thank you, I agree. Much better taste than me." I smiled, hardly willing to admit to myself how pleased I was by his words.

"They do. I must say, your wardrobe has improved a *ton* since you first got here," Dale said, looking me up and down, the statement in that purposely gray area between a compliment and an insult.

"All thanks to Gia and Effie." I gave her a tight smile as I pointed to our table. "Everyone's either on the dance floor or sitting over there. I'll see you both in a minute."

I headed to the ladies' room, located in the hallway near the elevators. When I walked out, I was taken aback to see Jonathan standing there, a serious expression on his face.

"I'm beginning to think you have a habit of loitering outside ladies' rooms," I teased.

"We need to talk, somewhere quiet," he said, giving me a pointed look.

"I know, we do," I said. "I was going to track you down this weekend if you didn't show tonight."

"Let's go to the bar in the lobby. Dale and I just checked it out, it's not crowded."

"But you just got here. We don't have to do this right this minute," I said. "What about Dale?"

"I told her I had work to discuss and I'd be back soon," he said. "She's holding court at the table. The guys are falling all over. Trust me, she's fine."

"If you say so," I said.

The lobby bar was dimly lit by dozens of Christmas tealight candles and cozy, with low tables flanked by plush chairs. The soft sounds of the orchestra in the ballroom poured from the speakers on the ceiling as we took our drinks to one of the tables out of earshot from other patrons.

"I didn't think you two were going to make it tonight," I said.

"Oh, I told Dale that we had to come," he said. "I needed to see you."

He took a sip of his drink and winked at me, and I pushed down the butterflies resulting from that one, tiny gesture.

This, I reminded myself again, was Jonathan Dardis, a known ladies' man and charmer, who was dating the beautiful Dale Motlow. We were friends and work associates. That's all we needed to be. He didn't think of me in any sort of romantic way, he was just flirtatious by nature. But why did the night suddenly seem more colorful, more shimmery, the music more romantic, now that he was sitting across from me?

"How's Bob doing?" I asked, forcing myself to focus on what mattered.

"When it comes to Meredith?" He looked at me, amused. "How do you think? He's at the end of his rope."

"I know he is," I said. "We all are."

I told him about my heated conversation with Meredith the day before. "At the end, I asked him, if he could get anything from the FBI, what would it be?" I said.

"What did he say?" Jonathan leaned in.

"I doubt you can fill this request, but I figured it was worth telling you," I said. "He wants copies of the Soviet messages transmitted from New York to Moscow in 1944. As many as he can get," I said, and he gave me a confused look.

"But you have thousands of those already. File cabinets full of them, don't you?"

"We do. And that's what I said. But he wants *uncoded* copies of those messages in Cyrillic, in Russian, *before* they were enciphered. To be able to compare the plain text messages to the same messages shrouded in code? Well, that would be a dream, for all of us in the Soviet section. But especially for him—just think what Meredith could do with that."

"That is a tall order," he said, tracing the table with his index finger, thinking it over. "I'll talk to Bob. We'll reach out to the New York field office. But I'll be honest with you. I've only been with the Bureau a short time. I don't know how we'd be able to get our hands on a bunch of four-year-old uncoded messages from New York to Moscow."

The Women of Arlington Hall

"I know," I said. "That's . . . well, he *claim*s that's why he hasn't asked. But if we could get our hands on information like that, he said it could be game changing for him, for all of us. So . . . you'll try?"

"Of course, I have to," he said. "First thing Monday. It might be our best chance of finally getting Bob and Meredith working together."

"Agree," I said. "And maybe our last."

"Whatever Bob says about it, I'll let you know Monday evening," he said. "Dale and I are going to the movies."

"Right, Dale. Okay, that's perfect," I said, ignoring the tug of jealousy in my chest at the mention of Dale. We were friends, this was fine. This was enough.

"So, I'll leave you a note if I miss you at Idaho Hall on Monday."

"Sounds good," I said.

We sat in silence for a moment, pondering this, sipping our drinks, listening to the soft clarinet sounds of "La Vie en Rose." I looked down at our hands almost touching across the small table, and, just for a second, I wished he would reach out and hold mine.

I looked up, and he was giving me a mischievous smile.

"What?"

"Let's make a bet," he said.

"What kind of bet?" I eyed him suspiciously.

"If Bob and I can get you the messages that Meredith requested, you owe me."

"Owe you what, exactly?" I frowned, sitting back, still skeptical.

"You will sing a song with the band at the Liberty Pub. I've already checked. People go up and sing with the house band all the time. I want to hear *you* sing with them."

"What? No, *no* way," I said, shaking my head.

"Come on, didn't you say you miss singing?" he said.

"I . . . I actually do," I said, longing for home, thinking of the sounds and the smells of my uncle's pub. "I can't wait to be home for Christmas, reunite with the band for a few days."

"Then it's a bet? If I get the messages, you'll sing?"

"Sure, it's a bet," I said. "Because Meredith said you'd have to break into the Russian consulate to get them, which means it's a bet I'm going to win."

"All right, now you've given me even more of an incentive to get ahold of them. Let's toast to it," he said, clinking my glass.

"And now we should go back," I said, finishing my drink and standing up. "Dale's going to be looking for you."

"I prefer it here, actually," he said as he got up, and I couldn't admit how much I did too. "But you're probably right."

He paid the bill, and we headed back through the lobby to the ballroom.

"Killeen?" he said into my ear, and I got a whiff of his cologne as we reached the entrance.

"Yes?" I felt a surge of electricity as his hand touched the small of my back, as we made our way through the crowds of people.

"This thing with Dale has been fun . . . but I am in the FBI. I've seen the clues, it's only a matter of time before it's over."

Chapter Seventeen

Friday, December 19, 1947

After I told Jonathan about Meredith's desire for the plain text messages, I received a note from him at the front desk at Idaho Hall, as promised, that said simply, *Bob and I are working on it. I'll keep you posted.*

For the next ten days, Bob made no visits to Building B, and I was busy enough to put Jonathan's note out of my mind, working our usual long hours in the Russian section and spending time outside of work Christmas shopping and planning for my trip home to Boston on the twentieth.

Late Friday afternoon, I was bringing Cokes back from the café for me and Effie when she met me halfway up the stairs.

"Let's go back to the café for a minute," she said, grabbing my elbow.

"Oh," I said. "What's the matter?"

"Bob Lamphere just arrived," she said.

"He did? Finally." I handed her a Coke. "Is he with Meredith?"

"Yup, he had a Christmas present with him."

"Anything can help his cause, I suppose," I said.

"But that's not all," Effie said. "Jonathan's with him too."

"Oh God," I said, feeling my stomach tighten up. She knew I had asked him for help. "I hope there's a good reason for that. We should go up."

"Just one more thing," Effie said, biting her lip.

"Effie, what is it?" I asked, trying to read her face.

She looked around the café, though it was completely empty. Even the cashier had clocked out for the day.

"So . . . I saw Bill Weissman at the Cairo when we were there," she whispered. "He was talking to a man from the British embassy, someone else from British intelligence, Archie told me."

"So?" I said.

"And Bill was also at the Liberty that night a while back. Did you see him there?"

"I did, but these are both really popular places, right?"

"I know, but don't you find it odd that he's always popping up where we are? It feels like more than a coincidence," Effie said, biting her thumbnail. "And then last night when I was leaving? I caught him standing over your desk."

"At *my* desk?" I said, angered now. "What the heck was he doing at my desk?"

"You had just left, and nobody else was in our section. I totally surprised him, and he tried to cover it up, like he had dropped something nearby, but I didn't buy it at all."

I tried to remember if I had locked up all my work in my desk before leaving.

"He was at Cecil's desk one night when I was leaving late," I said, feeling even more nerved up remembering various moments with Weissman, how I had never warmed to him. "What are you thinking? He's worked here for years, right? Is he keeping tabs on us for the colonel?"

"I don't know, but he's always given me the creeps," Effie said.

"Should we mention it to Gene? Or Frank or Meredith?"

"Maybe? But then I think maybe I'm just being paranoid . . ."

"No, I agree with you, I've never felt quite right around him."

"Me neither."

"All right, let's just keep our guard up when it comes to him," I said. "And we need to get back upstairs and find out what happened. That meeting might already be over."

The Women of Arlington Hall

As we suspected, by the time we got back upstairs, Meredith's door was closed, and Bob and Jonathan were already gone.

"What the heck happened?" I asked.

"That's what we're all wondering," Gia said. "They came in, dropped off a present to Meredith, and that was that. He didn't slam the door when they left, though. So that's progress, I guess?"

"Not much progress," Rosemary added. "But they did invite us to an unofficial FBI Christmas party at the Liberty tonight. I'll be on a train home, but Gia you're going to go, right?"

"If you two are going, I'll go," Gia said, pointing at me and Effie.

"Catherine! Come into my office now." Meredith said my name so loud I jumped, the blood draining from my face.

"Oh boy," Effie said, eyes wide. "Good luck in there."

"That's the second time he's yelled—and the first time it was also at you," Gia whispered. Pointing to my medallion, she added, "Maybe ask your friend Saint Rita for a little help."

"Seriously, good luck—let me know if you need us," Rosemary said, wincing.

I walked into Meredith's office holding the medallion. His expression was pure fury, and I didn't dare sit down. On his desk there was an unwrapped bottle of Harveys Bristol cream sherry, and next to it was a nine-by-twelve-inch gray envelope stamped *FBI Classified Material* that was stuffed full, with edges of what looked like photographs peeking out of the top.

"I heard you had some visitors," I said, stating the obvious as the hairs on the back of my neck stood on end.

"Yes." He glared at me. "They came with two gifts." He motioned to the envelope. "Said a little birdie told them that these might come in handy."

"What . . . what are they?" I felt the urge to dump out the contents and go through them myself.

"They are photographs of hundreds of cable messages from the Soviet Government Purchasing Commission on West Twenty-Eighth Street in Manhattan."

"Oh . . ." I said, blinking. "And are they . . ."

"Plain-text Cyrillic, all messages *before* they were enciphered, to compare against the enciphered ones, which we have here."

"But . . . this is amazing," I said. "Have you . . ."

"Catherine. Were you the one who told them that I wanted this?"

"Meredith, yes, I was," I said, throwing my hands up. "And is that so bad? They found exactly what you wanted."

"Illegally," Meredith said.

"What?" I said, frowning at them.

"I asked how they got them, and they said they couldn't tell me, because officially these photographs don't exist."

"Let the FBI worry about how they got them," I said. "Collective brain power, right? Maybe this will finally be the big break we need."

"You shouldn't have made that request, Catherine," he said, his voice still tight, but softening now. "You crossed a line. It was not in your purview. I could . . . I could have you fired."

"What?" I gasped, feeling physically ill.

It had been a gamble to ask Jonathan to get what we needed. But they had delivered what Meredith requested. Would he really have me fired over it? This job had given me the kind of life I hadn't even realized I wanted, and a real circle of friends. Would he really take it all away because of this?

"Look," I said, my voice shaking as I took a deep breath. "I know I crossed a line. I'm sorry. I was just trying to help. Like you, I've . . . I've always been somewhat of a loner. And I can't imagine what goes on in that mind of yours—nobody can. But also? Nobody can do this work completely alone . . . Not even *you*. And I know you know that. Please. Just look through it."

He didn't look at me, just silently stared at the envelope and bottle of sherry on his desk.

"I'm heading home for the holidays this weekend," I said. "Merry Christmas."

He spoke up just as I was about to close his door. "I'll give it a look over the break," he said with an exaggerated sigh, looking at me, his expression no longer angry, just solemn. "Merry Christmas, Catherine."

Chapter Eighteen

That evening, I sat on my bed, my back against the headboard, staring up at the ceiling at the octopus-shaped water stain in the corner, muffled sounds of laughter as well as the Andrews Sisters' hit "I'm Biting My Fingernails and Thinking of You" coming from somewhere down the hall. My suitcase was packed with my train ticket on top, ready to go. After my meeting with Meredith, my homesickness had returned with a vengeance, and I wished that I was already en route to Boston, to my father and brothers and my little bedroom off the kitchen.

It was just after six when there was a knock on my door, and Effie and Gia barged in before I could open it. I had told them both on the bus ride home about what had happened with Meredith, and they had given me a pep talk, but it hadn't helped my mood.

Effie went straight over to my closet, and Gia flopped down next to me on the bed, her cosmetic case in hand. They were both dressed for a night out, Effie in a green satin A-line dress and Gia in a cream-and-red floral one paired with a chunky beaded necklace, this one green and red for the holiday.

"You didn't pack that fabulous new red dress, did you?" Effie asked as she rifled through my clothes. "Ah, found it. Put it on, sugar, we're going to that Christmas party at the Liberty."

"*You* two are going," I said, pointing at them. "I'm going to bed early. I've got to be at the station tomorrow by six a.m."

"Oh please," Gia said, opening her case. "You can sleep on the train. We're not taking no for an answer. Now sit at your desk, I'm going to do your makeup and hair. I think you need to glam it up a little. It's Christmas."

"You can't just stay in and mope after the day you had. Come out with us, toast the holiday season, it will get your mind off of it," Effie said.

"All right, all right," I said, sitting in my chair, cheered by their concern. "I guess it wouldn't kill me to go to a party."

"Good," Gia said, as she stood over me, opening her case. "And besides, you've got to cheer up your friend Jonathan. Did you hear? Dale finally gave him the gate."

"Wait, really?" I said, my heart quickening in my chest.

"Really," Effie said, taking my black patent leather high heels out of my suitcase. "She's on the way home to Alabama now. For good. Her daddy's been promising to buy her a car if she moves home."

"I think Jonathan knew it was coming," I said. "I'm sure he'll have another stunner on his arm by New Year's."

"Sure, that's *exactly* what will happen," Effie said, looking over her shoulder at me, eyebrows raised before rummaging through my jewelry box.

Gia stopped pinning up the front of my hair and looked down at me.

"What? Why the look, Gia?"

"You aren't going to need a lick of blush tonight, given how pink your cheeks are right now," Gia said.

"Honestly, who do you think you're fooling, Cat?" Effie said, handing me the pearl necklace that had belonged to my mother.

"Who am I fooling about what?" I asked, though I knew exactly what she was asking.

"It's pretty obvious you have, well, at least a bit of a crush on him," Gia said, and I started to protest, but she kept talking. "For God's sake, even Cecil noticed, and he's not exactly quick on the uptake when it comes to stuff like this."

"Did you invite Cecil tonight?" I asked.

"Don't change the subject," Gia said.

"Look, even if he's not with Dale anymore, Jonathan and I are working together, with Bob and his FBI unit," I said. "Unless of course Meredith fires me."

"Meredith is *not* . . ." Gia stopped herself, her mouth twisted. "Well, he might fire you—you never know with him. He's fired people for less."

"Thanks, G. I appreciate your honesty as always," I said grimly.

"Gia!" Effie said, swiping at her arm and glaring at her. "You're not helping. Cat, I, for one, don't think he's going to fire you."

"I'm sorry, I only want you to be prepared for the worst because there's no predicting with him," Gia said.

"I know," I groaned, burying my face in my hands.

"But I have to say, the work you've already accomplished? It's more than any new employee has done in such a short time, and you know I'm not one to exaggerate. So that's in your favor. And he *did* learn your name in three months," Gia said. "That's definitely some kind of record. So . . . so maybe you'll be okay."

"Enough about that for now, let's just try to stay positive. And back to Jonathan," Effie said. "Archie's FBI—well, he's the British liaison to it—and we're dating. His supervisor is fine with it. So working together is not an obstacle."

"But you're with the IBM group, so it's one degree removed from the Russian section," I said. Shaking my head, I added, "Why am I even saying this? Even if Meredith spares me, I need to focus on keeping my job. And I'm not interested in dating someone who is a coworker, who back at Harvard had a reputation as the campus Don Juan. And I know he's not interested in me in that way. He never would be."

"Huh, okay." Gia smiled and glanced over at Effie.

"What?" I said, looking back and forth at them. "What do you mean, 'huh'?"

"It's just . . . are you trying to convince *us* there's nothing between you two, no spark?" Effie said. "Or are you trying to convince yourself?"

∾

The fresh wreaths hanging on the walls of the Liberty amid its permanent décor and the faint scent of pine were refreshing additions to the usual aromas of stale beer and frying oil. The pub had gone all-out with holiday decorations, including a life-size plastic Santa dressed in a leprechaun outfit next to the front door, as well as red monogrammed stockings and colored Christmas lights strung along the wall behind the bar.

Gia, Effie, and I navigated our way through the throngs of tipsy revelers to the bar, looking for familiar faces, and I couldn't believe that the first one I spotted was Bill Weissman, in the corner of the bar. He was talking to a middle-aged man, thin and distinguished-looking, with deep lines in his face and a prominent nose.

"There's Weissman *again*, end of the bar," I said. Effie and I had shared our Weissman suspicions with Gia while getting ready that evening.

"Who's he talking to?" Gia said. "Who invited him? It's mostly FBI or friends of FBI here, right?"

"Right," I said. "I have no idea. But again, he's been at Arlington Hall a long time. He knows a lot of people."

"There you ladies are. You all look beautiful," Archie said, coming up behind Effie and planting a kiss on her cheek. He was wearing a festive bow tie and new, darker-framed glasses.

"Archie, see Bill Weissman at the bar?" I said, pointing to Weissman. "You don't happen to know who he's talking to, do you?"

"Of course. He's essentially my new boss, though he works out of the British embassy," Archie said. "He's just arrived from London, name's Lindsay Philmore, extremely well-connected, went to

Cambridge. Philmore's quite the rising star. Rumor has it he'll be head of MI6 someday."

"What's his role here?" I asked.

"British intelligence liaison for both the FBI *and* CIA, which of course Hoover's not thrilled about," Archie said. "I just met him last week. A little full of himself, maybe—also very enamored of the CIA."

"He seems chummy with Weissman." Effie frowned.

"Their paths crossed in Europe. Philmore's lived all over the world too—raised in India, worked as a war journalist. Trust me when I say he'll tell you all about it," Archie said.

"Don't look now, but they're coming over," Gia hissed.

"Good evening. I wanted to introduce you ladies to the latest transplant from Britain," Weissman said, putting one of his chubby hands on Gia's shoulder, the other on mine, as he made introductions. Gia looked like she was about to smack his hand off but restrained herself.

"These are some of the lovely ladies of Arlington Hall I keep hearing about," Lindsay said, in an upper-class British accent. "Bob Lamphere told me all about you."

"How do you and Bill know each other?" I asked.

"Well . . . I . . ." Lindsay started to speak, seemingly searching for words, when Bill interrupted him.

"We were both in Africa during the war," Weissman said, nodding, bald head glistening as usual, and I wondered why the man was always sweating. "Lindsay and I go way back."

"Yes, I was an award-winning journalist during the war, covering stories in both Europe and North Africa," Lindsay said, and Archie coughed. "As the newcomer here, I need to go make the rounds, but I just wanted to say hello. I look forward to working with you all." He turned to Bill and held up his glass with a nod. "Another drink, my friend?"

"Certainly. Merry Christmas, everyone."

We offered our holiday wishes. Effie gave me a sideways glance as they walked away.

"Well, now it's a real Christmas party. Welcome, girls." I turned at the sound of Jonathan's voice, and I felt a little thrill when our eyes caught for a moment, before Bob came up behind him.

"So glad you all came," Bob said. He had dark circles under his eyes, his face unusually pale. "But I'm afraid I've got to go home soon. The baby's not sleeping, and my wife is at the end of her rope."

"I heard you two dropped off some presents at Arlington Hall today," I said. "Sorry I missed you."

"Yes," Bob said with a laugh. "*Presents*."

"So you saw both? The sherry and the other . . . ?" Jonathan asked.

"Oh yes, I might lose my job over the other present," I said. "Let's just say Meredith wasn't too thrilled with my forwarding his request."

"I've been wanting to tell you, Cat, I appreciate you trying," Bob said. "It's been an exhausting month, on the work and home fronts."

"Well, I'm not sure if it will make any difference," I said. "I had to try for your sake and ours."

"Thank you," Bob said. Looking at Gia and Effie, he added, "Seriously, thank all of you for your support. I've got to head out, but I've opened a tab. Drinks are on me for the rest of the night."

We all started protesting, but Bob held up his hand.

"I insist," he said, laughing. "Merry Christmas, ladies, see you all in '48. At least, I hope I will."

We thanked Bob profusely and wished him happy holidays, and Archie snagged us our usual table near the stage. Jonathan pulled out the chair next to him and offered it to me.

"Thank you," I said, squeezing in between him and Gia, as others sat down to join us.

"You're welcome," Jonathan said, concern in his eyes. "That thing you said about losing your job—you were just kidding, right?"

"It's tough to say," I said, telling him about my conversation with Meredith that afternoon.

"I hope he takes your advice and looks at what we gave him," Jonathan said.

"So do I," I said. Speaking into his ear, I added, "How did you get those files anyway? The plain text messages?"

"It's what they call a black bag operation," Jonathan said, his warm breath on my cheek. "That's all I can say about it, especially in present company. But Killeen?"

"Yes?" I said, and I got that feeling again, like everything was warmer and more festive. The Christmas lights sparkled brighter, now that he was here.

"It would kill me if you got fired over this."

"Me too," I said. "I feel like we're just getting started."

"We are," he said, gazing at me intently, like I was the only one in the room, and I didn't look away this time, as our knees touched under the table. I just bit my lip, wishing we were alone, somewhere far from this party. When did it happen exactly? When was the exact moment that this former irritating classmate and rival-turned-friend started to make me feel something else entirely?

There was laughter and loud cheering as the band announced a quick break, and I moved my knee and looked down at my drink, breaking the spell.

"I'm sorry about Dale," I said, pushing my feelings down. It might be over with Dale, but he was still Jonathan Dardis. Even though our knees touching made my head spin. We worked together, it was impossible, and next week he'd probably be charming someone new, maybe one of the secretaries at the FBI.

"Well, like I told you, it was just a matter of time." He shrugged, running his hand through his hair. "She's a great gal, but we were never really going to be long-term. A Southern Baptist and a Catholic? I'm just mad I didn't break it off with her first. I don't like to be on the losing end of anything."

"No kidding," I said with a laugh.

"Speaking of being on the losing end," he said, pointing his glass at me and giving me a mischievous look. "We delivered what Meredith was looking for. No matter what happens with it, I do believe you owe me one song, Killeen."

"I . . . what?" I said, and I remembered our so-called bet and held up my hands in protest. "Oh no. For the love of God, no. You weren't serious."

"Serious about what?" Effie asked, leaning across the table. "Everything okay over there?"

Jonathan explained our bet, and her eyes grew wide.

"Yes! I've been dying to hear you sing," Effie clapped her hands together. "It's about damn time."

"Oh, I'm all-in for this too," Gia said, taking a drag on her cigarette.

"I've spoken with the band already, told them how good you are, of course," Jonathan said. "They said they're happy to have you sing a couple tonight, that it would be nice to have a female vocalist for a change."

"Let's hear what you got, Cat Killeen. Get up there," Gia said, clapping.

"But . . ." I looked at him, frowning.

"Just one, please?" he said. The members of the five-piece band were just coming back onstage, their pint glasses refreshed. "Come on, I'll introduce you to these guys, I've gotten to know them a little."

I gave him a smirk as he stood up and held out his hand. A shot of warm electricity went through me as he pulled me up from the table.

He first introduced me to Trevor, the craggy-faced bandleader and fiddler. Trevor was originally from Howth, a seaside village northeast of Dublin. I told him my father was from Dingle in County Kerry, hoping it would give me some Irish folk singer credibility, but he just frowned, unimpressed.

Trevor introduced me to the other members, including the stocky, round-faced accordion player, who smiled at me with glazed eyes, visibly so drunk he was swaying, though none of the others seemed concerned about him.

"Are you as good as Jonathan says?" Trevor eyed me skeptically. He spoke in a brogue much thicker than my father's.

"I . . . I don't know. I hope so?" I said, sweating now from both the stage lights and my nerves.

"Because the last couple gals who asked to sing with us ended up being rubbish," the drummer said. He was the accordion player's brother and nearly identical in build and looks. "Everyone thinks they're the most talented person in the world after six pints of Guinness."

"She's not rubbish," Jonathan said. "I told you, Trevor, trust me."

"And I've only had one drink, not six," I said, but the drummer remained skeptical.

"Okay, what would you like to sing?" Trevor asked with a sigh. "A Christmas song or . . . what Irish folk songs do you know?"

"I know all the Irish folk songs," I said, wanting to prove the drummer wrong now.

"Well, listen to yourself," Trevor said, finally giving me a smile. "Go on, do you have any favorites, then?"

"How about 'I Know My Love'? In the key of D?" I asked.

"Ah, okay," he said, nodding now. "Good choice. We can play that. And you're sure you're up for this?"

"I'm sure," I said, but it was clear none of them had high expectations for me.

"All right, then," Trevor said. "Let's get ready, mates, 'I Know My Love', key of D, it is."

"Good luck, Killeen," Jonathan said, squeezing my hand as he stepped off stage. I gave him an exaggerated scowl.

As they warmed up their instruments, I took a deep breath and closed my eyes in an attempt to calm my nerves.

"Give it up for Cat!" Gia shouted, whistling through her teeth as Effie started clapping and whooping, even though the music hadn't even started.

"All right, everyone, we've got a special guest singer tonight just in time for Christmas," Trevor said into the microphone. "Please give a warm round of applause for . . ." Trevor looked at me. He had already forgotten my name.

"What's your name again, dear?" he whispered, hand over the mic, and a few people in the audience laughed.

"Catherine Killeen," I whispered back.

"Introducing Miss Catherine Killeen," Trevor said, moving aside so I could step in front of the microphone. I gave the crowd a small wave, my face still flushed, as I gripped the mic with sweaty palms and tried not to bounce my leg from the nervous energy coursing through me. The song was about a woman's love for an "errant rover" and her jealousy of other women.

It had been some time since I'd performed, and my self-consciousness was overwhelming, but after the first couple stanzas, that thrill of being onstage took hold, and my nerves started to evaporate.

Trevor and the other band members smiled and nodded at each other, clearly pleased with how I sounded. Meanwhile, Effie and Gia, Jonathan and Archie, as well as most of the crowd, were on their feet cheering and dancing to the music, which made me relax into the song and the moment and experience that pure bliss of performing music I had forgotten I loved so much.

> I know my love is an errant rover
> I know he'll wander the wild world over
> In dear old Ireland he'll no longer tarry
> An American girl he's sure to marry . . .

When I sang the words *American girl*, the crowd responded with more whoops and hollers, and I caught Jonathan's eye and he mouthed, *Brilliant*, clapping and shaking his head at me in awe, and I gave him a wink and looked away, too distracted by his smile. I had missed singing, missed being a part of something musical that filled me with an exhilaration and a joy that nothing else could.

As the last notes of the song played out, the crowd went wild, and I burst out laughing, basking in the relief and satisfaction of performing in front of a live audience for the first time in months. I stepped off the stage into the arms of Effie and Gia.

"You did not disappoint, my friend," Effie said.

"I'll be honest, I didn't believe you had it in you," Gia said, nodding as if she was appraising me anew.

"I did," Jonathan said. "Thank you for doing that. I needed it tonight."

"Would it surprise you to learn I did too?" I smiled at him, and for a moment I wondered what it would be like to kiss him, but I banished the thought. He was an errant rover, like the song. Someone tapped me on the shoulder, and I turned to see the drummer, his whole demeanor relaxed and warm now.

"I'm so sorry I doubted you, my dear," he said. "Any chance you'd be up for one or two more?"

"Of course she would—get on up there," Gia said, giving me a little shove.

"Go on. I knew when they heard you they wouldn't let you get away with just one," Jonathan said.

"Thank you, I'd love to," I smiled at the drummer. Back onstage I caught sight of Weissman and Lindsay Philmore near the bar's entrance. They had not left, and they were still talking, their faces serious as they watched me onstage, and it filled me with a sense of deep unease.

"Glad you're up for a couple more, Catherine," Trevor said. And, determined to distract myself from the odd pairing near the door, I chose a few more songs, starting with "Heave Away" because the crowd seemed primed for a rousing sing-along.

By the time I started to sing the familiar lyrics, Weissman and Philmore were gone. I sang one Irish folk song and then another, and then we did a couple of Christmas songs, and every time I went to take a break, Trevor would coax me to sing "just one more." It was such a delight to be performing again, it was impossible to say no. And, despite my harrowing day at work, I was overcome with a happiness and contentment I hadn't felt in a very long time.

At ten thirty, the band took a break to raucous applause, and as soon as I stepped off the stage, Jonathan grabbed my hand and pulled me down the dark hallway toward the rear entrance of the bar near the swinging kitchen door. The air was humid with the smells of grease and potatoes, the sounds of water running and the cook shouting orders to waitstaff.

"Where are we going?" I said, laughing.

"I have to tell you something," he said. We were facing each other now. My heart was beating in my ears, and I knew—I knew for all of my many pragmatic reasons—I should leave, but he stepped closer, our faces were inches apart, and I couldn't move.

"First off, you're incredible, Killeen. And beautiful, and talented, and competitive and stubborn. Being around you, working with you? It makes me want to be a better person. But there's something I . . ."

"Jonathan . . ." I whispered as he put his hand on my cheek, and I was breathless. He leaned closer to me, and I thought of all the reasons I should pull away, and yet I couldn't bring myself to do it.

"Cat, you have to understand . . ." He appeared to be struggling with what to say next, when suddenly a thunderous sound of pots clanging made me jump, and the cook stepped out of the kitchen through the swinging doors.

"Hey. You aren't supposed to be way back here, this area is *staff only*," he hollered at us, his white apron covered in stains, a cigarette hanging out of his mouth. "Go! Take your carrying on somewhere else."

We apologized and hurried out of the hallway laughing, our friends looking at us curiously when we returned to the table.

"We'll continue that conversation later," he said in a low whisper in my ear, hand on my shoulder, and I nodded, my face burning with the thoughts of what had almost happened as I watched him walk over to the bar.

But the cook's interruption had brought me back to my senses, and panic gripped me. Because really, what in the world was I doing? I couldn't kiss Jonathan Dardis, of all the men in DC. I was on the verge of either a breakthrough or a career disaster with Meredith. There was no need to make the situation more precarious by getting into some sort of romantic entanglement with Jonathan. The pub suddenly felt claustrophobic. I needed to get out of the Liberty and go home, before I did something I might regret later.

So, while Jonathan was still at the bar, and my friends were deep in conversation, before I changed my mind, I grabbed my coat and purse and slipped out of the pub into the cold December air.

Chapter Nineteen

Monday, January 5, 1948

After the holidays, on our first morning back at Building B, Effie, Gia, and I took the bus in at six thirty so we'd have to time for a quick cup of coffee with Rosemary before the day started. My Christmas break in Cambridge had started with a happy, tearful reunion with my father and brothers at South Station, and the ten-day vacation had been exactly what I needed for my soul. Between holiday festivities with cousins and aunts and uncles and even singing at the pub again, I kept myself distracted enough not to ruminate about Meredith and the FBI files and whether I was even still employed. But in an hour I would know for sure, and my nerves were getting to me.

"Cat, you're tapping your foot so hard you're going to break something," Gia said.

"Is that what that sound is?" Rosemary said, her voice raspier than usual because she was fighting a cold. When she glanced under the table, I stopped.

"Sorry, just a bit of a wreck about how it's going to go this morning," I said.

"You'll be fine," Effie said, patting my hand. "You would have heard by now if you . . . if . . ."

"If you were going to get canned," Gia said, offering me a Chesterfield from her bejeweled gold cigarette case. "But you should start smoking. It might help you calm all that nervous energy."

"Thank you for the offer, again, but I'll pass," I said, sipping my coffee. "Anyway, we've got thirty minutes or so until we should head upstairs. Tell me all about what you did over break, to keep my mind off everything else."

Rosemary had spent the holidays with her family in Philadelphia, where, much to her chagrin, her mother had once again attempted to set her up with the son of one of her parents' friends. He was a junior banker from another old-monied Pennsylvania Main Line family like hers. She and Margaret had just moved into their new apartment in a townhome in DC's Georgetown neighborhood.

Gia had worked at her family's beauty shop over the break and was still getting pressure from them to return home to help run the business. They couldn't understand why she would stay in DC just to be a secretary, and of course, she couldn't tell them she wasn't one.

Effie had celebrated Christmas with her family in New Orleans but had returned early to spend time with Archie, who had to head back to London for an indeterminate amount of time for some new assignments on that side of the pond.

"It's not that I won't miss him, he's a lovely guy," Effie said. "But as I said, girls, I like my freedom here. Being home reminded me why. So many friends getting married and having babies. And they cannot understand what in the world I'm doing up here."

"Just like my sisters," Gia said.

"Anyway, Archie's worried if they'll even let him come back to America now that Lindsay Philmore, the rising star in British intelligence, is here."

"That reminds me," I said. "I think I'm going to mention our suspicions about Bill Weissman to Gene."

We explained to Rosemary how we had seen him at the Liberty, among other places, and hovering over peoples' desks late at night.

"I've never trusted the man," Rosemary said. "He also seems to end up in meetings, even when he's not invited. And nobody ever questions it. Why is that? Frank loves him. Come to think of it, most of the men here seem to like him."

"Have you seen or heard from Jonathan since the break?" Effie asked, giving me a pointed look over her coffee cup.

"No, I have not," I said, and it killed me that hearing his name made me blush. And that he had occupied my thoughts over the holidays, more than my situation at work, more than anything.

"Look at you," Rosemary tilted her head at me with a sly smile. "Is there something I should know?"

"Absolutely not," I said.

"Uh-huh, sure, Cat," Effie said. "Oh my gosh, Rosie, you should have *seen* Cat sing at the Liberty. She blew the roof off the place."

Effie launched into the story of my singing debut at the Liberty, and I thought back to what a magical night it had been, up until the moment I had left. I had panicked, questioning my own judgment and blaming it on the thrill of singing onstage again and the free-flowing drinks. Gia saw me leave and had followed me out of the bar, taking a taxi back to Idaho Hall with me.

"I believe Cat pulled what is referred to as 'the Irish goodbye,'" Gia said, laughing. "You've never seen someone jump in a taxi so fast."

"I know, I'm sorry," I said. "I was just exhausted and had to catch a train so early the next morning."

"Cat," Rosemary said, raising her eyebrows with a smirk. "None of us believe that's really why you left. Be honest."

I had replayed the moment with Jonathan in the back hall more times than I could count, remembering his words, our faces so close. And I couldn't deny the number of times I had imagined what might have happened if the grouchy Liberty cook hadn't interrupted us.

"Ladies, the gang's all back. Happy New Year! How is everyone?" Cecil saved me from answering the question, bounding up to our table so fast that he spilled coffee on himself.

"Oh shoot," Cecil said, looking down at the constellation of brown spots on the front of his white shirt.

"I know what you're thinking. Do *not* take that shirt off," Gia said, pointing her finger at him. "Remember there are new dress-code rules now, most of them because of you."

"Gia, are we still on for bowling tonight, back to our usual schedule? I have it on my calendar. Seven, right?" Cecil plopped down next to her.

"Yeah, fine," Gia said in a soft, almost affectionate tone, not looking any of us in the eye. "I'll meet you there."

"Great, I can't wait." He grinned. "I'm going to go try to get these stains out. See you tonight, G."

He stood up and leaned in as if he was about to kiss her cheek but changed his mind at the last moment and hurried off with a wave instead.

Rosemary, Effie, and I turned our gaze to Gia, none of us able to hide our amusement or curiosity. It was the first time we had heard about her bowling outings with Cecil.

"*G*? What in the Sam Hill . . . ? Secret bowling dates?" Rosemary said, eyes wide as she watched Cecil exit the café.

"Not another word, Rosemary," Gia said.

"And did my eyes deceive me," I said, "or did he lean in to kiss . . . ?"

"Nope, not discussing it," Gia interrupted me, a small smile on her face as she stood up and headed out of the café.

"Oh, maybe you're not now, but you are later for sure. And I cannot *wait* to hear it," Effie said, as we got up to follow her. Then, pointing at me, she added, "And we're not done with you either."

∼

"Thank you for sharing your concerns, Cat, but I truly believe there is nothing to worry about regarding Bill Weissman," Gene said. She looked as impeccable as always, wearing a cranberry-colored wool dress with a black patent leather belt, shiny chestnut hair perfectly coiffed.

"Aside from the typical concerns women have around certain types of men. As I've told you, he's been known to come on too strong."

After heading upstairs from the café, I had spotted Gene and asked if we could have a quick, confidential talk before the rest of the office arrived. And I informed her about our ongoing suspicions regarding Bill Weissman.

"Okay," I said, unconvinced. "More than that, though, just . . . the snooping around our desks at night is the thing that really gets me. Why would he do that?"

"That I don't know," Gene said, frowning. "But look, I've known Bill for years now. He's worked here longer than just about everyone but me, and in all those years, no one has ever suspected him of anything nefarious. If I had any doubts about him, I'd have you take these suspicions to Frank."

"Okay . . . that makes me feel a little bit better," I said. I was still suspicious, and still believed my instincts about him were correct. "Anyway, I wanted to at least mention it. Since you've been here for so long."

"You make me sound like an ancient relic," Gene said with a laugh.

"I didn't mean it like that," I said. "You're just so wise and all-knowing about everything that goes on here."

"Why, thank you. And I'm truly not worried about him." She gave me a reassuring look that did not reassure me at all. "Speaking of my tenure here, confidentially, I have news."

"What is it?"

"I've been offered a newly created position with the CIA," she said. "I've discussed it at length with Meredith and Frank. I'm going to take it."

"Gene, I . . . wow, that is amazing. Congratulations," I said. "But it's such a loss for us. We'll all miss you terribly, Meredith especially."

"That means a great deal," she said. "I'll miss all of you too. Just between us, Rosemary is going to be offered the role as my replacement. What do you think of that?"

"I think that is a fabulous idea. She's been here for a while, she's so even-keeled and incredibly smart, I think she's perfect," I said.

"Yes, so do we," she said. "This will all be announced soon. I've got one final meeting with Meredith and Frank about the transition."

"Have you seen Meredith yet today?" I asked.

"No, not yet," she said, giving me a sympathetic look. She knew why I was asking, of course. "And I wish I had more information for you about his state of mind on things, but I don't."

At that moment, Rosemary knocked on the conference room door and peeked in.

"Meredith's looking for you," she said.

"Me?" Gene asked, getting up from the table.

"No, Cat," Rosemary said, and my heart sank. "He wants to see you in his office. Right now."

"Here goes nothing." I grabbed my notebook and the master book of code names that I planned on handing over to him if this turned out to be my last day.

"Good luck, Catherine," Gene said, reaching across to squeeze my hand.

"Thanks," I said, mentally preparing myself for the worst.

"I wish I could go in with you," Rosemary said, unable to hide her worry as we walked down to his office. "Actually, why couldn't I? Do you want me to go in with you?"

"No, it's okay," I said. "But thank you."

"I'm so sorry." Gia rushed over to me just as I was about to knock on his door. "I am way too sarcastic sometimes. The last thing in the world I would want is for you to lose your job here."

"I know," I said, as she threw her arms around me and gave me a quick hug, tears in her eyes. "Of course I know that."

I took a deep breath and knocked. Meredith said to come in, but he was facing his board so I couldn't see his expression. His office, the battlefield, was more chaotic than I'd ever seen it before, with its own weather system of cherry tobacco smoke haze. The bulletin board was filled with even more note cards color coded in yellow, blue, and pink, and there were rows of papers across his desk and even taped to the walls now. The envelope from the FBI was teetering on a pile of file folders, and I couldn't tell if he had gone through what was inside or if it had been sitting there untouched since the last time I was in his office.

"Did you bring the master book of code names with you?" he asked, not turning around. No *Did you enjoy the holidays?* No niceties at all. It could only mean one thing.

"I did," I said, suddenly on the verge of throwing up. It was happening. "I can just leave it on your desk . . ."

"What?" He whirled around, his curly hair more unkempt than usual. His eyes were bloodshot, and his clothes looked slept in. And he was smiling at me, in an almost goofy way. "Why would you leave it? No, sit. Sit down, Catherine. We've got tons of work to do. I thought you'd be back before the fifth, but then I was the only one back before the fifth. My wife wanted to kill me . . ."

"Meredith, what is going on? You mean you're not . . . not going to fire me?" I said, trying to absorb what he was saying.

"Fire you?" he said, letting out a laugh that was a little unhinged. "No, no, I'm not firing you. I mean, I know I lost my temper when I found out you tipped off Bob about what I needed. I was mad at you for interceding. But over the holidays, my wife, Blanche, read me the riot act about that, about my stubbornness, told me my perspective was all wrong. I was letting my ego get in the way, my dislike of Hoover too.

"Blanche said you were right, we had been in a rut, and we needed something to shake us out of it."

He paused, and I was finally breathing and no longer sick to my stomach. I still had a job. It was the best news I could have heard today.

"I'm rambling. I'm rambling because I'm not good at saying . . . I apologize for blowing up at you, and for threatening to fire you."

"Thank you," I said, exhaling. "So, did you look through the FBI files? The Russian plain-text messages. Were they helpful in any way?"

"Were they helpful?" Meredith swept his arms around the chaos. "Were they . . . Catherine, well . . . I'll just say it. These files? We've hit the jackpot with these files."

"You're joking," I said after a moment, getting choked up and blinking back tears. Not only was I not fired, but my risk had paid off.

"You know I'm not," he said. Nodding at the files, he added, "They are the break that we've desperately needed. Isn't that what you said? For book breaking, for reconstructing the KGB codebook. It's incredibly exciting, but quite troubling as well. This latest revelation is what has been keeping me up at night."

He grabbed one of the note cards off his corkboard and handed it to me.

"Oh. My. God," I said, putting a hand over my mouth, my arms breaking out in goose pimples as I read it.

"I know. Bob's instincts were right all along. This proves it."

Chapter Twenty

Friday, January 9, 1948

For the rest of the week, our team worked long hours to catch up with what Meredith in his brilliance had already accomplished with the FBI plain-text files—to see what else we could do to capitalize on his efforts, what other intelligence we might uncover in the thousands of KGB messages, focusing particularly on the ones from '44 to '45.

That week was also my first encounter with a Virginia cold spell, and as temperatures dipped into the twenties, the high winds made it feel ten degrees colder. Inside Building B wasn't much warmer than it was outside, and I was grateful I had brought my winter clothes back after the holidays. Many of us ended up wearing our coats at work most of the day, as the frigid air seeped through the cheaply constructed walls. But despite the terrible chill, the mood in the Russian section was focused and upbeat, almost jovial.

Friday afternoon, Bob and Jonathan were coming over for a meeting. It would be the first time I'd seen Jonathan since the Christmas party at the Liberty, and by lunch my appetite was shot, I was so nervous. I couldn't wait to see him, to talk to him about everything. But I didn't want to see him, because at some point I'd have to explain why I had left the Liberty that night without so much as a goodbye or Merry Christmas. What would I even say?

Hi, Jonathan. Sorry I left, but I knew I'd end up kissing you if I stayed. And I wanted to kiss you, but I shouldn't want to kiss you, because of our jobs, and let's face it, you're not exactly one for commitment. Also, I almost walked down the aisle with someone I didn't love, and I still don't trust my own heart. Anyway, hope you had a merry Christmas.

Even in my head it sounded ridiculous.

"Last year they promised to improve the heat in this place, but I think it might be colder in here. Hey, Cat, hello? Are you okay? Why are you in a daze?" Gia interrupted my thoughts as we walked back to our section with cups of instant hot chocolate from the café. She was wearing a bright yellow coat and had a thick black scarf draped rather dramatically around her head and neck, so all you could see was her face.

"Sorry, just a little tired, it's been a long week," I said.

"No kidding, and it's not over," she said. "This is definitely a working weekend."

"No doubt." I sighed.

"Oh, there you are, Cat." Rosemary waved to us when we got back. "Your meeting's been moved up. The G-men are arriving earlier than expected. And Gene and I stole—I mean borrowed—some electric heaters from the IBM group, so you shouldn't need your coat in there."

"Wow, Bob and Jonathan are eager beavers today," Gia said, as I dropped my jacket at my desk and headed for the small conference room.

"Can you blame them?" I said. "I'm guessing Bob especially has been champing at the bit all week."

"What about Jonathan?"

"Why are you asking?" I asked, knowing exactly why she had.

"Nothing, good luck." Gia gave me a smirk, clearly teasing.

Meredith nodded at me when I entered the conference room, and I took a seat next to him.

"Thank you for your work this week, all the late nights," he said, still looking down and shuffling through his papers.

"Of course," I said. "Thank you again for not firing me."

"You're welcome." He chuckled, which surprised me. "I need to tell the rest of the team how thankful I am too. I'm trying to be better about expressing my gratitude. Blanche says I need to work on that."

Bob Lamphere came in a couple minutes later, and we exchanged pleasantries about our holidays as Meredith got up and started erasing the chalkboard. Jonathan walked in just as Meredith had started writing on it, and he took the seat next to Bob.

Being so close to him made my heart ache in a way I had never felt before. Even with Andrew. How in the world had Jonathan Dardis, of all people, become someone who made me feel like this? Why did the sight of him now turn my insides to Jell-O? Jonathan had always been the kind of guy you warned your friends about, not the guy you fell for.

"Thank you for coming in today," Meredith said. "Bob, before the holidays, you and Jonathan gave me access to some plain-text pre-coded Russian messages you thought might help me, help us, and I behaved, well, rather rudely. So first, I want to apologize up front for my behavior, to both of you."

Meredith placed his hand on his chest.

"Apology accepted. I know that your role here comes with a great deal of pressure, so we understand," Bob said.

"We absolutely do," Jonathan added.

"Now the good news," Meredith said. "These messages have proved invaluable, comparable to hitting the codebreaking lottery. So again, thank you for whatever hoops you had to jump through to get them."

Bob let out a whoop and threw up his hands as if he were in the stands at a basketball game.

"That is exactly what I was hoping you'd say, my friend," Bob said, beaming at Meredith.

"That is amazing," Jonathan said with a nod. Now he finally, really looked at me, with a huge grin. Our risk had paid off. It felt like a small miracle. "I almost can't believe it."

"Oh, believe it. We're going to be able to decipher these other messages at a much faster rate moving forward, which is incredibly exciting," Meredith said, no discernible excitement in his voice, before he turned to the board to write out the latest revelations.

ENORMOZ

Liberal—American, atomic spy ringleader, attended City College, New York

Ethel—Liberal's wife's actual name, surname same as Liberal, now in her early thirties, knows of husband's work with Soviets

Max Elitcher—actual name, school friend of Liberal's at City College, New York, Communist Party member, possible Liberal recruit

"Now, here's what we have so far," he said, turning to us. "This code word, *Enormoz*, has appeared a few times, and we have enough context to suggest it is based on the English word *enormous* and it is related to our country's wartime nuclear fission research. Simply put? This word is the cover name for Russia's plot to steal atomic secrets from the United States."

It was still a shock to hear what *Enormoz* stood for, and Jonathan looked at me again, no longer smiling. You could hear the clicking of the little heaters as the four of us considered this revelation.

"Catherine," Meredith said, after a pause. "Why don't you explain the next part? You deserve a lot of the credit. Catherine's been instrumental to this process."

"Thank you," I said, blushing as I stood up. "So we believe the spy code-named Liberal is an American and the ringleader of the atomic spy ring. He also attended City College, New York. He has a wife, Ethel. We'll keep digging for clues about them.

"And we've also learned that Liberal was trying to recruit this man named Max Elitcher in '44. Not sure he was successful, but Max might help us identify him. There are several other code names connected to Enormoz, but these are the first newly discovered clues that we wanted to show you."

"Damn." Bob let out a whistle. "You weren't kidding about the jackpot."

"Yes," Meredith said. "I, rather *we*, should be able to make much more progress reconstructing the Russians' codebook now that we have the plain-text files, thanks to you."

"And this also proves what I've believed all along," Bob said. "This wasn't just a couple of scientists or engineers going rogue, passing secrets about the bomb to the Russians on their own. This was a highly sophisticated operation by the Soviet government, with multiple spies involved in stealing America's atomic secrets."

"Indeed. It was," Meredith said in a quiet voice.

"And I'm sure they're still at it. Everything changes now. Finally. *Finally*, we have enough to go on," Bob said, slamming his hand on the table in triumph. You could almost see the wheels turning in his mind. "I'm going to start launching investigations across the board, directing agents in the various field offices to chase down any clues, names, locations, anything you find in these messages moving forward. Starting with Max and Ethel."

"Elizabeth Bentley's testimony might also bear fruit now too," Jonathan said, and I nodded at him in agreement.

"Exactly, and we might now actually have evidence to corroborate all her testimony, or at least some of it," Bob said.

"How are you going to share this information with the field? Where are you going to say it came from?" I asked. "All of Frank's talks have me paranoid."

"We'll say it came from a 'highly trusted confidential informant,'" Bob said.

"And you and I should meet on a regular basis," Meredith said to Bob. "I think it's important that we work together, as a . . . as a team, moving forward."

"I agree," Bob said, and he looked like he might jump up to give Meredith a hug. "You realize what you've done here, Meredith?"

"What?" Meredith said, the tips of his ears turning red.

"You've not only uncovered the greatest covert threat against America in history. You've given us the keys to the enemy's house, and they don't even know we're inside," Bob said. "We have *real* leads. We might be able to find out who these people are and learn what they stole. We have a chance of bringing them to justice. I can't wait to tell Hoover."

"Will he inform Truman?" Meredith asked, looking equal parts proud and embarrassed.

"My guess is, once again, he will keep this from the president. According to the Bentley testimony, there might still be Russian spies in the White House. Hoover doesn't want to take the risk of them discovering that we have a way into their communications, thanks to you."

"We'll continue to work the problem here," Meredith said. "I'm lucky to have some of the best people on my team." He looked over at me when he said this, and my feeling of pride in that moment made all the late nights and weekends worthwhile.

"Yes, we'll do the same on our end. And I've been given the go-ahead to hire several more agents, here and in the other field offices. Also, Jonathan has just accepted a job in London, working under the FBI legal attaché at the US embassy, so he'll be our new contact over there for any Soviet espionage–related investigations."

"Oh!" I blurted out, not able to hide my shock. Bob raised his eyebrows at me, amused, and my face grew hot. "I mean, that's amazing news. Con . . . congratulations."

"Yes, congratulations," Meredith said.

"Thank you," Jonathan said with a tight smile, not meeting my gaze. The ache in my chest was an anvil now. He was leaving. But maybe this was a good thing. The work we were doing here was too important, and if he was gone, I could focus solely on that. I didn't need the complication, the distraction of feeling this way, of wondering when I was going to see him again, of what might happen between us. When he was gone, it would be easier to get him out of my head. But if this was for the best, why did I feel like crying?

"I'll miss having him as my right-hand man, but he'll be the liaison with British intelligence, and I need someone I can trust in that role."

After that, we discussed next steps for both sides. My euphoria about the success of our work had given way to a quiet despair. Jonathan was going to London.

And of course, as we were saying goodbyes, nosy Bill Weissman knocked on the door, wanting to talk with Meredith about translations he was working on, while also taking note of the names on the board. Meredith didn't seem concerned about that in the slightest. Despite everything Gene had said, I would never trust the man.

Just as Jonathan was leaving the conference room, he handed me a piece of paper, and when our fingers touched, he held onto my hand for just a few seconds. When we looked up at each other, so much passed between us unsaid that I couldn't breathe.

"So, you're . . . you're moving. To London?" I said, in a failed attempt to sound upbeat and casual.

"It's all kind of happened really fast," he said, his expression pained. "I applied in October, never thinking I'd get it. Hoover just officially approved it this morning."

"This is what you wanted to tell me at the Liberty," I said.

"Yes, I had just learned I'd been offered the role."

"When do you leave?"

"I go to Greenwich tomorrow to see my mom and sister," he said, his eyes filled with anguish. "Then I'll see my dad in New York and leave from there on Tuesday."

"Wow, that's . . . that *is* fast."

"I've got to go now. But please meet me tonight?" He pointed at the note. And as he walked away, I opened it and read it:

> Killeen,
> There's so much to say. I'm working late, but can you meet me at the Cairo at eight?
> X,
> J.

He was on his way out with Bob, but he turned around and looked back at me, and I gave him a nod to let him know I would be there.

Chapter Twenty-One

"Wait, you're meeting him at the Cairo at eight?" Effie asked. She was rifling through her closet, insisting on lending me something to wear. "But it's freezing tonight. Are you sure you want to go? Never mind, stupid question. I can tell by how you've been acting, you're definitely going."

"Definitely going where?" Gia asked, knocking on Effie's door. "Hey, did you do your hair and makeup yourself? It looks halfway decent."

"I'll take that, thanks," I said, laughing.

"Cat's meeting Jonathan at the Cairo for a rendezvous," Effie said, batting her eyelashes dramatically and holding a deep-violet dress up in front of me. "Yup, this is the one. Put it on."

"Oh, are you two finally going on a date?" Gia sat down at the desk chair and pulled out her cigarette case. "And before I forget, Cecil told me I must remind you both of the first annual ASA Bowling Championships next Sunday, and yes I know he has probably already reminded you a dozen times."

She spoke of him now with a new softness in her tone.

"What's going on with you two?" I asked.

"Are you changing the subject?" Gia said.

"She is, but I want to know too. What's really going on with Cecil?" Effie asked.

"Ladies, please, we are friends who bowl, nothing more," Gia said. "I will say he's grown on me, as a *friend*—there's something nice about a guy who's not all macho and posturing, like every guy I grew up with. Now, what's happening with Jonathan?"

"It's not a date," I said. "We've also become *friends* over the past few months, and while I will admit maybe there is a spark, nothing is going to happen now."

"Why the heck not?" Gia said.

"He's moving," I said, still absorbing the news, as well as how unhappy I was about it.

"What? Where?" Gia asked.

"London," Effie said, explaining the situation.

"Oh well," Gia shrugged. "That's that, then. It's over before it started."

"G, maybe this *one* time you could be a little less flip in your response," Effie said, shooting her a look.

"What?" Gia said, looking at me. "I mean, Cat, it's not like his track record with women is great. Spark or no spark, maybe you've dodged a bullet?"

"Very true," I said. "Maybe I should just cancel, then. What is the point, really? I'm working myself up about this date that's not really a date, and he's going to be gone tomorrow."

"No, you're trying to back out because of your feelings for him. What are you so afraid of?" Effie asked, standing with arms crossed in front of her, looking like the former teacher she was.

"It's the same reason you left without saying goodbye to him at the Liberty," Gia said.

"No, it's . . ." I stopped and looked at them. "Okay, maybe it is. I'm just—I'm a mess, really. I don't know what I feel."

"I'm not saying you're in love with the guy, but I have no doubt there's something between the two of you," Effie said.

"Is it that obvious?" I asked as they said "Yes!" in unison and started laughing.

"I know it is, stupid question," I said, heat creeping up my cheeks.

"Just go, have a great time, say goodbye. And don't overthink it like you always do, like you're doing right now," Effie said, sitting on the bed next to me, arm around my shoulder.

"All right, thanks, girls," I said, taking a deep breath.

"Good," Gia said. "Now that that's settled, let me fix your hair. Oh, and we've got to change that lipstick color too. It's all wrong for your complexion."

"You're never wrong, G," I said, then, looking at Effie, I added, "So, the plum dress, then?"

"Hmm . . . you know what, no," Effie said, putting it back. "Go get your red one. No one forgets a girl in a red dress."

～

When I stepped out of the taxi in front of the Cairo, big fat snowflakes were swirling in the frigid winter night air. Jonathan was waiting at the front entrance, and when he spotted me, he gave me a crooked smile, looking debonair in a navy wool overcoat, dark hair peeking out from under his fedora.

Meredith said when you change the way you look at something, the thing you look at changes. The same could be said for people, I now realized. When had I changed the way I looked at him? The way I felt about him? Maybe it was the moment on the rooftop at this very hotel, when something had shifted between us, it was hard to say. Again I wondered, how did it happen, this alchemy of falling for someone? Right at this moment, I desperately wished there was an elixir that could cure it, because everything about this was impossible, and the fact that he was leaving made it hurt to look at the way he smiled at me.

"You look beautiful, Killeen. Thank you for coming," he said, as he reached out and took my hand in his, and the warmth of it made me decide that, no matter what happened after tonight, the girls were right. I was going to enjoy this evening with him.

"Thank you. And after your news today, I decided I didn't have a choice." I met his eyes and gave him a shrug.

"You're right." He smiled.

"Are you here for the Ink Spots?" the doorman asked, as he pushed open one of the glass doors into the lobby, which felt unusually crowded, a palpable buzz of excitement in the air.

"Yes, sir," Jonathan said, holding up two tickets.

I gasped at the sight of a huge poster on an easel inside the entrance:

THE CAIRO HOTEL PRESENTS THE FOUR INK SPOTS ACCOMPANIED BY THE DC ORCHESTRA. GENERAL ADMISSION DANCE PARTY 9 P.M.–2 A.M.

A rectangular sticker with *SOLD OUT* in block letters was slapped diagonally across the middle of it.

"You mentioned in class once that you loved their music," he said, watching my face for a reaction.

"I do love them. I can't believe it." I laughed, hand in front of my mouth, unable to contain my excitement. "I had no idea they were in town. How in the world did you get tickets?"

"What can I say, the FBI has its perks sometimes." He winked at me.

"Like exciting job opportunities in far-off countries?" I said.

"Ah, yes, I'll get to that," he said.

In the ballroom the orchestra was warming up, and it was still early enough that we were able to find a small table for two not too far from the stage. The tables were draped in black linen, and with its dim, atmospheric lighting and small, fragrant white orchid bouquets throughout, the ballroom had more of a jazz club vibe tonight, in honor of its well-known musical guests.

As soon as the waitress left with our order, Jonathan reached out and took my hand again, and for a moment we sat there in silence. I looked down at our hands, filled with an ache of bittersweet longing as

I opened my mouth to speak, only to close it again. There was so much I wanted to say, but I couldn't seem to find the words.

Jonathan cleared his throat and spoke first. "Did you know that many employees of the FBI call the headquarters here in DC 'Dreamland'?" he asked.

"No, why is that?" I asked.

"Because it's a place that you go and dream about what your career might have been."

"Oh," I said, raising my eyebrows. "I'm guessing you didn't know that when you took the job here?"

"I did not," he said, as the waitress brought our drinks over. He explained that when he'd first arrived, he was thrilled to be working with Bob Lamphere in the Soviet espionage section. Bob had just been promoted to supervisor, had a great reputation, and had recently been recruited to DC himself. But then, after the first month, when they weren't making any traction with any of their Soviet spy cases and weren't being well supported by Hoover, Bob had told Jonathan that he was considering transferring back to New York, where he had more autonomy.

"And he encouraged me to apply for positions elsewhere, for the sake of my career. So, I applied for openings in New York and London, among others. This was all before we got wind of the so-called Venona Project, your team's remarkable progress in deciphering all these KGB telegrams. And it was well before Bob started making his visits to Meredith."

Our appetizers of shrimp cocktail and stuffed mushrooms arrived just as he said this, and we both sat back so they could be placed on the table. Rather than ordering entrees, we decided to order a couple more things to share.

"Anyway, I really can't believe I'm leaving right when things are finally getting exciting," he said.

"They are, but . . ." I frowned, examining my shrimp.

"What? What were you about to say?"

The Women of Arlington Hall

"Just that . . . don't you think it's crazy to imagine, of all the resources in the US government, that our two teams could actually be the ones to track down Russian spies here? I mean, let's be honest, Bob and Meredith are in fairly low-level roles at the FBI and ASA, never mind all of us working under them. Aren't we being a little naive?"

"I've asked myself the same thing, but then I think, why not Meredith and Bob? Why not us?" Jonathan said. "In any case, I wish I could be here to see how things unfold."

"Me too," I said, the pit in my stomach making my appetite vanish. He placed his fork down and looked at me, our knees touched under the table, and he reached for my hand again, stroking it with his thumb, making my heartbeat quicken.

"Cat . . ." He shook his head. "I wish . . . you heard him. Bob wants me there as a point person. And for a new agent, it's a big deal to be promoted to a role like this. Some of the guys were furious they offered it to me. I have to go. It's a career-making opportunity. Those don't come around often."

"Of course," I said with a sigh. "I get it. I would take it too. That is, if women were allowed to be FBI agents."

"I personally think you'd make a great FBI agent, better than me." He smiled.

"So do I," I teased, just as the orchestra director was introducing the main act.

"Ladies and gentlemen, I'm so thrilled to introduce one of the best vocal harmony groups in America today—Billy Bowen, Bill Kenny, Herb Kenny, and Charlie Fuqua, with Ray Tunia on piano. Please give a warm welcome to the Ink Spots!"

The four young Black men, wearing light-gray suits and silk ties, ran onto the stage to raucous applause.

"Thank you and greetings to you all." The tallest member of the group spoke into the mic in a deep, clear baritone. "Ladies and gentleman, our first tune, 'I'd Climb the Highest Mountain.'"

Another round of applause as the Ink Spots' guitarist played the solo introductory notes of the song, as he always did, and the four men started harmonizing. I looked at Jonathan and back at the stage in awe, because they sounded even more incredible in person.

"Thank you for this. I can't believe I'm watching them live—it's a dream." I smiled, clapping my hands together.

"Of course," Jonathan said. "I'm relieved you didn't have plans. I wanted to do something special tonight, before leaving."

"If you had told me you had tickets to the Ink Spots, I would have canceled any plans I had anyway," I said. "So . . . how long do you think you'll be over there?"

He paused.

"The average . . . the average tenure for this position is two to three years." He looked at me with such sad intensity that I had to turn away, just as the Ink Spots started to play "I Don't Want to Set the World on Fire."

"That's a long time," I whispered, biting my lip.

"It is," he said, reaching for my hand again. "And I could say let's write letters, try to see each other once or twice a year or something, but that wouldn't be fair to you."

"To either of us," I said, squeezing his hand.

"We're star-crossed, Killeen, but I do believe we might find our way back to each other someday. At least, I hope so."

"Me too," I replied, though my heart was aching, because we both knew the odds of it happening were not in our favor.

"So . . . let's dance? Just . . . just enjoy this last night, toast to our beautiful friendship." He stood up, still holding my hand. "Would that be okay with you?"

"I guess that would be okay." I gave him an exaggerated sigh. "But I still think quoting *Casablanca* is really corny."

Laughing at this, he led me out onto the dance floor, pulling me in, his arm tight around my waist. The way he smelled—it all made me a little woozy. Our faces were close enough to touch, and I wanted to bottle up the feeling of dancing in his arms, because who knew if we would ever have a moment like this again.

"I love this song."

"So do I," he said, his voice thick with emotion.

My breath caught in my throat. As I put my arm around his neck and looked up at him, he just tilted his head at me, like he couldn't quite believe I was there. Other couples on the dance floor glanced at us with knowing smiles, thinking we were something we weren't.

Still, as we danced, everything else in the room fell away, and I enjoyed how delicious this moment in his arms felt, how the whole night seemed to glitter as bright as all the chandeliers hanging from the ceiling.

We ordered more food and drinks and danced to every slow song. We talked and laughed and told each other stories about family and friends that we'd never shared before. We didn't say another word about work for the rest of the night.

It was nearly one in the morning when we finally got our coats and left the Cairo, and I was gripped with the pain of missing him, even though he was still with me. He insisted on us taking a cab together, dropping me at Idaho Hall before heading home. As he put his arm around me in the back seat of the cab, I leaned into the warmth of his chest, watching the snowflakes swirl around in the dark winter sky.

The driver pulled up to Idaho Hall, and Jonathan told him to wait as he walked me to the door to say good night.

"So, this is goodbye," he said in a soft voice when we reached the steps.

"It is." I nodded as we faced each other, holding hands, looking into each other's eyes. There was so much I wanted to say but couldn't bring myself to say it.

"Thank you for tonight. I needed it . . . I had . . . just the best time."

"So did I. I . . . thank you too," he said.

It was overwhelming to feel this way, only to have to say goodbye before we had even gotten started. So, I gave him a kiss on the cheek and a tight hug, breathing him in one last time, and then willed myself to step back, my eyes filling with tears despite myself.

"You should go," I said, blinking fast and giving him a playful push, smiling through tears. "Send me a postcard?"

"Sure." He laughed, though he looked like he might cry, slowly walking backward. "Goodnight, Killeen."

"Goodnight, safe travels," I said, my voice catching on the word *travels*. He waved and turned around, and I watched him walk down the path toward the cab.

I walked up the staircase to the door to Idaho Hall, before turning to see him striding back up the path toward me as the taxi pulled away, and I ran toward him, almost slipping on the ice.

"I'm sorry, I can't . . ." he said, grabbing my hand and wrapping his arm around my waist. "I can't leave here without . . ."

"Shh . . . I know," I said, as we crashed into each other like on that very first night we saw each other at the Liberty.

Only this time, I threw my arms around him, and we both gasped when our lips met, kissing with a passion and intensity that I thought only existed in the movies. He put his hands in my hair, and I put mine inside his coat, and as he pulled me closer to him, he let out a small groan, pressing his lips against mine even harder.

It was the kind of kiss that stopped time. One that might ruin me for any future kisses. As we melted into each other, there was no doubt this moment was going to make it impossible to ever forget him. And I don't know how long we stayed there locked in that embrace, but it was far longer than we should have, consumed with each other as the snowflakes kept falling, though neither of us felt the cold.

Part Two

There is no foreseeable defense against atomic bombs . . . America has a temporary superiority in armament, but it is certain that we have no lasting secret.

—*Albert Einstein, "The Real Problem Is in the Hearts of Men,"* New York Sunday Times, *June 1946*

Chapter Twenty-Two

Monday, August 27, 1949

Dear Dad,

It was so good to see you and the boys last weekend. I miss you all so much already, and I promise I'll try to get home again in a few months if my work allows, definitely over Christmas and hopefully at least one other time before Mickey's wedding next April. I still can't believe he's getting married! I'm so excited to have a sister-in-law. Betty is lovely, and I'm glad I got to spend more time with her.

I know from our talk that you're still worried that I'm working too hard down here, but I promise you I'm not. Like I said, I truly still love every minute of this job, despite the long days.

And I have great news. Effie, Gia, and I just found an apartment—we move on September 1! We have been looking for so long, I was beginning to wonder if we'd ever find a place. The new place is on the second floor of an apartment complex called Melrose Manor, an eight-minute bus ride from work. It's a sun-filled three-bedroom with one bath—to share a bathroom with only two other people is going to be a dream! Maybe one of these days, we can finally get you on a train down here, so you can see it for yourself.

I'm heading out to our bowling tournament, so I have to run, but I wanted to write a quick note with my brand-new forwarding address.

Love you, miss you, and I'll write more very soon!

Xoxo,

Cat

I sealed the letter, wondering if I'd ever be able to tell him and my brothers about the actual work we did in Building B at Arlington Hall. I had imagined their reaction more than once, how impressed, how incredibly proud they would be, how the guys at my father's station would never hear the end of it.

Over the past eighteen months, the heads of the ASA and FBI had been stunned that two obscure teams, led by the eccentric, multilingual codebreaker Meredith Gardner and the rough-and-tumble FBI agent Bob Lamphere, had come together and accomplished the impossible: re-creating the Soviet KGB codebook.

After the first envelope of plain-text Russian messages Jonathan and Bob had provided Meredith, several more batches had followed, and we all knew better than to ask how the FBI had obtained them. Slowly and then seemingly all at once, the version of the codebook on Meredith's desk took on a fuller and more complete shape. And the so-called unbreakable KGB telegrams from the war years were no longer unbreakable. Thanks to Meredith's brilliance and thousands of hours of painstaking work by the team, we could decipher entire messages.

Bob referred to this as the golden time for our teams, in all the things we were able to accomplish together. Often, as soon as we deciphered a message and sent it over to him, he would launch an

The Women of Arlington Hall

investigation and try to track down the Russian spies or informants that might still be in the US.

At various points in time, he had agents in over a dozen cities following up on clues and code names that had been revealed in the messages. The possible recruit Max Elitcher, one of the original real persons identified, had unfortunately been a dead end. And the atomic spy ringleader Liberal and his wife Ethel remained an elusive mystery, but Meredith was sure that in time we would be able to identify them.

Our first major breakthrough came in late 1948, just after Truman was elected—although, per Hoover's directive, the president had still not been informed of the work we were doing. In December of that year, we learned that there was a Russian spy, code name Sima, real name Judith Coplon, still working for the Justice Department in DC. The FBI arrested Coplon in New York City, when she was caught meeting with her Russian handler, a bunch of stolen classified government documents in her purse.

> Judith Coplon and Russian Indicted on Four Counts as Spies

The clipping of the front-page article from the March 10 edition of *The Evening Star* was pinned to the corkboard above my desk. I glanced at it as I finished brushing my hair and getting dressed in my bowling shirt and pedal pushers to go meet the girls.

The morning after her arrest, I had walked by the newsstand, stopping in my tracks at the sight of Judith Coplon's name splashed across the front of several major newspapers. I kept the clipping on my bulletin board as a proud reminder, an example of the real-world consequences of our work.

The corkboard had become a hanging scrapbook of my life in DC. In addition to articles, there was a poster from the Ella Fitzgerald "First Lady of Swing" concert at the Howard Theatre, many movie theater ticket stubs, a few bowling tournament ribbons, and several pictures of me, Effie, Gia, and Rosemary. One of us sitting on the beach in Virginia, another of us picnicking on the National Mall, and of course a team photo of the Flying Saucers, Cecil standing proudly in the middle, holding Gia's pink bowling ball. There were a couple photos of me onstage with Trevor and the band at the Liberty, as I'd started singing with them one Saturday a month, more when my work schedule at Arlington Hall allowed, which wasn't often.

Also included in my collage were the postcards from Jonathan that I had been meaning to throw away. I hadn't seen him since our night at the Cairo, and I had no idea if he had come back to the States at all since then. But if he had, he hadn't contacted me.

At first, the postcards had arrived almost weekly, with pictures of Big Ben or Parliament or a random pub or garden, and a quick note about his life there. They always ended with *Yours, J.* There were no other terms of endearment, no *I miss yous*, no mention of returning to the States. I had sent just as many postcards to him, signing off in kind. But after a while, his postcards trickled down to once every other month or so, and now I hadn't received one since April.

I was starting to let go of the fantasy that he'd come back to DC, that we would have this fairy-tale romantic reunion. The lingering ache of what might have been ebbed and flowed, sometimes fading into the background of my life, only to bubble up with renewed intensity when I least expected it. And I still relived that night, especially our first and last kiss, more times than I could count.

"Hey, Cat, you ready?" Effie knocked and hollered through the door. "Gia's already left. Next bus will be here in five, and you know Cecil will lose his mind if we're late."

"Coming," I said as I opened the door.

"Are you all right?" she asked, hand on her hip, looking me up and down.

"Fine, why?" I said. "Just finished a letter to my dad, telling him about our new place."

"Yes, we're finally saying au revoir to Idaho." She glanced around my room, nodding at the corkboard. "Still haven't thrown out the postcards, huh?"

"I'm getting to it." I grabbed my purse and locked the door.

"Good." She placed an arm through my elbow as we walked down the hall. "Archie has a friend named Brendan I want you to meet. Also British, works at the embassy. He's bringing him to the bowling afterparty. He says he's handsome, though we know men are not always great judges of that. Also, I'm not sure about his teeth—you know, the stereotypes about the English and their teeth are kind of true . . ."

"Effie, I told you . . ." I started to say. Archie had managed to be assigned to the US again for the foreseeable future, which Effie seemed happy about the majority of the time, except when he brought up marriage or visiting his family in England.

"Sugar, yes, but it's time to forget Jonathan Dardis. You've only been on a few dates with other guys since he left, and I know it's because you're still pining for him. It's time to get out there. Nothing serious," she said.

"Ugh, I don't know . . ."

"Just promise me you'll think about it? It would be good for you," Effie said. "Just meet him. No pressure. He has no idea I want to set you guys up."

"I'll think about it," I said with a sigh, just to appease her. "As long as he has decent teeth."

∼

I continued to be a hopeless bowler, but I had grown to love the Flying Saucers, because even when we lost, we'd still end up laughing until our sides ached, a fact that Cecil did not always appreciate. Our team did not win the second annual ASA Bowling Championships, much to his dismay, but we did come in a respectable third. Gia was our bowling ace and always seemed to help us climb into the top three teams. The new team from Building A, the Lucky Strikes, dominated the competition from the start. After it was over, everyone headed over to the end-of-season party for all the teams at a popular burger joint close to the Arlington Hall campus.

"There he is. There's Brendan sitting with Arch at the bar. See him?" Effie asked me as we sat down at a high-top table. "I just met him. And he has no visible dental issues."

I looked over to see that Archie's friend Brendan had thick blond hair and an aquiline nose, was built like an ex-rugby player, and yes, he was handsome.

"I can't see his teeth from here. Are you sure about that?" I asked, jokingly.

"Whose teeth?" Rosemary asked, joining our table along with Margaret, as Effie explained who Brendan was. They were both very tan after a few days' vacation at Rosemary's family home on Saint Thomas in the US Virgin Islands. Margaret could still be a little uptight for Effie, Gia, and me at times, but since she was Rosemary's best friend and roommate, she ended up hanging out with us fairly often.

"He's not *bad*-looking," Margaret said, pushing her glasses up as she looked at him, and judging from her expression, she didn't think he was exactly good-looking either.

"I'm not sure I'm in the mood to meet him tonight. Maybe another time?" I said to Effie.

"Yeah, give her a break, Eff, she's still mourning our championship loss," Rosemary said.

"Fine," Effie said, with a pretend pout.

"Lindsay Philmore's at the bar too," I said. He was still a bit of an enigma, friendly with a distinct air of snobbery, and hard-partying. He had shown up for more than one afternoon meeting at Arlington Hall reeking of whiskey and cigars, and that had not endeared him to any of us, especially Meredith.

"Oh yes, the one and thankfully only," Effie groaned. "Archie keeps hoping he'll head back to England soon. He's a lot to take."

"Bob was saying the same thing," Rosemary said. "Apparently, he arrived at an FBI meeting the other day drunk as a skunk. Also, he *much* prefers the company of the CIA, so you can imagine how Hoover feels about that."

"How can a boorish guy like that be next in line to head up British intelligence?" I asked, watching Philmore down a glass of something amber-colored.

"Good question. I haven't heard many positive things about him, and I hear *a lot* up at the main hall," Margaret said. "Hey, Cat, will you please help me get the first round of drinks?"

"Is Gia here?" Margaret asked after we had taken everyone's orders.

"She is." I followed Margaret as she weaved her way through the crowd. We found a spot on the opposite side of the bar from Philmore and Brendan.

"I wanted to get you alone for a second," Margaret said in a low voice, pushing her glasses up her nose again, her eyes serious. "There's something you should know."

"What is it?" I said, my body tensing up as I tried to guess what it could be, what security protocol I might have unknowingly violated at work.

"You remember your intake interview, when I mentioned your uncle in New York was flagged in your background check?" she said.

"Oh God, yes," I said. "Peter Walker. He came up *again*?"

"In a review of your personnel file this week." She nodded, cringing. It was clear she didn't enjoy delivering this news.

"What are you talking about? Why this week?"

"It's this hysteria that's gripped the country. It's out of control. Colonel Carpenter insisted on a review of the personnel files of everyone working in Building B. Again."

"So? They've known since I started that he's a member of the CPUSA," I said, trying to control my frustration. "I was cleared for my job ages ago. And I've never met this man. What am I supposed to do?"

"I honestly don't know," Margaret said. "But I wanted to warn you."

"They wouldn't fire me for this, would they?" I felt physically ill. How could this still be a concern after all this time?

"I mean, to be honest, anything's possible these days," Margaret said with sympathy. "I'm sorry to alarm you. Maybe talk to Meredith about it? Before someone else does?"

"I will. It's absurd that this is an issue again."

The harried bartender finally saw Margaret signaling him, and we ordered our drinks. I'd been naive to think my uncle would never come up again, given the current state of the world.

Over the past two years, communist hysteria in America had reached a fever pitch. Among many factors, in the summer of '48, a former Soviet spy named Whittaker Chambers, as well as none other than Elizabeth Bentley, had publicly testified in front of the House Un-American Activities Committee in Congress, fueling the flames of panic with their revelations about Soviet agents infiltrating every level of government in the United States.

"Thanks very much for giving me advance warning," I said.

"Of course," Margaret said. "It's possible nothing will come of it."

"Let's hope so," I said, still uneasy. I hadn't thought about Peter Walker in months.

Margaret didn't hear me. She was smiling and looking over at Rosemary, who had just thrown her head back, laughing at something Effie said.

"I love her, you know," Margaret whispered.

"We all do, and she's done so well taking over for Gene in our section," I said, also grinning at the scene. "I wonder what they're laughing at."

"No, Cat, I mean, I am in *love* with her," Margaret said. "With Rosemary."

"Oh," I said, looking over to see tears in her eyes, and my mouth dropped open. "*Oh* . . . I, I didn't know."

"Of course you didn't. Why would you?"

And suddenly I saw Rosemary and Margaret's friendship over the past couple of years, their entire relationship, in a whole different light.

"I'm . . . I'm not even sure what to say," I said, because I hadn't seen what was, in hindsight, right in front of my eyes.

"You know, she almost didn't take Gene's job?" she said, her eyes still watery. "She was so afraid people at work would find out about us and we'd both get fired. But I insisted she take it because I knew she'd be brilliant at it. And she's terrified to tell you all, but you're her best friends here, besides me. I know you and I aren't as close. I know I can be little . . . well, let's just say intense. But I want you to know, because it's exhausting, all the pretending, living this lie, especially with her family this past week. But I told Rosie, it's time for you all to know. That you would understand. I hope . . . I hope I'm not wrong."

As our drinks arrived, Margaret took off her glasses and wiped away her tears as I paid the bartender. I felt naive that I hadn't put the pieces together before now. And it broke my heart at how anxious and emotional the usually buttoned-up Margaret was after telling me.

Did I understand? Not exactly. I'd never known two women in a relationship before, but I knew they existed. It felt awkward, as I tried to think of the right words.

"As you know, my mother was Russian and Jewish. She became estranged from her family the moment she got engaged to my father," I said, and Margaret just nodded, so I kept talking. "One of the reasons I called off my wedding—I kept going back to my mother's choice. She sacrificed everything, gave up her family to build a new one with my father. Why? Because my father was the love of her life. And I absolutely knew I didn't feel that way about Andrew. I cared about him, but not enough, not like that. All this is to say that the real thing, true love? I think it's so very rare, and . . . well, if you've found that? I'm . . . I'm just so happy for you both."

We were quiet for a moment, watching our circle of friends from afar.

"Thank you." Margaret gave me a look of gratitude. "Just telling you? It makes me feel less . . . suffocated, if that makes sense."

"I'm glad," I said, trying to imagine the pain of hiding, always being afraid of what would happen if people found out the truth of who you really were. "Come on, we better bring these drinks back. They're getting impatient over there."

"Thank you again, Cat," Margaret said as we headed back.

"Thank you for trusting me," I said. "Can I . . . do you want me to talk to Effie and Gia?"

"Yes, please," she said. "It will be an enormous relief to both of us, to be free to be ourselves with you three."

Chapter Twenty-Three

Friday, September 16, 1949

"Okay, so Sunday, provided we don't have to work, we need to go shopping," Effie said, as the bus pulled up in front of Arlington Hall. "I definitely want to get a toaster, and I could use some new towels."

"And we should do a big grocery shopping too, stock up, just so we don't have to think about it," I said.

"Agreed," said Gia. "But *I* get to pick out the fruits and vegetables. I'm the only one of us that knows good produce."

"Whatever you say, G," Effie said, giving me an amused look.

"Also, Cecil has offered to paint our rooms. It's allowed in the lease, so we should pick paint colors this weekend too," Gia said.

"Are we paying Cecil for this?" Effie asked.

"Do . . . do we know if Cecil's a *good* painter?" I said, hand on my chin, questioning Gia. She and Cecil remained close friends. Whether they would ever become more than that was anyone's guess, though Cecil was forever the optimist.

"Of course. Do you think I'd let him near our walls if he wasn't?" Gia said.

Our apartment was a small but sunny corner unit, with a combined living room and kitchen area, one bathroom, and three modest-sized bedrooms off a narrow hallway. After we had scrubbed it from top to bottom the first couple days and added some brightly colored throw pillows, frosted blue glass table lamps, and other cozy touches to the living area, it now had a much warmer and homier feel to it. And it was absolutely luxurious compared to living at Idaho Hall.

The day was warm and breezy as we walked down the hill to Building B, past the crimson dogwood trees. Maybe it was because of our apartment, or the gorgeous weather, or how well work was going, but it felt like a new chapter, like the first day of school, when you were filled with anticipation of all the good things that might happen.

Gia and I said goodbye to Effie, and when we headed into the Russian section something immediately seemed off. The coworkers who were already sitting at their desks were way too quiet for a Friday morning. Except for Cecil, who bounded over to us at Gia's desk, nervous energy personified.

"So, Bob's in Meredith's office. He showed up at like seven this morning. He wasn't supposed to be here today," Cecil said, fidgeting with the buttons on his shirt.

"Do you have a clue why?" I asked.

"No, but I got a look at their faces. They were grim," he said. "Like 'someone died' grim. Whatever the reason? It's not good."

"Great," Gia said, rummaging through her purse for her cigarette case. "We are working Sunday for sure."

"Hand me one of those, G," Rosemary said, joining us. "The energy in this place this morning is giving me a bad feeling. Margaret just told me the colonel and some of the other ASA heads left Arlington Hall for the White House at the crack of dawn."

"Oh no, that never happens," I said, my sunny outlook now overshadowed by a sense of foreboding.

We all tried to work for the next half hour, but I kept staring at the papers in front of me and not really seeing them, tapping my foot under my desk, glancing up at Meredith's door. When it finally opened, Meredith peeked out and called for Rosemary, along with me, Gia,

Cecil, and a few others, and said to meet him in the smaller conference room in ten minutes.

I took a seat across from Bob. He was haggard, two days' worth of dark stubble on his face. He did not greet me with his usual friendly chitchat, just nodded a quiet hello.

"All right, everyone's here that needs to be here," Meredith said, his voice flat and dejected. "Frank and Colonel Carter aren't available, so it's just us. Frank told me to remind you all that if you reveal to anyone outside this room what Bob's about to tell you, you will be executed for treason by the United States government. Bob, go ahead, I'll let you tell them."

"Lucky me," Bob said, rubbing his hands over his face and sitting back in his chair. "So, I have a story to tell—buckle up because it's one for the history books. Though you won't be able to tell your grandchildren why you learned about it before the rest of the world.

"In early September, the B-29s of the air force's 175th Weather Reconnaissance Squadron were doing a routine patrol of the Pacific, circling back up over the Arctic, just downwind of the Soviet Union. These planes are what the air force calls 'sniffers,' and their classified mission? Detect atomic explosions from distant geographic locations."

My arms broke out in goose pimples, and I shivered. He paused for a moment, looking around the room, struggling to deliver news that none of us wanted to hear.

"While one of these planes was flying east of the Kamchatka Peninsula in Russia, its red-alarm lights started going off. Back at the base, they confirmed that this B-29 had detected radioactivity. The Soviets successfully tested an atomic bomb at the end of August in northeast Kazakhstan. Four bloody years ahead of what the CIA predicted," Bob said. "They've got the bomb. America no longer has a monopoly. There are now two atomic superpowers in the world. And . . . and my absolute *worst* fears about the Soviets have now come true."

My mind flashed to when my family got the telegram stating that Richie had been killed in action. I remember Mickey reading it to me, his hand shaking as he held the paper, his voice cracking. I'd never seen him cry before. I had sunk to my knees on our kitchen floor, not able to understand what he was saying, like my brain couldn't quite absorb the terrible news that Richie was gone. I still remembered every second of that devastating moment in a visceral way—the smell of burnt toast, the coffee spilled on our linoleum floor, the wrenching sound of my father's uncontrollable sobbing.

This moment, though not as personal, was reminiscent of that one. There was a ringing in my ears as I took in what Bob was saying. It was a before-and-after moment for the world, and I knew I'd remember the anger and chill that went through me at the words *They've got the bomb* for the rest of my life.

People's expressions ranged from horrified to stunned to furious. Cecil had jumped out of his chair and started pacing near the door, but even he was too shell-shocked to speak.

"I had to sit through a brutal meeting last night with some of the FBI brass. They are mad as hell and frustrated, naturally. And they grilled me—did the Soviets build this bomb using scientific information stolen from the US? And if they did, why weren't the Soviet spies who stole this intelligence from us in jail yet?"

"But whatever they stole, it happened years ago. That's not your fault," Cecil said. "Why would they be furious with you?"

"They want a scapegoat," Bob said with the smallest shrug, and it was awful to see him so beaten down. "And since they can't punish the Soviet agents, as head of the Soviet espionage unit, I'm the closest thing. I sat back and took it for the most part, because remember, I still can't reveal to most of them what you're working on here—even the president *still* doesn't know. Anyway, I feel the weight of this, the shame of it, like I've let the Bureau—hell, the entire country—down."

"I truly believe, based on what we know so far about Project Enormoz, that Russian scientists were aided in their effort to build the bomb by information stolen from the US," Meredith said.

The Women of Arlington Hall

"So do I. Just the mere existence of Project Enormoz validates that," Bob said. "But we still haven't been able to prove it."

"Yet," I said, speaking up for the first time. Meredith gave me a nod of approval. "Can't prove it *yet*. Doesn't mean we won't."

"Cat's right," Rosemary said. "We've been making progress . . ."

"Look, I know how hard you've all been working on this," Bob said, interrupting her and getting up from the table. "Not only Meredith, but all of you. I see the long hours you put in and the painstaking effort this work takes.

"We've had some success, yes, but now I need to ask you to work harder than ever, because this quiet cooperation between me and Meredith and all of us? It's just taken on immense importance, not only to the FBI, but to the nation.

"We need the names behind the code names—we've got to find Liberal and his friends in this atomic spy ring. We need some wins, to bring some of these traitors to justice. Although, to be completely honest . . . right now? In this moment . . . I'm not . . . I'm not feeling confident that we can."

∼

The rest of the day the mood in the office was somber, and I knew I wasn't the only one feeling defeated. Bob's news, his lack of faith, had demoralized us all.

It was after six o'clock and everyone had left, but I was too restless and aggravated about the day's events. I kept going over the book of code names, all our notes. Had we missed something? Meredith had compared deciphering the KGB messages to the elephant and the blind man parable—sometimes we could think we'd cracked something important, but it only amounted to the elephant's tusk. It barely touched a piece of the massive espionage operation underneath. Just as I considered packing up for the night, Meredith opened his door and looked out.

"Hi, I didn't even realize you were still here," I said.

"Glad I'm not the only one." He waved me over. "Please come in."

I walked into a cloud of pipe smoke, his office having even more of a mad-scientist aesthetic than usual, and I looked at the musings in chalk, the five columns of papers tacked to the corkboard, trying to decipher his genius, to find meaning in his most recent iteration of chaos.

"That meeting, that was . . . pretty devastating," I said. Even that was an understatement.

"It was," Meredith said, letting out a breath. His tone was neutral, his demeanor less morose than earlier. "The world just became much more dangerous. The global balance of power has shifted. But Bob should not have said that at the end. It wasn't good for morale."

"I think he's just been taking so much heat at headquarters," I said. "I just . . . maybe you're used to it, but having this kind of knowledge before the rest of the country? There's an almost physical heaviness to it, being the first to know . . . I'm not explaining myself . . ."

"I understand," he said. "But that's why I'm still here. We've learned this news. Now we need to do something about it."

"So, what . . . what have you been working on?"

"Everything, maybe nothing," Meredith said, motioning to the papers all over his desk and on the walls. "The way I see it, we can mope around, or we can do what we do best."

"Which is what, exactly?" I asked, not sure where he was going with this.

"Work the problem. Go over all the clues we have, review every code name of every Soviet agent with a possible connection with Enormoz. Go through all the past messages we've deciphered, see what we might have overlooked. Leave no stone unturned. Bob's our friend as well as a colleague. We need to do this for him."

Bob's our friend. It's the first time I'd heard Meredith speak endearingly of anyone other than his wife.

"I agree," I said, heartened by his attitude.

"Do you have time to review some materials with me?"

"I do," I said. "But I need to talk to you about something first."

"More important than this?" Meredith asked, his tone impatient.

"It is only because it could impact my role here."

"Ah, let me guess. Is this about your uncle? The physicist named Peter Walker, works at Columbia?"

"Yes," I said, grimacing. "So, you know about him? I've never even met him."

"Personnel showed me your file the other day, with this new ridiculous review that the colonel wanted. Quite honestly, I think it would be odd if he worked at Columbia and *wasn't* a communist," he said with sarcasm. "You've more than proven yourself, Catherine. I trust you implicitly."

"Thank you," I said, relief washing over me. "I can't tell you how much I appreciate hearing that."

"All this anti-communist hysteria is absurd," Meredith said, shaking his head. "And now it's about to get so, so much worse. Soon, everyone in the entire US government will have someone in their background who's considered 'a concern.'"

"I hope you're wrong," I said, relieved that Meredith wasn't worried, that I could focus on what was in front of us.

"So put your worry about that aside. We've got no time for that now," Meredith said, giving me a pointed look. "Let's get to work so we can divide and conquer with the team this weekend."

Chapter Twenty-Four

"Thank you for coming in this weekend. There's, there's . . . there's apple cider donuts. It was my wife's idea," Meredith said, his voice a little shaky as he stood in front of the Russian section at eight a.m. on Saturday morning, arms crossed, looking awkward but determined. "You all know I'm not one for speeches. Or . . . talking most of the time, let's be frank."

A few quiet laughs and nods at his self-deprecation, and he continued.

"I need to say a few words this morning. It's important, so bear with me. We are some of the only people in the world who know that the Soviets now have the bomb. But we are also some of the only people who can actually do something about it.

"You've worked with me long enough. You know I'm not good at compliments, but listen . . . Nobody in the world is better at this work than the group of you sitting here. *Nobody.* You all came in here as ordinary Americans—with superior intellects—but still, living ordinary lives. But together? Well, you've all proved to be so very extraordinary."

He paused and looked around the room. All of us were silent. I wasn't the only one who had a lump in my throat.

"As Bob said, we now need to work even harder. We have more to discover—who were the spies working on Enormoz? Where are they now? What clues have we yet to decipher in these messages so that the FBI can finally open an investigation that leads directly to them?

"I feel it, I can't explain it, but my instincts tell me we are on the verge of success. We just need to keep going, to not give up. We all can make history. Let's do just that."

"We won't let you down, Meredith," Cecil said, and a few others around the room chimed in with similar sentiments.

"All right, that's enough," Meredith said after a moment, his ears bright red. "Grab a donut and let's get to work."

Weekend plans had been canceled without complaint, and there was no grocery shopping or picking paint colors for me, Gia, and Effie. For the next two days, we rehashed and reviewed hundreds of deciphered or partially deciphered KGB messages. We went over old ground, working with Meredith on some of the more difficult messages we had yet to break. We were all bleary-eyed and exhausted, and nobody worked harder than Meredith Gardner himself.

On Sunday morning, I brought him a coffee and a chocolate muffin from the café, and we sat in his office looking at yet another list of scientists on his chalkboard. This time, it was the British scientific delegation, fifteen in all, that had been hand-picked by J. Robert Oppenheimer to come to the U.S. to work on the Manhattan Project. WORK 186-86 Enemy House—clarify.

"One of the men on *this* list is most definitely a Russian spy," I said.

"Agree." Meredith nodded. "Walk me through why. Let's review what we've got so far."

"A newly deciphered message from the KGB's New York office in June 1944 states that a spy code-named Rest passed a highly classified report on the gaseous diffusion process, one of the key scientific techniques to prepare uranium to make an atomic bomb, to another spy, a courier code-named Gus. It included a portion of a scientific paper published nine days earlier. All this intelligence seems to have come directly from the Manhattan Project."

"Good work, go on," Meredith said, so I kept going through my notes.

"And now we know from an earlier KGB message that our spy Rest came from the UK. To quote, 'Rest arrived in the Country'—aka America—'as a member of the Island's'—aka England's—'mission to Enormoz.' So Rest's real name is up here. He is one of these scientists from the British delegation," I concluded, pointing up at the names.

"Yes, this is all excellent work," Meredith said. "And we also know that when this group first arrived, many of them spent time at Columbia, studying gaseous diffusion." Meredith looked up at me when he said this.

"What? Seriously?" I said.

"Seriously," Meredith said.

Columbia. Where Peter Walker worked.

"Should I call my uncle?" I said, half joking.

"No," Meredith said. "You should focus on this list. It's an Ivy League institution. Of course Columbia, like Harvard and MIT, would be affiliated with the Manhattan Project somehow. We're talking about a collection of the most brilliant scientific minds in the world."

"Good point." I nodded. "I'll focus on the list."

"So Bob is in touch with the Atomic Energy Commission to learn who wrote that paper, and to also confirm which of the scientists listed here went to work at the secret compound in Los Alamos, referred to as Camp Two by the Soviets. Share this with the team. We need to mine the messages, find out everything we've got on Rest, any personal details that will allow us to make the connection between the code name and one of the scientists we have on the board."

"Will do." I examined his face, the bluish circles under his eyes. Nodding at his rumpled shirt and tie, the same one he had been wearing the day before, I added, "You should eat that muffin. You look pale. Did you go home last night?"

"Keep working." Meredith ignored my comment and ran his hand through his hair, causing one curl in the front to stick straight up in the air as it often did, like a barometer measuring his stress level. "Can't you hear that clock ticking? Any day now, Truman's going to tell the country the Russians have the bomb. We need to give Bob some real names he can go after."

"Got it, boss," I said, giving him a little salute that elicited an eye roll.

By late Sunday afternoon, only a half dozen of us remained, as our coworkers with families finally took the last hours of the weekend off. Rosemary, Gia, and I were discussing where to go grab some dinner when Bob walked into the office, clean-shaven, seemingly well rested, and smiling.

"You look a whole lot better than you did a couple of days ago," I said.

"No kidding," Gia said, looking him up and down.

"Thanks, still getting beat up over the news, but I'm better," he said. "I've got something I need to show Meredith—all of you. It couldn't wait till Monday. I think we've finally caught a break."

Just then, the muffled sounds of Meredith yelling from inside his office made us all look at each other in alarm.

"Is he . . . is he in there alone?" Bob asked, pointing at Meredith's closed door.

"Of course," Gia said. "He tends to talk to himself more when he doesn't get much sleep."

"Who's still here?" Meredith called out, his tone excited as he opened the office door. "Bob! Good, perfect timing. Gia, Cat, Rosemary, come in. Grab an extra chair or two."

We all squeezed into Meredith's office. He even pulled his desk back to make room, careful not to move any of the piles of papers and files on it.

"We're finally getting somewhere," Meredith said, pacing behind his desk.

"I agree," Bob said. "So yesterday after you told me about the paper cited in that KGB message, I tracked down the paper at the Atomic Energy Commission to see who wrote it. I had to get one of them to show up on a Saturday to let me in."

"Please tell me that it's one of the names up there." Meredith pointed to the names of British scientific delegation on the chalkboard.

Jane Healey

"He is," Bob said with a chuckle, rubbing his hands together. "The author of the paper is a scientist named Klaus Fuchs," Bob said, nodding at his name on the board. "One of the most prominent members of the British delegation mission. We did a deep dive on him."

"And *we* did a deep dive on the spy code-named Rest," Meredith said, talking faster than usual, pacing behind his desk. "Let's see what, if anything, matches up."

"Right. Just because Klaus Fuchs wrote the paper doesn't necessarily mean he's a spy. There are a lot of other names up there," I said.

"Exactly what I was thinking," Gia said. "Anyone could have swiped the paper and shared it."

"Right, so why don't you tell me what you've got on Rest?" Bob said.

"A few details that might be helpful," Meredith said. "First, Rest definitely worked at Camp Two, aka Los Alamos."

"As did Klaus Fuchs," Bob said with a nod.

"Second, Rest took a trip to Chicago in February 1945," Rosemary added, something we had discovered earlier in the day.

"Oh, interesting, I'll look into that," Bob said, making a note.

"Would you happen to know if Klaus Fuchs has a sister living in America?" Meredith asked, revealing another clue we had discovered. "Because Rest does."

"She lives in Cambridge, Massachusetts," I added. "Rest spent Christmas with her in 1944, according to a KGB message from New York to Moscow on November 16, 1944."

"Bingo!" Bob said, clapping his hands together. "Klaus Fuchs has a sister named Kristel Heineman. She lives in Cambridge, Massachusetts, with her husband and children. Friends, I think we might have found him."

"Are you joking? You better not be joking, Bob," Meredith said, a slightly manic look in his eyes.

"Oh no, you know I'm not." Bob smiled at him and held out his hand, and they shook, and we all started clapping. "We've got a name, now we have to corroborate everything, make sure we're right. If we put Klaus Fuchs at his sister's in Christmas of '44, check and see if he was in Chicago in '45 . . . We've still got more to do, but this is a huge breakthrough."

"Klaus Fuchs is probably Rest," I smiled. "We've got an actual name."

"I can't believe it," Rosemary said, letting out a huge sigh. "I think I might cry."

"Jesus, Mary, and Joseph," Gia said, sinking back in her chair like she was about to pass out. "It's about time."

"Truman hasn't even told the country about the Soviet's atomic bomb test, and we've already got a prime suspect for the Soviet spy who stole the atomic secrets," Bob said. "The bad news? Fuchs is back in London, and the arm of United States law doesn't extend that far."

"So now what happens?" Meredith asked. "Assuming we can corroborate everything and think Fuchs is our man?"

"Britain's MI6 needs to bring him in for questioning ASAP," Bob said. "I am writing up a top secret report, telling them everything we know. In the meantime, I'm opening an FBI criminal investigation on him here."

"*If* they can get to Rest and get him to talk, we might finally get some of these other dominos to fall. Here are the major spies in the atomic ring so far," Meredith said, going to the chalkboard:

Rest—Klaus Fuchs?

Liberal—engineer, leader of spy ring, City College, wife Ethel

Gus—courier for Liberal and Rest

Kaliber—scientist, also City College connection possibly

"I'd definitely share what we have on the spy named Gus with MI6," Meredith said. "Question Fuchs about him first, see if he has a name."

"Gus and Rest met on more than one occasion, according to several messages," Rosemary said, going through her notes.

"Also, Ethel, Liberal's wife, is at the center of all of this," Meredith added.

"Ah, yes, the mysterious Ethel," Bob said.

"We've been able to decipher more of this message about her," I said, flipping through my notebook. "This is from November of '44.

"'Intelligence on Liberal's wife: surname that of her husband. Christian name Ethel. Married five years. Twenty-nine years old. Finished middle school. A fellow countryman. Sufficiently well-developed politically. She knows about her husband's work . . . in view of her delicate health, she does not work.' 'Countryman,' as we know, means a member of the CPUSA. 'Does not work'—we believe that means she's not a spy herself. That and the fact they mention her by her real name."

"Well done," Bob said, taking notes. "We're finally getting closer to ID'ing Liberal and his wife."

"Will you go to London?" I asked, and of course my thoughts turned to Jonathan.

"I want to go interview Fuchs myself, of course, but I'm not sure if the bosses will let me," Bob said, rubbing his face with his hand. "Right now, I just want them to get to him before he disappears."

"Isn't Jonathan Dardis still working with British intelligence in London?" Gia said. I shot her a look, and she just winked at me.

"Funny you should ask," Bob said. "He was, up until a week ago. But he recently put in for a transfer and got the green light. He's coming back to the States, working for the Bureau's Soviet espionage unit again, this time with a promotion."

"Back here in DC?" I hoped my voice sounded casual, refusing to look over at Rosemary and Gia.

"No, not DC. Though it was his first choice," Bob said. "He's headed to New York City."

∼

When we finally got home after nine on Sunday night, Effie, Gia, and I sat in our living room, the windows open to enjoy the cool September night air as we devoured an enormous pepperoni pizza from Federici's, a tiny Italian restaurant two blocks from our new apartment.

"So, you honestly, truly didn't know?" Gia asked. "That Margaret and Rosemary were . . ."

"A couple?" I said.

"Yes." Gia rolled her eyes and handed me a bottle of Coke from the fridge.

"I had no idea, and I can't believe you *had* figured it out and never told me. And now I feel like an idiot that I didn't see what was right in front of us."

"Oh no, I also had no clue," Effie said, and looking uncomfortable, she added, "And honestly? I . . . I still don't get it. I really don't get it. I mean, maybe it's because I just really like men? Or because of my Baptist upbringing. I don't know . . . it's not something I understand. At all."

"It's the religion thing. That's entirely why," Gia said in a matter-of-fact tone. "You're not even supposed to *imagine* relationships like that, even though they've been around since Ancient Rome. Listen, my aunt, Zia Carmella, and her best friend, Antonina, have lived together for over thirty years. Thirty years! And nobody in my family acknowledges they're a couple. But also? Everyone *knows* they're a couple."

"And how do your relatives treat them?" Effie asked, which was my question too.

"Like family. Because really, unless you're an awful person, what else are you going to do?" Gia shrugged, helping herself to another slice of pizza and tucking her legs back under her on our sapphire-blue sofa, which we had purchased from the last tenant.

"Even my grandparents, God rest their souls, treated Antonina like a daughter," Gia added. "Meaning that my grandmother often told her when she was getting too fat or needed a haircut, and my grandfather teased her about how bad she was at bocce."

"Look, Rosemary is one of our best friends, so I will do my best to come around," Effie said. "But it's just not exactly comfortable to think about."

"I understand that. Because you're right, Gia, about the religion thing," I said, putting my feet up on our new walnut coffee table. "And look, I know we're going to be tired in the morning, but I needed this tonight."

"Okay, on to more pressing matters," Gia said. "We need to discuss a certain FBI man returning from London."

"Amen," Effie said. She took a sip of her Coke and pointed at me.

"You heard about Jonathan?" I looked at Effie.

"Of course," Effie laughed. "The question is, what are you going to do about it?"

"Nothing," I said, but just the thought of him being closer had sent me into a tailspin of emotions earlier in the day, that familiar ache in my chest returning with a vengeance, and a thrill at the thought of seeing him again.

I had replayed our kiss so many times over the past eighteen months, every second of it was burned into my brain. The tinge of gin on his breath, his hands on my face, mine inside his coat as the snowflakes swirled around us.

"But Bob did say Jonathan *wanted* to be back in DC," Gia said.

"But he's not going to be," I said. "And we've barely been in touch. It... Don't get me wrong. It was nice, but it meant nothing. It was just one kiss."

"That is such a lie." Effie shook her head at me.

"What do you mean? Did he stay over that night? The night you went on a 'date that wasn't a date'?" Gia asked.

"What? No, no, of course not. He called another taxi and went home," I said, my face growing hot because we had both considered it, but it would have made his leaving even more difficult for me to bear.

"That's not what I meant, Gia," Effie said, laughing. "I meant there was something between you two, real feelings. Also, Cat, you are blushing so much right now it's ridiculous."

"I can't help it," I said, laughing too, putting my hand on my cheek. "It was a memorable kiss, but that's all it was. I keep reminding myself that he's kissed a lot of girls in his time."

"True," Gia said with a nod. "What did he say when he left that night?"

"He said goodbye," I said, remembering the feeling of being in his arms. "And that we were star-crossed. But that we might find our way back to each other someday."

"Huh. Star-crossed is a really good line," Gia said, considering. "I bet he's used that one a lot."

"Gee, thanks G," I said with heavy sarcasm, giving her a comical scowl.

"Oh, don't listen to Gia," Effie said. "I for one am curious to see what happens when you see him again. In the meantime, there's that fella Brendan from the British embassy I've been dying to introduce you to. And Lindsay Philmore and his wife are having a party next Saturday. They're living in a gorgeous brick home on Nebraska Avenue, next to the navy center. Archie said we're all invited. It's the perfect opportunity. And we're going, even if we're still working ourselves to the bone."

"I'll go," I said, deciding I needed a distraction from Jonathan's return. "You can even introduce me."

"Perfect," Effie said, pleased. "Philmore's parties are becoming legendary. Gia, you can invite Cecil too."

"I will, but I'll have to give him the UFO talk again." Gia rolled her eyes, though she spoke of him in an obviously affectionate way. "There was a sighting in Fargo, North Dakota, and it's all he's been talking about. I thought he'd be over this obsession by now, but it's only gotten worse."

"Are you ever going to put the man out of his misery and actually date him?" I asked, raising an eyebrow at her.

"How do you know we're not already dating?" Gia said.

"Get out of town!" Effie said, so delighted she jumped up from the couch. "Are you? Really?"

"No. But I like to keep you girls guessing," Gia said with a sly grin.

Chapter Twenty-Five

Saturday, September 24, 1949

THE WASHINGTON TIMES-HERALD

Truman Statement on Atom

By United Press

Washington, Sept. 23—The text of President Truman's statement today announcing a recent atomic explosion in the Soviet Union:

I believe the American people, to the fullest extent consistent with national security, are entitled to be informed of all developments in the field of atomic energy. That is my reason for making public the following information.

We have evidence that within recent weeks an atomic explosion occurred in the USSR. Ever since atomic energy was first released by man, the eventual development of this new force by other nations was to be expected. This probability has always been taken into account by us. Nearly four years ago I pointed out that "scientific opinion appears to be practically unanimous that the essential theoretical knowledge upon which the discovery is based is already widely known. There is also substantial agreement that foreign research can come abreast of our present theoretical knowledge in time." And, in the Three-Nation Declaration of the President of the United States and the Prime Ministers of the United Kingdom and of Canada, dated November 15, 1945, it was emphasized that no single nation could in fact have a monopoly of atomic weapons.

This recent development emphasizes once again, if indeed such emphasis were needed, the necessity for that truly effective enforceable international control of atomic energy which this Government and the large majority of the members of the United Nations support.

In August 1946, a reporter named John Hersey had written an article in *The New Yorker* magazine, after interviewing dozens of the survivors of America's atomic bombing in Hiroshima, Japan. These men and women gave gruesome, detailed, firsthand accounts of the aftermath, of the massive, noiseless flash of brilliant white light that killed thousands instantly, of buildings leveled, the horrific, devastating injuries, ranging from severe burns to multiple broken bones to blindness. Hersey painted pictures with his words: a young mother sitting on the side of the road holding tight to her dead infant daughter, stubbornly waiting for a husband who would never return. A trio of orphaned children lying in a hospital together, burned and battered, crying hysterically over their lost parents.

Hersey also detailed people falling ill with terrible symptoms in the days and months after the bomb—high fever, vomiting and fatigue, their hair falling out, sores that didn't heal—what doctors would ultimately recognize as the ravages of radiation disease.

In August of '45, when America bombed the Japanese cities of Hiroshima and Nagasaki, my first reaction had been one of tremendous relief. I had lost one brother in the war, and the bombing almost guaranteed that the war would end and Seamus would come home alive. But in the years since, after reading that article and others, I had questioned the catastrophic human cost of the atomic bombs. How many innocent Japanese children had died? How many lives had been ruined forever? And what kind of terrible Pandora's box had America opened?

The words of that *New Yorker* article came back to haunt me as I sat at my desk Saturday evening reading Truman's statement, waiting for my friends to freshen up before we headed to Lindsay Philmore's party.

The statement was printed above the fold on the front page of the newspaper and my arms were covered in goose pimples as I finished reading it. Even though I had known before the rest of the country, something about seeing it as front-page news was chilling in its own special way. Now, Americans' fear and paranoia of a potential nuclear war was rooted in a dark new reality, thanks in large part to a group of traitors in the United States, the newly identified Klaus Fuchs among them.

"There she is," Rosemary said from the other side of the office. "Nice dress, Cat. The girls headed downstairs, our taxi's waiting outside the gates. I said we'd catch up with them."

At Gia and Effie's insistence, I had brought a change of clothes, my burgundy dress with a V-neck and hourglass silhouette. Rosemary's platinum hair was freshly bobbed, and she looked her usual casually elegant self, wearing black wide-legged slacks and a teal silk blouse.

"Eff insisted that I bring a change of clothes and go," I said as we went down to join them. "But honestly, I would much rather be in my pajamas reading an Agatha Christie novel. It has been a hell of a week."

"I'm feeling the same," Rosemary said. "In fact, that's what Margaret is doing right now, and I cannot wait to join her. But I promised Eff."

"Me too," I said with a yawn.

"I wanted to say thank you by the way, but we haven't had a second alone these days," Rosemary said, as we made our way up the hill to the security gates. "And to be honest, it's hard for me to speak about, because I've conditioned myself to never discuss it, to pretend and live this lie. But thank you for understanding, about Margaret and me."

"Oh no, I mean, Rosemary, you're one of my dearest friends. I . . . If you're happy, that makes me happy."

"I'm so happy. With her." Rosemary blinked fast, her eyes welling with tears. "I . . . we can't tell our families, *ever*. I mean, my father . . . I can't even think about it. It's exhausting sometimes."

"Most secrets are," I said.

"The relief I feel just to know that you all see me for exactly who I am now. At least I'm no longer carrying the heavy weight of this enormous lie when it comes to you three. It means the world to me, and to Margaret."

We had just passed through security, and I wrapped my arm around hers and gave it a squeeze. She had seemed different, lighter, more relaxed now that we all knew.

"Hey, quit the chitchat and get your butts in the car, ladies," Gia hollered, leaning out the window of the back seat of the yellow taxi. "We've got a party to go to!"

∼

Lindsay Philmore and his wife and their five children lived in a gorgeous brick center-entrance colonial with black shutters on Nebraska Avenue. We arrived a little after seven, and there were several cars parked up and down the street, a sign the soiree was already in full swing, the sounds of jazz music and raucous laughter coming from the home's open windows.

The four of us stood in front of the walk as the cab drove away, and I longed again for my pajamas and Agatha Christie novel.

"You know, it's so crowded, nobody would notice if we didn't go in." I raised my eyebrows.

"You read my mind, Cat." Rosemary laughed.

"We're going in; stop being drips, you two." Effie grabbed my hand, pulling me toward the house.

"All right, if nothing else, I want to see how they decorated," Rosemary said. "It is a beautiful home."

"And they better have good food. All I've eaten today is a stale blueberry muffin," Gia said.

"The only thing I've heard about these parties is how much booze is flowing, so honestly I'm not sure about food," Effie said in a low voice as we rang the front doorbell. "A lot of CIA fellas and their wives will be here. Archie says Philmore *loves* to socialize with the CIA. More of his crowd—Ivy League, upper-class types."

When nobody answered, Gia opened the door and we stepped inside the entryway to blaring music and a packed house of people talking and laughing in clusters under a haze of cigarette smoke, mixed with the savory smells of rosemary and chicken roasting in an oven somewhere inside. To the left of the entranceway there was a formal dining room, a cozy living room to the right. It was tastefully decorated with a soft palette of complementary floral wallpapers, highly polished oak floors, and priceless Oriental area rugs.

"Where are the Philmores?" I looked around, recognizing some of the faces from work. "Shouldn't we at least greet the hosts?"

Just then, Lindsay Philmore came down the hall from what appeared to be the kitchen in the back of the house, holding a full martini in each hand. Tonight, he looked less disheveled than usual, wearing a light-blue button-down shirt and a blue-and-white-checked tie.

"Ah, it's the women of Arlington Hall," he said, coming over to us. "Welcome, welcome, so glad you could come."

We thanked him as he greeted each of us with a kiss on the cheek. His breath smelled strongly of vodka.

"I've got to deliver these. The bar's in the breezeway, back there off of the kitchen." He tilted his head in that direction. "We've hired a bartender for the night. Go on, get yourselves some drinks, have a grand time. I'm sure you'll see some familiar faces."

We followed his orders, greeting various folks we recognized from Arlington Hall as well as a few from the FBI as we made our way to the makeshift bar and ordered drinks from a white-coated bartender.

The party spilled out into the expansive backyard, and after getting refreshments, we sat against the back patio's retaining wall, watching couples swing-dance to the music of Guy Lombardo and His Royal Canadians, under strands of twinkling lights strung above an improvised dance floor. The evening breeze smelled of the pale-pink rosebushes that lined the perimeter of the yard, and it was preferable to the claustrophobic, smoke-filled rooms inside.

"I noticed Weissman's here," Gia said.

"Of course he is. Does that guy ever miss a night out?" I said. None of us had gotten over our paranoia about Weissman and his snooping ways. "I'll never trust him."

"I'm with you. And no, he's never missed a night out," Gia said. "And is it me, or does he always seem one drink away from inappropriately groping someone?"

"Is . . . is there an *appropriate* way to grope someone?" Rosemary frowned, and I couldn't help but laugh.

"Where'd Eff go?" I looked around the patio. "She was just here."

"I found them," Effie said, in a singsongy voice, making her way over to us, holding Archie's hand. Brendan, "the new Brit," was right behind them.

Seeing him up close for the first time, I assessed he was not hard on the eyes, as Gia would say. Dressed in a white shirt, bold yellow-and-navy-blue plaid tie, and dark trousers, he was about six feet, with thick, dirty-blond hair and a cleft chin.

After introductions were made, Gia darted away to see if Cecil had arrived, and, as if on cue, Rosemary spotted a friend of Margaret's from Arlington's main hall, just as Effie and Archie decided to go check out the buffet inside. I silently groaned, knowing they'd left me alone with Brendan on purpose.

"Was it . . . was it something I said, to make your friends scatter like that?" Brendan gave me a knowing grin.

"I'm sorry, they . . ." I rolled my eyes. "I assure you it wasn't. They'll be back soon. Did you know the Philmores before coming here?"

"You can't be in British intelligence without knowing Lindsay Philmore." Brendan smiled and sipped his martini. From somewhere inside the house came the sound of glass shattering followed by a burst of hysterical laughter.

"I'm beginning to understand that," I said.

"I'm sure you've heard his perfect pedigree: favorite son of MI6, Cambridge University, and all that?" Brendan said.

"Oh, of course I have. Everyone here is well aware of it, trust me," I said.

"I don't doubt it," Brendan said with a bit of a smirk.

There was an uncomfortable pause in our conversation. I took a sip of my drink, and though I still longed to go home as soon as I could, I decided it would be rude to just walk away from this handsome English stranger.

"So, what's your story with British intelligence?" I asked. "And how'd you end up here?"

Brendan explained how after he graduated from Manchester University in '39, he had served in the British army stationed in the Middle East during the war. While he was there, he was recruited by British intelligence.

"I'd always wanted one of these liaison posts in America," Brendan said.

"What do you think of DC?"

"It's . . . an adjustment," he said with a laugh. "I quite like it, but DC is definitely a different world from London, isn't it? I must say, it's fascinating to see what's happening with the FBI and the new CIA, the power struggle between the two."

"Oh, yes, and you have a front row seat to that, don't you?" I said.

"I do," he laughed. "But tell me about you, I've been talking too much."

I told him my background, leaving out Richie, as I always did when first meeting someone. But I talked about Radcliffe and my decision to move here, including my "runaway bride" status because it was less embarrassing to me now that it was more of a distant memory. He was easy to talk to, and he really listened, a skill that many men lacked. I told him where I worked, and though I was sure he suspected what I did, he understood when I told him I couldn't discuss it.

"You've certainly taken an interesting path, given the state of the world right now," he said.

"So have you," I said, nodding at him.

"Do you like the work? The job? Is it everything you thought it would be, when you ran away from your wedding?"

"You know what? It's . . . it's more," I said with a proud smile because it was true. "It's so much more. Don't get me wrong, it's hard, it's high-pressure and intense and frustrating . . . but I wouldn't trade it for anything. And the friends I've made. That's been the sweetest part of it all."

I didn't add the bittersweetness of the one friend who had moved to England. I was sure Brendan had crossed paths with Jonathan at some point in time. I was about to ask him if they had, when a couple swing-dancing on the patio twirled right into me, knocking my rum and Coke out of my hand, splashing some on the front of my dress.

"Oh no! I'm sorry, I'm so sorry," the woman said, light-brown hair in a bouffant, swaying tipsily. "Can I get you another drink?"

"It's fine," I said, as Brendan handed me a napkin to wipe the splashed Coke off my arm. The dance floor had grown increasingly crowded. "Want to find another place to sit? We're bound to get bumped again sitting on the wall."

"Yes, or . . . would you . . . would you like to get out of here?" Brendan asked, a little nervously, which was endearing. "Just go for a tea or coffee, or a drink, just somewhere a little bit quieter?"

"Um . . . sure, that would be nice," I said. I tried to think of a reason to say no, but I didn't really have one. Because he was kind and intelligent, and I hadn't been out on anything resembling a date in months.

"Brilliant," Brendan said, smiling widely now. "I've heard of a couple of places not too far from here that we could go."

"Sounds good. I'm just going to go find the bathroom and blot this Coke off my dress before we head out," I said. "I'll be back in ten minutes."

"Great," he said, walking back inside with me. "I'll meet you in the breezeway by the bar. I'll try to find Archie and Effie to let them know."

I braved the crowded house once more. In a short time the volume of both the music and talking had gotten louder, and based on people's behavior, Effie was right about the booze flowing. I spotted one man already passed out on the couch in the living room, a broken pair of dark framed glasses splayed across his face. A woman directed me to a bathroom, down the hall off the kitchen.

The bathroom door was locked, and I could hear women inside talking, so I stood in the hall and waited.

What appeared to be Lindsay's home office was diagonally across the hall, the door was half open, and, hearing his voice, I decided to do the polite thing and thank him for the party before leaving. I could see paneled floor-to-ceiling dark wood and an enormous gold-leafed mirror on the wall opposite the door. I saw Lindsay in the mirror's reflection, standing behind a massive walnut desk, martini in hand. I was about to knock, when I heard Bill Weissman's voice.

"You've got nothing to worry about," Bill said. "Your reputation remains stellar."

"But McAllister, I think he was too careless. He could sink me . . ." Philmore said, his voice panicked and slightly slurred. "His embarrassing incident in Tangiers, his drunken escapades and homosexual affairs . . ."

Something told me this was not a conversation I should interrupt, so I stepped back from the door.

"Catherine Killeen, is that you? Were you looking for something?" Philmore's voice called out, and I cringed, knowing he saw me in the mirror.

"I'm so sorry to interrupt," I stepped halfway in and held my hands up. "I was just on my way to the bathroom to clean up this spill on my dress, and I wanted to say thank you for a great party. And I still didn't even get to meet your wife, to thank her for her hospitality."

"That's all right, dear, she's up with the children, the little one is sick. You're leaving so soon, though?" Philmore looked at me with glazed eyes, beads of sweat dotting his forehead.

"Yes, we're working tomorrow," I said. "I don't want to be out too late."

"That's right, our work is never done in Building B, is it? Especially these days." Weissman nodded at me from a burgundy leather sofa opposite the desk before taking a long sip of an amber drink in a short glass. His tone was tense, more clipped than normal.

"That's for sure," I said, nodding back, hating the awkwardness of the conversation. "Well, I should . . ."

"Yes, those *fearless leaders* of yours, the duo of Gardner and Agent Lamphere, they're quite the Boy Scouts, aren't they?" Philmore's voice was sour with sarcasm and disdain. He downed his martini before pointing a pinkie finger at me, adding, "Straight out of a gumshoe detective novel with their relentless pursuit of truth and justice and all that rubbish."

"They're the best at what they do." I glared at Philmore, astonished because, yes, he was drunk, but really, how *dare* he? "It's an absolute honor to work with them. And their relentless pursuit . . . the work we do, is more important than ever . . ."

"Yes, just make sure you stay on their good side, right, dear Catherine? Wouldn't want any skeletons falling out of your cupboard, say, a communist uncle, would you?"

"What did you say?" I narrowed my eyes at him, anger laced with a bit of paranoia. I supposed he was high enough up in British intelligence to see anyone's personnel file he wanted, but the way he brought it up sounded like a threat. "What are you talking about? Why would you bring that—"

"Oh, I think—" Philmore interrupted me and Weissman cut him off.

"That's enough, Philmore." Weissman raised his voice and stood up, glaring at Philmore. He then looked at me, his voice quiet. "Look, it's been a stressful week for all of us."

Philmore just snorted at this and grabbed a half-empty bottle of scotch off the shelf behind his desk.

"But I . . ." I said, and Weissman nodded at me to step into the hallway, and we both did, with him standing too close as always.

"He's drunk, Catherine, that's all," Weissman said in a whisper. "He won't remember he said any of that."

"But he brought up my uncle, why . . ."

"As I said, in the morning he won't remember a thing. It's best that you don't either. Do you understand?"

"No," I said. "I don't. I . . ."

"Just . . . *let it go*," Weissman said. "Trust me."

I trusted him even less than when I had arrived at the party. Their conversation was beyond odd, and again I wondered why they seemed to know each other so well, enough for Philmore to confide in him about the problematic McAllister, whoever that was. But at this point, it was Philmore's party, and there was nothing I could do but file away my suspicions. Though the whole interaction had shaken me.

"All right," I said.

"Now I'm going to try to wrestle that bottle of scotch out of his hand. Goodnight," Weissman said, shutting the door of the office in my face as two women exited the bathroom giggling and nearly tripping over each other.

A communist uncle.

I splashed water on my face in the bathroom and took some deep breaths to try to calm down. Philmore had shown his true colors, and I'd been caught completely off guard. I wished I had said more and considered knocking on the office door and doing just that. But given how inebriated he was, and Weissman's behavior just now, there was no point.

I blotted the Coke splash on my dress, reapplied my lipstick, and smoothed out my hair. After that encounter I needed a good night's sleep. It was time to go home. Brendan would have to take a rain check.

Brendan was in the breezeway talking in a group that included Effie, Rosemary, and Archie, and a tall, dark-haired man who was facing away from me. There was something familiar about the build of the man's shoulders, the dark, wavy hair, and I stopped short a couple yards away, my heart beating in my ears. No. It wasn't possible. I didn't need one more thing to deal with tonight. Philmore's oddly threatening comment was enough.

Effie's urgent, wide-eyed glance over at me confirmed that it was him, which was unnecessary. I'd know him anywhere, even after all this time.

As if he sensed my stare, Jonathan Dardis turned around and did a double take, followed by that devastating smile and a heartfelt look that made me catch my breath as all the memories of him came flooding back: the first time our fingers brushed, dancing to the Ink Spots under sparkling chandeliers, a song in an Irish pub meant for him. And, more than any other, the crush of a kiss under a sky of snow.

But that night eighteen months ago was just a brief snapshot in time. Nothing had been promised. "We're star-crossed, Killeen, but I do believe we might find our way back to each other someday. At least, I hope so," he had said. Gia was right. It was a good line, nothing more. And his postcards had all but stopped.

And yet, standing here in front of him, I still cared, that ache in my chest roaring back, as strong as the night he left. And I hated that.

Because in the end, he'd given no real sign that he felt the same. I grasped my Saint Rita's medallion. No cause was more hopeless than my heart in that moment.

"Killeen!" Jonathan rushed over to me, laughing as he pulled me into a tight hug, and the feel of his arms again, the way he smelled, it was almost too much to bear, so I pulled away first, taking a step back, my face flushed.

"Dardis," I said. "Wow. It's . . . what are you doing here?"

"I took the train down early this morning. I've been in meetings at headquarters all day," he said, and it killed me that he looked more handsome than ever. "Actually, I stopped by Idaho Hall after work. I didn't know you moved."

"I did, I sent you a postcard with my new address. You . . . you didn't get it before you went to New York?" I said, and all I could think about was the fact he'd gone by to see me.

"No," he said, shaking his head. He hadn't stopped looking into my eyes, and it was unnerving and thrilling at the same time. "God, you look—you look terrific. How have you been?"

"Great," I said, nodding way too much, and now the awkwardness of the time and distance settled over the conversation. "Fine, working hard, like everyone here. I'm sure you are too. Congratulations on your promotion. How's New York City?"

"Thanks. New York, it's going well, hectic, never dull," he said, and he ran his fingers through his hair, another uncomfortable pause as we searched for what to say. "Are you singing at the Liberty at all?"

"Yes. Once a month. They'd love me to do more than that, but it's too much with work," I said.

"Look, do you want to . . ." Jonathan started to ask me something but was interrupted by Brendan.

"I didn't realize you were *that* Catherine. Jonathan's told me all about the brilliant Catherine Killeen from Radcliffe. I should have put it together." Brendan put his arm around Jonathan's shoulders.

"I . . . am, and thank you, I guess?" I said, looking back and forth between the two of them, desperately wanting to ask what had been said about me, but restraining myself. "So, you two do know each other. Of course you do, that makes sense."

"Yes, we met shortly after I arrived in London," Jonathan said, and I wasn't sure I'd ever seen his face so red. "We've worked together off and on."

"Shared a few pints too, gone to a few shindigs." Brendan laughed. "Cat, do you still want to go grab that drink, or whatever you're up for?"

I hesitated, and did I imagine the look of hurt in Jonathan's eyes simply because I wanted it to be there, wanted him to still feel something for me too? But how many women had he dated in London, how many hearts had he broken there? Eighteen months, and nothing more than a few postcards. Of course there had to have been others for him.

"Sure, of course, let's go." I smiled at Brendan, though I yearned to go home and hide under my covers, to fall asleep and forget about this bizarre soiree.

It was time to get out of this house, this party, and going with Brendan would accomplish that. And if I was honest with myself, it would signal to Jonathan that I hadn't been "pining away" for him all this time, waiting for the moment he walked back into my life.

"It was good to see you," I said to Jonathan as Brendan looked on. "Will you be back in DC often?"

"I hope to be," he said, avoiding my gaze now, then, as if correcting himself, he added, "I mean, I'll have to be, once in a while at least, to check in with Bob and the team down here."

"Okay, maybe I'll see you next time," I said.

"Sounds good," he said, in a noncommittal way. "Take care, Killeen."

Brendan and I said our goodbyes to the rest of our friends, and he guided me through the crowd, his hand on the small of my back. Just before I stepped out of the breezeway, I turned to see Jonathan watching us walk away. We looked in each other's eyes again, and I felt a sudden urge to run back to him, into his arms. But instead, I gave him a sad smile and mouthed the word *goodbye*.

Chapter Twenty-Six

Friday, December 16, 1949

After the Philmores' raucous party, Brendan and I had gone out for coffee and split a crêpe Suzette at a tiny French café near American University. He had been nice and interesting, thoughtful and self-deprecating—a perfect gentleman in every way, the kind of man any woman would want to date. But I had been so preoccupied, between Philmore's outburst and Jonathan's surprise appearance, that I could barely enjoy his gracious company.

And at the end of the night, when he asked me if he could see me again, he couldn't hide his disappointment when I gave him a vague non-answer about both of us being so busy with work that we'd have to see what happened.

The first few times I had run into Lindsay Philmore in Building B after that night, I'd remained calm and friendly around him, waiting to see if he would mention any aspect of our conversation the night of his party. But he never acknowledged it, which made me think Weissman was right, he had been too drunk to have any recollection of that moment in his home office.

But McAllister, I think he was too careless. He could sink me...

Recalling Philmore's words, I was still incredibly curious about the origins of his friendship with Weissman, where and how they had met, and why Philmore was confiding in him. And who was McAllister? In what way could he sink Philmore? Of course, Jonathan would be the perfect contact in the FBI to ask, but I hadn't seen or heard from him since the night of the party.

He did not return to DC in October or November, and I kept telling myself it was for the best. But whenever Bob arrived for meetings, I found myself doing a double take to see if Jonathan was with him, despite myself.

It was a chilly afternoon in mid-December, and I was in the small conference room cleaning the chalkboard for my next meeting when Gia came in and threw an envelope down on the table next to my notebook.

"This came in the mail for you," she said. "I ran home at lunch to get my wallet, and it was there."

"Oh," I said, when I registered my name and address in Jonathan's handwriting. "I've really been trying to forget that he's back in the US."

"Well, based on the look on his face when he saw you at the Philmores' party, it was clear that he hadn't forgotten about *you*," Gia said, pulling out a chair. "Far from it."

"But it's not like he's been in touch since, and he hasn't been in DC as far as I know."

"I'm sure he's working as much as we are, if not more. The FBI is feeling the pressure too. Give him a break."

"I don't know," I said, tracing the letters on the envelope with my finger.

"Are you going to open it?"

"Not yet," I said, getting back to the board. "We need to focus on the meeting, review what we've got before Bob and Meredith arrive."

"Oh, come on, you must be dying of curiosity," Gia said.

"About what?" Cecil said, bounding in, wearing his winter coat, a bright blue scarf wrapped around his head. "I brought you your coat, Gia. Cat, do you want me to go get yours?"

"No thank you, Cecil." I smiled as he draped Gia's coat over her shoulders, just as Rosemary walked in.

"Cat got a letter from Jonathan Dardis, and she won't open it," Gia said.

"Oh, Cat, why the heck not?" Rosemary asked. Wrapping her arms around herself, she shivered and added, "Cecil, will you be a dear and go steal one of the little electric heaters from the IBM group again? They like you better than they like any of us."

"Absolutely, of course, be right back," Cecil said.

"He really is the nicest man in all of Arlington Hall," I said, watching him run out the door.

"That's for sure," Rosemary said.

"Enough about Cecil, just open the letter," Gia said, adjusting her coat and pointing at it.

"No, not now, it'll just distract me too much," I said. "I'll open it after work."

Cecil came back and set up the space heater just as Meredith and Bob arrived. Both had a look of perpetual exhaustion these days. Meredith was dressed in a button-down shirt, vest, and plaid bow tie, dapper as usual, but more disheveled every day, and his curly hair was starting to take the shape of a bird's nest. He desperately needed a trip to the barber. And Bob had those dark circles under his eyes again, and I swore *his* hair was becoming grayer at the temples every time I saw him.

In these meetings with Bob and Meredith, we would review any newly deciphered messages relating to the dozens of investigations that had been opened by the FBI's Soviet espionage section. Over time, some of the cases ultimately ended up being dead ends, while others, such as one regarding White Russian émigré circles in New York City, proved to be quite important. And we'd conclude these meetings with the most critical investigation we had been working on thus far: the atomic spy ring that included Rest, aka Klaus Fuchs.

"I feel like they're mocking us, all these code names," Rosemary said, as we once again put the code names of the atomic spies up on the board. Gia, Rosemary, Cecil, and I had become part of a core team supporting Meredith, and we were all a little more relaxed than in the earlier days of working with him.

"So do I." Bob laughed cynically. "And I have Hoover breathing down my neck over this every damn day. But I do have very good news, the best kind. Klaus Fuchs is talking, *really* talking, to British intelligence now. I think they're going to get a confession out of him soon."

"Oh, thank God, that is amazing," I said.

"Can we get him to talk faster?" Gia said, gesturing to the board. "So we can track down some of these mystery people?"

"Believe me, I'm pushing them to," Bob said.

"Okay, back to business, let's review what we've got—latest clues regarding Klaus Fuchs and friends," Meredith said. "Catherine, I'll let you do the honors."

"Here's the latest," I said, writing notes next to the names written on the chalkboard.

REST—Real name Klaus Fuchs, sister Kristel in Cambridge

LIBERAL—Leader and recruiter of ring, engineer, attended City College, wife Ethel, sister-in-law that lives in NYC

GUS—first-generation American with accent, visited Klaus in Cambridge at sister's house, chemist, owner of pesticide firm, new physical description

KALIBER—Los Alamos engineer, NYC connection

"Yeah, so when our guys in Boston interviewed Fuchs's sister Kristel and her husband, they gave a description of the spy code-named Gus," Bob said, flipping open his notebook. "He's age forty to forty-five, five foot eight inches, dark-brown hair, round face, stocky build."

"Seriously? You just described like ninety percent of the men who live on my street in New York," Gia said, and when Meredith shot her a harsh look, she added, "Well, sorry, Bob, but that description doesn't exactly narrow it down."

Bob burst out laughing, and all of us joined in because it was true, and it was obvious we all needed a laugh amid all the stress we had been under.

"I was going to say the same thing, Gia, but you beat me to it," Bob said, rubbing his hands over his face. "On a serious note, we also know that Gus revealed to Kristel that he was a chemist at a firm developing pesticides, and that he was bitter because his partner had cheated him out of money."

"That's a little more to go on," I said.

"We'll go back over all the messages related to Gus again, see if there's any other clues," Meredith said. "We've got Klaus. We're close to some of these others."

"I know we're all tired, but we're making progress." Bob paused for a moment before he continued speaking. "I'm so proud of my team, and the team here. I know the hours you've put in, the sacrifices you've made to help the dozens of investigations we have ongoing now. And we would never have found Klaus Fuchs without you."

Cecil sat up a little taller, and we all nodded and murmured words of thanks.

"I've been working with Lindsay Philmore, lobbying Hoover," Bob said, standing up and looking closer at the list of names, as if something more might be revealed. "I plan on going over to London after the holidays to interview Fuchs myself if I must. To get his confession and his help identifying the rest of this ring."

"Thank you, Bob," Meredith said. "I agree. We all deserve to see this come to a satisfying end."

~

I felt his eyes on me before I heard his vaguely accented voice.

"It's Friday night. You should be home, or out with your friends," Bill Weissman said. He was standing near the entrance of our offices, coat and briefcase in hand, giving me a look that made my skin crawl.

"I could say the same thing to you," I said, putting away the file I was reading, closing my tired eyes and putting my fingers on the bridge of my nose in an attempt to soothe them, but mostly to avoid looking at him. "You seem to keep later hours than just about anyone here."

"Except for you, and Meredith of course," Weissman said, nodding at Meredith's office. His light was still on, and through the blinds I could see him inside, standing in front of his chalkboard.

"Nobody works more than him," I said. "Are you headed home for Christmas?"

"Yes, to New York, to see family," he said. "Family is everything. Isn't it?"

"It is." I nodded. I'd had enough small talk. It was time to acknowledge my encounter with him and Philmore at the party. "Bill . . . since I have you alone, why did Lindsay Philmore comment about my 'communist' uncle? Obviously, he must have viewed my personnel file. My uncle came up when I was first hired because he's a member of the Communist Party of America . . ."

Bill paused and tilted his head, as if he were debating something. "Well, Catherine," he said, "aside from him being drunk, it's becoming more understood in intelligence circles that the Communist Party of America's connection to Soviet espionage is not incidental by any stretch. It's a significant aspect of their activities."

"What are you saying?" I said, squinting at him, tired and paranoid, thinking back to Philmore's drunk, accusatorial tone. "There must be thousands of members of CPUSA. My uncle is just a physics professor."

"Of course," Weissman said with a distinct edge of sarcasm.

"Bill, there is no way I would have passed the background check to work here if my uncle was a spy," I said, getting aggravated now, unable to read him. "If you know something about him that I don't, something incriminating, just tell me."

"First of all, I think you give the American government too much credit when it comes to the thoroughness of their background checks. As for your uncle, I don't know anything. Philmore might, but he didn't tell me. Just understand it's entirely possible that your uncle may be more than just a physics professor. After all, look at Klaus Fuchs."

"I'm going to ask Philmore next time I have a chance," I said.

"You can, but he doesn't really owe you that information. And whatever he knows may be classified."

I opened my mouth to say something else and closed it again. He appeared to be enjoying my frustration. As I watched him turn to go, I decided I had one more question for him.

"Who is McAllister?" I said, loud enough for anyone who might be left in the section to hear, and he whipped around.

"Ah, so you *did* hear that part of the conversation that night. You shouldn't eavesdrop on the future head of MI6. It could get you into a world of trouble," Bill said. His voice was calm but mildly threatening, and his eyes flashed with anger.

"The eavesdropping wasn't intentional," I said.

"McAllister is none of your concern or your business, frankly. Just a difficult colleague of Philmore's, nothing more. Now I must go, or I am going to miss my bus. Goodnight, Catherine."

I told him goodnight and watched him leave. Nothing about our conversation had allayed my suspicions about him or Philmore.

My stomach let out a loud growl, and that was the cue I needed to stop ruminating about the two men for now, pack up, and get my coat on. I had barely eaten lunch, and I was already late to meet Effie and Gia at the Liberty for burgers and their delicious, salty French fries. And it was also time to finally open the letter from Jonathan that was sitting in my purse. I had managed to throw myself into work and put it out of my head for the afternoon, but now it was consuming my thoughts again.

Meredith was still in his office with the door closed, hands on his hips, studying his chalkboard, looking in no hurry to leave.

"Hey, Meredith, I'm heading out." I knocked, and he jumped, turning to me with a baffled expression.

"Sorry to startle you. Just wanted to say goodnight. I'll be in tomorrow."

"Yes, yes, me too," he said. He was always distracted to some degree, but tonight there was something about his demeanor. His face was drawn, and he looked down at his desk with a worried expression.

"Is . . . is everything all right?" I asked.

"No, not particularly." He sighed, his shoulders stooped.

"Do you want to talk about it?" He seemed so deflated I had to ask, though a part of me hoped he would say no. After Weissman, all I wanted was to get out of here and see my friends.

He sat down at his desk and put his hands over his face for a few moments, not saying a word. I was about to tiptoe away when he spoke.

"Shut the door and have a seat," Meredith said.

After I did what he asked, he looked across at me with tired eyes and let out a long sigh.

"You might as well know," he said. "Because I'm going to assign a few more people to work on it—this is about someone in British intelligence."

"What about them?" I frowned.

"Over the past week I've deciphered a new group of KGB messages from the war. And I know for certain there was a Russian spy working at a fairly high position at the British embassy, here in DC. And this person was able to send large batches of British and US classified intelligence to KGB headquarters, Moscow Center."

"What? I just . . . unbelievable. Although at this point, I don't know why I'm surprised," I said, looking around at the chaos of Meredith's office, feeling desperate for our work to result in more *real* names. We needed a break. It was beating us all down. "I feel like the only government institution the Russians didn't plant a spy in is here at Arlington Hall."

"As far as we know," Meredith scoffed. "The thing that gets me is . . . well, it's very possible this spy is still active in British intelligence in London. What if he's helping Klaus Fuchs escape to Russia as we speak?

Bob just told the Brits, and their response was dismissive. They basically shrugged their shoulders. Can you believe that?"

"Why? I don't understand."

"Nor do I," Meredith said. "They're unconvinced, though I shared most of what I had learned."

"What about Lindsay Philmore?" I said. His name tasted bitter in my mouth.

"Bob talked to him. Philmore brushed it off as well," Meredith said.

"No, I mean . . . look, what if . . . what if Philmore is part of the problem?" I said.

"What? What do you mean?"

I told him about the conversation I had overheard at the party and about my interaction with Weissman just now, as well as the many times we'd seen him loitering around people's desks at night.

"Catherine, Lindsay Philmore is the highest-ranking British intelligence official in the US," Meredith said, dismissively. "And Weissman is a veteran in Building B. You can't make accusations like that without proof."

"I know, I know," I said. "But I'm telling you, something is off with those two. Do you know a McAllister with British intelligence?"

"I do not, no," Meredith said, his tone clipped. He got up and started pacing behind his desk. "But now I need you to put your suspicions about them aside and focus. Help me with this new revelation about this spy who was at the British embassy during the war, who could not have been Philmore because he was *not* here at the time. Will you do that?"

"Yes," I said. I knew I wasn't just being paranoid, but I also knew when Meredith was getting aggravated and needed me to just listen and follow his lead. "Of course I will help in any way."

"Good, because something about it all doesn't sit well with me. That's why I'm still here, going over old messages, new messages. All my notebooks. I'm having that intuitive sense again, like I'm missing a clue that is just beyond my grasp."

"Have you narrowed it down to any suspects?"

"Not yet, but thank you, that's my plan," he said, staring up at the ceiling. "Before you came in, I was thinking about when I was teaching at the University of Akron, before the war. I was finishing up my dissertation, an extensive and thoughtful journey regarding the fundamental meanings of words in High German."

"That sounds . . . um, fascinating," I said, eyebrows raised, not knowing what else to say.

"I can tell you're humoring me." He smiled. "But it was. Sometimes . . . sometimes I wish I was still there."

"How come?" I asked, but from his wistful tone I had already guessed the answer.

"That work was a purely intellectual pursuit," he said, leaning back in his chair. "What we are doing here, with Bob, I feel the brutal responsibility of it, what it might mean, the arrests it might lead to, the impact on our country's security . . . I feel it, *all* the time. I'll never adjust to that part of the job."

"I understand that," I said in a soft voice, because the work kept me awake on many nights. "And I am not in your position. I can't comprehend the burden you feel."

We both sat there for a moment, and I tried to imagine myself in his shoes, this shy, brilliant man who had probably envisioned a lifelong career in academia studying languages, a life a world away from what we were doing here in Building B.

"Anyway, you don't need to hear me complain. And I've got to get home for a late dinner, or Blanche is going to kill me," he said, snapping out of his reverie. "Tomorrow's Saturday, so I'll bring donuts. Thank you, Catherine."

Chapter Twenty-Seven

On the first bus stop after Arlington Hall, a guy in an olive-green fedora and beige raincoat climbed on and hurried past me, taking a seat in the back. He was just under six feet tall, probably in his late thirties, with thick, dark eyebrows and a Roman nose. I only noticed him because he looked familiar, possibly a member of the Lucky Strikes bowling team that recently beat us, but I was too tired and hungry to be friendly.

It was sleeting when I got off a block from the Liberty, and the man was the only one left on the bus as it drove away. By the time I managed to get my new black-and-white polka dot umbrella open, my hair was already soaked, wet tendrils sticking to the sides of my face.

Trevor and the band had the night off, which was a shame, because I'd been forced to cancel the last two times I had been scheduled to perform with them due to work, and singing a few songs tonight would have been a welcome distraction.

The Liberty was decked out for the holidays again. This year the Irish Santa was joined by a big plastic snowman with a top hat and pipe. Seeing my friends at our favorite table, the coziness of what had become our favorite hangout in DC, even the greasy, smoky smell of the place was the perfect antidote to a very long, frustrating day at work.

"Ah, look what the cat dragged in," Gia said when I hurried inside. She scooted over so I could slide in, after hanging my wet things on the empty chair.

"We were starting to get worried," Effie said, as I helped myself to some of her French fries after ordering food for myself from the waitress. "Rosemary headed out; said she'd see you tomorrow."

"Effie was just telling me all of her excuses about why she can't go on a trip to London to meet Archie's family," Gia said.

"Why not, Eff?" I asked.

"Because I like things the way they are." Effie sighed. "He's fun and he treats me well, and I *do* care about him, but let's be honest: meeting the family means it's serious."

"Um, hate to break it to you, Eff, but you've been together for over a year. That also means it's serious," Gia said.

"Have you talked about marriage?" I asked.

"No, he's brought it up, but I just—I don't know," Effie said. "We're so different. I'm from New Orleans, land of hot weather and hotter spices; he's from the land of scones and rain. I know it's going to reach a point where I have to decide . . . but I'm not there. Yet."

"And how is he with that?" Gia asked.

"So far, he's all right with it, but I know he won't be forever. Or even much longer," Effie said. "I'll figure it out eventually. Anyway, enough about my Archie woes. Did you open the letter?"

"I did not," I said, my stomach doing a flip at the thought of it. "I don't know why I'm so nervous about it. It's ridiculous."

"Open it up. It's time," Gia said, pointing at my purse.

"All right, all right," I sighed, rifling through my purse. I ripped the letter open and read it to myself first.

"Well?" Effie said. "Come on, Cat. We're dying."

I took a sip of water, cleared my throat, and read it to them.

Dear Killeen,

I hope you're well, though I'm guessing your days are at least as long as mine given what we're working on these days. I'll finally be back in DC the week before Christmas for the first time since September. I'd love to see you, to catch up, if you're available. I don't know what else to say, except that I miss our friendship.

Yours,
Jonathan

"How do you feel? Do you *want* to see him?" Effie asked.

"I do, but then I think . . ." I started to speak but didn't know what to say.

"You want it to be more than friendship," Effie said. "It's okay, we already know that."

"Do I, though? I mean, it's hard for even me to believe that after all this time the feelings are still there," I said. "But he's in New York and I'm here, and we both work so much. And what if he just wants to be friends anyway?"

"You're overthinking, you *always* overthink." Gia shook her head. "Just talk to him, you won't know anything until you do."

"Gia's right," Effie said. "What are you more afraid of, that he still might have feelings for you too, or that he just wants to be friends?"

"Both . . . ?" I said, pain in my heart as I traced his handwriting. "Look, I canceled my wedding and took the job at Arlington Hall, to not choose the path that like ninety percent of the girls in my neighborhood choose. And I threw myself into this work and met the very best friends."

"Damn right you did," Gia said, toasting her glass to me as Effie squeezed my hand.

"And it remains the best decision of my life," I continued. "And yes, I've been on a few dates here and there since he left. But when he was here, he changed my mind about who he was . . . and that night before he left was . . ." I could feel my face turning red at the thought of our kiss. I blinked as if that would shake the memory out of my head. "I just feel like he might be a distraction. I moved here to figure out my life. What if he pulls me off track . . ."

Gia gave Effie a look.

"What? Why are you looking at each other like that?"

"I know Catholic guilt is ingrained in you," Gia said, "but don't you think it's time you stopped punishing yourself for calling off a wedding to a guy that was clearly not the love of your life?"

"And pulling you off track from what, exactly? Look, Cat, for a smart woman, to call him a 'distraction'? You're thinking about this all wrong," Effie said.

"How so?" I said, feeling defensive.

"What she's saying is, you're not a nun," Gia said, as the waitress brought over rum and Cokes as well as my cheeseburger and fries. "And you have nothing left to prove in terms of whether you belong here, career-wise. You're brilliant at your job. Stop being so afraid of the what ifs."

"Exactly. This work we do is amazing, historic even. But it shouldn't be your whole entire *life*. Love isn't a life distraction. Love is the point." Effie said this and then, her mouth in a tight line, added, "And I realized in saying this that I just answered the lingering question about Archie. He is lovely, but I'm still not sure I'm in love with him. And let's face it, that is *not* a good sign."

"Who said anything about love? Anyway, what if I turned this on you?" I said, pointing a french fry at Gia. "Are you ever going to give Cecil a chance?"

Gia glowered at me over her glass, but then broke out into a Cheshire cat smile, her cheeks turning the color of her fuchsia dress.

"Wait? Are you . . . what's going on? And you better not be lying to us this time, G," Effie said.

"Okay, here goes," Gia said, taking a deep breath. "Cecil Peterson is a very odd duck. He is abnormally obsessed with UFOs and bowling and, lately, collecting rare stamps from Australia, for some reason? Don't even get me started about that. Also, he has zero fashion sense and still chooses to take off his shoes at the most inappropriate times.

"He is the opposite of every guy I grew up with, including all my sisters' husbands—meaning he's the opposite of selfish and has zero bravado or arrogance, even though he's one of the smartest people we all know."

Gia started blinking fast, waving a hand in front of her face. Effie's looked so excited she might scream, and I couldn't stop smiling between bites of cheeseburger.

"All I've ever wanted is a guy that shows up for me. And Cecil does. If you had told me this two years ago? I would have spit out my drink, laughing at how ridiculous the idea was, but . . . girls, speaking of love, I . . . I *love* him," Gia said, putting her hands up in surrender as she started laughing, her eyes still watery. "It's crazy, I mean it's *really* crazy, but I do."

"Oh, Gia," I said, giving her a hug.

"Well, this is just about the best news I have heard in months," Effie said, clapping her hands.

"Yeah, okay, enough of me blabbering," she said, lighting a cigarette, her cheeks still flushed. "Secret's out, back to business, so my point in that confession is, if I can give Cecil a chance, at the very least, you need to hear whatever Jonathan Dardis has to say."

Chapter Twenty-Eight

Jonathan called me at work on Monday, and with Effie, Rosemary, and Gia standing over me, making faces, trying to make me laugh as I talked to him, we made plans to meet on Tuesday evening. We chose the restaurant and bar in the basement of the Manger Hay-Adams Hotel, right near the White House. It was a place well loved by both the Washington political set and famous patrons of the hotel, including Charles Lindbergh and Sinclair Lewis.

I didn't see anyone famous when I entered the front lobby, though a man brushed past me and made me do a double take because he looked a lot like the man I had seen on the bus ride home the week prior, the one with the olive fedora and eyebrows. When I turned to get a better look, he was already out the front doors. I chalked it up to paranoia—all of us were keyed up these days. Between the anti-communist hysteria in the country and what we in Building B knew was actually real, sometimes it felt like there might be Soviet spies hiding in the shadows everywhere.

The restaurant was decorated to the hilt for Christmas, with garlands and bows draped along the oak bar and strands of Christmas lights framing the mirrors behind it. With its dark wood paneling and dramatic crimson red upholstered chairs and banquettes, it gave an impression of understated elegance, and the dim lighting made it feel intimate and romantic, or maybe that was just my mood.

Because FBI headquarters was around the corner from the Hay-Adams, Jonathan had told me he'd try to get there early to get us a table, and just as I was going to ask the hostess if she had seen him, I heard his voice in my ear and felt a hand on my elbow, and the butterflies in my stomach that had flown off to London with him were not only back—they had multiplied exponentially.

"I went upstairs to try to meet you out front. We must have crossed paths," Jonathan said, with a warm smile.

"Oh, hi," I said as he leaned down and gave me a quick kiss on the cheek.

"Hi, yourself," he said. "You showed up."

"You didn't think I would?" I said, teasing.

"I wasn't sure," he said. "You sounded a little strange on the phone."

"That's because my friends were eavesdropping and driving me crazy." I laughed.

"Speaking of your friends, you must know about the annual unofficial, completely unsanctioned FBI Christmas party at the Liberty on Thursday?"

"Of course," I said. "We're all going, are you?"

"Yes, as a matter of fact I am." He gave me an amused look as he led me to a cozy booth, far from the noise of the politicians yucking it up at the bar.

"It's actually not as crowded as I expected," he said.

"Maybe people have taken off for the holidays already?"

"Maybe," he said. We got settled and ordered drinks and appetizers from a young waitress in a slim black satin dress. And then we were sitting there across from each other, and when we finally really looked into each other's eyes, I was afraid he might be able to hear my heart beating.

"You're doing that thing when you're nervous, tapping your foot," he said, looking down at it. "I remember you did that before tests. Are you nervous?"

"No, of course not," I said, as I stopped tapping it. "I'm sorry, maybe a little. I don't know, it's just been so long since you and I have had a real conversation. Since . . . anything."

"I know. I've been nervous all afternoon," he said.

"Really? *You?*"

"*Really*," he said as the waitress put our drinks down, an old-fashioned for him, a gin fizz for me. "I wanted my time in London to be shorter. I'd been applying for transfers back to the States for a while. It's good to be back in New York, but it's not here . . . Anyway, I'm rambling on . . . all this to say I've . . . I've missed you. If nothing else, I just wanted to see you again. To get . . . reacquainted."

"I'm glad," I said, holding up my glass. "To getting reacquainted, then."

We clinked our glasses together. *If nothing else . . .* Did he want nothing else? And I had missed him too, but why couldn't I bring myself to say it?

"Tell me about London—and New York. I want to hear everything," I said, distracting myself from overanalyzing every moment we were together.

"Are you sure?" He smiled.

"Absolutely."

He talked about how London was still recovering from the war years, with many streets still not cleared of debris. There was rationing, and a lot of the buildings barely had heat. He told me stories of his days at the embassy and nights on the town, and all about the weather (terribly gray) and the food (not much better in color or variety). If he dated a woman or two in London, he left that part out, and part of me wanted to know, but mostly I preferred he not tell me.

"Did you by chance meet a British intelligence official with the last name McAllister?" I said.

"Ron, yes," Jonathan said. "Ron McAllister. He's head of the American Department in the British Foreign Office. What about him?"

"He's friends with Lindsay Philmore, yes?"

"Very close friends. They went to Cambridge together," Jonathan said, as we ordered another round of drinks.

"Huh," I said.

"Why do you ask?"

"Nothing really," I said. So maybe Philmore's drunken rant was just about an argument among old college mates. I lowered my voice. "I'm glad you chose someplace we could talk with relative privacy; I did want to talk to you about something work-related. The Elizabeth Bentley files."

"Okay, I'm listening," he said, and our hands brushed as we both reached for the bread basket at the same time. I thought he was going to take hold of mine but then seemed to hesitate. "I have to tell you, it's so good to talk to you like this again."

"You too." I wished I could read his mind in this moment. Did he ever think about the night we kissed? Did he still have feelings for me too, after all this time? But, of course, rather than asking, I chose suffering, the ache in my chest getting worse every time he smiled.

"As you know, we're still trying to identify the rest of this atomic spy ring," I said, whispering now. "Before I left tonight, I read through the transcripts from Elizabeth Bentley's grand jury testimony, hoping something in it might corroborate some of our newest information from the deciphered KGB messages."

"Now you've piqued my curiosity, Killeen. What've you got?"

"She mentions two men, chemists that she met while working for the Russians. They both testified at the grand jury trial, claimed total innocence. But our atomic spy friend Klaus Fuchs had a courier code-named Gus who was a chemist or engineer, according to Klaus's sister," I said. "Bentley's chemists were two men named Abe Brothman and Harry Gold."

"You think one of them might be our man, Gus?" he asked, nodding, and I could see him weighing the possibilities in his mind.

"I think there's a strong possibility, yes," I said.

"I think you could be right. We've got someone assigned to the Bentley files; I'm guessing they'll come to the same conclusion. Do you know there are seventy-five thousand chemical manufacturing firms in New York City?"

"I did not." I laughed. "How do you know that?"

"Because once we knew Gus the courier was involved with a chemical manufacturing firm, we put together a database of all of them. We've also reopened the files of the various chemists, engineers, and physicists the FBI has encountered over the last decade."

"Ugh, and I thought my work was tedious," I said.

"I know, just reading through the list gave me a headache. But your lead . . . maybe it's the piece we've been looking for," he said.

"We'll see," I said.

"We will see." He gave me a wink, and I didn't know if he was talking about the two of us or Gus the courier.

And it occurred to me that there was an irony in being able to decipher unbreakable Russian codes but being useless when it came to decoding what was in someone else's heart.

∼

"Yes," I said. "It was fun, and we talked all night, and after the initial awkwardness? It was like no time had passed."

"But the end of the night—no kiss, nothing?" Effie asked as we headed down the street to the Christmas party at the Liberty, huddled close together because there was a bitter cold wind whipping at our faces as we walked.

"No, just a quick kiss on the cheek before I got into the cab," I said, thinking of our goodbye, the look Jonathan gave me as he shut the cab's door.

"On the ride home, I started to think that maybe our last kiss before he left didn't mean much to him. Maybe he remembers it differently, like it was just a lark to him. And we're both consumed with work right now. So, we're friends. This is . . . friends is fine."

"Uh-huh." Effie looked at me. "Keep telling yourself that."

"I know I can't lie to you," I said.

"No, you cannot," Effie said. "Call me crazy, but did you ever, I don't know, consider *talking* to him about how you feel?"

"God no, and risk being humiliated? What if I'm right about him wanting to just be friends? Anyway, on an unrelated note, I've wanted to ask you, does Archie ever mention working with a Ron McAllister?" I had told her and Gia about Philmore's drunken threat, but I'd never mentioned what I'd overheard him say about McAllister.

"Yes, of course. He's a very close mate of Lindsay Philmore, as he would say," Effie nodded. "He used to work here, actually."

"Work where?" I asked.

"Here in DC at the British embassy, during the war," Effie said. "The only reason I remember that is because Archie says he boasts about it all the time, like he was Churchill's man in America during the war or something. I guess he's kind of obnoxious."

A man opened the door of the pub for us, just as Trevor and the band were playing the ending notes of a song and the crowd erupted in applause and rousing cheers as they announced a quick break. Rosemary waved to us from our favorite table; she was sitting with Margaret and Gia and Cecil.

I put my things down, sensing someone's eyes on me, and a chill went through me when I recognized the man I'd seen on the bus. This time I was certain it was him and that it had been him at the Hay-Adams Hotel too. He was standing near the entrance of the pub wearing a gray fedora this time, but it was definitely the same thick, dark eyebrows and prominent nose. He ducked out at that moment, almost as if he knew I'd spotted him.

"Hey, are you okay?" Rosemary tugged at my hand. "You look like you've seen a ghost."

"Maybe I have?" I said, feeling lightheaded and anxious, as I considered the fact that someone might be following me.

"Talk to me," she said, as I sat down next to her.

"Remember way back when I started, you mentioned the vodka Collins rule, to order one when we felt like someone was asking too many questions or seemed suspicious?"

"Of course, we haven't had to use it in a very long time. Why?" She scanned the pub and looked back at me. "What's going on?"

I told her about the man and the two times I had seen him before.

"He's gone now?"

"He's gone. I'm not sure if he followed me and Eff in here, or if he was here before we arrived," I said.

"When the girls are all together, *not* here, alone, you need to give us a description so we can be on the lookout."

"You don't think I'm being paranoid?" I said, still unnerved by the thought of being followed.

"No, in fact, I think these days, if anything, we're not being paranoid enough." She stood up. "Let's go get you a drink."

Jonathan stepped up to the bar just as Rosemary was paying our tab and greeted us both with kisses on the cheek, and now I was lightheaded for an entirely different reason.

"What will it take to get you to sing with the band tonight?" Jonathan asked.

"More than you can afford." I laughed.

"I'm going to bring this rum and Coke over to Eff. See you at the table," Rosemary said with a wink.

"Thank you again for the other night," Jonathan said. "It was fun."

"Thank you. I agree it was," I said. "When are you heading back to New York?"

"First thing in the morning, and then going to see my family for Christmas," he said. Did I detect a wistfulness in his tone? "I'm . . . I'm not sure when I'll be back down, probably middle to late January. Maybe we could grab dinner or drinks or something then?"

"Sure," I said, my heart sinking because I'd hoped he'd be back sooner. "That would be great."

"I'm really sorry it won't be sooner," he said, as if he had read my mind, and his expression told me he truly was.

"Oh no, it's fine. I understand, trust me." I nodded, and there was that awkwardness between us again, of all the things I wanted to say, and all the things I wished he would.

"Oh, and I have to tell you, about what you mentioned the other night." Jonathan leaned over and spoke this in my ear, his voice lower, his lips so close to my face I could feel his breath on my skin. "Those names—the chemists, Brothman and Gold. We'd already opened investigations on both."

"Oh, that's fantastic news," I said. Switching to a work topic made things relaxed between us again.

"Isn't it?" He clinked his glass with mine. "I'm telling you, this year I think we're finally going to get our big break—our teams, I mean."

"Attention, attention everyone." Trevor the bandleader tapped on his mic as the band assembled onstage, fresh pints of Guiness in hand. "A very special friend of the band is here . . . She's been too busy for us lately, but we're hoping she can join us onstage tonight."

Trevor looked right at me and gave me a smile and a wave.

"Did . . . did you put them up to this?" I said to Jonathan, smiling and waving back at the guys onstage, my face growing hot at being singled out in the crowd.

"No, I swear, I did nothing." Jonathan held up his hands as if to prove his innocence, and the cheering from my table of friends confirmed he was telling the truth.

"Come on, Cat, get up there!" Gia said, letting out a whistle.

"Catherine, not to put you on the spot, but will you do us the honor of just a couple of songs?" Trevor held one hand to his chest, his other one held out to me as the crowd started to clap and cheer. And the hopeful looks from these five band members that I had grown to adore were too much to refuse.

The Women of Arlington Hall

"Your fans await, Killeen. Come on, get up there," Jonathan said as he grabbed my hand and pulled me through the crowd. And both of us held on a little tighter just before I let go and stepped onstage next to Trevor.

I could have begged off, told Trevor he'd have to take a rain check. But the truth is, I loved singing with this band, and performing in front of a crowd that was in the throes of holiday revelry was the perfect distraction. I could get lost in the music for a short time instead of worrying about being followed, or about Jonathan.

"What's it going to be?" Trevor said, a twinkle in his eye. "Your choice, darlin'."

"Let's do the very first song I ever sang with you-all," I said. "'I Know My Love'?"

"Brilliant." Trevor smiled and, looking at his bandmates, added, "We ready, boys?"

The music started and the crowd, especially my friends, gave a rousing cheer when I started to sing.

> I know my love by his way of walking
> I know my love by his way of talking.
> I know my love dressed in a suit of blue
> and if my love leaves me, what will I do?
> And still she cried, "I love him the best"
> And a troubled mind sure can know no rest
> And still she cried, "Bonny boys are few
> And if my love leaves me, what will I do?"

On the "troubled mind" lyric, I caught Jonathan's eye for a few seconds, but the lyrics felt too intimate, and I feared my feelings for him would be obvious, not just to him, but to the entire pub, so I finally had to turn my eyes away, scanning the crowd and smiling. He was leaving, again. Friends was easier, not complicated or messy, if only I could convince my own heart of that fact.

I spotted several familiar faces in the crowd, including Lindsay Philmore, and just the mere sight of him made me uncomfortable.

As the song ended and the crowd cheered, wanting more, the hairs on the back of my neck stood on end, and the blurry puzzle pieces I had been grasping at in my mind swirled—Philmore's words to Weissman that night about his friend McAllister, their unlikely friendship and their vague connections to foreign lands and experiences. Like Meredith had described, intuitively I knew there was something there, just beyond my reach of understanding.

As the band began to play "Heave Away," I started singing and caught Lindsay's eye. He held up his drink to me in a toast, and I nodded back and tried to ignore the deep sense of foreboding I felt when he smiled at me.

Chapter Twenty-Nine

Monday, February 6, 1950

But McAllister, I think he was too careless. He could sink me . . .

On this particular Sunday night, there were many reasons sleep was elusive, but it was Lindsay Philmore's conversation with Weissman that made me sit up in bed at three thirty in the morning, the goose pimples all over my arms having nothing to do with my drafty bedroom. McAllister had worked at the British embassy during the war years. What if *he* was the Russian spy working at a very high level that Meredith had discovered? And if he was, would it be a stretch to suspect that his best friend, Lindsay Philmore, might be a spy as well? Was that why he was worrying about McAllister "sinking him"? And why tell Weissman, unless he was somehow involved too?

I lay back down on my pillow, the branches outside my window making a mosaic of thin, dark, fingerlike shadows on my bedroom ceiling. Maybe I was losing my mind, jumping at my own imagined ghosts, worrying about men in fedoras following me, because my paranoia was finally making me insane?

We were all exhausted and stressed from the brutally long hours of work in the Russian section over the past couple of months, as we tried to find and identify the rest of the members of the atomic spy ring associated with Klaus Fuchs. We had made amazing progress, but it had taken a toll. Rosemary was never without a cigarette; Effie's nails were bitten to the quick. Gia drank coffee by the pot all day long. And I had too many nights like this, where no matter how many tricks I tried, I couldn't turn my mind off, ruminating on the latest messages we were working on, about the uneasiness I felt every time I ran into Philmore or Weissman. And of course, Jonathan was never far from my thoughts these days either.

It was almost five when I mercifully drifted off to sleep, until my alarm jolted me awake at seven. In the morning light, my thoughts about Ron McAllister were no less troubling.

"You up?" Effie said, banging on my door. "It's a big day for Building B!"

"Yup, getting dressed," I said, my voice hoarse. A minute later Gia knocked on the door and handed me a big orange ceramic mug of Italian coffee.

"God bless you, you're the best," I said holding the mug in both hands and taking a sip.

"I know," she smiled. "Hurry up, I want to have enough time to hit the newsstand."

In late January, Klaus Fuchs, the German-born physicist turned Russian spy, had, finally, given British intelligence a long, detailed confession regarding his involvement with Soviet espionage. His testimony detailed his time as part of the British scientific delegation picked by Oppenheimer to come to the U.S. to work on the Manhattan Project. Fuchs was one of the scientists in the delegation that had spent time doing work at the project's secret laboratories in Los Alamos, New Mexico.

Because the British could not use the top secret evidence that Bob had provided from our deciphered KGB messages, they could not prosecute Fuchs for espionage. They could, however, charge him with violation of the Official Secrets Act. And so, on February 2, Klaus Fuchs was formally arrested and charged in England, pleading guilty to all counts. He was expected to receive the maximum penalty of fourteen years in prison.

We managed to make it to the newsstand, purchasing every single US national newspaper we could find before hurrying to catch our bus to work.

"So, Jonathan's back in town?" Effie asked as we waited in the security line for Arlington Hall, holding our stacks of newspapers.

"According to the note he sent me last week, he should have arrived last night," I said. His letter was still in my purse and, with its arrival, I again felt the heady anticipation of seeing him, along with that bittersweet ache that was only growing stronger.

"And you're supposed to go out with him tonight?" Gia asked.

"Yes," I said. "In his note he talked about meeting after work at the Cairo. He's supposed to call me to confirm."

"And what are you going to do when you meet up with him?" Effie gave me a pointed look.

"I am going to . . . attempt to talk to him about how I feel, how I still *have* feelings, even though the thought of it makes me want to throw up," I said with a groan. "But as you two and Rosemary have reminded me more than once, I am a college-educated, grown woman, not some moon-eyed high school girl with a crush."

"Damn right," Gia said with a smile.

And I knew that I would have eventually come to that conclusion, though my friends had helped me reach it a little sooner. He was in New York, I was here, but it was time to take this risk. And if the feelings weren't mutual, I would at least know where I stood with him and I could get on with my life. The not knowing was driving me crazy.

The four of us were the first to arrive at the conference room for our all-hands meeting with Meredith and Bob, and we spread all the newspapers across the conference room table, the headlines stunning to see:

> Hoover Set to Tell Body of Senators That Fuchs Sent Data to Soviets

> H Bomb Data Given to Soviets, Britain's Top Atomic Scientist is Held, Allegedly Confesses Spy Activities

FBI's Hoover Tells Senators Dr. Klaus Fuchs Had Become Paid Russian Agent in 1939

Rosemary came in as soon as she spotted us, and the rest of the team started to arrive, a few people gasping when they saw the papers. It was an extraordinary and surreal moment, to know that all of us shared a direct connection to the world events on the front pages of newspapers around the globe.

We passed around the papers, reading parts of the various articles out loud to one another. Cecil read *The New York Times* piece with obvious pride in his voice. Rosemary's tone reading the *Washington Times-Herald* was one of shocked disbelief. Klaus Fuchs, code-named Rest, was now sitting in an English prison.

When Meredith walked in with Bob, they both looked lighter, less weighted down by the tremendous pressure they'd been under since the news that the Soviets had the bomb. When the room was quiet, Bob began to speak, Meredith standing behind him, leaning against the board. Bill Weissman was, notably, absent from the meeting.

"I don't have a lot of time, so I asked Meredith if I could say a few words first," Bob said. He shook his head and ran his fingers through his hair, smiling as he looked across the room. "Oh, but per Frank and the colonel, as usual I must remind you of the secrecy oath you took and that you could be executed for treason if you violate it. But let's be honest, you've all been here long enough. If you don't understand that by now, you never will."

As a few people laughed at this comment, Bob picked up the front page of *The New York Times*, the one with Klaus Fuchs's picture and the headline "British Jail Atom Scientist as a Spy after Tip by the FBI He Knew of Hydrogen Bomb," holding it up high and pointing at the photo of Fuchs.

"The work you do here? It's the biggest secret in US intelligence in the history of the country. And it is by far the FBI's best secret weapon. You most certainly were with this case.

"You've all worked hundreds of hours, long days, and weekends. You've helped discover dozens of code names of Soviet spies, deciphered countless KGB messages, and because of all of that? We just brought Klaus Fuchs, the man who stole some of America's biggest atomic secrets, to justice. You've made history, even if they can't include this part of the story in the history books. And you all need to savor this moment and be proud of it. Because Meredith and I are so damn proud of you."

Cecil let out a whoop. There was another ripple of laughter, and then everyone in the room stood up cheering and applauding, for Bob, for Meredith, and for what we had done together. Effie was one of many in the room who were wiping tears from their eyes. Bob clapped Meredith on the back, and the cheering got louder when Meredith turned to shake his hand.

"Obviously, I couldn't have said it better. I'm also . . . I'm so proud, it's hard for me to articulate, as it is with most things," Meredith said with a chuckle. "The only thing I want to add is, and I've said it before: this was an underdog project. Nobody expected much of this group, or of me and Bob to be honest. *Nobody*. We've stunned the powers that be here at the ASA and the FBI in what we've accomplished. And now we've shocked the world. But to be clear, we can take a quick victory lap, but this is really a starting gun. We've only got one of them. We've got more to track down, and I know we can do it."

"On that note, I've got to head out," Bob said, checking his watch. "Since Fuchs's arrest, all hell has broken loose over at the FBI. We can barely keep up with the number of investigations we're launching. Hoover says this case may be the crime of the century, and I believe he's right. We're very close to finding more of these traitors thanks to your work. That's all I can say. I'll let Meredith take it from here. Keep up the good work, everyone."

This led to another round of applause, and now I couldn't help but start blinking back tears of pride to be a part of it too, even if it remained America's biggest secret for the rest of my life.

Killeen, can you meet me at the Lincoln Memorial at seven thirty? I'll be at the bottom of the steps on the right-hand side. We'll go somewhere from there. It's important. If you can't make it, please call the office. I'll be here until seven. I have to see you.

I frowned again at the While You Were Out slip with the message from J. Dardis that had been left on my desk.

"So you have a romantic date night at the, uh, Lincoln Memorial? He does realize it's February, right?" Gia said, as we both got ready to leave.

"Yes, I'm sure," I said. "It's odd, but we'll probably go somewhere close by to eat or something. Maybe he has a meeting nearby? Who knows."

"Well, if you two want to come back to the apartment, we'll be there hanging in tonight. Rosemary's coming by, maybe Margaret and Cecil too."

"Sounds good. We might see you later," I said, putting on my newly purchased, navy-blue wool coat and grabbing my bag out of my desk.

Meredith's light was still on. He had been running back and forth between meetings all day, with Frank and the colonel and other higher-ups in the ASA. And then Bob had returned after lunch, and they had been hunkered down in his office for at least a couple of hours. But now he was finally alone. I'd be a little late meeting Jonathan, but I had to talk with him.

"You coming?" Gia asked, slinging her red purse over her shoulder.

"You go ahead, I need to ask Meredith something."

When I knocked, he looked up, and something about his expression gave me pause. It had been a triumphant day for our team. But Meredith's expression was grave, his face pale.

"Are you okay?" I said.

The Women of Arlington Hall

"Catherine . . . uh, I'm fine. *Fine*," he said, letting out a deep breath. "I'm heading out soon. What can I help you with?"

"I wanted to talk to you about those KGB messages you mentioned a little while ago, regarding the high-level spy at the British embassy during the war—"

"What about them?" He interrupted me before I could finish, avoiding eye contact as he shuffled papers around on his desk.

"Is it possible . . . have you, has Bob considered Ron McAllister? We know he was working at the British embassy during those years. And remember what I told you, about what Philmore said at his party about McAllister?"

"I'm sorry, but this conversation is going to have to wait. I have to go." He stood up, stuffing files and a couple of his gray notebooks into his battered briefcase. "I promised Blanche I'd be home at a decent time tonight. You should go too. You're always here, working too late."

"Oh . . . okay. Meredith?" I said, frowning as he continued to pack up his things, not looking up at me. He'd never accused me, or anyone, of working too late. "There's something you're not telling me. What's going on?"

"I can't discuss it," he said a little too loudly. "I'm sorry to raise my voice. It's just . . . it's been a long, hard day."

"It's okay," I said. "I thought it was an incredible day . . . I wish you would tell me what changed . . ."

"And you're not privy to *everything* that goes on in this organization, Catherine. It's time . . . You need to go home."

His words hurt my pride. I admired Meredith so much as a mentor, and I thought we had reached the point where we were almost friends. Clearly, I was wrong.

"Yes, of course," I said, trying not to show how much his condescending tone had stung. "Good night."

Chapter Thirty

I arrived at the Lincoln Memorial a little after seven thirty. There were a few stars already visible in the clear evening sky, the wind had died down, and it was mild, almost balmy for February. The Memorial towered over the Reflecting Pool, and at night it was stunning, the thirty-six columns of its Greek Revival temple backlit, and inside of it sat the imposing white marble statue of the sixteenth president. Lincoln was facing the US Capitol and cast in a dramatic light so that every feature of his face was visible.

I tried to put aside my abrupt conversation with Meredith, my related worries and fears about Philmore and Weissman, all my racing thoughts. As I searched the eerily quiet memorial grounds for Jonathan, my heart beating loudly in my chest, suddenly my instincts told me his reasons for meeting here had nothing to do with romance.

He was leaning against the granite wall on the right-hand side of the memorial's steps, looking up at the statue, and I had to remind myself to breathe.

"Hey," I said, and he whipped his head around to look at me.

"Killeen, you made it, thank God." He hurried over and pulled me into a hug.

"Did you think I wouldn't?" I said with a laugh, melting into his tight embrace, the strength of his arms, before he pulled away.

"Did you see anyone following you? Think hard, did you notice anyone at all?" he said, hand on my elbow as he surveyed the area around us.

"No . . . why do you ask?" I said, afraid to hear the answer. I was right, this was not the happy reunion I expected. "Because, well, not tonight, but I . . . I *have* seen someone, someone I thought might be following me, on more than one occasion lately. I'm almost sure of it."

"I *am* sure of it," Jonathan said, still looking in all directions.

"Dardis, what the hell is going on?" I said. "Tell me. Right now."

"I will. Come on, let's go see Abe. We can talk up there, where I'm sure nobody can hear us," he said, his hand on my elbow as we walked up the forty-eight steps to the top, the giddiness in my stomach replaced with that deep pit of dread again.

We entered the empty central chamber where Lincoln's massive statue sat, our footsteps the only sound on the pink marble floors.

"I'm sorry for the cloak-and-dagger stuff," he said, after he had checked the other two chambers to ensure we were alone.

"So am I," I said. "What is happening? Why are we here?"

"Well, for one I know it's not bugged," he said, putting his coat down and motioning for me to join him on the top step. I sat next to him, and both of us were quiet for a moment, looking out across the shimmering Reflecting Pool to the Washington Monument in the distance.

"Who's following me?"

"An agent named Raymond," he said in a low voice.

"A Soviet agent? Following me?" I said, shivering.

"No, Killeen. Raymond is an FBI agent," Jonathan said with a deep sigh. "You're being tailed by the FBI."

"What . . ." I gasped, trying to understand what he was saying. "Why is the FBI following *me*?"

"Philmore and Weissman . . ."

"Oh no." I bit my lip and shook my head back and forth because I knew what was coming. "No. I . . . I think I know why . . . Go ahead tell me."

"Philmore, backed by Weissman, recently demanded the FBI start 'lightly' tailing you. They said you have been highly suspicious on several occasions, including eavesdropping on a top-secret conversation they had in Philmore's home study. And Weissman said you stay late; he alleges it's because you're going through file cabinets and desks, possibly stealing intelligence."

"What?" I gasped. "He . . . Jonathan, you have to know this is all bogus, I would never . . ."

"I know, I know," Jonathan said, putting his hands up. "That's why I am here. And the FBI would probably not have even agreed to someone tailing you, were it not for something else that recently came to light."

"What are you talking about?" I felt physically ill, bracing for what was coming.

"We recently received an anonymous tip in the New York City field office that your uncle, the Columbia professor Peter Walker, was passing intelligence to the Soviets from contacts at Los Alamos and Texas during the war."

"What . . . No . . . No! You have got to be joking!" I said with a bitter laugh. I jumped up and started to pace back and forth, my boots clicking on the marble floor. "Oh, this is rich. There's no way after all this time, after he was flagged in my background check, and then brought up again. Now? *Now* the FBI learns that he's a spy. Not just a member of the Communist Party?"

"Unfortunately, the more we learn, the more it's become clear that the CPUSA is essentially a front for Soviet espionage operations in the US. We've all been joking that it should be called United Spies of America."

"Great. This is just terrific," I said sarcastically, recalling Weissman saying something similar. "And this explains why Meredith was just acting strange too, more distant with me."

"Yes, well, in just the past few days Meredith has, unbeknownst to you or your team, been able to verify some facts from the KGB messages, exclusively for Bob, to compare them with the details from the anonymous tip." Jonathan paused, his face anguished. "Killeen, Peter Walker, he's . . . his code name is Quantum. In '43, he provided secret intelligence regarding gaseous diffusion and remained in contact with both spies—Gus and Liberal—after that. Meredith told Bob the other night that he's now certain Quantum is Peter Walker. They just informed *me* because I'm part of the Soviet espionage section in New York."

I kept pacing. My uncle was a suspect. My hands had started shaking, and I hugged myself and tried to get a handle on the anger and fear coursing through me.

"Is it possible that I was hired to work at Arlington Hall not *despite* my relationship to Peter Walker but because of it?" I said, my voice wavering. "Because this feels like it's . . . it's like, how in the world could nobody—the FBI, the ASA—how could they not have known until now, this moment in time?"

"I thought of that, but honestly? We've been taking a second look at all the members of CPUSA, because so damn many of them are turning out to be involved in espionage, and then Meredith found what he found, and the pieces fit for Peter Walker. You know the only reason we're identifying so many of these people is because of the work you're doing in Building B."

"The irony." I laughed even though I wanted to cry. "Before you go on, I need to tell you why I think Philmore and Weissman are setting me up."

I told him everything—about our long-held suspicions about Weissman, what I'd overheard him and Philmore discussing in the study at Philmore's party, including Philmore's snarky comment about my uncle, and concluded with the night I confronted Weissman about it in Building B.

He listened quietly, though his expression turned angrier.

"Also, Weissman tried to convince me that Philmore would be too drunk to remember anything from the night of his party," I said when I was through.

"Oh, trust me, neither of them forgot a thing from that night," he said, bitterness in his voice. "And the other reason the FBI agreed to start tailing you? Philmore received 'evidence' from a 'high-level source' in British intelligence in New York City, linking you directly to Peter Walker."

"How perfectly convenient for Philmore," I said. "What evidence did they find, exactly?"

"A witness who has seen you meeting with Walker in Cambridge and New York City," Jonathan said. "And a couple letters—supposedly correspondence between the two of you as well."

"Jonathan, I . . ." I stopped and tried to calm myself because I was on the verge of either bursting into tears or screaming. It was too surreal to be true. How was this my life? Why were they doing this to me? "This is madness. I swear on my mother's grave I have never met the man. Whoever this witness is, is lying! And correspondence? Whatever they've got, it's bogus. It's completely fabricated."

"*I* believe you," he said. "But this is—"

"I think we're going to find out about those two," I interrupted him and kept ranting. "As well as McAllister, the one at the British embassy during the war. *They're* the ones that are guilty of something, I feel it in my bones. That's why they're doing this. It's too easy—deflect suspicion by throwing a young female codebreaker with zero power under the bus, even *without* the connection to my uncle. My God, Peter Walker was just the icing on the cake for them!"

"I think you could be right, but at the moment it's your word against—"

"Against two men with seniority, including one who is in line to be the future head of MI6 in the UK?" I said.

"Exactly. Please, sit down," he said, reaching out his hand, patting the space next to him on his coat.

"I'm only sitting because I feel like I'm going to pass out." I took his hand and dropped down on the step, still shaking from the shock of these revelations. "Meredith once said he trusted me implicitly. But tonight? I tried to tell him about the possible theory I had about Philmore's friend McAllister, but he brushed me off. Now I know why. I don't think he . . . I don't think he'll believe me . . . I . . . I really hope that you do."

My voice cracked at the end, and no amount of blinking could keep the tears from falling. And for the first time in months, an overwhelming wave of homesickness came over me. Would I still have taken this job if I had known it was going to lead me to this disastrous moment?

"I believe you. Of course I believe you. That's why I met you here tonight," Jonathan whispered in my ear, putting his arm around me and pulling me close. And leaning against him felt so good, it made me wish this night had been the one I had been imagining instead of the current nightmare it had become.

"Why are you telling me all this now, here?" I whispered back, after I had taken a minute to compose myself. Of course, he had learned all of this because he was based in New York. And the risk he was taking by sharing it all with me? He could lose his job, or worse.

"Because any day now, they're going to bring you in for questioning. I'm not sure if they have enough to press charges, but if they do, you're looking at conspiracy to commit espionage and violation of the Official Secrets Act."

"Which, as we are always reminded, means I could be executed for treason. Oh my God, you weren't even done with the bad news," I said, wiping the tears on my cheeks away. "What am I going to do?"

"That's up to you," he said. "What do you want to do?"

"I have no idea. I need to think," I said.

The two of us sat there together for a short time, lost in our own thoughts, elbows touching, looking out at the Reflecting Pool, the silhouettes of several elm trees standing like guards down both sides. In the distance, the Washington Monument appeared majestic, glowing silvery white in its evening spotlight.

"I have an idea," I said in a quiet voice after several minutes, talking to myself more than him.

"Tell me."

"I think I need to pay him a visit," I said.

"Who?" Jonathan frowned. "Philmore?"

"No," I said. "I think it's time to meet the man who has been hanging over my life since I took this job. I'm going to go to New York City. To meet the mysterious Peter Walker."

Chapter Thirty-One

For the next hour, Jonathan and I sat on the steps in front of Lincoln and came up with a plan. My friends would cover for me at work, informing everyone who needed to know that I was taking a few days off, to go home to Cambridge due to a family emergency. Tomorrow morning, I would take the train to New York City and stay at La Belle Aurore, a small, discreet hotel near Columbia that Jonathan knew of. I'd visit my uncle during his regular office hours at the university, without advance notice.

"And you're going to ask for . . ." Jonathan said.

"I'm going to ask him to help clear me somehow, to get my name out of this mess, maybe even give me evidence that implicates Philmore, or some of the members of the atomic spy ring," I said. "He owes me this *one* favor after ruining the life I've built here, after never wanting to know his own niece and nephews."

"This is . . . I don't know, it's such an enormous risk," Jonathan said, hands in a steeple in front of his face.

"So is not doing anything," I said. "What am I supposed to do, Jonathan? Wait around for a knock on my apartment door? For Meredith or Bob to tell me the FBI is bringing me in for questioning?"

"You're right. That's why I told you all of this. To come up with a plan, but I . . . I'm just sorry you have to do this on your own, Killeen. I only wish I could do more to help."

"You've already done enough. You've taken an enormous chance in telling me all of this. You could lose . . . well, everything. I don't know how I'll ever be able to repay you."

He took my hand in his, and when our eyes met, I had to choke back tears again.

"Repay me? You don't . . ." he said, looking down at our hands. "Enough of that talk. Let's review, because you should get one of the earliest trains out in the morning."

Jonathan went on to explain that Peter Walker was being tailed by the FBI in New York, and it was clear that he was well aware of it, because it had become a game of cat and mouse. His apartment complex in Knickerbocker Village on the Lower East Side had several tunnels underneath it, so it was impossible to keep track of his comings and goings there, and there were also multiple exits to Hamilton Hall, where his office at Columbia was located.

"All of that said, you'll pose as a student, get a book bag, dress discreetly, and maybe wear some sort of disguise—glasses, whatever. Just so, if anyone gets photos of you with him, you can't be identified."

"Now you *really* sound cloak-and-dagger," I said, shaking my head. "I still cannot believe this is happening."

"I know." He looked at me with a sad smile that broke something open in my heart. "I wish more than anything that it wasn't. I'll try to be in New York the day after tomorrow. I'll check in by leaving a message at the hotel. Let's get a cab. We'll drop you at your apartment first. I want to make sure you get home safe tonight."

We walked down the steps hand in hand. To anyone who happened to see us out together, we looked like a couple on a date, without a care in the world. If only that were true.

"In case you want to hear one bit of good news, we're getting close to the courier, Gus. Gold and Brothman, those two we talked about, we believe it's one of them."

"That is excellent news," I said, though it didn't do much to improve my mood. "Now if you all can just hurry up and get the rest of them, clear things up. I've kind of got a major personal stake in this now."

"No kidding," he said, squeezing my hand.

We were quiet on the cab ride to my apartment, and I leaned my head on his shoulder and closed my eyes, an ache in my chest, imagining an alternate reality where this was the first of many dates to come. But that wasn't meant to be, and now I questioned if it would ever happen.

He offered his hand to help me out of the cab and walked me to the front door of my building. We stood and faced each other, as the cab idled, just like the night we had kissed in front of Idaho Hall, a lifetime ago. And there was a pain and longing in my heart, for something so much more than another goodbye.

"Remember to tell the girls as little as possible about what's going on. They just need to cover for you. They don't need to know everything. And . . ."

"Jonathan, wait, I have to . . . you *love* this job," I said, interrupting him. "I remember how proud you were the first time you told me you were a G-man. Bob always says you're a rising star in the FBI. Why are you doing this? Why would you risk all of it?"

He looked down at the ground for a second, and then he grabbed my hand and looked at me.

"Don't you get it?" he said, his voice choked up. "You know, for someone so smart, Killeen . . ."

"Thank you," I said, as he seemed like he was struggling to find the words. "Thank you. For risking your whole career, for giving me a chance to save myself."

"Of course," he said. "There's so much more to say. But we'll save it, for after."

"If there is an after. If I'm not in prison." I bit my lip, blinking fast, trying not to cry again.

"You listen to me, Killeen." He pulled me into an embrace and whispered in my ear, "You'll get through this. *We'll* get through this."

He put his hand under my chin and tilted my head up, and I knew he was about to kiss me, but I pulled away because, as much as I wanted to, I couldn't. It was too much. I was almost dizzy with the sense of foreboding about what was to come, about what I had to do. And my heart couldn't take it—another kiss goodbye, another first and last kiss all at once.

"I'm sorry," I said, seeing the sadness in his eyes. "It's just I can't . . ."

"I understand. I'll be in touch, and I'll see you soon," he said, walking backward, finally dropping my hand when we were too far apart to hold on. "Remember what I said."

I nodded and waved to him as the cab drove away, thinking of his words. *You'll get through this. We'll get through this.*

I wiped one last tear off my face. I wasn't sure we would.

∽

"There she is." Effie gave me a mischievous smile when she opened the door, but then her face fell. "Wait, have you been crying? Oh no, what happened? Is it Jonathan? I'll kill him."

"No, honestly, I'm fine," I said, but then I felt myself tearing up again, touched by her concern.

Rosemary and Gia were sitting in our cozy, colorful living area. There were several lit candles and a cheese ball surrounded by assorted crackers on the coffee table. Gia was wearing pink floral flannel pajamas, her hair up in a bun; Rosemary was in flared sailor pants and a cream-colored cashmere twinset. The hit song "Chattanooga Shoeshine Boy" by Red Foley was playing on the radio.

"Is anyone else here?" I asked.

"No, just us. Margaret went out with some of the girls from the main hall, and Cecil went bowling with the accounting guys," Rosemary said.

"What's going on, Cat?" Gia said, examining my face. "You look . . ."

"Oh, nothing's going on, we had a great night. I'll tell you gals all about it," I said, keeping my voice calm and talking a little louder than normal as I held my fingers to my lips. "Hey, Eff, will you get me a Coke? I'm going to turn the radio way up. This is my favorite song."

"You hate this song. Effie's the only one that loves it." Gia frowned at me.

I did hate the song, but I turned the volume way up on the radio as Jonathan had instructed, because he was almost certain our apartment was bugged. I grabbed a pen and notepad from the kitchen drawer and wrote a note, holding it up to them as we huddled close on the living room couches.

Jonathan thinks apartment's bugged. Going to New York City to see my uncle tomorrow. I need your help. Cover for me at work, say it's an urgent family emergency.

"Why are you going to see him now?" Rosemary whispered.

"It's a long story, and all I can say is I think I'm being set up," I whispered back.

Effie gasped, and Gia swore under her breath.

"Are you . . . is your life in danger?" Rosemary leaned forward, her voice soft as she grabbed my hand and looked me in the eye. "Be honest."

"I don't *think* my life's in danger . . . no . . ."

"Well for goodness' sake, Cat, that's not exactly reassuring," Rosemary said.

"All I know is, my job and my life as I know it? They're definitely in jeopardy," I said.

"Who the heck is bugging the apartment?" Effie said with a hiss.

I wrote, *FBI. Surprised?* on a piece of paper and held it up.

"No, not in the slightest. My father and uncles have never trusted the FBI," Gia said as Effie turned the music up even louder, and we all kept our heads close together, talking in whispers. Gia lit her cigarette and then Rosemary's before adding, "I know New York. I'll go with you."

"Thank you, but you can't," I said. "I wish you could, believe me, but I need to go see him discreetly and get out of there as quickly as possible."

"Aside from covering at work, how can we help?" Effie inched closer to me and squeezed my hand.

I jotted down a note about posing as a Columbia student and Jonathan suggesting a disguise, and Gia jumped up from the couch and ran into her room. She came out with her makeup bag, a couple of pairs of fashionable eyeglasses, and the most gorgeous wig I'd ever seen—fiery red hair, long and thick, styled in tumbling, glamorous waves a la Lana Turner.

"Why in the world do you have this fabulous wig in your room?" Rosemary laughed, coughing on cigarette smoke, and I had to remind her to keep her voice down.

"That is beautiful, but exactly, why?" Effie asked.

"Remember my family owns a beauty shop, and this was one of my sister Dee's favorites, so of course I took it with me when I moved here." Gia grinned, dumping the wig on my lap.

"I don't know. I'll take the tortoiseshell glasses, but I was just thinking of wearing a hat. This is a little much," I said, holding it up with two hands like it was a live animal.

"Nonsense," Gia said, and she was already behind me, pulling my hair back and pinning it, and before I knew it, she had secured the wig on my head. "Tada—there, perfect."

"Wow." Rosemary was still laughing. "I'd never guess. You look almost *nothing* like you."

"I was skeptical, but if you're looking for a disguise, this is definitely . . . different," Effie said.

I ran to the bathroom mirror to look and burst out laughing. The color wasn't too bad for my complexion, but it was bizarre seeing myself with a whole new head of hair.

"I look ridiculous." I walked out of the bathroom and sat back down on the couch. "But thanks for the laugh. I needed it."

"But you don't look like yourself." Gia was smiling, but then her face got serious again. "That's all that matters. I have a few guesses as to what's going on, you . . ."

"Please don't guess," I said, as the radio still blared and I sat there wearing the wig, trying not to panic about what I was about to do.

"This is a little insane, Cat," Rosemary said as if reading my mind. "I'm worried about you. What if this plan doesn't work?"

"I can't think about that." I took the wig off, examining a strand of the red hair, as a wave of exhaustion came over me, more emotional than physical. Would my uncle agree to help me, or would he laugh in my face? Or make the whole situation even worse for me somehow? "Anyway, thank you for covering for me, for being the best kind of friends. Now I've got to pack and get up early . . ."

"Nope, you're going to sit and tell us what you can about meeting up with Jonathan tonight," Effie said, scooting even closer to me on the couch.

"Exactly, I could smell his cologne on you when you came in." Gia gave me a pointed smirk. "Spill, then you can pack."

So I sat down and gave them a recap of what I could, the highest-level details, simply saying Jonathan was taking a risk for me and that we had sat at the Lincoln Memorial for a while talking. My cheeks flushed when I told them about our last words to each other.

"Oh honey, he's got it bad," Rosemary said.

"Exactly." Effie nodded, putting her arm around my shoulder.

"And he didn't even use the line about being star-crossed," Gia said.

"That's true," I said, feeling the rush of being in his arms, along with the pain of not knowing when I would see him again. "But clearly our star-crossed days aren't over. Not yet."

Chapter Thirty-Two

The train ride from Union Station in DC to Penn Station in New York City took a little less than four hours, and more than once I wished I had taken Gia up on her offer to come with me, because my anxiety about meeting Peter Walker had only increased the closer I got to my destination.

La Belle Aurore hotel was not the bare-bones establishment I had expected. It was small and intimate. The subtle scents of orange blossoms and exotic spice permeated the interior, the lobby was decorated in deep jewel tones of topaz orange and teal, with an intricate tile floor, and the glow of the copper lantern-style light fixtures provided a mysterious ambience.

I had just enough time to take a quick shower and throw on a change of clothes, choosing a black wool skirt and emerald-green cotton sweater, bobby socks, and my old saddle shoes, which I hadn't worn since my Radcliffe days. After debating with myself, I secured Gia's wig with hair pins, tucking my curls underneath, and put on a pair of cat-eye sunglasses with tortoiseshell frames borrowed from Effie.

Peter Walker's office hours at Columbia were from two to four p.m., and, wanting to be his last "student" of the day, I planned to arrive at three forty-five. Wearing my wool coat and carrying a leather book bag Rosemary had lent me, I did a double take when I looked into

The Women of Arlington Hall

the gilded mirror next to my hotel room door and saw the red-haired woman looking back at me.

"No, this is absurd," I said out loud, taking out the pins and pulling the wig off my head, smoothing out my curls. I kept the glasses on and tucked my own hair under my black wool beret. I could be discreet but I wasn't disguising myself, despite Jonathan's' suggestion. Of course it wouldn't help my cause if by chance the FBI spotted me with my uncle, but at the end of the day I had done absolutely nothing wrong. I wasn't the one who had something to hide.

Seeing my actual self in the mirror calmed my nerves and gave me a boost of confidence. I had chosen to come to New York to save myself, to save the life I'd created from being sabotaged. I wasn't going to let anyone do this to me without a fight.

The only pall on my otherwise happy childhood had been my mother's absence, and the family who had cut her off and, in turn, cut off her widowed husband and children. Anna Walker's family had been a mystery to us, a black box that was rarely discussed unless my brothers or I hounded my father with questions.

While the existence of my uncle, Peter Walker, had been hanging over my career at Arlington Hall, the absence of her, and of her estranged family, had cast a long shadow over my life since the day I was born. So, this trip essentially had two purposes. There was no telling if either would be resolved with this gamble that I was taking, this bet on my own life, meeting this relative who was a complete stranger. He might slam the door in my face as soon as I told him who I was, and I tried to brace myself for any possibility.

On the brisk fifteen-minute walk to campus, out of sheer paranoia I paid careful attention to my unfamiliar surroundings, hyperaware of anyone who might look like they were following me. I arrived in front of Hamilton Hall, and a young man carrying a pile of massive textbooks managed to hold the door for me. Peter Walker's office was number 307 on the third floor, and ascending the stairs, I rehearsed what I planned to say to him for the thousandth time.

257

Dr. Peter Walker
Department of Applied Physics & Mathematics

Seeing his nameplate on his office door made me break out into a sweat. His door was closed, and I could hear two people talking inside, so I sat down in one of the chairs next to the door set out for waiting students and took some deep breaths in an attempt to control my nerves and keep calm.

If I thought about it too much, I'd run from the building and never come back. So I distracted myself and thought instead about Gia, Effie, and Rosemary supporting me unconditionally the night before, covering for me, even without knowing the exact circumstances. I hoped Meredith and the rest of the team had bought my family emergency excuse; it was only a partial lie, really.

And my thoughts turned to me and Jonathan on the steps, our words, his arms around me. I tried to guess where he was now, and whether he had regrets about telling me what he knew.

Five minutes later, the door opened, and I shot out of the chair, holding tight to my book bag to keep my hands from shaking.

Breathe, Cat. You can do this.

I kept saying the words in my mind over and over.

"Thanks, professor. See you next week," A sandy-haired young man stepped out and nodded to me.

"He's all yours," he said.

"Uh . . . thanks," I replied, trying to smile.

I knocked on the half-open door and peeked in.

"Come in, come in," Peter Walker said, waving me inside, still looking down at his desk, a head of dark, curly hair streaked with gray. "Though if it's about last week's exam, I haven't even graded them yet."

"I'm not here about that," I said.

"No, then what . . ." He looked up at me and stared. My mouth dropped open because of how much he looked like Richie: dark, curly hair, prominent jawline, blue eyes just like mine.

"Then. . . can I help you?" he asked, sitting back in his chair now, still studying my face with a look of curiosity.

"I really hope so," I said, taking off my hat. "But I honestly have no idea."

"Dear God," Peter Walker said, his hand over his mouth, eyes wide with shock. "It's like I'm seeing a ghost. I'd know you anywhere. You're . . ."

"Catherine," I said, my face turning several shades of red as I held out my hand. "I'm Annie's daughter, although I know you called her Anna. I'm your niece. Catherine Killeen."

His eyes welled up with tears as we shook hands, and he stared at me as if I was an apparition or an alien from outer space. He then offered to go to the kitchenette on the floor to get us both coffees, I think more so he could compose himself than anything else. I enthusiastically agreed, as his reaction had moved me more than I anticipated, and I was also fighting back tears.

His large oak desk was covered with scientific journals and student papers. A locked metal file cabinet stood in the corner next to a bookshelf that was packed with textbooks and volumes of technical materials, although one shelf was dedicated to works of classic literature and political philosophy.

Multiple degrees and awards from scientific societies were framed and hung on the wall behind his desk on either side of a large paned window. The rest of the office walls were covered with various awards and black-and-white photographs of Dr. Peter Walker with different groups of men in white lab coats, looking celebratory. There was even one of him posing with a young, smiling, bespectacled Klaus Fuchs. It was a surprise that he hadn't taken it down since Fuchs's arrest.

Also on his desk was a black-and-white photo of a tremendous, glowing mushroom cloud in the middle of a desert labeled, *Trinity test explosion*, the date—*July 16, 1945*—scribbled in the bottom right-hand corner. The August 1946 *New Yorker* article "Hiroshima" by John Hersey was framed and hung on the wall as well.

"Have you read that piece?" Peter walked back in as I was looking at the article, nodding to it as he handed me a cup of coffee in a faded blue mug with the Columbia crest. He was more composed and professorial now than when he had stepped out a minute earlier.

"I've read it more than once," I said.

"Me too," he said.

"Why . . . why do you have it framed?" I asked.

"It's the same reason I have a picture of this." He held up the little photo of the mushroom cloud, his expression serious, and I felt slightly ill. Was he holding these up as evidence of his scientific accomplishments?

I waited for him to explain, not knowing what to say.

"These serve as my daily reminders of what we've unleashed on the world. And my small part in it," Peter said, his tone one of mournful regret as he put the photo down. "Please, please sit down."

When we were sitting across from each other, he just shook his head as in disbelief. "My God. I'm sorry, but you look so much like her. Except for the . . ."

"Freckles?" I said, and he smiled. "Yes. I have a picture of her that I keep on my dresser."

"I have a few pictures of her, from growing up," he said, his eyes welling up again. "I . . . I'm not sure how long you're in town, but I could show you."

"I would love to see them." I frowned. "But . . . aren't you wondering why I'm here? After all this time?"

A strange calmness came over me now that I was sitting here with the actual person, no longer a vague mystery of a man, a mystery that had grown a little threatening in my mind since I had started working at Arlington Hall.

He took a sip of his coffee and looked up for a moment, like he was carefully choosing what to say next.

"I do believe the fact that I'm a blood relative has caused you some difficulty in your government job in Virginia. Am I right?"

The Women of Arlington Hall

"Yes. I should have known you would know that." I looked around the room, examining the lamp on his desk, among other items. "Is this . . . it is safe to talk here, in your office?"

"Is it safe? Do you mean could someone be listening in?"

"Yes." I held my coffee mug in a tight grip.

"Who do you think might be listening, exactly?" he asked, eyebrows raised, amused.

"With my luck these days? Absolutely anyone who can," I said with a sigh.

"Interesting," he said. "You didn't say how long you were in town."

"I only plan to be here a day or two at most," I said. And then, realizing there was zero time to beat around the bush, I told him my purpose. "My sole reason for coming to New York is because I need your help. If I'm being honest, I desperately need your help, and yours alone. But I don't have much time, and if you don't think you can help me . . . I'm sorry, I'm getting ahead of myself . . ."

"Yes, you are," he said. "Because I have no idea what you're talking about."

"But if this isn't a good place to talk . . ."

"I have a double lock on the door, but if you feel we need to be *that* cautious about what you need to tell me, I can think of a better place," he said. He took a notepad and pen, jotted something down, ripped off the page, and handed it to me.

I looked up at him and frowned. How could this place be more secure than a locked office?

"It's owned by friends. Trust me."

If only I knew that I could.

Chapter Thirty-Three

Two hours later, I walked into the Bird in Hand restaurant on Broadway, and when I told her my name, the teenage hostess brought me to a booth in the far back. It was a cozy diner that smelled of hash browns, coffee, and cigarettes, with a long red Formica bar and comic-book-style pictures of roosters decorating the wood-paneled walls.

Peter Walker stood up when I arrived, taking my coat from me and handing it to the hostess. Just then, the waitress came over and I requested a Coke after she placed a martini on the table for Peter.

"I took the liberty of ordering us some piroshkis—fried pastries—as an appetizer. You'll love them. And you must try the stroganoff," he said. And then, lowering his voice, he added, "This restaurant is owned by a dear friend. We can talk safely, I assure you. Many highly confidential conversations have taken place here over the years."

"Okay," I said, looking around nodding, still not completely comfortable, but not having a choice at this point.

"Now do you want to tell me why you have come all the way here to meet me?"

The waitress put my Coke down in front of me, and I took a sip, thinking of how I had rehearsed what I was about to say next.

"I'm being set up," I said. "I know what you do for a living at Columbia, but I now also know of your other activities during the war. I don't think any of this is going to come as a surprise to you."

"No, even before Klaus's arrest, it's not a surprise at all," he said in quiet voice.

I then told him everything about Philmore and Weissman, the overheard conversation, and their accusations and supposed evidence linking me to him, and he laughed.

"That was quite a chance they took, the two of them," he said. "Quite bold."

"Well, Philmore is kind of a star in British intelligence. He can do no wrong." I shrugged.

"And he never thought you'd call their bluff, by coming here, to ask for my help."

"Exactly," I said.

"This took some courage," he said, nodding, impressed. "You seem so much like your mother, more than your face, I mean."

"My father has told me that too," I said.

"My biggest regret in life is not reconciling with her, you know," he said, blotting a drip of his drink on the table with his finger. "And after she died, so many times I've thought of contacting your father, just to meet you and your brothers. I'm so incredibly sorry about the loss of your brother Richie."

"Thank you," I said, getting emotional again, trying to hold back the tears. I was overcome by how much it meant, how moved I was to hear him say these things. I took a deep breath and couldn't help myself from asking the next question. "Is that . . . *that's* your biggest regret? Really?"

"You mean as opposed to helping America build the atom bomb? Or maybe you mean my sharing scientific research about that atom bomb with Soviet scientists?" he said, draining his martini.

And there it was, an open confession, with not a hint of shame or regret.

"My grandparents, your parents, came here as immigrants," I said. "This country gave them—gave *you*—everything. I just don't understand how you could betray . . ."

"Have you ever heard about the girls' dance camp in Ruidoso, New Mexico?" he asked, cutting me off.

"Um . . . no, I . . ."

"Of course you haven't. Few people in America have," he said, grim-faced. "It was located fifty miles from the site of the Trinity test bomb. The camp was given no warning before the bomb exploded. The girls were all jolted out of bed in confusion and woke up to witness a massive mushroom cloud in the distance. They started playing in the radioactive fallout, mistaking it as 'warm snow' falling from the sky. They covered themselves in it, some of them even opened their mouths so it dropped on their tongues. The effects of that radioactive fallout? None of those girls will live to see their fortieth birthday. That is a guarantee."

"My God," I said, my hand to my mouth, sickened at the images of those little girls playing in poisonous snow.

"And that is just one small example of what the test bomb did *here*, never mind the horrors you read about in that Hiroshima article," he said with passion. "You may think I betrayed my country, but you must understand, scientists like me? We believe in the international sharing of information, making knowledge available to all.

"There was a strong sense among many of us in the Manhattan Project, particularly at the end of it, that no nation should be the sole owner of that kind of catastrophic power. We thought it was gross negligence for the United States not to share information about the atom bomb with the Soviets, their 'ally' at the time. For America alone to have a monopoly on atomic power? It is far too dangerous."

"But sharing that information, that wasn't your decision to make—any of you," I said, incredulous at his hubris.

"Why not? We were the ones responsible for building it," he said. "We all felt it had to be done."

He looked at me as I considered this, considered his perspective on his choices.

"Thank you for giving me some context for your . . . decisions," I said.

"Thank you for listening," he said. "So . . . how can I best help you?"

"You *will* help me?" I said, feeling hopeful for the first time since I'd arrived in New York.

"I suppose I can write a letter," he said, waving his hand around. "It would state that I have never met you and all evidence against you to the contrary is fabricated."

"That would help, and I will take it, thank you," I said, pausing before the next part. "But given your background and um . . . history, I'm thinking I might need more than just a letter."

"Very true," he said. "So, what are you suggesting?"

"In addition to a letter, if you could please give me something more," I said. "I need to prove I don't have any loyalty to you or . . . or your cause. Now, I'm not asking you to give yourself up . . ."

"Well, thank God for that." He laughed. Just then, a couple who looked to be in their thirties entered the restaurant, both looking furious, their body language tense as they sat down across from each other. The hostess seated them in a red leather booth closer to the front, but I had a clear view, and they were having a heated argument as soon as they were seated.

"I'm looking . . . I'm looking for more evidence, more clues to help us track down some of this atomic ring," I whispered. "To prove to my bosses and the FBI that I'm still on the right side of this . . ."

"After what I just told you, are you *sure* you are on the right side of this? And you do realize you're asking me to give up one of my fellow comrades?"

"Listen, I do understand the moral ambiguity here, and why a scientist like you might make the choices that you have made," I said. "That said, I'm still certain that stealing the most sensitive intelligence from the United States and giving it to a foreign power is treason, yes? And let's be honest, not all the people we are after do it for altruistic reasons like you."

"Now that is very true," he said. He sat back and considered this. "Some do it for money; others do it because they have a fanatical loyalty to party and country."

"I risked everything to come here to see you." I looked at him, suddenly feeling weary and losing hope. "To come here and ask for your help. You're basically . . ."

"Do not worry," Peter said. "I will write you the letter, and provide you with some . . . *materials* . . . that will support your efforts and get you back in your boss's good graces. Let's meet back at my office tomorrow morning first thing. I'll have them for you then."

"Thank you," I said, breathing a deep sigh of relief, almost wanting to give him a hug. "I can't thank you enough. I . . . I hope you aren't putting yourself in any danger . . ."

"Oh, Catherine, I have been playing this game longer than you've been alive. Do not fret about me," he said, smiling, and he truly didn't appear worried in the slightest. "Let's order some more food, shall we? With what little time we have, please, indulge me. I want to hear more about your life, beyond this problem you've been having."

All I wanted was to go back to the hotel and try to sleep, but there was no way I could say no. He was helping me; I might possibly get out from under the accusations. Though I wouldn't believe it until it happened.

We ordered food and our dinner conversation actually took my mind off things for a brief time, as I shared stories of my life growing up in Cambridge, what my brothers were like, as well as my time at Radcliffe and decision to move to DC. I also showed him my mother's gold Saint Rita medallion that I had started wearing at age five, as soon as I knew it was hers.

"She got it when she converted to Catholicism." I held it out to him.

"Of all the saints, she chose the patron saint of impossible causes as her favorite?" He looked at it.

"Yes," I said. "Nobody has ever told me why, though."

"No doubt she was thinking of our parents," Peter said, sadness in his eyes.

"Tell me about them, about what my mother was like growing up." I said it with a yearning that surprised me, given how much else I had to worry about. But here was the only person I'd ever met who knew my mother before she was a Killeen.

So he told me all about my very strict, old-school Russian grandparents, of growing up with my mother, the pranks they would play on each other, her love of performing in school plays, her rare intelligence and natural gifts as a nursing student. He explained the stubbornness of my grandparents in not reconnecting with her after she married my father, and, after my mother's death, their heartbreak and deep regret over never reconciling with her.

"But still, they never came to see us, to meet her children?" I said.

"They were so stubborn, a different generation," he said. "And I think maybe it was all too painful to face, so they buried their grief, as well as the love they could have shared with you."

"Oh," I said, as my eyes welled with tears once more, because there was something so incredibly sad about his words, about my now-deceased grandparents burying their love instead of opening their hearts to me and my brothers when we most needed it.

Everything he shared filled up a well in me I hadn't realized was empty—my mother before my father, her own family history, the branches of the family tree that had always been a missing piece in my life story. And I only wished my brothers were here to listen to Peter as well. And when the waitress put our check on the table, I found myself a little bereft that our time was over.

"Have you ever heard the Yiddish word *bashert*?" he asked, after he insisted on paying.

"No," I said. "What does it mean?"

"It has a couple of different meanings. But it often refers to events that are believed to be predestined, fated. Sitting here with you, I keep thinking of that word. Don't you think it's extraordinary that of all the jobs in the world, you took one that led you to your late mother's brother?"

"I don't know . . ." I said. "Even when you were first mentioned in my background check, I just thought if I was cleared, it was fine. I didn't think we would ever have a reason to meet, because why would we, after all this time? And then this . . . mess happened with my job, my life . . ."

"Well, I am sorry for what you've been through, but I am absolutely not sorry to *meet* you." He smiled.

"Thank you, I . . . I feel the same," I said. "I didn't understand how much I needed to hear all of this, about her."

"Tell me, this friend who helped you, in the FBI. Is he someone special to you? A boyfriend?"

"I . . . that's an interesting question," I said, my cheeks growing warm as I thought of our goodbye outside of my apartment, wondering if we'd ever get the chance for another, under less fraught circumstances. "He's been a good friend to me. He might be more than that."

"By the way that you're blushing, I think he might be too," Peter said.

"Yes, well, we'll see," I said with a small, wistful smile. "And you? Never married? No special someone?"

"No, almost, but no . . . I never did," he said, a hint of regret in his voice. "When I was young, I thought there was so much time for love, so much future ahead of me for those things. I focused too much on my work as a scientist, my work as a comrade. And now that I am old? I realize that time is even more fleeting than you can ever imagine at your age. And finding love—true, lasting love? Well, that is a rare thing. And I understand now why my sister, your mother, went against our parents, left her life and her religion behind to marry a poor Irish firefighter. I know now, it *was* that rare thing."

"It was." I nodded, thinking of my father and the way he spoke of my mother still, of how their love story still echoed through my childhood, though I had not been alive to witness it.

"Yes. By the way, one of the other meanings of *bashert* is soulmate," he smiled. "My advice? If you ever find that kind of love, do not let anything get in the way of it."

"I will keep that in mind," I said, thinking again of Jonathan, wishing he was with me now.

As we headed out of the restaurant, Peter stopped by the table with the couple who had been fighting when they arrived. They seemed in much better spirits now.

"Julius!" Peter said, putting his hand on the shoulder of the man in the booth. He was wearing wire-rimmed glasses and had dark-brown hair, slightly receding, and a small mustache over full lips.

The Women of Arlington Hall

"Peter, my friend, it's good to see you," the man said, standing to shake Peter's hand and give him a slap on the back.

"Look at you two, out on a date alone," Peter said. "Where are those beautiful boys of yours? Don't they usually come here with you on Tuesday nights?"

"Mrs. Abramowitz took them for the evening, so we could get out for a bit. It's difficult to hear myself think with those two running around," the woman said, rolling her eyes as Peter leaned down and gave her a kiss on the cheek. She was very petite, with thick, wavy brown hair cut short, and round dark eyes.

"Catherine, let me introduce you to the Rosenbergs. They also live in the Knickerbocker Village housing complex," Peter said. "This is my niece, Catherine Killeen."

"Hello, Catherine, I'm Julius," the man said, giving me a brief handshake. "And this is my wife, Ethel."

Liberal speaks of his wife Ethel, aged twenty-nine, married five years...

The words from the KGB telegram from November 1944 flashed through my mind as I greeted them. Liberal's wife, Ethel, would be about thirty-three years old now, and the Ethel sitting in front of me in the booth looked to be around the exact same age.

I was glad I had my coat on, because as soon as Peter said her name, a chill went through me and my arms broke out into goose pimples. I contemplated how many women in their thirties named Ethel lived in New York City. Hundreds? Thousands? This was a restaurant owned by a friend, a safe place to talk, meaning safe for anyone with ties to CPUSA. Was Julius Rosenberg the leader of the atomic spy ring, codenamed Liberal? Was this the mysterious Ethel who "did not work"?

"Nice to meet you, Julius," I said, turning to the woman, attempting a casual smile as I checked to be sure I had heard her name right. "And Ethel is it?"

"Yes," the woman said with a shy smile back as we shook hands. "It's nice to meet you."

We exchanged a few more pleasantries before leaving, and then I stood in front of the Bird in Hand with my no-longer-estranged uncle. Did Peter know that the Rosenbergs would be there tonight? Was he giving me information, or was it a strange coincidence, given the circles he traveled in?

I stared at him, waiting to see if he was going to tell me if the people he had just introduced me to were the ones we'd been searching for all these months. But he just smiled; he was not going to make it that easy.

"So . . . you'll really help me?" I said after a moment, as I gazed at Julius and Ethel Rosenberg through the front window of the restaurant, trying to memorize what they looked like.

"Of course I will," he said with conviction. "I will help you out of obligation to my late sister, whom I loved dearly and should have never, ever let go. I can do this one thing for you, for her."

He paused for a second before continuing. "After Fuchs, the walls are closing in on a number of us now. Things are going to have to change dramatically. Some will leave the US, and some will have no choice but to stay." He shrugged, as if it was an inevitable part of the "game," as he called it. "But I will do this for you, while I still can, because very soon I am going to have to make some hard decisions about my own future."

"Well again, I can't . . . I can't thank you enough," I said, and as he leaned down, he gave me a quick kiss goodbye on the cheek, and I imagined a life where I had known him and my mother's parents growing up, and a part of me mourned it now in a way I never had before.

"You're welcome," he said, his eyes darting up and down the street. "We should leave, heading in different directions, just in case."

"Okay, so I will meet you at your office tomorrow morning?" I said.

"What?" he asked, still distracted.

"Tomorrow, at your office? Eight o'clock?"

"Oh yes, yes," he said, not meeting my eye. "I promise. I will get you what you need."

Chapter Thirty-Four

After dinner, I went back to my little hotel, disappointed, but not surprised, that there were no messages from Jonathan at the front desk. That night I tossed and turned in the unfamiliar bed, wishing I was back in my apartment. I finally fell asleep for about an hour, but was up again at one in the morning, staring out at the lights of New York City, listening to the police sirens, wondering what the day would bring.

I couldn't stop thinking about the restaurant encounter with the married couple, Julius and Ethel Rosenberg. I started going over the history of the atomic spy ring in my mind, particularly the details about Liberal's wife, Ethel, that we knew for certain:

Intelligence on Liberal's wife: Surname that of her husband. Christian name Ethel. Married five years. Twenty-nine years old. Finished middle school. A fellow countryman. Sufficiently well-developed politically. She knows about her husband's work . . . in view of her delicate health she does not work.

The odds were that it was not a coincidence at all. Liberal had to be Julius Rosenberg, who lived in the same complex as his friend and "comrade" Quantum, aka Peter Walker. I wished I could call Meredith to tell him, or even Bob, but I knew that was impossible.

My thoughts turned to my uncle and his lack of remorse for his actions, betraying his country by sharing scientific secrets along with Klaus Fuchs and others, changing the course of history as a result.

His unapologetic gall in what he had done was shocking, but now I understood his humanity and rationale too.

Sometime just before three a.m. I fell asleep, waking up at seven to get dressed quickly, grab some coffee in the hotel lobby, and head to Columbia.

It had gotten colder overnight; the New York sky was whitish gray, and a light, pretty snow was coming down. The tiny flakes swirling around me made me think of the story of the girls at the camp in New Mexico, and I shuddered, quickening my pace, not wanting to be late for our eight o'clock meeting.

There were several cars parked in front of Hamilton Hall when I arrived, including two black Fordors and one gray Ford, all with government plates. I stopped short about twenty feet from the building when a man in an overcoat and fedora came out of the front entrance carrying a huge cardboard box, putting it in the trunk of the gray Ford. Then two more G-men emerged from the building with boxes. I shuddered, filled with feelings of dread. If the FBI was here, this did not bode well for my meeting with Peter.

It occurred to me I could run, but then what would I do? Hide like a fugitive in a hotel in New York City? Flee the country? That would be crazy when I hadn't done anything wrong. At least I hadn't done anything wrong up until yesterday, when I had finally reached out to my uncle, a confirmed Soviet agent, for help.

I braced myself for what I had to do next. The only way out of my situation was through, whether Peter Walker had delivered on his promises or not. I had to face whatever was happening in that building.

Inside, students were milling about, whispering with one another and giving curious looks to the men in almost identical overcoats and fedoras, carrying box after box down the hallways and out to their cars. At least one of the FBI agents gave me a double take as I went upstairs, but I kept going until I reached the third floor.

A man walked out of Peter Walker's office, no overcoat, looking down at his notebook, and I recognized Bob Lamphere immediately.

"Bob," I said, a little breathless from the climb and the fear of what I was about to discover. He looked up at me, his eyes wide.

"Catherine! Oh, thank God you're okay. After we got here this morning, we weren't sure," he said.

"Why?" I frowned, and then I looked past him into the office and gasped at the complete disarray. The walls of the office were bare. The pictures, the diplomas and awards, the Hiroshima article—everything was gone, just hooks and wall mounts indicating they had once been there. The desk and file cabinet drawers were open and empty. Even the tiny photo of the Trinity explosion was missing. The only thing that remained were the books on the bookshelves, and they were being packed up by agents.

"His apartment is also emptied of all personal effects," Bob said, and it sounded like he was talking at the other end of a tunnel because it was hard to process what was happening. It was making me feel woozy.

"But I . . . I was with him just hours ago," I said. "He offered to help me. Where . . . where on earth did he go?"

"Yes, we know you were with him yesterday evening. Here, you look like you need to sit," Bob said, lowering me into the chair that I had sat in just the day before. "We think he fled to Mexico. Since the Fuchs arrest was made public, several Russian spies have left the country. Mexico is a top destination."

"Mexico." I took a deep breath and closed my eyes, trying to keep it together, because falling to pieces in front of Bob or anyone else was not going to help my cause.

"I know why you came here, and I understand," Bob said, a mix of compassion and obvious frustration in his voice. "But this going rogue, coming up here on your own to try to fix this? I wish you and Dardis had talked to me. You have to come down to the field office for questioning now. Obviously."

"I . . . I understand," I said, angry and embarrassed that my plan had failed. "Where is Jonathan?"

"Oh, well, he's on his way back from DC, a day later than expected. I'm taking over his work on the Soviet espionage unit. When he gets to New York, he'll find out he's been suspended. I don't think I need to explain why," Bob said, and I buried my face in my hands.

~

The room they placed me in at the FBI field office in the US District Court office in Foley Square was painted sanitarium yellow and smelled of cleaning products, cigarette smoke, and stale urine. There was a rickety metal table and four well-worn folding chairs, their thin, upholstered seats ripped and dingy-looking. Bob made sure someone brought me cups of coffee and water. I contemplated how long I would be able to keep this situation from my father and brothers and prayed I had not ruined Jonathan's life, as well as my own, by going to see a man that I never should have trusted.

After an hour the door finally opened, and Bob came in with a husky guy probably in his fifties, sporting a thick black mustache, with heavy bags under basset hound eyes.

"Catherine, this is Agent Harvey. He's going to be doing most of the questioning," Bob said.

"Nice to meet you, Catherine," Harvey said, shaking my hand. "Okay, so let's start with . . ."

"Before we get started, could I have a word alone, with Bob?" I gave Harvey the sweetest smile I could muster under the circumstances. He looked over at Bob.

"Just give us five minutes, please. I've known Catherine a long time now," Bob said.

Harvey did not seem pleased, but he sighed and left, saying he'd be back in five.

"I'm sorry I've created such a mess," I said. "You have to believe me, though."

I told him everything—my suspicions about Philmore and Weissman, and everything I had discussed with Peter Walker, including what he had promised me, to clear my name.

"Oh no, you didn't really think he'd betray his comrades for you?" Bob gave me a look of pity.

"I really—look, I know it sounds naive, but I did." I sighed, feeling ridiculous for thinking it. "But listen, I think he might have already betrayed them. You need to go back to Knickerbocker Village. I think one of his friends who lives there is Liberal."

"What? What are you talking about?" Bob said, throwing up his hands in aggravation. "Catherine, you are in enough hot water without sending the FBI out on wild goose chases."

"Hear me out. I swear to you I'm not." I explained going to dinner at the Bird in Hand and meeting Julius and Ethel Rosenberg, and that Peter Walker knew they were going to be there. His eyes lit up when I mentioned Julius's name.

"Wait, Julius Rosenberg was the man's name? You're positive?"

"Of course. And his wife was *Ethel*, who looked like she was in her early thirties, definitely around the same age Liberal's wife would be now," I said.

"I know that name, Rosenberg. He's come up in at least one investigation before, though I'd have to look back," Bob said, taking out his notebook.

"I . . . I mean, Peter Walker's gone now, so yeah, who knows," I said. "But last night? I honestly felt he had introduced me to them on purpose."

"I think I'm going to go look him up, maybe pay him a visit," Bob said. "Catherine, I believe you, because I *know* you. I know that you are not a spy and that you were not conspiring with your estranged uncle. But Philmore and Weissman are well respected."

"Uh-huh." I rolled my eyes.

"I know they come across as a little cagey," Bob said. "But nothing has come to light about either of them. And believe me, I've had my team check. For your sake."

"Thank you for that," I said.

"You're welcome," Bob said. "But I'm not going to lie: the evidence Philmore has? The letters, the forgery is perfect. It looks like your handwriting, and then he has his witness, the young MI6 agent who claims to have seen you. And especially after all of this? You could still be charged. It's not up to me."

"So what do I do?" I said, despair washing over me. My life as I knew it would be over. No more Arlington Hall, no friends, no possible future with Jonathan. And I thought of my father and brothers, how devastated they would be. How disappointed and ashamed. Bob could tell I was barely holding it together.

"Answer all of Harvey's questions," he said, his tone sympathetic. "It will probably take more than one day. You'll stay in the same hotel tonight. We'll have it under surveillance to make sure you don't head to Mexico too."

"You know I would never . . ."

"*I* know that, but just do everything by the book from now on. Promise me? In the meantime, I'm going to have someone follow up this potential Rosenberg lead. Meredith is also trying to gather some more information that might help your cause."

"Meredith believes me too?"

"Of course he does," Bob said in a quiet voice. "He's not exactly what you'd call an emotional guy, but it's no secret you're one of his favorites."

And that's when I finally burst into tears.

∼

Agent Harvey questioned me for almost three hours, making me rehash everything that had transpired with my uncle the day before, trying to see if my story changed by making me repeat it multiple times. He also questioned me about the alleged sightings of us together prior to this week, and the two supposed letters I had written him in the past that MI6 had "discovered."

My story, and my denials regarding the fake evidence against me, never wavered, but I had a whopping headache after sitting in the stuffy, foul-smelling room for hours. And at five o'clock, Bob told Harvey that it was time to call it a day, and we could reconvene in the morning.

The Women of Arlington Hall

Bob offered to give me a ride back to my hotel, but I told him I needed some air and would prefer to walk at least part of the way there, and he agreed to it.

"There'll be two agents parked out front overnight," Bob said as he stood inside the entrance of the Foley Square office building. "Not so much because we think you're a flight risk, more because we're really hoping your uncle surfaces and comes to see you."

"Got it," I said, "Thank you for believing me. I'll see you tomorrow."

We said our goodbyes, and I watched him leave as I buttoned my coat and pulled on my gloves. When I stepped outside, I took a deep breath in, relieved to be in the fresh air, despite how freezing it was.

"Finally! I thought they might keep you there all night." Gia was standing on the steps, shivering but smiling at me in her banana-yellow wool coat.

"What, how?" I ran over to her, and we hugged as tears stung my eyes. "What are you doing here?"

"I know you're trying to keep this from your father and brothers," Gia said. "I get it. But you need *some* support. Me, Effie, Rosemary— we're your family too. I was the one nominated to come check on you. Effie and Rosemary wanted to come, but that would have raised some serious eyebrows in Building B."

"Do people know what happened?"

"Not exactly? They do know that your 'family emergency' is a little more complicated than originally thought. And clearly if you've spent the day being questioned by the FBI, it is," Gia said. Studying my face, she added. "How are you? You look like death."

"Thanks." I smiled. "I'm better now that you're here. Thank you so much for coming."

"Come on," she said, hooking an arm around my elbow. "There's a coffee shop just across the street. Let's warm up and get you some food."

Minutes later, we were settled into a black-and-white leather booth in the back of the empty diner with large cups of coffee in front of us. Gia signaled the waitress to also bring two slices of apple pie.

"Have you eaten since you got here? You're looking too thin," she said.

"Again, thanks for your brutal honesty." I smiled.

"So, can you please tell me a little more about what is going on? Because we are all worried sick. I swear Meredith looks like he's going to have a stroke, he's such a wreck about you."

"I'll tell you, confidentially, though most of it you already know from our work. But I've been talking for hours, so forgive me if I keep it brief."

I told her, starting with what Jonathan and I had discussed the night I saw him, then moved on to my reunion with my uncle, to what had happened since I had arrived at his office that morning.

"Well, hell, Cat," Gia said, sitting back in the booth, a stunned expression on her face. "This is even worse than I expected."

"It's . . . it's not great." I bit my lip and nodded. "But questioning went all right today, and Bob Lamphere is on my side and has some leads, so . . ."

"Before I forget, this is the card for Rosemary's family lawyer." She took an ivory-colored embossed business card out of her wallet and put it on the table between us. "He's a bigwig, and Rosemary said if you end up needing a lawyer, call him, and I quote, 'The Biddles will pick up the tab, no questions asked.'"

"That's . . . incredibly generous," I said. "But I hope it doesn't come to that."

"Oh, and Effie packed some extra clothes for you just in case. Here," Gia said, handing me the small floral travel bag she had been carrying.

"What about *your* clothes?" I frowned, taking it from her, touched by my friends' care.

"I already dropped them off at my parents'," she said. "Why don't you come and stay there with me? It's no palace, but it's more comfortable than a hotel. And I guarantee my mother's food is better."

"Thank you, I'm just—I'm not sure I'm allowed." I cringed.

"Well, if you're here for more than another night or two, I'll talk to Bob myself and insist," Gia said as the waitress placed five-inch-tall pieces of apple pie in front of us.

"Thank you, G," I said, my voice cracking as I tried and failed once again to keep my emotions in check.

"You'll get through this," she said, reaching across the table and squeezing my hand, echoing the words Jonathan had said to me. "Eat your apple pie. You need your strength. And . . . I have some news that might cheer you up, at least a little."

"I doubt that," I said, forcing myself to take a bite of the apple pie.

"There's another reason I'm here, not that I wouldn't have come anyway, but I'm killing two birds," Gia said.

"What? What is it? Is one of your sisters having a baby again?"

"You think that qualifies as something that would cheer you up? You know me better than that."

"Okay, tell me," I said.

"I'm here to inform my parents that I am going to be getting engaged soon, to a slightly younger man who is extremely tall, brilliant but a little odd, and neither Italian nor Catholic."

"Gia," I said, choking on my third bite of apple pie. "Gia? Cecil? Oh my . . ."

"Yup," she said, smiling. "What can I say? I'm crazy about my UFO-obsessed man. And I want to thank you."

"Why me?" I said, giving her a questioning look.

"Because you made me look at him in a different light, to see the incredible goodness beyond his many quirks."

I jumped up and gave her a hug. She was right. It was the kind of happy news that took me out of my own dire circumstances.

"All right, that's enough," she said, laughing as I sat back down. "But it's too bad you can't be there when I tell them, because my father is going to have an absolute fit. It's going to be a total *show*. Honestly? You'll probably be able to hear him yelling from your hotel."

Chapter Thirty-Five

Gia promised to return to the FBI office to see me the next morning, saying that she would be there for me for any coffee or lunch breaks I was allowed. I arrived back at the hotel an hour later, and, as promised, there was a black Ford across the street, two agents sitting in the front seat with a perfect view of the hotel entrance. Before going inside, I gave them a small wave, and the younger of the two gave me an enthusiastic wave back, while the older one scowled at him.

Off the lobby, there was a pianist in the corner of the cocktail lounge playing "As Time Goes By," and a half dozen couples were sitting at small, round tables enjoying the music with their drinks. Something about the song, about seeing those couples, made me feel nostalgic and melancholy, and my momentary cheer from Gia's visit faded, replaced by pure anxiety and dread.

By the time I reached my hotel room, my mood had turned dark, and the only thing to do was wash up and go to bed. Stepping into the hot, steamy shower, I let more tears fall. My harebrained plan to ask my uncle for help had only made my situation worse, and I was furious at myself for putting my trust in a stranger. He had made a promise, and I had naively believed his act, his emotional reaction to meeting me, his supposed love for my mother, and his bitter regrets.

And now he was gone, choosing to save himself and leave me under more suspicion and facing possible charges. How could I have been so stupid? Had I been so desperate to connect with someone in my mother's family that I'd just assumed he'd be a decent, upstanding person because we were blood relatives?

I changed into my yellow flannel pajama set that Effie had packed for me, and as I was towel-drying my hair, there was a knock on the door that made me jump.

"Yes," I said before opening. "Who is it?"

"Cat, it's Jonathan."

I unlocked the door with shaking hands, because I'd never wanted to hear someone's voice as much as I wanted to hear his. He was standing in the hall in his overcoat, giving me a small smile as he held up a pizza box and a bottle of wine, and my heart felt like it could burst wide open.

"Hi," he said. "I thought you might be hungry. How . . . how are you?"

"I've been better," I said, promising myself I wouldn't cry as I opened the door so he could come in. Given that I was already in my pajamas, I was definitely crossing a line, inviting him into my hotel room. But after everything that had happened, I was beyond caring about decorum.

"Should . . . should you even be here?"

"No, of course not." He placed the pizza and wine down on the dresser. "But the thought of you all alone in this hotel after what happened today? Bob knew from the look on my face that nothing was going to stop me from coming here to see you."

"What about the guys sitting in the car out front?" I asked, moved by his words, but still worried at the consequences.

"I took the side entrance, and honestly? Those two aren't exactly the crème de la crème of the force, so I'm not too worried."

"Jonathan, I feel horrible about your suspension," I said. "This is such a mess, and now it seems what you did for me was all for nothing. I don't even . . ."

"No, stop. Please," he said, taking my hands and looking into my eyes. "Because I need to say some things that I should have said a long time ago. I was broken when I came back from the war, drinking and dating a new girl every week and spending my father's money, just trying to forget what happened over there. But then came the opportunity with the FBI, the training, the purpose, and I finally started to grow up, to figure out my life."

"I know . . . and now—" I said, holding his hands tighter as he pulled me closer into him, making me catch my breath.

"I should never have gone to London," he interrupted me, hand on my cheek now, tracing my jaw with his thumb. "I should never have left after that night we first kissed. I've regretted it ever since. But I wanted to prove that I deserved someone like you. I thought . . ."

"Shh . . ." I whispered, and he kissed me with fierce intensity, as the longing that had been building inside both of us since that night in the snow finally hit us like a hurricane. And everything else in the world disappeared except for us, in this moment in time, and it was all that I needed.

I inhaled the scent of him, cologne tinged with sweat, and pressed up against him just as he pulled me in tighter.

With my heart beating out of my chest, he took off his coat, and then we kept kissing, kneeling on the bed, his hands under my pajama top, as I unbuttoned his shirt, breathless and not able to keep from exploring each other. He impatiently ripped his white T-shirt over his head, and I threw my top to the floor as he gently tugged at my pants.

I kissed his bare shoulder, and with a quiet groan he pulled me down onto the bed, and I was underneath him, looking into his eyes, running my hand down his back.

"You're so beautiful," he said, his voice rough with emotion.

"I wanted it to be you at the door. Only you." I sighed, wrapping one of my legs around his. "Please, stay with me tonight?"

"Of course. We're going to take our sweet time, forget our troubles for a few hours." He smiled as he kissed my collarbone, one hand tangled in my hair. "I've been waiting for a night like this, with you, for longer than you can possibly imagine."

∽

We finally fell asleep around two in the morning, and I woke a few hours later just as the sun was coming up. Jonathan was fast asleep next to me in bed, his hair sticking up in all directions, making me imagine what he must have looked like as a little boy. I grabbed a blanket, wrapped it around myself and walked over to the window to look out at the sights and sounds of the city waking up, the morning delivery trucks and newspaper carriers, a coffee shop across the street, orange neon "Open" sign glowing, already doing a steady business.

I had an urge to crawl into bed next to him and never leave. But after getting caught up in an unforgettable, blissful night, it was time to face reality and get ready to go back to the FBI office in a couple of hours. My dread had come rushing back with the sunrise.

A half hour later, I walked out of the bathroom dressed for the day, a towel around my head. Jonathan was sitting up against the pillows, still shirtless, and I suddenly felt a little nervous and shy, wondering where we would go from here. But then he held out his hand to me and grinned, and those feelings melted away.

"Look at you, already showered and dressed," he said. "Come here."

He pulled me into his arms, and I leaned against him as he pulled the towel off my head and kissed my hair.

"What happens for you now?" I said, and he groaned.

"I know we have to talk about it, but I wish we could just stay in this bubble of a hotel room and forget everything."

"You read my mind," I said. "But . . . ?"

"So, I have to go in for an interrogation this afternoon about why I did what I did, why I told you everything that I told you. I shouldn't have let you come here on your own. And I'm so sorry your uncle left you high and dry. You must be devastated."

"Yes, but mostly I feel like a complete fool," I said.

"I wouldn't have let you do it if I didn't think it was worth taking the risk," he said.

"I'm also scared, and frankly furious that Philmore and Weissman are trying to pin all this stuff on me, and that I made it worse . . ."

"Hey, hey, we'll get through this," he said, stroking my hair. "I told you."

"But what if we don't?" I said, sitting up. "What if we lose our jobs, or if, God forbid, they still end up charging me?"

"They might even charge me, Killeen. Who knows at this point? But even if the worst happens, we'll figure it out, together." He leaned down, holding my face in his hands. "Do you know why?"

"Why?" I said, my eyes welling up.

"Because I am completely crazy about you," he said, kissing the tear on my cheek. "I have been for longer than you know. And I'm not letting anything come between us ever again."

We kissed, gently at first, but then more intensely as he pulled me on top of him and his hands slid underneath my sweater.

"You know, you've still got a whole two hours until you have to be at Foley Square," he said.

"Is that right?" I smiled, melting into his arms, forgetting about the world one last time while I could.

Chapter Thirty-Six

"Thank you for coming back. But I'm not sure they'll let you come inside with me," I said, as I gave Gia a hug in front of the FBI offices.

"Oh yes, they will," she said. "I asked Bob when he was on his way out of the building yesterday. At first he said no, but I told him I had an uncle who would make a few calls, so they would have to let me come in with you, and he rolled his eyes and said fine."

"You have no idea how happy I am about that," I said as we headed inside.

"You look pretty chipper for someone who might be charged with conspiring to commit espionage today." Gia raised an eyebrow at me. "What's going on?"

"Yes, well, I had a visitor last night," I said, and I filled her in on Jonathan showing up at my hotel.

"I *knew* it," Gia said, giving me a playful shove. "Well, if you end up in prison, at least you'll have a night to remember."

"Okay, I love you, but no more sarcasm please," I said. "I'm too much of a wreck about what's going to happen today."

"I'm so sorry," she said, giving me another hug. "It's mostly because I'm so nervous for you."

"I know," I said. "Now, how did breaking the news to your parents about Cecil go? Okay?"

"Oh no, it was a complete disaster. My father isn't speaking to me. I told them how tall he was, so my mother was sobbing and carrying on about me having long, pale-skinned babies."

"Oh no, that's not good," I said.

"I think they'll come around. This is just what they do," Gia said, though she didn't sound convinced. "They did this with my sister Dee when she said she wanted to marry her husband, Frankie. My mother cried for days because 'Frankie is so stupid he'd eat rocks.'"

"Ouch," I said.

"Yeah, sadly in his case it's true, though," Gia said.

We reached the reception area on the third floor, and Bob came out to greet us, holding a cup of coffee, a bulky manila envelope under his arm.

"Gia, I am happy to have you here for Cat, but you know I can't let you come into the interview room with her," Bob said.

"Fine." Gia sighed dramatically. "I'll go get a coffee and the papers downstairs."

I followed Bob back into the foul-smelling interview room and sat down, ready to get on with it.

"Where's Agent Harvey?" I asked when we were both seated.

"I told him I'd handle things from here," Bob said. "There are some developments we need to discuss. This was dropped off by a bike messenger early this morning."

He placed the bulky ten-by-twelve manila envelope on the table in front of me. It was addressed to *Catherine Killeen, care of Agent Bob Lamphere.*

I looked up at Bob in shock, the hairs on the back of my neck standing on end.

"I've only seen his handwriting once, but . . . I think that's . . ."

"It's addressed to you. Just *open* it already." Bob pushed it across to me. "I was going to do it myself, but I decided to wait and let you do it when you got here."

I tore open the top of the envelope and dumped the contents on the table. There were two business-size envelopes inside, one with my name on it, one just marked *FBI*, and two sealed bags with photographs, marked *Personal* and *Business*. I opened the letter addressed to me and started reading.

> Dear Catherine,
>
> By the time you read this letter, I will be gone. I had been planning my departure for some time, but when you arrived at my office, it forced me to put my plan into action sooner than later. As I said during our dinner, I've known from our own sources inside the US government that the FBI, with the help of your team at Arlington Hall, has been getting close to identifying several of us. Making the decision to help you precipitated my plans to leave.
>
> I'm sorry you were greeted with such an unpleasant surprise when you arrived at my office, and I hope your day at the FBI was not too grueling. The contents of this package should ensure that it does not happen again.
>
> I promised that I would get you what you needed, and here it is. Inside the envelope marked *FBI* is a letter stating that I had never corresponded with you nor met you in my life and that any evidence against you is fabricated. Now they may dismiss the letter, but they will not be able to discount the evidence contained therein. For what it's worth, the letter was also notarized by a dear respected colleague at Columbia shortly after our dinner.
>
> This package also contains photographs identifying certain Russian agents that have been eluding the FBI for a long time. And I am certain it

will help your cause, and the combination of the letter and the evidence will let you get on with your life and that job that you seem to love.

Why would I betray my comrades for a niece I have only just met? My dear Catherine, think of it as a way of apologizing for not being a better brother, for not reconciling with my beloved sister, nor having the courage to defy my parents and be the uncle that you and your brothers deserved growing up. It is part of my process of repentance, what we call teshuvah in the Jewish faith.

Regarding my decision to share atomic intelligence during the war, as I tried to explain, many of the scientists at Los Alamos pushed for the science to be available internationally and thought that an American monopoly on atomic weapons was far too dangerous. You've read the article about Hiroshima and heard my story of the girls' camp—to this day I'm surprised that *more* of my fellow scientists did not make the choice that I did.

Ultimately, a few of us felt passionately enough to take matters into our own hands and share scientific secrets with the Soviet Union. In the end, history is something that is shaped by ordinary people. That is what Klaus Fuchs, and others like myself, tried to do. For that, I still have no regrets.

Americans tend to think of the world of espionage as black-and-white, good guys versus bad guys, but ultimately there are only many shades of gray on both sides of this conflict.

I do hope that someday we meet again, as it healed something in my soul to see your face the other day, to see part of the brilliant legacy my dear sister has left behind. I do believe our paths were destined to cross. I'm just sorry that our time together was short. I will send you a postcard from wherever I end up in the world.

With affection,
Peter Walker

The photos in the personal packet were of my mother as a toddler, as a grade-schooler with braids, and in a theater program from a play she was in as a teenager. After all I had been through, it was almost too much to take, to finally see these scraps of history, this woman I had never known, gone too soon.

And as Bob read the notarized letter out loud to me, I dared to feel hopeful and relieved for the first time since I'd walked into the FBI's offices that morning. Peter had not abandoned me or used me as a scapegoat; he had delivered on his promise to help. Would it be enough for the FBI to let me go? To get my job back?

Bob then turned to the photographs marked *Business*, his expression going from neutral to pleased as I held back from jumping up to look over his shoulder. Finally, he handed me one of them. It was dated March 1945, grainy, and taken from a distance, but I recognized both men, walking out of a pub in London.

"That's Klaus Fuchs and . . . oh my God . . . is that *Lindsay Philmore?*" I said.

"Indeed, it is," Bob said.

"I *knew* it! I knew it before I even overheard Philmore at his party," I said, slamming my hand on the table. "But then he and Weissman accused me, and—"

"I know Cat, I know. Calm down," Bob said, laughing as he handed me another photograph. "That's Lindsay's best friend, Ron McAllister, in front of the British embassy in Washington, with his very pregnant wife."

"But that doesn't tell us anything," I said.

"No, but thanks to a recently deciphered message, we know that whoever the mole was at the British embassy paid several visits to his pregnant wife, who was living in New York at the time. This is your uncle confirming our suspicions. And finally, this one, this one is the most interesting."

He handed me the last photo, and I gasped. It was a much younger Julius Rosenberg, standing with two other men, smiling. I read the back of the photo.

"*Julius and David, Young Communist League party, October 1939.*"

"Who are the other two?" I asked. "Do you know?"

"That is Julius with his brother-in-law David Greenglass," Bob said. "Who happened to work at Los Alamos as part of the special engineering unit working on implosion."

My mouth dropped open as I looked up at Bob and down at the picture again.

"But wait, there's more," Bob said, clearly enjoying my reaction as he took out his notebook, thumbing through his notes. "I remembered where I had heard the name Julius. It was in Elizabeth Bentley's confession in '45. She mentioned meeting with an 'engineer named Julius at New York's Knickerbocker Village apartment complex.'"

"So, Julius is Liberal, the ringleader?" I said, taking it all in.

"With a wife named Ethel, safe to say he's our number-one suspect." He nodded. "And we think Greenglass is the spy code-named Kaliber, and the spy code-named Gus is Harry Gold, the chemist."

"Oh my God," I said, looking up at him, stunned. "I keep thinking about Meredith's board, the code names in the atomic spy ring, clues but not names. I was beginning to think we'd never find out who they were."

"No kidding," Bob said, and he looked as exhausted as I felt. "And it's about damn time. I know in your uncle's letter, he mentions doing it for noble reasons, but the egos of these men. They're traitors, every damn one of them."

"One question: How is Weissman connected to all of this?" I said.

"We don't really have evidence that he is, except the conversation you overheard, which he denies," Bob said, and I started to protest, but he held up his hand. "Now I know, I *know* you were telling the truth, but still, we can't do anything on hearsay."

"Could you get him out of Building B?"

"Not yet," Bob said, and I sat back in my chair, fingering the photo of my mother as a toddler at Brighton Beach in Brooklyn.

"So Weissman aside, did he give you enough? Is this enough, am I . . . am I going to be charged?" I said, at the edge of my seat now. "Or fired, or held, or whatever? Do I need a lawyer? Because apparently I have one I can call . . ."

"This is more than enough," Bob said, waving his hand across the table. "Now, you went rogue under, let's face it, incredibly bizarre circumstances, though in the end you didn't violate your secrecy oath. You didn't tell your uncle anything he didn't already know."

"You know I didn't," I said.

"And you certainly didn't conspire to commit espionage. But there may be some sort of probationary period before you can return to Arlington Hall."

"Do you really think they'll let me return to my job? Really?"

"I don't want to get ahead of myself, but there's this letter, these photos, and as I said, you're a favorite of Meredith's. I think they will figure out a way to take you back."

"I pray you're right," I said, still uncertain, but a tremendous weight had been lifted, and everything seemed brighter, even the ugly yellow walls. "So, I'm free to go?"

"Yes, Cat, you're free to go." Bob grinned.

"Thank you, thank you so much!" I jumped up and gathered my things, but then I stopped myself.

"What?" Bob said. "Did you forget to tell me something?"

"What's going to happen to Jonathan?" I asked.

"Ah, Jonathan," Bob said. "He's suspended, as you know. And there'll be an internal investigation. Given how this appears to be playing out, the odds are in his favor. I've always said he's a star, and I, for one, still want him on my team."

"That's great news," I said, my heart soaring.

"That said, Cat, I wouldn't be surprised if Hoover made an example of him by shipping him to some far-off field office for six months to a year. He's done it before, as a way to punish an agent for an indiscretion. And let's face it, this is an enormous one."

"Oh no," I said, my hopes sinking, a pain in my chest at the thought of him being so far way again. "I guess we'll have to just see what happens."

I thanked him once more, and we said our goodbyes, but just as I opened the door to leave, he spoke. "For the record, Cat, what Dardis did for you? Risking his entire career, being willing to throw it all away?"

"Yes?" I said, and Bob just tilted his head at me smiled.

"Well, if that isn't love . . . I don't know what is."

"I know," I said.

Chapter Thirty-Seven

"I wish you could stay in New York," Jonathan said the next morning as we stood at Penn Station with our arms around each other.

"Me too," I said into his ear.

The night before, we had gone out to dinner in Little Italy with Gia and some of her sisters and their husbands and laughed and drank wine and ate fresh pasta until our stomachs ached. And instead of staying with Gia and her family, I had gone home to Jonathan's apartment in Greenwich Village, where we had fallen into bed with each other and stayed up until the early morning hours, not wanting the night to end.

"Hey, lovebirds, that's enough. Wrap it up," Gia said, coming up behind me.

"You know it's different this time," Jonathan said, looking down at me. "Even if I end up in, I don't know, South Dakota or wherever for a while, it's temporary. I'm coming back."

"I know." I swallowed, trying not to get choked up and failing completely.

"I'm coming back to *you*," he said as he gave me one last, lingering kiss goodbye.

When Gia and I arrived at our apartment that evening, Effie, Rosemary, and Margaret had a welcome-home celebratory dinner prepared, consisting of Effie's fried chicken, green bean casserole, and mashed potatoes. And it felt so good to be in my friends' company, to know that most of the uncertainty that had been swirling around my life, my future, was over. It eased the sting of saying goodbye to Jonathan. But that night, falling asleep, all I could think about were our two nights together, and when we would get the chance to be together again.

It wasn't until the next morning while we were waiting in line to go through security at Arlington Hall that I started getting worried about what the day would bring.

"I don't know. I feel like Frank, or someone, is going to meet me on the other side of this and ask me to hand in my badge," I said.

"No, they would have fired you outright by now," Gia said.

"G's right. They would have just packed up your things and shipped them to our apartment," Effie said.

"Probably true," I said, exhaling as the guard nodded and greeted me as we passed through. "Of course, I dread having to deal with Weissman now that I know the FBI launched an investigation into me because of *him*. Ugh, I really can't believe he's still here."

"I know, but just steer clear," Effie said. "Don't even give him the time of day."

"I'd like to give him a hell of a lot more than the time of day," Gia said.

"Cat! Cat! You're here, you're back!" Cecil came running up to us on the path to Building B, swooping in and giving Gia a kiss on the cheek and then picking me up off the ground with his hug.

"Cecil!" I smiled. "It's so good to see you."

"Are you okay, after everything?" He looked at me. "Gia told me enough."

"I'm doing much better. Thank you, my friend," I said.

"Terrific. And I must tell you about Roswell . . ." Cecil said.

"Cecil, please just let her get a coffee before you tell her about the UFOs in Roswell," Gia said, grabbing his hand.

"Oh right, coffee." He kissed her hand and nodded.

Effie and I went downstairs to the café to get coffees, and naturally, the first person we walked right into was Bill Weissman, the man I had planned to avoid at all costs. His face went pale, and I gritted my teeth and gave him my phoniest smile, though I was so angry I was shaking with rage.

"Bill, just the man I didn't want to see," I said.

"Catherine, uh . . . you're back . . ." he said with a stutter, clearly shocked at the sight of me.

"I am, no thanks to you," I said.

"Catherine, you have to understand . . ." He looked at Effie as if for help, but she just glared at him, arms crossed.

"Oh no, no. Stop right there," I said, holding my hand up to his face. "You don't get to explain anything to me. You don't get to rationalize almost ruining my life! Conspiring with Philmore of all people. How *dare* you? And the thing is, you almost got away with it. Just . . . stay away from me. Do not speak with me. Ever. Do you understand?"

"I understand perfectly," he said with a nod, but he was stone-faced now, the apologetic tone gone, something glimmering in his eye, reminiscent of the night I had seen him with Philmore. As if he was still plotting, conspiring. "Good day."

"Well done," Effie said as we watched him walk upstairs. "For a minute there, I thought you might sock him."

"For a minute there, I considered it," I said. "He disgusts me."

"You're not alone in that," Effie said.

When we arrived back in the office, I received warm greetings and hugs from many of my coworkers, who had caught wind of at least part of my story. Meredith's door was open, and he must have heard some of the commotion because he peeked out, and we caught each other's eye.

"Catherine." He beamed at me.

"Meredith." I smiled back and gave him a wave.

"Can you please come in for a minute?"

"Of course." I grabbed a notebook and pen and felt like skipping into his office, but I restrained myself.

"Welcome back," he said.

"Thank you, it's such an enormous relief that you took me back," I said. "I know I need to meet with Frank and some of the other administrators up at the main hall. I understand I might be on some probationary period . . ."

"Not if I can help it," he said. "We are on the verge of deciphering messages that will identify more of this spiderweb of an atomic spy ring. I already told Frank; I need you too much for any of that nonsense."

"Oh," I said, swallowing, choked up hearing those words from him. "I . . . I don't know what to say, but thank you."

"Regarding what happened, I need to apologize. I understand why you did what you did. You must have felt so desperate when Dardis told you everything," Meredith said, his mouth in a tight line. "And shame on me, because I should have told you about your uncle myself, about the so-called evidence against you. You are a trusted and valued member of this team. But I was torn because . . ."

"Meredith, believe me, I understand the situation you were in," I said, moved by his words. "I probably wouldn't have told me either."

Just then, Rosemary knocked on the door and stuck her head in.

"Sorry to interrupt, but Meredith, you wanted me to tell you. Bob and Frank are here, with a couple other agents," she said.

"Not for me?" I said, gripping the arm of the chair, slightly panicked.

"No, definitely not for you," Meredith said. "But I wanted you to be here for this. I told Bob to wait until you were back today."

"For who, then?" Rosemary said, leaning against the doorframe.

"They're here for Weissman."

"Seriously?" Rosemary said, looking down the hall and back at Meredith with wide eyes.

"Wait, what?" I said.

"I'm afraid that we've had our own mole, right here in Building B. Since '45," Meredith said with disdain.

"All this time, he's been snooping around, leaning over our shoulders . . ." Rosemary said.

"Staying late," I added, my anger rising again. "And then he accuses *me* of exactly what he's been doing all this time?"

"Well, yes, the FBI has had him on their radar, and I think he knew it, so he and Philmore accused you as a way of deflecting. I don't know. He probably thought it would buy him some time," Meredith said.

He went on to explain that the FBI had recently interviewed a man who had been identified as a spy in the aircraft industry. The man told them that his KGB handler in the US in the early forties was named William Weissman. That Weissman helped him buy a camera to photograph documents, among other assistance.

"He's been doing this since the early forties?" I said, eyebrows raised.

"And then they hired him. He passed a background check to work *here*? Unbelievable, just unbelievable," Rosemary said, arms crossed. "You know, every single woman in this office has at one point or another expressed discomfort about him."

"All of that women's intuition was correct all along," Meredith said.

"Yup, it always is, and nobody ever believes it," Rosemary said.

"What happens now?" I asked.

"They're bringing him in for questioning," he said. "He's suspended from the ASA on suspicion of disloyalty. That's, at least, the beginning of the consequences. But the damage he has done, what he's shared? Well . . . it's devastating to even think about."

"Hey, the guys are bringing him in," Bob said with a knock on the door. "But did you hear about Philmore?"

"Are they bringing in Philmore as well?" I asked. "Because that would be too good to be true."

"No, Lindsay Philmore is gone. Along with his friend McAllister," Bob said.

"Where?" I asked. "Mexico?"

"Not quite," Bob said. "British intelligence has information that indicates the two of them have defected. To Russia."

Chapter Thirty-Eight

Friday, August 11, 1950

Dear Killeen,
Will I ever get used to calling you anything else? I'm not sure. I miss you so much. I try to remain distracted with work. There is plenty to do in El Paso in that regard. As promised, it wasn't a demotion, just a relocation. But I'm not sure Hoover could have sent me to a more far-flung place than this border town. I wish I was at least close enough to see you on the weekends. This might as well be on the other side of the world.

Reading the newspaper headlines over the past couple of months has been difficult to comprehend. You know I can't say much more in a letter except that we should both be proud of our contribution, that our hard work over the past couple of years is finally paying off.

The nights are long, and the days are brutally hot here, and I keep waiting for someone from the Bureau to tell me that I've done my time and can come back to the East Coast. Last week when I talked to Bob, he promised me he was still working on a transfer for me, that Hoover was considering it. But he's been saying that for a month now, and I'm frustrated.

After four months, I miss you more than I can say. I want to finally get an end date on my time here, so I can start counting the days until I see you again. I'll be honest, Killeen, you know I love this work, but if I don't get out of this field office purgatory soon, I may have to consider other career options. I told you I was coming back to you, and that is the most important thing to me now. I promise you that.

Thank you for your letters. Every time I see something in the mail from you, it makes my long, hot day in this place so much brighter.

I'll give you a call on Sunday night like we planned. I can't wait to hear your voice.

Yours,

Jonathan

"Another letter from Jonathan?" Rosemary asked, leaning against my desk with her cup of coffee, a rolled newspaper under her arm.

"Yes." I sat back in my chair, holding the letter like a promise. "Still no news about when they're going to let him come back."

"I'm sorry," she said.

"Thanks," I said. "I keep trying to plan a visit, but it would take me two days by train. Not exactly a weekend getaway."

"Definitely not," Rosemary said. "Speaking of, you're still coming this weekend, yes? The house will be all ready for us when we get there, refrigerators stocked. You'll have your own bedroom and bathroom."

"Yes," I said. "But shoot, I'm supposed to talk to Jonathan—our brief Sunday night phone call every few weeks."

"Oh, that's fine, we have a phone," Rosemary said. "And you can talk as long as you want. My family's accounting firm pays the bills; they won't bat an eye."

"Thank you, that's too generous," I said. "You know, I was picturing a cozy little beach cottage, but the fact that I'll have my own bed and bath—how big is this house?"

"Oh, it's pretty big." She smiled. "It's got seven bedrooms, nearly as many bathrooms."

"Rosemary, that's not a cottage, that's a mansion." I laughed.

"Maybe." She smiled. "I'm just happy we'll have it all to ourselves. We all need it after the way the summer's been going. Speaking of, did you see this?"

She put the newspaper she was holding on my desk. It was today's New York *Daily News*. I read the headline and the lead paragraph out loud:

FBI Arrests Atomic Suspect's Wife as Spy

Mrs. Ethel Greenglass Rosenberg, 34, mother of two, was arrested yesterday on charges of conspiring with her husband and her brother to steal atomic secrets and transmit them to the Soviet Union.

Starting in May, the roundup of the rest of the atomic spy ring had begun, just as Meredith and Bob had hoped it would. Harry Gold, the spy code-named Gus, the courier, was arrested and the first to confess, identifying Klaus Fuchs and David Greenglass as his sources at Los Alamos.

Then, in June, just as America entered the Korean War, David Greenglass, aka Kaliber, Ethel Rosenberg's brother, was arrested. He in turn gave up his brother-in-law Julius, code name Liberal, the linchpin in a vast network of Soviet spies involved in Enormoz, as we had long suspected.

It was Greenglass's wife alone who had said Ethel knew everything about Julius's activities. As a result, Ethel Rosenberg had been summoned by a grand jury on August 7 and had pleaded the Fifth Amendment.

"They gave her one more chance to answer questions, and she refused, so that was that," Rosemary said, as we both kept reading the article.

"They have to be doing this to put pressure on Julius to confess," I said. "I'm still surprised they arrested her; they don't have much of a case against her, from the looks of it, just her sister-in-law's words."

"And I thought my sister-in-law was bad," Rosemary said.

"Her own brother David is no better."

We kept talking about the Rosenbergs as we headed into Meredith's office for our meeting with him and Bob.

"Good morning, ladies, any word from Peter Walker?" Bob asked, as he did every time we saw each other. My answer was always the same.

"Nothing. Anything new about Philmore and Weissman?" I asked.

"Philmore's in Moscow, living the life of a disgraced British intelligence officer," Bob said. "Weissman is disgraced, but proving difficult to charge because we can't use any of our deciphered KGB messages in court."

"That's so ridiculous," Rosemary said. "After all the damage he did over the years."

"Indeed. We'll keep trying. So . . . you both saw the morning papers?" Bob said, his expression troubled, nodding at the copy of the *Daily News* that I was now holding. Meredith had his back to us this whole time, writing on the chalkboard, grumbling to himself.

"I keep thinking about her two boys," I said. "Who's taking care of the Rosenbergs' sons?"

"The thing is, they're just doing this to force Julius's hand," Meredith said, in an agitated tone as he turned around. "They *named* her. She didn't have a code name. The KGB had never considered her consequential enough to give her one."

He had written the code names that we had been tracking all along on the board.

ENORMOZ

REST—Klaus Fuchs

GUS—Harry Gold

KALIBER—David Greenglass

LIBERAL—Julius Rosenberg, "wife ETHEL—does not work."

"Even David Greenglass's wife had a code name, and she's not arrested," Meredith said, looking to Bob for an explanation.

"I know," Bob said. "But still, I find it hard to believe she didn't know *anything* about what Julius was up to. And remember, people believe the Russians would never have invaded Korea if they didn't have the atomic bomb, a bomb they developed via secrets that were stolen from us by the people on this board, among others."

"So, what are you saying?" I asked, feeling slightly ill, because I knew what he was getting at.

"Look, once more we're a nation at war, with American boys once again dying on distant battlefields, while anti-communist hysteria rages on thanks to people like Senator McCarthy. I'm *saying* that I worry that this country is looking for vengeance," Bob said. "And at the moment, the Rosenbergs are the perfect villains, and the only known targets on whom to exact that vengeance."

"Julius Rosenberg deserves any punishment he gets," Rosemary said. "But Ethel? Really?"

"No, she doesn't in my opinion," Meredith said, looking at his rows of code on his corkboard. "So, we keep working as we always have. I've got some new atomic spy leads I've recently uncovered that I want to review, two former Los Alamos workers in Chicago, now working on the hydrogen bomb. There are others that we can go after, bigger fish than Ethel Rosenberg. Let's brief the rest of the team."

Later that afternoon, I knocked on Meredith's door, and he was doing that thing he did, staring off at something nobody else could see.

"Yes? Catherine, sorry . . . What can I help you with?"

"We're supposed to be leaving early today, going to Rosemary's house for a long weekend?" I said. "She's up at the main building right now. But we were both saying, we could change our plans and work this weekend. I feel—I don't know if guilty is the right word, but Ethel's arrest, and we could work . . ."

"Stop," Meredith said, holding up his hand. "Tell me, when was the last time you took time off, a weekend away like this?"

"Aside from seeing my family over the holidays, it's been over a year, at least."

"That's what I thought. We've all worked so hard for so long," Meredith said, sitting back in his chair, looking at me with tired eyes. "And the thing my wife reminded me the other night, again . . . we're not going to decipher every message, identify every person. *Ever.* There will always be more code names, there will always be more work to do. And I'm afraid there will continue to be more bad news in the world that, somehow, *we'll* feel responsible for."

"You're right," I said. "But it's hard not to become obsessed. To want to try to solve the world's problems, or at least the ones in front of us."

"I agree, but we can't continue to let it take over our entire lives. And we can't control what is going to happen to the Rosenbergs, as much as we want to," Meredith said, his voice quiet. "Ethel and Julius Rosenberg made their choices long ago. We just happened to discover those choices.

"After these arrests, I don't know . . . I have realized that I need to spend a little more time away from here with my wife and kids, or I'll lose my mind. It's too much. You girls, you're younger than I am, you should start doing more of the same."

"Are you actually suggesting that we take time off?" I teased.

"It's not a suggestion, it's an order," he said. "So go, get out of here. Tell Rosemary I don't want to see any of you until next Wednesday."

"Really?" I said, unable to contain my shock.

"Really," he said.

"What about you? Are you actually going to take time off?"

"Yes, I promised my wife, we're going to Cape Cod at the end of the month," he said.

"Good," I said. "I'll hold you to it."

"Now go before I change my mind." He smiled. "Have fun."

I left his office, only to peek back in one more time.

"Thank you, Meredith. For everything."

"You're welcome, Catherine. Thank *you*. Good night."

Chapter Thirty-Nine

Monday, August 14, 1950

Somewhere beyond right and wrong there is a garden. I will meet you there.

—Rumi

The postcard from Mexico City, addressed to me, had arrived the day we left for Rosemary's family's beach house. The quote was from the poet Rumi, but no doubt the writing was Peter Walker's. He spoke of a metaphorical garden. Whether we'd ever meet in real life again remained to be seen.

I traced the quote on the postcard, thinking of my uncle in Mexico and the decisions that had led him there. The choices a person makes in life are shaped and influenced by a complicated calculus of time and circumstances and chance. Did I agree with Peter Walker's choices, betraying a country that had given him and his family everything? I didn't. But I understood him and the humanity behind his reasons now.

I put the postcard back in my overnight bag and took out Jonathan's most recent letter, rereading it for the fiftieth time, imagining his arms around me, the last time we were together. The fact that we had no date for when we would see each other again was making me crazy.

And now that I am old? I realize that time is even more fleeting than you can ever imagine at your age. And finding love—true, lasting love? Well, that is a rare thing.

I thought of my uncle's words, placing Jonathan's letter on the bed as I took out my favorite pale-pink cotton dress, my shoulders stinging from sunburn as I pulled it over my head. It was Monday of our girls' weekend at Rosemary's family's beachfront house in Delaware. The Biddles' beach house was called *Stella Maris*. It was a sprawling, weathered clapboard home with sea-foam-blue shutters, a large courtyard, and an even larger swimming pool. It had been eighty degrees and sunny every day, and three days in, I knew that this trip with my friends had been exactly what we all needed. Meredith was right. It was time we all tried to find a balance between our intense work and the rest of our lives.

The days away had also given me clarity. It was time for another before-and-after moment in my life, again of my own choosing. Only this time I wasn't running away; I was running toward something. Toward someone. And it had nothing to do with a job or career, but everything to do with what I wanted for my future.

"Cat, you coming down?" Effie knocked on my door, and I told her to come in. Her hair had bleached out from the sun, and she was wearing a blue piqué sundress with matching headband.

"The girls are having drinks and snacks on the porch, although it seems odd to call it a porch, given that it's bigger than my parents' entire home. Wait . . . what's wrong?"

"Nothing, just . . . I've decided to use a few more of the vacation days that I've accrued."

"Excellent idea," Effie said, looking at the letter in my hand. "But for what?"

"I'm going to go to El Paso," I said. "I know it's going to take me days to get there, but I don't care. I need to see him. Who knows . . .

maybe I'll even stay . . . I'm just . . . I miss him so much, Eff. And I'm . . ."

"In love with him," Effie said. It wasn't a question, because she knew the answer.

"Yes," I said, putting the letter back in my bag. It was as simple as that.

"You should absolutely go," Effie said. "I don't blame you one bit. But for now, come downstairs and have a drink with the girls. The sunset should be beautiful tonight."

"Sounds perfect," I said as we headed downstairs. "I'll figure out my plans tomorrow."

"You know, I'm actually starting to really like Margaret," Effie whispered. "Last night when we were playing cards, she was kind of hilarious."

"Agree. I told you it just takes some time to get to know her," I said. "And she makes Rosemary so happy."

"*So* happy," Effie said.

We arrived at the massive wraparound porch, with its stunning views of Rehoboth Beach just across a narrow dirt road, only two other sprawling homes visible in the distance. Gia, Margaret, and Rosemary were sitting in wicker chairs with their drinks, admiring the view of the ocean, the seagulls bobbing and weaving against a blue sky with cotton-candy white clouds.

"Rosemary, come on, exactly how rich is your family?" Gia asked. "Because this is the fourth house—that we know of."

"Do you know about the one in Bar Harbor, Maine?" Margaret said. She was very tan, freckles across her nose from the sun. She had let her hair grow long, and it was in a braid down her back. She looked so different than the Margaret I had met on my first day at Arlington Hall. Happiness changes a person from the inside out.

"That makes five houses," Gia said, holding up five fingers. "The Bar Harbor one is news to me."

"Well, cheers to the Biddles, and to Rosemary for generously inviting us to stay at one of the most beautiful homes I've ever seen," I said.

We all clinked our glasses together in a toast.

Rosemary went inside to get more refreshments, the screen door slamming behind her as she carried out a tray of snacks for us, placing them on the low wicker table. We sipped our drinks, chatting and laughing as the sun set over the ocean.

"Hey, Rose, is that one of your neighbors?" Effie asked, the headlights of a car far off in the distance coming down the dirt road.

"No, as far as I know, neither family is here," Rosemary said, standing up to get a better look.

"Is it Cecil?" I asked.

"He's not coming until tomorrow," Gia said. "He's bringing a friend, Eff. From the bowling team."

"Is he related to Rosemary? Because I think the next guy I date needs to own a home or two just like this one," Effie joked. She and Archie had permanently broken up since he had returned to London for good. As the car got closer, we could see it was a pale-blue convertible, driven by a man. Nobody else with him.

"Are you expecting any relatives?" Margaret asked, looking at Rosemary, a little nervous now.

"No, definitely not," Rosemary said, holding tight to Margaret's hand.

"Cat, call me crazy, but the guy in that car looks a little bit like Jonathan," Gia said.

"Don't be ridiculous, G. He's serving his time in El Paso," I said, also standing up to look now, just to get a glimpse. And now the five of us were lined up on the porch, watching the car approach.

"Uh . . . Cat . . ." Effie said, when the car was finally close enough to get a clear look at the driver.

I started blinking, shaking my head, my hand up to my mouth because it wasn't possible.

"I don't think you're taking that trip to Texas after all," Effie said, putting her arm around my shoulder, smiling.

"I knew it!" Gia said. "Hey, Dardis!"

"It really is Jonathan." Rosemary laughed, as the car pulled up across the street and parked.

"Go, Cat! Go—what are you waiting for?" Margaret said, giving me a playful shove, and I ran across the dirt road and straight into his arms.

"I found you. Thank God, I found you," he said as he picked me up and spun me around, and then he pulled me into his arms and kissed me despite the audience, and the girls cheered before disappearing inside the house.

"I just told Effie I was coming to see you. But you found me instead . . . how? How are you here now?" I said, as I put my hand on his unshaven face.

"Cecil gave me the address." He smiled. "I thought he might have gotten it wrong."

"But the FBI, your career, what are you going to . . ."

"Well, they're either going to let me stay on or fire me," he said. "But a few friends have recently moved to the CIA. I have options."

"Good," I said, relieved, still touching his face, not quite believing we were on a beach, together, in Delaware.

"Cat, don't you understand? That doesn't matter. The only thing that matters is you and me." He leaned down, kissing me again, arms around my waist. "I should have learned that from London. And I'm sorry that I had to go all the way to Texas to realize it. I woke up three days ago and said, '*Enough*. Not one more day. Not one more month or two or six. I'm not doing that again.' I needed to be with you now. And always."

"Always." I smiled through happy tears.

"I took a sixty-hour train ride to get back to you. Because I am completely in love with you. You are the one I've been waiting for. The love of my life," he said, his hands on my cheeks.

"I am head over heels in love with you," I said, laughing.

I was overcome again as he pulled me into another kiss, because it was hard to comprehend that it was possible to be this happy.

"Where'd you get the car?" I ran my hand down the door after we had finished kissing. "It's a pretty sweet ride."

"You like it? It's a Mercury convertible. I borrowed it from a friend."

"Nice," I said, and we both gave each other a look.

"So?" he said, putting his arms around me again.

"So? Want to take me for a drive in this behemoth?" I said.

"Killeen, are you asking if we're going to ride off into the sunset together, like in the movies?" He gave me that crooked smile that was going to do me in for the rest of my life.

"Something like that," I said. "It's a better ending than *Casablanca*."

"Of course it is," he said, as he opened the passenger-side door for me, taking my hand to help me climb in.

There was the sound of pebbles and rocks crunching underneath the wheels as he turned the car around, the Ink Spots' "Ask Anyone Who Knows" playing on the car radio. And as we pulled down the road, my friends ran out onto the porch again, waving wildly and hollering goodbyes to us. I leaned out of the back of the convertible, waving and blowing kisses back at them, holding tight to Jonathan's hand as we drove away.

Author's Notes

This is a work of fiction, but it is inspired by and incorporates true events and real people. Codebreaking and the early days of the Cold War are both complex and layered subjects, and to write a novel inspired by that era means honoring the historical facts. When writing historical fiction, my intention is to never alter the historical record in a way that is problematic or offensive. But ultimately this is a novel, not a textbook, and writing fiction requires taking some artistic license. These author's notes will hopefully help you understand my choices in that regard, and why sometimes I had to alter things to fit the narrative, while remaining loyal to the truth of the historical era and the events that took place during that time. Of course, any errors in fact are mine alone.

I'm often asked how I get my ideas. I've had this idea since 2018, when I came across an article in *Smithsonian* magazine entitled "The Women Code Breakers Who Unmasked Soviet Spies" by the brilliant author Liza Mundy. That is where I first learned of the Venona Project, which is now considered one of the greatest feats in the history of US cryptology, a project that continued until it was cancelled in 1980, and was only finally declassified in 1995. For the article, Mundy interviewed one of the last living female codebreakers from Venona, ninety-nine-year-old Angeline Nanni. I was captivated by her story and have read the article dozens of times since, trying to figure out how I could write a novel honoring the women of the Venona Project. Like many story ideas, this one took some time to marinate before I was ready to write it.

The cryptology seminar that Jonathan and Cat took together at Harvard/Radcliffe was fictional, but it was based on the courses that the US Army and Navy initiated, partnering with colleges like Radcliffe during World War II in an attempt to recruit women for roles in cryptology. The joint seminar in the story is based on these secretive cryptology courses that were offered at elite colleges across the United States.

The timeline of the major events in the story is accurate; the more minor events are as accurate as I could make them, though some dates might be altered slightly in certain cases to fit the timeline of the story.

The art and science of codebreaking is dense, and in the early chapters I tried to provide a primer for authenticity's sake. There was a *NOVA* episode from 2002 called "Secrets, Lies and Atomic Spies" that was incredibly helpful in breaking the process down in an understandable way. The "Attack at Dawn" code problem that Gene gives Cat to test her is taken directly from this episode. Two terrific books—Robert Lamphere and Tom Shachtman's *The FBI-KGB War* and Howard Blum's *In the Enemy's House*—were also helpful in this regard, and invaluable in understanding the story of the incredible, historic partnership between Robert Lamphere and Meredith Gardner.

Speaking of those men, FBI agent Robert "Bob" Lamphere and the ASA's genius codebreaker Meredith Gardner were real people, and their partnership is truly one for the history books. What they accomplished in the Venona Project, in breaking into the KGB's telegrams from the war years and tracking down atomic spies in the US and abroad as a result, was historic. It goes without saying that they deserve all the credit they have received since the project was declassified. However, in many sources, I read about the men and women who worked in Arlington Hall with Meredith, assisting and supporting him, as well as the team of agents that reported to Robert at the FBI. What if a female codebreaker working with Meredith fell for one of the young FBI agents working for Bob? That is the origin of Catherine and Jonathan's story.

Catherine Killeen and her friends are all composites based on the many brilliant, fascinating female codebreakers working at Arlington Hall, including women like Angeline Nanni, Gloria Forbes, Mildred Hayes, Carrie Berry, Mary Boake, Josephine Miller Deafenbaugh, Joan Malone Callahan, Helen Bradley, Juanita McCutcheon, Ruby Roland, and Gene Grabeel.

Rosemary's relationship with Margaret was inspired by the relationship between two real women of Arlington Hall, Ann Caracristi and Gertrude Kirkland. Kirkland eventually left government work, but Caracristi would go on to become the first female deputy director of the National Security Agency.

Jonathan Dardis and his coworkers are composites based on the agents working with Robert Lamphere at the time.

Cecil, Frank, and the other male characters working at Arlington Hall are also inspired by some of the men who worked there. The stories of UFOs that are Cecil's obsession are based on actual news stories of the time period, though some dates and details have been altered.

Bill Weissman and Lindsay Philmore are based on two real Soviet spies, but I changed their storylines to such a degree that it was necessary to fictionalize the characters entirely. Bill Weissman is based on William Weisband, who worked at Arlington Hall for many years before the team there was devastated to discover he was a Soviet spy. Lindsay Philmore is based on the famous and notorious Soviet spy Kim Philby, who rose up the ranks of MI6 and stole intelligence secrets from the British for the Soviets for several years. Lindsay Philmore's friend Ron McAllister is based on the real MI6 member and Russian spy Donald Maclean.

It is important to note that, of the three hundred Americans spying for the Soviets during World War II, only a hundred were ever identified. To this day, many are still only known by their code names. One of these was the spy code-named Quantum, who provided secret information related to gaseous diffusion in 1943. In the narrative, Catherine's uncle, the fictional Peter Walker, turns out to be Quantum.

In reality, Quantum's name is still not known, though there are theories as to his identity.

The Justice Department employee Judith Coplon, code name Sima, was the first Russian spy in the US that the team identified based on the KGB messages.

Meredith, Bob, and their teams did identify Klaus Fuchs, the Rosenbergs, and the rest of their atomic spy ring, though the dates of discovery are in some cases slightly altered from the actual dates they were uncovered. How they were able to put the pieces together from a codebreaking and investigative perspective is, of course, somewhat simplified for the sake of the story but based in truth.

J. Edgar Hoover did not attend a meeting with Meredith and Robert at Arlington Hall, although he was well aware of the Venona Project and kept tabs on it throughout his tenure.

President Truman was never informed of the Venona Project because there were suspected spies working in the White House at the time.

Elizabeth Bentley was a real Soviet spy who turned herself in to the FBI. All the details about her life and confession are based in fact.

According to declassified FBI documents, the Rosenbergs did rendezvous with other members of the CPUSA at a restaurant in New York City called the Bird in Hand.

Special Report Number One—the one that Meredith and his team sent to the upper levels of the US government—was not as revelatory as later reports, but I condensed the multiple reports into one for the purposes of narrative.

All Soviet spies had code names for KGB communications and cover names for working in the field. Often, they had multiple versions of both. For simplicity and to avoid confusion, I focused solely on the code names of the spies in the story.

Both the Soviet KGB and GRU, the Soviet military intelligence agency, were involved in spying in the US, but again, to avoid confusion I put all Soviet endeavors under the umbrella of the better-known KGB.

The Cairo Hotel was real and was part of the DC nightlife at the time. The Liberty Pub is a fictional bar. The Ink Spots did play in DC during the late forties but not at the Cairo as far as I know.

Idaho Hall was one of ten dormitories at Arlington Farms, where many young women working at Arlington Hall lived both during WWII and in the years right after the war.

The Italian American Bowling League of New York City is fictional.

The *New Yorker* article "Hiroshima" by John Hersey, from August 1946, is an incredible real piece of journalism that is worth reading.

The story of the dance camp in Ruidoso, New Mexico, and the girls there playing in "warm snow" that was actual radioactive fallout from the Trinity test bomb is heartbreakingly true.

Acknowledgments

Though writing this novel was, as always, a very solitary experience, publishing and getting it out into the world takes the effort of so many people. I may be a bit biased, but I think I work with some of the most talented professionals in the book business.

To my longtime former editor, Alicia Clancy: Thank you so much for acquiring this latest novel and for all of your hard work and excellent editorial instincts on my behalf over the years. I wish you so much success in your new endeavors.

To my developmental editor, Faith Black Ross: What an absolute gift it has been to work with you on all five of my books. I can't even begin to thank you for your brilliant and meticulous notes and for always pushing me to write the best possible book I can. You are one of the absolute best at what you do, and I am blessed to have had you as an editor for all these years.

To Nancy Holmes, my managing editor: Thank you for taking over this project so seamlessly, and for all your hard work on this novel. I'm thrilled to be working together and look forward to many more projects!

I am so thankful to the entire team at Lake Union Publishing, particularly editorial director Danielle Marshall, who plucked *The Saturday Evening Girls Club* manuscript from obscurity years ago—so thankful for your support, and I wish you so much success in your next chapter professionally. Thank you to the fabulous Gabriella Dumpit and the entire marketing and sales staff, and thank you to the amazing team of copyeditors and proofreaders who always make the book better in every way.

An enormous thank-you to my agent, Carly Watters at P.S. Literary, for your amazing support and expertise at every step of the publishing process and beyond. I'm so very grateful to have you on my team.

Thank you to the wonderful Ann-Marie Nieves of Get Red PR: You are a rock star in the book publicity business, and I'm so very grateful for your hard work and your friendship.

I'm thankful to the staff at the Center for Cryptologic History at the National Security Agency for so generously sending me materials about the Venona Project, including the invaluable book *Venona: Soviet Espionage and the American Response: 1939–1957*, edited by Robert Louis Benson and Michael Warner.

An enormous thank-you to Lisa Barr, Fiona Davis and Joy Jordan-Lake for taking time out of their very busy lives to give this story an early read and write such lovely words of praise for this novel. You all inspire me so much with your talent and kindness and support of the literary community.

Speaking of the literary community, I am constantly blown away by the generosity and kindness of my fellow fiction authors. I'm so grateful to write for a living, but the publishing industry can be very difficult at times, and it means so much to be able to have such terrific friends on my side. Sending love and gratitude to the many authors that I have been blessed to connect with in this business—thank you all!

To all the wonderful libraries and rock star librarians who have supported me from the start, thank you! I also have to say a huge thank-you to my local independent bookstores in Massachusetts, which have so generously worked with me: Book Ends in Winchester, Whitelam Books in Reading, and Molly's Bookstore in Melrose.

To all the book clubs that have chosen my novels over the years, thank you from the bottom of my heart. Your incredible support is one of the best parts of this author life.

To my readers around the world, many of whom have become friends: I would not be able to do any of this without your wonderful support over the past eight years. A million thanks for reading my stories, for telling your friends about my books, for writing reviews and sharing on social media, for listening to my Historical Happy Hour podcast, and for showing up to my webinars and in-person events.

My parents, Tom and Beth Healey are, quite simply, the best parents in the world: Thank you for being everything you are to our family—love you both so much.

To my daughters, Ellie and Madeleine: Being your mom is the best job I've ever had. You both inspire me every day with your kindness, creativity, and brilliance, and I love you more than I can say.

To Charlie: Thank you for being my marketing department, tech department, cheerleader, sounding board, and, most importantly, the love of my life. My writing dreams would not have come true without your unwavering support. I love our story best of all.

Book Club Questions

1. Before reading this novel, had you ever heard of the US codebreaking operation known as the Venona Project?

2. Did the book introduce you to any new historical details or events that you hadn't previously known about?

3. Were any aspects of the early Cold War years in America surprising to you?

4. Which character in the story was the most compelling to you? Why?

5. As a woman in the 1940s, Cat took the road less traveled in terms of her career path. What are the many ways things have changed for women in terms of life and career opportunities? What, if anything, is still similar?

6. Cat's uncle was a traitor to his country, but his reasons for that were nuanced. Discuss the choices he made and why. Do you agree with those choices? Why or why not?

7. What were some of the major themes that emerged in the story?

8. Did you notice any parallels between historical events in the story and contemporary challenges or debates?

9. Do you think any of the characters in the story would be considered neurodivergent today?

10. Was there a scene that completely took you by surprise? Did any character's actions surprise you?

11. What symbols, motifs, or cultural elements had a particular significance throughout the story? In what way were they significant? How did they tie into the historical settings or the overall themes of the book?

12. Did you find the ending of the novel satisfying? Was the resolution fitting given the historical context?

About the Author

Jane Healey is the author of *The Saturday Evening Girls Club*, *Goodnight from Paris*, *The Secret Stealers*, and *The Beantown Girls*, a *Washington Post* and Amazon Charts bestseller. She is also the host of the *Historical Happy Hour* podcast, where she interviews fellow historical fiction authors about their latest novels. A graduate of the University of New Hampshire and Northeastern University, Jane shares a home north of Boston with her husband, two daughters, a cat, and a dog. For more information on the author and upcoming events, or to schedule a virtual book club visit, please see her website at www.janehealey.com.